Widdershins

ALEX ALEXANDER

Widdershins

– Adverb

In a direction contrary to the sun's course,
        considered as unlucky; anti clockwise.

"She danced widdershins around him"

THE BIT BEFORE

The boy had the face of a babe. He was twelve but sickly. His endless spluttering cough was one you might expect to hear from a man seven times his age. He was skinny, so skinny that his dirty clothes hung over his body like wet rags over a stick.

The scarred man had taken him there, to the corner of the slums, to an empty place no one dared go.

It was there that the brutish, thuggish man gave him his freedom, telling him to walk into the narrow streets and not come back.

The boy could barely hold himself upright. He begged his master to reconsider. He coughed and wheezed and cried.

But the man had no care for tears. He loosed the club that hung by his waist and started a slow count from three.

The frail, pasty boy saw the ridges and grooves and brown once red stains in his master's club. He knew what happened when the countdown was allowed to end; so he fled, down the street and into the Narrows...

...until the fog and the darkness and something else unseen consumed him.

one

Laburnum was a city of two moons and two halves. There was the half north of the river and the half south of the river. North were its proudest establishments. The House of Lords, the High Court, the Royal Palace, the Academy and the majestic Guild of Philosophers. This was the heart of civilisation. It was from here that science, logic and order had been birthed, packaged and spread across the known world on ships and galleys of oak and iron.

Just next door, south of the river was a very different sort of place. The cobbled streets were narrow, the buildings shoddy, green spaces were few and clouds of soot perpetually hung in the air, floating west from the factories of an industrial revolution at its peak.

This part of the world stank. Never did a place have such a distinct odour. The stifling damp of wet horse hair, the piquant zest of a drunkard's armpit, the smell of rotting meat and mouldy milk, seasoned with the fresh excrement of rat. And not just rat, it stank of dog muck, cat muck, horse muck, cow and pig muck, geese and chicken and fox muck. Oh yes, and human deposits too. It was a signpost to the blind that said: welcome and behold, this is the city of Laburnum. Though, the only thing to be *beheld* was often a nose.

There were pockets of poverty all over the south. Places ordinary folk steered well clear of, even if it meant going down several different back roads and getting lost. The biggest of these had been carved out of maps and blacklisted by the Laburnum Tourist Board. Even the locals in the south tried to ignore its existence, as if it were that estranged uncle who always says the wrong thing at dinner parties. They had many names for it: Bog End, The Rags... Rat Bottom was a particular favourite. But most people called it by its common name: The Slums.

This was where all the poorest of the poorest ended up. Where people who had fallen off the rungs of society found a notch to exist in.

The buildings were broken in, falling apart and rotting. The streets were awash with dirt and filth and in some places had become indistinguishable from the sewers below, riddled with stagnant water and the furry backs of rats.

It was a quiet place. There were no horses trotting to and fro, no coach waggons going rickety rackety along the cobbles, no one trying to sell a newspaper, not even a copy of *The Tiny Issue*; a paper written by people who couldn't write and sold to people who couldn't read for a farthing.

The slums were engrossed in a grotesque silence. A silence occasionally broken by the cry of a starving child or the moan of a forsaken pauper.

The inhabitants of such a place were caricatures of its worn out buildings and forlorn streets. They were the kind of poor that made beggars look somewhat well put together. A scratching, spluttering, desperate sort.

If there's one universally acknowledged truth about desperate people, it's that they're extremely good for business.

At least, the Bowler Gang thought so. They were the ruling class of the slums. The fat cats that had floated to the top. From their HQ, an abandoned textiles factory, they orchestrated citywide crime. Burglary, smuggling, coin clipping. You name it, they did it. They were the leading criminals in the south. They were also the leading producers and distributors of the infamous Speckled Gin. A substance so strong that it was guaranteed to remove all a person's problems after just two sips. Mind you, it also rotted brains and spoiled eyes. For those latter reasons, it was banned in Laburnum, but no City Watchman would venture into the slums to police the ban.

The gang was also the leading employer of children in the slums. There's nothing at all altruistic about this. Children were often sold to them for bottles of Speckled Gin, or wandering orphans were enlisted into the ranks. This had proven to be quite a lucrative business model. They didn't have to pay them, yet the children did most of the work. Distilling gin, clipping coins and when they were old enough, they could become fully fledged associates of the gang, stealing from southern markets and robbing southern houses. If they did well and survived long enough, they were bestowed with the highest honour, a bowler hat, which separated the members of the gang from the workers of the gang.

It's time now to meet one of the Bowler Gang employees. A certified slum dweller, a ragamuffin, a guttersnipe. His name is Nicholas.

...

Or, it would have been *Nicholas,* had he been raised north of the river. Down sowf, people tend t'talk different. And so 'e went by the name o': Niclas.

Niclas lugged in a fresh sack of juniper berries and slumped it on the floor in front of an empty copper still. All around was a forest of shiny vats, chemistry pipes and glassware that branched out between water baths and hot coal furnaces.

The workforce, all young boys just like Niclas, were working in groups. Some were tasked with keeping the furnace hot and the baths bubbling. Some were tasked with stirring the stills, while trying not to breathe in the wobbly fumes. Some were barrelling up the latest batch of Speckled Gin and wheeling it to the stores.

Niclas had done every task there was in the distillery. He knew it inside out, and had so far managed to avoid any accidents. Accidents which were all too common, considering none of the boys really grasped the science of what it was exactly they were doing.

'Niclas!' Someone shouted from the stairwell. It wasn't a pubescent voice, more the voice of a croaky man, trying to shout through the pipe-smoke-infused phlegm lodged in his throat. 'Boss wants to see ya!'

All the boys stared round at Niclas.

'Wot you done?' said one.

'Good luck, mate,' said another.

Something in the tone of their voices and the shape of their faces said a quick farewell to Niclas. It wasn't usual to be called on by the boss. The only time a boy was called on by the boss, was for a beating.

Niclas ran through the events of the last week in his mind on his way to Mr K's office. There wasn't really anything he could think of that he'd done wrong. But one could never be too sure of this, the boys were often blamed for all sorts. If Mr K as much as misplaced his pipe, he was known to give his club a good shining on their bony buttocks. But this time, it felt different.

Mr K's office wasn't the office that springs to mind when you think of an office. There was a desk, yes. And a chair. But on the desk were a number of non-officey type things. Like wooden clubs, knuckledusters, a knife that was a bit too threatening to be a fruit knife; and, a fleet of empty gin bottles. Except for the bottle nearest Mr K, that was half empty. The boss of the Bowler Gang was a bottle half empty kind of guy. Half full bottles were the work of fantasists.

''Ello, 'ello, Nicky boy. 'Avin' a good day are we?' said Mr K.

Niclas stood up straight, twiddling his thumbs behind his back and staring down at his blackened toes. None of the boys could look Mr K in the eye for more than a fleeting moment, but they all knew his face well. His nose was stubby and red, his eyebrows were bushy like whiskers, and his eyes dark like his cold blooded heart. And, from his brow to his cheek, down the right hand side, the embossed burn of the letter 'K' told stories no scribe could tell.

'I ain't down there, Nicky, so quit lookin' down there.'

Niclas raised his head and caught sight of the broad shouldered bull sat in the moth eaten chesterfield behind the desk.

'Frightened are you?' Mr K's voice was rough. Like an old, rusty razor grating over plucked turkey skin.

'No, sir. I ain't. I's just… confoozed, that's all,' said Niclas.

'No need t'be. I've 'ad me eye on you, Nicky boy. You've been doin' well in the gin department.'

'Yessir.'

'You're older now. Nearly a man.'

'Yessir.'

'I remember when you first come t'this place. You was but a little brat… Not much taller than this 'ere desk. Took to work like a dog takes to a sausage. I know your late mam would be proud of the young man I see before me today. Come a long way you 'av'.'

'Yessir.'

'Listen. You know 'ow it works round 'ere don't ya? Boys come in, do the chores, do the labour, rise up the ranks and then one day I come along and pop one o' these 'ere 'ats on your 'ead. And just like that, you're in the gang.'

'Yessir.' Niclas almost smiled, but didn't. It was the greatest thing a slum boy could do, become a real, *bona fide* member of the gang. All of the lads aspired to it… though, none had ever seen it happen.

'You get respect when you wear one o' these.' Mr K tipped his hat. 'People don't just treat you different round 'ere. All over the slums people be sayin', "look! One of 'em. One of 'em Bowlers." You can walk up to people and just ask 'em to give you stuff. They don't argue with Bowlers. You won't get touched by no law enforcement sowf o' the river either. They treat proper members with the proper respect they deserves. Do you get me?'

'I fink so, sir.'

'Now. It ain't easy. It's a mark o' status. A badge. You don't get just anyone wearin' one o' these. You gotta proooove yourself, Nicky boy. You gotta go out there and provide for our family. Provide for all these little buggers workin' 'ard below just like you done.' Mr K's smile was shiny, gold and silver plated; it twinkled in the dusty light.

'Do you know 'ow t'filch?' said Mr K.

'Filch, sir? Like steal?'

'Yeah. That's it.'

'Uh… I guess, sir.'

'Good. I want you to show me your best filchin'.' Mr K stood. He was a lot taller than Niclas, probably seven foot; but there was nothing lanky about the man, he was a giant.

'See this pocket watch. This 'ere's exactly wot you gotta be lookin' for when you're doin' a bit o' filchin'. It's shiny. That's always a good indicator o' worth. It's 'eavy too. Another good sign. Now. Watch very carefully. I'm gonna leave it 'ere, right in the middle o' the table, then I'm gonna turn round like so… doin' me own fing… and… you…' Mr K peered back over his shoulder.

Niclas looked at the watch, then at Mr K's back. It was pretty easy stuff this filchin' malarky, he thought.

When Mr K turned his head away, Niclas grabbed the watch

and pocketed it. Though Mr K hadn't seen him do it, he'd heard the chain rattle and let out a slow depraved chuckle.

'Good. Good. You're fast. You got to be fast. Always fast. And confident too. It's all 'bout confidence and speed, Nicky. If you do summin quickly and with conviction no one'll ever question you. The best filchers ain't got special fingers or wider pockets, they're just good at lyin'. And not just lyin' wiv their tongue either. Lyin' wiv their face. That's the real skill.'

Niclas' face had a big proud smile on it. No one ever got praise from Mr K. Maybe he'd get better rations this week. Maybe even one of the two circulating pillows.

'I want you to go up town. I'm not talkin' Bog End. I'm talkin' proper town. Do you know where Carrot Street market is?'

'Uh… I fink so. Yeah. Just a little norf o' Birch Lane and a little sowf o' Char–'

'Good. The market there's got lots o' shiny stuff. Lots o' little glittery fings. I want you to go there and filch the most valuable fing you can. Fink o' it as a little test. The first step on your way to wearin' one o' these.'

Niclas hesitated.

'Alright wiv that?'

'Yessir. Can do, sir. I'll get summin proper good, sir. Fanks for the opportunity 'n' all, sir. Is that… everyfing, sir?'

'Yeah. Get out.' Mr K sat back down and took a swig from his bottle.

'Fanks again, sir. Fanks so much…' Niclas backed up to the door, turned to exit through it and felt his heart sink.

'*Wait.*'

'…Sir?' he said, turning back.

'Where you goin' wiv me pocket watch?' Mr K said this without a smile, his face hard and cruel.

'…Sorry, sir. I… Sorry.' Niclas sidled up to the desk and dropped the watch, like a little bird dashing to and from a crocodile.

'Fanks. Sorry. Bye,' he said, and escaped out the door with awkward finesse.

Out of Bog End, a little north of Birch lane and a little south of
Chardy Street, the traders and merchants were shouting out once
in a lifetime deals under the colourful marquees over their stalls.

'Twoforahalfpenny! Twoforahalfpenny! Ladies and gentlemen,
wot a bargain this is. Get your very own boot brushes. Twoforahalfpenny!'

This is Carrot Market. Where anything can be bought from
black striped eels to cashmere scarves and the latest perfumes all
the posh folk north of the river wear.

Niclas had been to Carrot Market a few times before, but only
ever in the company of Archie and Clyde, Mr K's most loyal
thugs; and only ever as a mule to carry back the sacks of botani-
cals and juniper berries. This was his first time alone. And his first
time *filchin'*.

There were lots of people there, more than he remembered; and,
despite his earlier enthusiasm, he was now well and truly brick-
ing it. What if someone saw? What if he got pinched? The City
Watch didn't treat guttersnipes nicely, and they treated thieving
guttersnipes even worse.

These kind of thoughts weren't useful. They were as distracting
as pink elephants. And everyone knows it's best to keep pink elephants where they belong, chained up in your imagination somewhere.

Niclas scanned the stalls for shinies. There was a lot of stuff on
offer. Mostly junk. Rusty iron trinkets, copper pipes, earthenware
bowls, workman tools; none would do. What he really needed
was a shiny, weighty pocket watch…

…Something twinkled out of the corner of his eye. It was a
twinkle that whispered into his ear and said rather politely,
"Ahem! Oi, Thief. Over 'ere."

Niclas made his way over.

On the stall's counter was a blue velvet cloth, and on the cloth, a constellation of twinkling jewels dancing in the pale sunlight. There were rings, necklaces, earrings, bracelets and charms, and there, in the middle of it all, a silver pocket watch. The shiniest silver pocket watch Niclas had ever seen.

The trader looked to be occupied, closing a sale with a lady at one end of the stall. He hadn't even noticed Niclas yet.

'My lady, you simply must have these earrings. They have quite a slimming effect on yourself, if I may say so.'

Niclas glanced over his shoulder. No one was looking. They were all too busy to notice him. If there was ever a clear coast, this was it. He tweeted a nonchalant whistle, exuding a bit of confidence just like Mr K had said, leaned in and swiped the watch.

This particular trader, however, was no fool. No matter how preoccupied he seemed, the eyes in the back of his head never left his merchandise. They had been stuck on Niclas since he'd arrived at the stall, and had sounded the alarm the instant the boy's dirty finger tips touched the watch.

The trader's hand clasped hold of Niclas' wrist like a striking adder. Their eyes locked together, each waiting for the other's next move.

'Thief!' said the trader, filling the boy with venomous fright. He tried to pull his hand away, but the grip was rooted. People were beginning to stare, stop what they were doing, whisper to one another. It was a standoff. The tighter the trader squeezed, the tighter Niclas held the watch.

'Guards! Thief! Thief!' The trader, suddenly livid, spat the words into Niclas' face.

Niclas swayed. He couldn't get free and the City Watch were coming. He could hear their boots on the ground. He'd be nicked for sure. Pinched. Beaten. Strung up to hang. Or worse. What was worse than being sent to the gallows you might wonder?

Worse was imagining what Mr K would do if he returned to Bog End empty-handed. It was too much, he was taking the watch.

With a brute thrust of his shoulder, he turned the stall over and sent its valuable contents tumbling onto the street. The trader lost hold and Niclas pulled the timepiece away. He stepped back from the fallen stand, hesitated to take in the drama he'd caused, and then, seeing that the proverbial horse dung was about to hit the proverbial fan, legged it.

'Guards! Thief! Stop him!' The shouts faded behind.

He was soaring, cutting through the crowds, through the scents and colours of the flower market, through the hanging, dripping meat of the butcher's stall, through the clothes market, where big hats, long dresses and laced corsets were pushed aside like curtains. He danced out of a tangled dress, the lady behind the stall wagging her finger and yelling scurrilously. Her shouts shoved him backwards into the fish stall, which collapsed and sent cold ice and fresh salmon slithering down his back. The cold was electrifying. Just what he needed to fire himself back to his feet.

'Sorry 'bout that,' he said to the open mouthed fishmonger.

'Halt! You there!' A guard pushed his way out of the crowd. 'Stop in the name of the law!'

The guardsman wore the brown leather uniform and copper chest plate of the City Watch. At his waist, a silver rapier and a flintlock pistol: both of which stabbed and shot fear without being drawn.

Niclas decided he wasn't going to stop in the name of anyone. He sped off, taking the chase into the nearest alley. Whistles rang out behind as his bare feet slapped across the cobbles. Ahead he could see the locks along the canal. Bog End wasn't far, if he could make it, he'd be safe. He just had to make it to the end of the alley. And he was making it. He was definitely making it, and was about to get ahead of himself with a cheeky smile, when a guard stepped out in front of him. He skidded, turned, ran back the other way, and a rapier came slithering out into the air, its cold icy tip finding the ridge of his Adam's apple. The other guard had caught up.

'Don't move,' commanded the swordsman. Niclas wondered if this applied to breathing. He held his breath just in case it did.

'Thief! He's got my watch. Dirty rotten thief!' said the trader, appearing at the back.

'Is this true boy? Have you been thieving?' asked the guard.

'No, sir. I ain't. I swear!'

'Why were you running then?'

'I just got scared, that's all. People was shouting, whistles was blowing. I ain't done nuffin' wrong. Nuffin'. I swears it.'

The trader moved in, reaching for the boy's pockets.

'Keep yer 'ands off me! I'm no crook!' said Niclas, swatting him away.

'Why you dirty little guttersnipe!' cried the man. 'He's a thief *and* a liar.'

'Empty your pockets,' said the guard behind, shoving Niclas forward.

Niclas sighed. He turned his pocket inside out and presented the interior to the trader who looked at him askant.

The rapier slid in against his neck again and lifted his chin to face the guard.

'The other pocket, boy.'

Niclas reached in nice and slow, and clasped the timepiece. He stalled. The rapier pressed against his flesh. He blinked timidly, swallowed and pulled out the silver chain; at the end, swinging like a pendulum, the shiny, weighty pocket watch.

It's a well known fact that the poorer you are, the fewer rights you have. Guttersnipes, being at the bottom of Laburnum's food chain, have no rights whatsoever. And so, it wasn't that far fetched for Niclas to believe his time was up. They could cut his throat, toss him in the canal and never speak another word of it.

The guard snatched the watch from his hand.

'It's a crime to steal, boy. Don't you know it?'

'I'm sorry, sirs. I'm well sorry. I's never bin sorrier.'

'I want him hung. He's a slum boy, got no future besides crime anyway. It'd do the whole city good to see his little carcase revolving at the end of a rope,' said the trader.

'No! Please, sirs, I ain't 'ad a choice in the matter. I ain't. Please... You gotta let me go. Give me a warning, a slap on the old wrist. I won't do it again, I swears it.'

The guards looked at each other and weighed up the options. They could run him through and chuck him in the water. Or, they could take him to the Guard's Tower and have him processed. The first option was certainly more appealing, there was a lot less paper work.

And they would have probably done just that, had they not had a strange, unexplainable change of heart.

'To the Guard's Tower with him,' one said, to everyone's surprise.

They marched Niclas away from the edge of Bog End to the jail waggons, then on, north of the river to the Guard's Tower.

But all the time they were followed. The scene in the market had attracted a lot of attention, but one particular set of eyes lingered long after the commotion had settled.

Two green eyes belonging to a cat.

***

The furnace cast an orange glow across the dungeon, and the shadows of torturous tools flickered in the firelight.

Niclas had been hoisted six feet up in a dangling cage. It was a tight fit and both his arms and one leg hung out of it.

Below, humming to himself in twisted nonchalance, the torturer crossed the room and set a branding iron down on the coals. From Niclas' vantage point, he could see the small white circle of the man's scalp, sitting like an island at the top of his long, slimy hair.

'I'll be wiv you in a minute,' he said, casting a grin up at the boy. He reminded Niclas of the famished rats of home. He had pointed ears, a shrunken chin and a rodent's overbite. His back was hunched and he hobbled when he walked, elbows bent at his side and his fidgeting hands leading the way.

He picked up a roll of parchment and folded it out.

'Wot 'av' we 'ere?'

'Please, it weren't me, you got to believe me!' said an elderly man, rattling his cage across from Niclas'. He had been quiet up until then. So quiet Niclas thought he was dead.

'Smugglin' is it? On the first o' this 'ere month, you was caught in possession of three and forty gallons o' Speckled Gin – oooh, nasty stuff.'

'I demand a lawyer,' said the prisoner.

'Lawyer, eh?' The torturer was a man who did everything by the book, and the book had a very clear passage about this bit. 'Can you afford a lawyer?'

'...'

'I'll take that as a no.' He returned his eyes to the scroll. 'The punishment for such a crime is life imprisonment, on the basis that you confess your crime promptly. If you will not confess, you must seek representation... court o' law... proven innocent... fair trial... We can probably ignore all this can't we? Let's see... blah... blah... blah... 'ere we are! *If you cannot afford representation*, and you will not confess your crime then the jurisdiction lies with the acting officer of the law – that's me. So, tell me, do you confess your crime?'

'I didn't do it.'

'I have to ask you again. It's a legal thing.'

'I'm innocent.'

'Yes. Everyone's innocent. As you 'av' clearly stated that you will not confess, and as you cannot afford representation to make your case, I, as the acting officer o' the law, hereby find you in breach of the 1620 Smugglin' Prevention act of Parliament, and am granted the power to sentence you.' The torturer signed the bottom of the parchment rolled it up and tossed it onto his table.

'…But…'

'You can choose how you go if you'd like. Death by sword, death by choker, death by club, death by water, or – a personal favourite of mine, death by boiling. Both my iron maidens are in use I'm afraid… and there's a three week waitin' list for the gallows. Probably a pear of anguish around here somewhere though.'

'No, stop! I confess. I confess. I did it. It's the Bowler Gang in Bog End. Said they'd pay me a pretty penny if I took the boat along the canal. I never knew what was in it. I swear it.'

The torturer sighed. 'Come now, man. Keep with it. We've done that bit, you've already chosen not to confess and we're onto your sentencin'. So… which is it?'

'B… B… But…'

The torturer raised his hand to his pointy ear. 'Did I hear… boiling?'

'But… I confessed.'

'Excellent. It's a rare one, I'll give you that.' With the yank of a chain, the torturer pulled the man's cage across the ceiling and above a large wooden tub of bubbling water.

'You can't do this. You can't! I have a son! I have grandsons!'

The torturer's hand wandered to a nearby lever, where it hovered as he took in these last words. His hesitation inspired hope. False hope. He shrugged and gave the steel arm a swift jerk and the chain shot free, rattling through the rusted mechanism. There was a splash, a short scream and Niclas tore his eyes away. The torturer kept his eyes fixed. He enjoyed watching the struggle people made as they were boiled alive, and often wondered what must go through their minds in those final effervescent moments.

Once the splashing had stopped and the ambient bubbling resumed, the torturer turned his attention upwards.

'Right, lad, filchin' was it?' he asked, unrolling another scroll.

Niclas trembled.

'I tell ya, the amount o' times I've 'ad one o' your lot in 'ere for thievin'. Suppose you know wot's comin'?'

'No, sir…' Niclas had a clue. His eyes had been watching the branding iron warm in the furnace. The letter T at its end was glowing white. The torturer swiped it up and headed for the levers below the cage.

'Your age, lad?' he asked.

'Err… I dunno, sir.'

'You don't know your own bleedin' age?'

'No, sir.'

'When's your birthday?'

'Birfday, sir?'

'Yeah you know. The day your sweet mother brought you into this cruel world.'

'I don't 'av' no mother, sir.'

'Well you must 'av' done at some point. Say, you've never had a birthday? No one's ever gone round singin' for-he's-a-jollygood-fellow?'

'…No, sir.'

The torturer shrugged. 'That's too bad. Right, well, let's get a good look at you. Yeah… Hmmm… I'd say you look about five and ten. That sound reasonable?'

'If you say so, sir.'

'Sure you're not four and ten?'

Niclas shook his head, uncertain.

'If you was four and ten you'd be considered a babe in the eyes of the law. That means a good solid branding, a few lashes to the back and a kick on your arse out into the street.'

'Yessir…'

'But you're five and ten, right?'

'I dunno, sir.'

'Well… I'm gonna call it. I think you're five and ten. That's between babehood and adulthood, so… you should really know better than to be going round filchin'. Yep! I'm afraid I'll 'av' to take a finger.'

Niclas gasped and his fingers fled into the shelter of clenched fists.

'Please, sir, please don't take me fingers. I needs 'em.'

'For wot, pocket picking?'

'No sir, I promise, I won't ever steal again. I'll be on the straight and narrow from now on.'

'Sorry, lad, regulations is regulations. I gotta follow the book. Besides, it's not very often I get to remove body parts. There's summin very therapeutic 'bout choppin' off someone's phalanges.' The torturer searched his table for the required implements. Unable to find what he was looking for, he stalled and rubbed an ear lobe.

'Please, sir, I don't want to lose 'em. Please, sir. I begs you, I begs you.'

'Don't be vain, lad. Now I err… I seem to have misplaced me saw, so, don't you be going nowhere. I'll be as quick as I can.'

The torturer left the room through a large iron door, leaving Niclas alone to ponder which of his eight fingers and two thumbs would be the least missed.

The loss of his fingers wasn't even the worst of it. He was going to be branded with the hot iron. A letter "T" for "Thief" on his face for all to see. Mr K wasn't fond of branded guttersnipes. Once marked, the children became no use to the Bowler Gang. Niclas remembered the last time a boy returned to the gang's warehouse after getting caught filching. His burn was fresh and still blistering on his cheek but Mr K showed no sympathy. Nor did he beat him. They went for a walk and an hour later only Mr

K returned. No one ever saw that boy again. It was an unsaid rule among the boys, that if you were caught and branded, it was best not to go back.

All was silent in the dungeon, save the creaking cages and shuffling coals. But as the boy dangled in the air, stroking his hands and trying to stifle fresh tears, he heard a noise from within the shadows.

Rats. It sounded like rats, and Niclas would have cast it to the back of his mind as just that, had it not sounded again.

'*Pssst*, boy.'

This time he thought he heard a word, but he saw no space for a speaker to hide and no cages with living people to speak.

'Are you deaf, boy?'

'Where are you?' said Niclas.

'Shush, he'll be back any minute. There isn't much time,' said the voice. 'A question, boy, what would you give to be free?'

'Free? Like escape?'

'…Yes.'

'Err,' Niclas looked his cage up and down and gave his head a glum shake. 'I'd probs give whatever I could, but I don't see 'ow—'

There was clank from the levers below and the chain rattled free. With a sudden swoosh and clanging clang, the cage crashed into the floor. A very startled Niclas looked up, his hands clutching the bars and his heart pounding.

'Listen, boy, I have the keys to your cage and I can free you.'

'Let me out. Let me out. Quick!'

'Wait,' demanded the voice. 'Have you any family, boy?'

Niclas didn't understand the meaning of the question but knew that the quicker he answered the quicker he'd be out. Possibly with all fingers and thumbs intact.

'I ain't gots no family, no, sir.'

'No life ahead of you but the slums? No future ahead of you but poverty, crime and misery?'

'…… Probs not.'

'And are you a thief?'

'I'm not a bad person, I promise. I won't ever steal again if you let me out of this 'ere cage,' said Niclas rattling the bars.

'Let's not jump to conclusions, boy. I want you to make me a promise. Can you do that?'

'Anyfing, sir, anyfing.' Niclas couldn't stop his eyes from twitching towards the door.

He envisaged the torturer's return and the consequences that would follow if he were found on the floor. It would be more than a finger he'd lose. He'd be put on the stretching rack, have his toes hammered in or have the hot poker put right up his–

'I need your help with a matter of great importance,' said the voice. Something was beginning to feel odd. Had Niclas had the time, or the capacity to think about it, he might have found it suspicious that someone was pottering around the Guard's Tower, looking to recruit some help. But time was short.

'Yessir, I'll help with your matter of great *impotence*. I promise.'

'Swear it.'

'I swear it.'

'Swear on your life.'

'I swear it on me life, sir.'

There was an exasperating silence. Then the cage keys chimed against the ground.

Niclas reached out. His soon-to-be-saved fingers tapped the copper ring closer. He snatched it up and shakily began to unlock the cage, eyes dancing between the lock and the door.

Then, like a fly slipping out from beneath an upturned glass, he was free.

'Where you at?' he called.

He looked around eager to meet his liberator. But there was no one there. No one at all. Except a black cat, which ambled over and sat before him. Niclas gave the cat a dubious frown and turned to address the room.

'This your cat, sir?' he asked.

'Listen, the only way out is…'

At first, Niclas thought it entirely ordinary that the source of the voice should be a cat. But after a moment's thought, he felt his eyes grow and his jaw drop. Then, as if in delayed response to an iron mallet thumping his knee, he leapt up and made a high pitched, squawky sort of gasping sound. A bit like this: '*Wu-ah-huh*! You're talkin'?'

'Good of you to notice. You'll need to get over that quite quickly, if you're to get out of here alive.'

'But… you're a… Am I dreamin'? Are you real?'

The cat sighed. It had expected this. 'No, I am not real. I am a hallucination. A figment of your imagination. Does that make you feel better?'

Niclas didn't know what a hallucination was, and he wasn't fond of figs, thus, he just stared, unable to close his mouth.

'Sorry, sir, you've got me all in a muddle. I ain't never seen–'

'Shut up!' snapped the cat. 'Your only way out of this is the chimney. You look as dirty as a chimney sweep, so it should be no problem for you. When you get to the top, you'll be very high up, so try not to fall. You'll see the clock tower towards the west. That's where we will meet, in Potfoot Alley directly behind it.'

Niclas could have asked many more questions, but seeing the cat was frightfully serious, he asked only one.

'Chimney?'

The cat darted its nose to the furnace. There, above the orange coals was a large stone column.

'*You want me to climb that?*'

'Climb or you hang. What'll it be?'

The climb seemed endless, like one of those forever stretching corridors in a nightmare. There was a bright dot of light in the distance above, but it wasn't getting any nearer. It helped to count the bricks as he passed them. Granted, it didn't help much. His hands, arms and clothes were black with soot. The stuffy air filled his lungs and the heat nipped at his feet. At least it can't get any worse, thought Niclas. Of course, that kind of thinking is practically asking for it.

The iron door slammed below and the whistling torturer sauntered back into the room. Niclas froze. His lungs shuddering beneath his shirt as he listened and imagined the look that was formulating on the torturer's face. His whistling had stopped, and there was no other sound in Niclas' ears other than the thump of his own heart.

Below, the torturer was but seconds from turning on his tail and running out to fetch the nearest Guard. Had Niclas kept still, he would have done just that. But it wasn't going to be that easy, because just at that moment, a tickle of soot decided to settle at the back of his throat. His eyes watered, his nose crinkled and a cough echoed out of his mouth, down the chimney and straight into the torturer's pointy, rat-like ears.

After a short bout of silence, Niclas stopped cringing and opened his eyes to look down.

…

The torturer's head shot into the shaft and he growled like a dog.

'I don't believe it!'

Niclas replied with a frantic, scuttling climb.

'Guards!' shouted the torturer, flustering. 'Guards! Guards! Guards!' His shout got louder each time. 'Guards! Guards!'

Then it stopped, just as quickly as it had started. Niclas stared below. He couldn't hear anything and that was a great deal more worrying than before.

''Ello! Yoo-hoo! You're gonna regret this.' Something about the way the man said this made Niclas regret everything all at once.

The torturer, to the tune of a sadistic cackle, grasped the bellows and fed the coals. The embers blazed and the fire burst into life.

Niclas felt faint. The air was instantly hotter, thicker, unbreathable and rising faster than he could climb. He felt as though he were trapped in an oven. His skin was pouring with sweat, and his hands slipping on the brickwork. His chest was heaving under the weight of dense air and spluttering. A black cloud engulfed him. He couldn't see or breathe so he closed his eyes and held his breath. Which was just as well, as one breath of that black smoke and the game would be up. He climbed blind, hand over hand, foot over foot. Then, just as he lost the will to go on, light coruscated through his eyelids and his hand shot out of the chimney, pulling him into the city's semi-fresh air.

After an inconvenient and time consuming coughing fit, he stood, wiped the black from his eyes and stared out at the view.

There were wide canals, busy streets and enormous, extravagant buildings, the biggest he had ever seen. He saw the Royal Palace, a large shimmering mansion encircled by fountains, gardens and statues. Before its golden gates lay the Guard's Square, around which stood the city's most prestigious establishments. There was the House of Lords with pointed spires and stone busts carved around its walls. There was the High Court with its huge dome roof and Scales of Justice. And there, beneath his feet, the Guard's Tower, the tallest tower in the city.

He was north of the river. He'd never been north of the river. The air was… nice.

He wasn't sure which way was west, but after a bit of squinting and turning, he soon spotted the clock tower. It was ringing out on the hour, a loft of pigeons breaking free from its rafters and swooping over the rooftops below.

That was where the cat was. But it was late in the day and Mr K would be waiting far away south of the river. It was probably best to get back to Bog End and not keep the boss waiting.

But…

He had made a promise, and Niclas was a boy of his word.

Down a very precarious, wonky drain pipe Niclas went and into the streets below.

It was a foreign place for a guttersnipe to be. The streets were cleaner north of the river, they were wider and the people going about them were a lot better dressed. Niclas felt like a tourist in his own city, and not a welcome one. The top hatted gentlemen and ladies in blooming dresses stared at him the way they stared at rats.

'You there, I say, what are you up to?' One gentleman called. Niclas didn't reply, he stumbled over his own feet and hurried to the nearest quiet place he could find, a narrow alleyway. It was best to keep off the main streets, he thought, unless he wanted to give autographs.

The alleys Niclas was used to down south were the sorts of places you expected to find trouble. But these ones north of the river were as sophisticated as alleyways could get. No one lived there for a start. Nor was there a designated peeing wall. Nor an entrepreneur with the only roll of toilet paper in the neighbourhood and a purse that was several shillings too light – yes, that was actually a thing.

Niclas waited for a bit, wondering if perhaps he'd misheard the talking cat. He suspected people often misheard talking cats, which was probably something to do with the fact that talking cats couldn't exist. Or could they?

'You're filthy,' said the cat, appearing at his side. Out of the dungeon's darkness, Niclas had a better look at his liberator. It was a black cat with a small white patch under its neck, and two unnaturally green, piercing eyes.

'I will confess, I had my doubts about that chimney scenario. It would appear that you're quite the climber.'

''Ow'd you do that?'

'I beg your pardon?'

'Talk?'

'It's easy,' replied the cat, 'I open my mouth, position my tongue and vocal chords in a variety of arrangements and aspirate.'

'But you're a cat,' said Niclas.

'Very observant,' said the cat.

'I don't get it.'

'Hmm…' The cat stared up at him compassionately. 'It's likely there are many things in this world you *don't get*. Why we have day and night, why the wind blows, why people call tomatoes a fruit, yet buy them from the vegetable stall.'

'A fruit? Really?'

'Yes. It's best you don't think about such things, if you can't get your head around them.'

Niclas scratched his head. He had never really thought about why the wind blew, or what caused day and night, and the very thought of thinking about the thought baffled him.

'D'you 'av' a name?' he asked.

'Of course.'

'Well, wot is it? Mine's Niclas.' The boy proffered his hand to shake.

The cat looked at it with disdain.

'Balthazar. And I don't touch.'

Niclas inspected his sooty hand and withdrew the offer.

'Balfazar you say?'

'Bal-tha-zar.'

'Yeah. Balfazar. Got it.'

The cat rolled its eyes.

'This is Poshside ain't it. Never bin north o' the river. It's proper clean, ain't it. Smells nice too. Sorta.'

'Yes. Marginally better. And here I'm afraid someone of your current appearance sticks out like a lump of coal in a jewellery box.'

Niclas wasn't sure what to say. He apologised.

'We have some business to discuss, but I need to visit the bank first.'

'The bank?'

'Yes, where I keep my money,' said Balthazar.

'You've got a bank?'

'Hmm... It's best if you don't think about that either.'

Niclas had heard about banks. They were places where rich people kept their coin stacks. They weren't the sorts of places frequented by guttersnipes, or furry animals for that matter. He imagined them to be big buildings, probably in the centre of town, probably surrounded by folk wearing top hats. He hadn't imagined that he would end up in another doorless alley, but apparently, that was where the entrance to this such bank was.

It had a funny looking entrance, not so much a door as an inlet into the sewers, barely big enough for Balthazar to squeeze into, certainly not big enough for Niclas to follow. So he waited, as instructed, watching the minute hand on the clock tower above.

It had been eleven minutes precisely and it was starting to get dark; though, not as dark as south of the river. The northern districts were well lit by gas lanterns. Even the alleyways, which were corridors of blackness down south, had their own lighting here. And they had crews of men who went around lighting them. Niclas thought it must have been a very respectable job, and gave a salute to the light marshals as they went by. Needless to say, they ignored him and returned to their waggon.

'It's a crime to beg north of the river. Be gone, boy, before we call the watch,' one called back.

'Oh, I ain't beggin', sir. No, sir. I'm waitin' for me master, sir.'

'... Righto lad, righto.' The man gave a crooked look, climbed on his waggon of flaming torches and mushed the horses away and down the street.

A rattling sound of coins came from the drain, then a brief pause, followed by the sound of Balthazar cursing.

He appeared from the sewer dragging a small brown purse by his mouth. He dropped it and caught his breath.

Niclas could see the shillings poking out the side. His eyes bulged.

'Is that?' he couldn't believe it.

'Don't get any ideas, boy. If you help me, there will be plenty more of this.'

'There's a bank. Wot? In there? I almost didn't believe you! Is it a special bank wot's only for cats? Or can dogs use it too–'

'Enough questions. Pick it up.'

Niclas lifted the pouch from the floor and poured into his hand pennies, sixpences, shillings, and a weighty coin that must have been a pound. It was around about then his instinct to run tapped him on the shoulder and gave his knees a sharp nudge. He looked at the cat and tried to judge how fast it was. Of course, it didn't matter, it was only a cat, what was it going to do? Mind you, it had said there'd be *plenty* more. That had made him curious and had appealed to his greed more so than his instincts. It could be worth seeing where this was going. With a small coin purse like that he could eat for weeks – months – maybe a year! His stomach agreed.

'There's a place a bit south from here, on the edge of the Brewery Quarter. You'll be able to get cleaned up and dressed in something a little less (the cat paused to find the least offensive adjective) repulsive.'

'Wot kind of a place?'

'A nice place where they don't ask questions.'

'Oh. I never bin to any nice places before, sir. Not bin t'many places at all really.'

'Everything will be fine. All you have to do is say the following,

31

"I have come of age, been released from the workhouse, come straight here with my father's inheritance and would like to rent a room." A room with a bath, don't forget that bit.'

'Wot's in-ear-ett-ence?'

'A generous sum of money left to you by a dead person.'

'But I don't 'av' no in-ear-ett-ence. I ain't got no father either to tell the troof.'

'Ah, yes. You see, it's a little lie. You are capable of lying aren't you?'

'Guess so, sir, don't take much lyin', you just say summin that ain't. But...'

'But what?'

'But I still don't 'av' no in-ear-ett-ence.'

Balthazar stared blankly at Niclas, as if trying to figure out the boy's mysterious inner workings. Then his eyes moved to the purse of coin in the boy's hand.

'Oh... I get it. This is the in-ear-ett-ence ain't it?'

'...'

'But... Sir, why 'av' I got to lie?'

'...' Balthazar waited to see if the penny would drop. It didn't. 'Because explaining that you're a thief who's just escaped the Guard's Tower and been given a bag of coins by a talking cat is a little hard to follow. Do you follow?'

'I see your point, sir.'

'Excellent. Let's go. Oh, and, when you arrive you'll be asked if you'd like a tumble after your bath. To this, you will respectfully decline.'

'Wot's a tumble, sir?'

'It's a rather expensive dance.'

'Dance?' asked Niclas.

'Expensive,' replied Balthazar.

The Brewery Quarter is in the north of the city, but only just.

It spills over from the south, a stronghold of debauchery and filth. It's not quite southern or northern in atmosphere, it has its own character entirely. The locals themselves regard it as a different dimension; so different that it has its own time zone; but this is probably because the locals are in a constant state of intoxication, stumbling from one public house to the next.

Niclas hadn't seen so many people making so much noise in one place before. People were singing in the street, playing fiddles on the rooftops, fighting in the alleys, shouting out the windows, peeing in the gutters (men, as well as women), and drinking in every conceivable location. There was laughter too, lots of it.

Balthazar led him through the merry crowd and stopped at a door. A sign hung above it with a woman's leg painted on it. Bright, lipstick-red calligraphy said: The Queen's Garter.

The cat nodded to the door and Niclas pushed it open.

Inside was a warm, musky room, tinted with a rich saffron hue. The noise of the street was muffled behind the closed door and replaced with the gentle pluckings of a harp. The harpist sat in the corner of the room, playing and humming softly. She must have been the most beautiful woman Niclas had ever seen. Nor had he ever heard a more beautiful song. For a moment, the rattling of horse carts and shouting and barking from the outer world disappeared completely.

'Ahem…' said Balthazar, breaking the trance.

Niclas smiled at the lady with the harp, she smiled back.

He continued on towards the far counter.

There were booths all around the room. In them were important looking gentlemen and women dressed in tight colourful corsets and dresses. Some even had their bare arms on display! The ladies who were by themselves smiled at Niclas, some offered him a seat. At the end of the room was a high counter. There sat an older woman in a dark red dress, who, seeing Niclas' incongruent demeanour, gave a crooked bronze smile. She had been quite good looking herself, perhaps thirty years ago.

'Can I 'elp you, luv?' she asked.

Niclas hesitated, looked at the cat by his feet, realised it wasn't going to help him and stuttered out a shy greeting.

'I needs a room, miss.'

'We gots plenty o' rooms, m'luv, wot'll it be?'

Niclas looked to his feet again, intriguing the woman as to what was down there.

'One which 'as a balf, miss.'

'Yes,' said the woman, narrowing her eyes. She could see that Niclas needed a bath, but was yet to see anything to persuade her she would be the one to provide it.

Niclas looked down. Balthazar mouthed, "the purse." This jogged his memory and he dropped the weighty bag on the table. At once the uncertainty fell from the woman's face and her hospitable warmth returned.

'A room wiv a balf wos it? Gots plenty o' those m'luv.'

'I've come of age see. Left the workhouse I 'av'. I gots moneys. Me father's moneys. In-ear-ett-ence.' Niclas said, with great difficulty.

'Well then, gots some nice rooms upstairs, believe this'll do.' The woman took a key from the wall behind and slid it across the table. 'It'll be a crown a night, unless you want the premium suite,' added the woman, 'that one'll be two and a half crown and comes with *a nice and friendly wakeup call.*'

Niclas looked again at his feet and then hurriedly back at the woman.

'No, miss, the first room will do us fine.'

'Alrighty.'

'Uh… Wot's that in shillin's, miss?'

'A crown's five shillin', m'luv.'

Niclas counted out five shillings, the only coins he could count, and exchanged them for the key.

'Would you like a tumble afta your balf, little sir?'

This, Niclas remembered well. 'Sorry, miss, I don't know 'ow t'dance, so I must re-spec-full-e decline,' he said proudly.

'Alrighty, little sir; but if you fancy learnin' – to dance – we can arrange some lessons. There ain't no better place to learn than the Queen's Garter.'

'Thanks, miss, I'll bear it in mind.'

'Alrighty. Now if you'll just make your mark, little sir, the room's all yours.'

'Mark?' Niclas was confronted with a book, upon which were listed the names of those staying in the inn. He stared blankly at the quill and the paper and looked to his feet.

'Everyfing alright, little sir?'

'Yeah, it's just I've never made a mark before, see.'

'Oh, no problem at all, m'luv,' said the woman, turning the book to face her and picking up the pen. 'Wot name would you be going under then?'

'Niclas.'

'Niclas…' she held on for a surname.

'That's right, Niclas.'

'Niclas wot?'

'I begs your pardon, miss?'

'Wot's your second name, m'luv?'

'I only gots one name, miss, ain't important nuff to 'av' me no other names. Just Niclas.'

'Very well, *Niclas*,' here she added a wink, which made him feel a touch uncomfortable. ''Ead on up.'

Niclas started up the stairs, but his foot found only the first step before the woman called him back.

'That your cat, little sir?'

'Yes, miss,' said Niclas.

'We 'av' a no animals policy, 'case customers 'av' allergies and the like.'

Niclas looked at Balthazar and racked his brain for a reply.

'Gunna 'av' to keep it outside, little sir.'

Balthazar shook his head and began walking over to the woman, whispering in strange tones under his breath.

'Miss,' said Niclas, stopping the cat. 'I don't asks for much, but this 'ere cat is all I gots left of me good 'n' dead father. I ain't never bin separated from 'im, not in the workhouse, not nowhere. Please, miss, 'e's trained good 'n' proper. Knows to do 'is business outside.'

The woman gave this heartfelt speech some consideration. She watched the loving cat rub its back against Niclas' leg and purr as if the two formed an inseparable pair. She beckoned him closer with her finger.

'Alrighty, little sir, but don't 'av' it gallivantin' up and down this 'ere establishment in front of t'other guests. It wouldn't be appropriate.'

'Thanks, miss.' Niclas bowed his head and continued up the stairs. Balthazar followed.

Niclas was spellbound by the room. There was a four poster bed, a chair and a small dresser with a mirror on top; all of which were made of polished mahogany and dressed in plush velvets and silks.

'This bed's proper big!' said Niclas. 'Bet there's room for a whole family under them fancy covers. And this,' he paused to stroke the quilt, 'I've never felt a finer feel.'

'It'll do,' said Balthazar. He *had* felt finer.

Niclas crawled onto the bed and bounced up and down a few times to rate its comfort.

'I've bin sleeping on the floor for all me years, I never knew such beds existed.'

'May I suggest bathing before you get too comfortable. As nice as that quilt may be, it is not a towel.'

'Crikey, me own water closet 'n' all!'

Niclas jumped up and headed for the bathroom.

Something stopped him. Above the dresser he saw a boy with scruffy, mousy brown hair and a face full of coal. He reached out and stroked the reflection, smearing soot on the glass.

'Everything alright?' asked Balthazar.

'Yeah,' said Niclas, ruefully. It was as though he'd never seen himself before.

He had certainly not had a bath before. Not one like this anyway. Once the taps were sussed, he stepped into the tub and sank up to his chin. At first he clung to the sides in case he sank below the waterline. He had always been uneasy around large amounts of water. But he soon let go, and, doing so, found it to be the most tranquil experience of his life to date.

The calm was short lived. He made beards of bubbles, practised his swordplay with the scrubber and splashed and splashed – the way any boy does in his first bath.

The room came with nightwear. Pink satin shirts with the initials "Q.G." sewn into the breast pocket. It wasn't exactly Niclas' colour, but he wasn't choosey.

He sat on the bed, buttoning it up and admiring his clean fingernails. Who knew? They were actually pink underneath. When he turned his hands over, he frowned. The ends of his fingers had shrivelled up like raisins.

'You were in the bath too long, that's what happens,' said Balthazar, jumping up on the bed beside him.

'Why?'

'Science.'

'Oh,' said Niclas.

'You know science?'

'Can't say I knows 'im well, sir – I can call you sir can't I?'

'You can call me whatever you wish, providing you pronounce it correctly.'

Niclas grabbed his stomach and winced.

'Hungry?'

'Yes, sir.'

'When did you last eat?'

'Can't remember, sir,'

'We'll have you fed, clothed and groomed.'

'Groomed, sir?'

'Looking the part.'

'Part, sir?' Niclas had gotten so caught up in the comfort of the Queen's Garter that his promise to the talking cat had completely slipped his mind. Until now.

'If you're going to be working for me, you must look decent. The guttersnipe trends won't get you far in this city.'

'O, maybe they 'av' a laundry place 'ere.' Niclas looked over at his previous rags on the floor of the bathroom.

'No, no. Forget those. We'll get you new garments. Garments suited to a squire.'

Niclas was a bit too excited by this. So excited, he laughed.

'I'm gonna be the best lookin' guttersnipe norf o' the river.'

'Yes.'

'So. Wot's I gots to do?'

'Pardon?'

'Wot's will I be doin' workin' for you, sir?'

'You can start by pouring me some water.'

'Righto, sir.' Niclas reached for the jug on the bedside table and poured a glass. A pretty easy task to begin with, yet not completed without spilling a drop.

'I will need you to run errands for me about town. There are certain things I am incapable of doing. Certain places I cannot go.' The cat lapped at the rim of the glass.

'Like wot, sir?'

'Have you been to the Scholar Quarter?'

'Can't say I 'av', sir. Didn't get out much before, sir.'

'It's where all the educated members of society hang out. The Philosophers' Guild, the Academy, the City Library. Very quiet place, not like around here. It's the sort of place a man can sit on a bench and read a book all day without once being asked for loose change.'

'Is there uh… much readin' involved, sir?'

'No. But I will need you to visit the library for me, to make use of your expertise.'

'Expert-ease, sir?'

'I need you to acquire something.'

'Acquire, sir?'

'Take something.'

'Take, sir?'

'Yes. It's a book. But it's not the sort of book one can borrow. You'll have to steal it.'

'Filchin', sir! But I promised never to nick as much as a farvin',' said Niclas, grasping his noisy stomach again.

'You made a promise to me, boy. I do hope you're not thinking about breaking it.' There was a tone in this that scared Niclas more than Mr K's fiercest strike.

'I wasn't, sir, I swear I wasn't. It's just… well, I didn't fink I'd ever 'av' to filch anyfing again. Not afta wot 'appened. Not afta I nearly lost me fingers.'

'No harm shall come to you, boy, you have my word.' The cat smiled. It was the first time Niclas had seen a cat smile. The majority of it is in their eyes – their narrow, mischievous eyes.

'Wot do you want me to steal?' he asked.

'Please,' said Balthazar. 'If it makes you feel better, let's not use the word steal, it feels so… *criminal*. We'll give it back of course, once we're done with it. So it's not really stealing at all.'

'Ok…' It didn't make Niclas feel any better. If anything it just made him feel worse. And confused. Of course, he was normally confused, but on this occasion he was even more confused than usual.

'Trust me, boy. I would get it myself, had I a pair of hands and posable thumbs,' said Balthazar.

'Wot's so special 'bout a book, sir? If you don't mind me askin'.'

'Come now, there's no need to worry about it tonight. We'll have to sort your clothes out first, and your hair could do with a trim.'

Niclas' stomach groaned.

'And food, sir.'

'Yes, and food,' said the cat.

***

The following morning, two thugs were waiting by the stables outside the Guard's Tower. One had his hands deep in his pockets, and had taken a lean against the lamp post. The other was eating an apple, chewing with his mouth as wide open as he could get it. Both were dressed like gentlemen, though scruffily, in what wasn't really second, or third, but possibly fourth-hand clothes. And both wore a black bowler on top of their head.

'This apple's sour,' said Archie.

'Don't like apples,' said Clyde. 'Ain't got the teef for apples me. I used to love 'em, spesh the sour ones. But once one's pulled out a few o' your teef, you go off 'em completely.'

Archie stopped mid-bite and examined his apple.

'I mean you can go see one o' these dentists,' Clyde continued, 'but it costs a right fortune to get a new pair o' teef. They can give you these porcelain ones wot don't stain though. I knew a bloke wot 'ad 'is teef removed, and they paid 'im to do it! Can you believe that? 'pparently 'e 'ad eight out and it only took a minute.'

Archie thought better of it and tossed the apple over his shoulder.

He pulled his pocket watch out from his shabby coat and stared at the rusted, damp, spore-ridden glass.

'Usually round this time, innit.'

'Yeah. 'Less they've 'ung 'im. Sometimes they string 'em straight up you know. Depends wot mood they're in.'

'Nah, if they was goin' do 'im in, they wouldn't 'av' taken 'im in. Once 'es in the system, 'es got to be processed properly. I 'ad a cousin wot was in the Watch, take it from me, I know these fings.'

'O, 'ello, some northern ladies one o'clock. Check 'em out. Check 'em out.'

'That's three o'clock.'

'Two o'clock.'

'Quarter to three at the very least.'

'Whatever, ain't they gorge.'

'Nah, I like a proper woman. Nuffin' like a good souvern girl. One who slaps you back. One who when you spit in 'er face, will spit your spit right back at you. That's a lady.'

Clyde nodded in agreement.

'Eh?' said Clyde. 'You don't reckon 'e's done a runner?'

'A runner. Who? Nicky?'

'Yeah?'

Archie thought about it for a few seconds, taking in the busy street around them.

'Nah,' he said at last. 'Why'd 'e do that? Ain't got no moneys. Ain't got no family. Ain't got no friends. Ain't got no manners. Ain't got no know-how eiver. Be dead by the end o' the week 'e would. It's a 'ard world out there, you forget. Dog eat dog.'

'I knows it. You knows it. But does 'e know it? Bit slow this one.'

'Hmmm... 'ang on, 'ere we go!'

The side gate across from the stables opened and out of the Guard's Tower came a handful of Watchmen. Two, freshly brand-ed criminals were ushered back onto the streets, and sent on their way in the direction of the nearest pub; the first place all rehabil-itated offenders go.

'Don't look like our boy.'

'Nah. That's coz they ain't.'

'P'raps they've kept 'im in.'

'Nah. Not for filchin'. He'd 'av 'ad to steal summin proper important to get more than one night. Ain't got the cells see, ain't got the room for guttersnipes. Always toss 'em out afta one night. Maybe a brandin', sometimes a clippin', but always toss 'em out by mornin'.' Archie looked at his watch. There weren't very many minutes left of the morning.

'Wot we goin' do 'bout it?'

'Don't know. But boss ain't goin' be pleased.'

'You know…' said Clyde, 'I 'ad a feelin', sorta in my ankles. I 'ad a feelin' this one'd do a runner.' Clyde was over enthused. He stroked the club hanging from his belt preparatively.

'Calm it, calm it. He might 'av' just run into some trouble inside, that's all. Might've kicked up a fight or summin. Might o' professed 'is innocence.'

'Yeah. And wot if he ain't?'

Archie didn't answer back. He ground his plaque layered fillings together and spat a slug of apple and smoke flavoured spit onto the cobbles.

***

Niclas was introduced to the baker for breakfast. He had a cinnamon swirl, a gooey almond croissant and a sausage roll; and ate them all on the spot as soon as he got them, placing the order for the next course when he was halfway through the current one. The baker found him odd. He was ill-mannered, scruffy looking, hungrier than a lion, and not quite right upstairs, telling his pet cat how good the sausage was and that he really should get one. But he had a big fat purse of coin, and that was all that mattered.

Next, the cat took Niclas to the barber; where, when he was asked: "What can I do for you, young man?", he replied, "A haircut, sir." The barber, puzzled at first, saw the coin purse and soon found himself awash with unrestrained creativity. Using a tiny pair of scissors, a light-catching razor, and a large ivory comb, he transformed Niclas' mane of hair into short back and sides with the top combed over.

Then, it was onwards to the tailor. There, Niclas picked up a grey shirt, a pair of brown trousers and a green waistcoat. Niclas was impressed by his new look, except the boots. They were strange heavy things that he was reluctant to wear. They crushed his toes and made the everyday task of walking unnecessarily painful. He told Balthazar it would take some getting used to, "on account o' 'em bein' 'is first pair o' shoes."

The rest of the day was spent back at the Queen's Garter.

Niclas took off his shoes as if his life depended on it. He slumped onto the bed and cradled his bloated belly.

'Cor blimey! Wot a day!' he said, staring down at his new socks.

Balthazar made his way to the windowsill, where he liked to sit and watch the drunken crowds below.

'Never 'ad a finer day, sir. I 'ads breakfast, lunch and gots me a pair o' socks. Not a fan o' 'em breeze blocks you call shoes, but boy do I feel good. Wot's the plan tomorrow, sir?'

'Tomorrow, you start work.'

'Will I be goin' t'the library as you said, sir?'

'Yes. That's right.'

'Can't say I'm not nervous, sir. First day nerves 'n' all.'

'You'll be just fine. I wouldn't put you in harm's way. You'd be of no use to me if you were in harm's way.'

'Fanks, sir.'

'Now look into my eyes.'

Niclas looked up into the cat's bright green, yet darkening eyes. 'And... *sleep.*'

The Scholar Quarter had been built in a different age. An age where limestone had been in fashion and architecture had been a bit grander in general.

There were lots of grassy squares about, each dedicated to some so and so who had done something a little less deserving of a statue but a little more so than a mere bench. Niclas hadn't ever seen that sort of stuff before. Down south, the nearest thing to a park was Mudslinger's Common, which, as you can imagine from the name, wasn't much of a green space at all.

At the end of New Road, the spine of the Quarter, was a pillared building of terrific proportions. From each of its tall, narrow windows hung red banners, and there were huge burning braziers instead of gas lamps.

'Wot's that place?' asked Niclas.

Balthazar wasn't interested in the building. He was, however, interested in the movement going on outside it. Men in crimson robes with an air of sanctimony about themselves were coming out of the main entrance and down the steps. Though there were only two and they were quite a way off, they seemed to unnerve the cat.

'Sir?'

'*The Academy.*'

'Wot's them men wearin' silly dresses for?'

'Best to keep away from there. The Library is this way, come.'

The Library was down a side street, a very large side street at that. It had huge stone steps and an enormous door, which in itself was bigger than most buildings. Niclas wondered if it had been built for giants. He'd heard about giants. Though he was pretty sure they weren't real. But surely this was proof that they were? Why else would people build such big doors… unless they'd read the blueprints wrong.

'Now you remember everything I told you?' said Balthazar taking a seat at the top step.

'Fink so, sir,' Niclas said with lukewarm optimism.

'Once you find the forbidden section, do your best not to get caught; if you do get caught, just play stupid… I'm sure that shouldn't be too hard for you.'

'Righto, sir.'

'And you remember what the book looks like?'

'Fink so, sir. Big leathery thing. Big black stone in the cover. Looks unlike any other book. Zol… Zal… Zor… Zoo-ee-coo-coo-com? Somethin'or'other.'

'*The Zolnomicon*. I shan't spell it again. The name's not important, it won't be labelled anyway. But if you look in the right place, you're certain to find it.'

'Ok, sir. And I'll defo knows it when I sees it?'

'Oh, certainly. It is unmistakable.'

The library was a high ceilinged building filled with halls that looked like caves built by men. Each was ribbed with towering bookshelves. Some books were within reach, but most needed a rolling ladder to get to. Niclas was glad the forbidden section wasn't up there. It was likely there were birds nesting up there, or a family of cirrocumulus that had gotten lost.

The hallways, like the offshoots of a star, circled around the centre of the library. In the middle, sat a large circular desk with parapets made of books. Every few seconds the crunch of a stamp slamming down on a returned book would echo out. Each one made Niclas jump.

The shelves were marked with hanging signs. *Marine Biology, Agricultural Science, Lunar Studies*. To Niclas they all said the same thing in slightly different squiggles. But it didn't matter, he'd been told he wouldn't find what he'd come for on any regular shelves. This sort of book wasn't the sort of book that was put on display. It was the sort of book that was hidden away so well, that not even the librarians would have known where to find it.

The Forbidden Section was easy to locate. Though he couldn't read the sign either, it was written in red and there was a red rope stretched out over the entrance to the stairwell. It was as clear an indication of *out of bounds* as can be.

Niclas made his way over to the entrance, trying his best to look inconspicuous, which had the reversed effect of making him look a great deal conspicuous.

But no one in particular was interested in what he was doing. There was a lawyer trying to find a case file in the *Law Histories* section and a nearby librarian rehoming a copy of *The Hitchhiker's Guide to Tea*. No one had even noticed Niclas enter the library, it wasn't like when he visited a shop or a market, all eyes didn't suddenly loom over him, waiting to catch him out on some intended criminality. Probably because everyone in the library was far too absorbed in their own bubble to notice someone else's bubble. And even if they had noticed him, there was no reason to believe he had any bad intentions – people with bad intentions and libraries didn't tend to go together; less common than olives in a bowl of porridge in fact.

Yet, perhaps it was Niclas' lack of fortune, or his odd, not so dashing good looks, or maybe it was just the way he seemed to tiptoe and dart his eyes around like a thief in a pantomime, but someone did pay him a little more attention than most.

She was sat with a book at a nearby table. It was *Professor Columbo's History of the Colonies* and she had just reached a boring bit, which, in this type of book, was all too common. She glanced up from the over-inked pages, and caught sight of Niclas, looking about as roguish as a sheep in wolf's clothing.

Niclas, completely unaware his every action was now being broadcast, sidled over to the red rope, ducked under it and snuck down the stairs.

The steps spiralled down and cold air breathed up from below. Downstairs was more stoney than upstairs. It was darker too. The gas lamps on the walls were a deep orange in glow, but not really that bright. The bookshelves were smaller, and the ceiling was lower, low enough that Niclas could stroke it, which he couldn't seem to stop himself from doing.

The space was cramped, the shelves closer together. The books down there were caked in dust and cobwebs and were some of the oldest books in the city, probably some of the oldest in the known world. Their spines were tattered and their pages were a tea stained yellow. On the right hung the sign: *Records of the Academy*. On the left: *Reports and Inquiries*. Then there was *Auld Istories* and *Auld Filosophies*. None of the books looked like the one he was after. He'd have to go a lot deeper to find that one.

Soon there were no bookshelves at all, just piles of old manuscripts and chests piled up on one another, over filled with dusty old tomes.

Niclas let out a heavy sigh. It was clear that the book wasn't going to be as easy to find as Balthazar had suggested. This was the Aladdin's cave of old books. It could take years to find the right one – and only if a person could read. Niclas, who couldn't read street signs, was entirely dependant on luck to be on his side; which of course, it never was.

It was best to start somewhere, he thought. He began rummaging through the chests, looking for a thick, leather-bound tome, untitled, with a black stone in its cover. Lots of books were untitled, and most of them were leather-bound, but not a single one had a stone of any kind whatsoever.

'What are you doing down here?' came a voice from behind.

Niclas stiffened up, the book in his hand dropped back into the chest and he swallowed a hard, dry gulp that hurt a bit as it went down.

'Excuse me?' The voice didn't sound threatening. It was well spoken. A *toff* for sure, definitely not a thug, but he didn't feel assured by that. Slowly, as if expecting to be shot, he turned around to face it.

'I said, what are you doing down here? It's forbidden, didn't you see the sign?'

There stood a young girl with fair hair and a firm look on her face. She wasn't much older than he was, not that her age made him feel any more at ease.

'Uhh…'

'Yes?' she said quickly.

'Well, wot you doin' down 'ere 'n' all?'

'I beg your pardon?'

'Well… you shouldn't be down 'ere, miss. It's forbidden, didn't *you* see the sign?'

'Oh, don't try that on me. I'm only here because you're here. Now, answer me, what are you doing here?'

Niclas swallowed again, painfully.

'I work for the libraries miss. I'm just makin' sure all the books are in the right places, innit?'

The girl said nothing at first, she looked Niclas up and down and narrowed her eyes.

'That's likely to be the worst lie I have ever heard.'

'You callin' me a liar, miss?' said Niclas, with a dash of spurious exasperation.

'Yes. I am. You're far too young to be a librarian. Now, I suggest you tell me what you're up to, or, I'll fetch an *actual* librarian and we'll see shall we?'

'No need for that, miss. I's only playin', that's all. Just havin' me a browse. No 'arm meant.'

'You're a thief then?'

'Wot! No! I ain't no thief! I swear I ain't. I ain't never stolen anyfing in me life.'

'There is no such word as ain't,' said the girl. 'You either are not or am not. And you *are* a terrible liar.'

'Don't be calling' me a liar, miss, I don'ts lie.'

'Stop it. You just did, again. You're a hypocrite too.'

'I ain't no hippo's pit, miss. I ain't lying t'ya, I ain't—'

'If you say that word one more time, I will call a librarian on principle alone.'

'…Sorry, miss, me speakin' ai…' Niclas paused to think.

'Is not,' said the girl.

'Is not… no good.'

'Sign of a poorly read mind, that's what my tutor always says. I have read many books and I have a good knowledge of many things. I've just finished *Dr Shorlock Gnomes' Science of Body Language* you know.'

'Body sandwich?'

'Language.'

'Wot's that?'

'It means I can tell you're lying. I can read your movements. The way your eyes are flickering, the way you're playing with your hands, the way you're sweating.'

Niclas was suddenly even more uncomfortable, apparently that was possible. He paid attention to everything about himself, from where his feet were pointing, to how quickly he was breathing.

'So… let's try it again, shall we? What are you looking for? The truth, if you please.'

'Troof… troof is…' What was the truth? That he'd been rescued from the Guard's Tower by a talking cat, verbally signed a contract of employment and had been sent out to steal a book, which he wouldn't be able to read but that he was pretty sure his new feline master would? When you put it like that, the truth really was an inconvenient one.

'I don't know wot the troof is, miss.'

'You do speak funny don't you? Are you from Cheapside? South of the river or something?'

'Uh, nah, I ain't ever bin sowf o' the river, miss. Never ever. Not in all me life.'

'Where are you from then?'

'I'm from…' Niclas' little pea brain suddenly went into over-drive. It wasn't very good at working on the spot. If he said he was from south of the river, she'd make him as a thief for sure. Northern folk, especially lady northern folk seemed to point their fingers and yell "Guards!" at southerners; no southern person had any business this far north of the river, not any reputable business anyway. But where else could he say? His own geographical un-derstanding of where he was, was about the same as a rat that's been spun around in an empty barrel of gin fumes, blind folded, placed in a maze and asked to find the cheese. As far as he was aware, north was south and south was west and west was proba-bly also north. But his little pea brain took hold of the situation, raised its metaphorical hand against his chest and said, "I'll take it from here."

'Brewery Quarter. Queen's Garter. That's where I live.' Niclas felt the words come out, but wasn't really sure how they had done so. It certainly didn't have anything to do with him.

'You live in the Brewery Quarter?'

'Yeah. All me life.'

The girl didn't look like she was going to buy this. That's why it was all the more surprising when she said: 'Well, that explains a lot.'

'It does?'

'Certainly. I'm glad we're getting somewhere. Now, what brings you here?'

'…'

'Well?'

'I'm lookin' for a book, miss.'

'… Yes, this is a library. The thought had crossed my mind that you'd be in here for one of those. But why down here?'

'I was told I'd find it down 'ere, miss… It ain't like t'other books. It's a special one.'

'Special?'

'It's a bigg'n, I knows that. It's leather-bound. Probs got no title on the cover. And it's got a big black stone on its front.'

'Interesting… What is it about?'

'About?'

'Yes. History? Science? Language? A memoir?'

'Dunno, miss.'

The girl was so taken aback by this that she literally craned her neck backwards as she looked askant.

'That's helpful,' she said.

'Not really, miss…'

'Surely you know what it's about? Why else would you be looking for… oh… I see… you're getting it for someone aren't you?'

'Wot? No? Wot makes you say that.'

'Well, besides the look you just gave me, it's obvious isn't it.'

'I don'ts know wot you fink's going on miss, but I finks you're probs wrong.'

'How curious…' said the girl, thinking aloud.

'Curious? Wot's curious?'

'Someone has blatantly asked you to get this book for them. The question is why? Why can't they get it themselves?'

It was an interesting question and Niclas for once had the answer. He so badly wanted to tell her but he flat-out knew it was a terrible idea.

'Don't know wot you're talkin' 'bout miss.'

'Hmm… Of course you don't.' Something about the way she stared back at him, made him feel frightfully on edge. It was her body language thing, he was sure of it.

'Come on then. Let's start with these chests. All the really old books will be in there. Preserves them better.'

Niclas didn't move. He watched as the girl crossed him and began rooting through the nearest dusty coffer.

'You're gonna 'elp me?'

'Of course. I doubt you'd ever be able to find anything. And how am I going to know what this is all about, unless you do.'

The two of them went through the chests like wildfire. Two very different interpretations of wildfire. The girl moved fast, but treated each and every book with the same reverence as you'd treat a great grandmother, carefully placing them out of the way where they couldn't get hurt. Niclas was faster, but tossed the books over his shoulder in a fierce dig, like a dog trying to find its bone at the bottom of a sandpit.

'You're certain this book actually exists?' asked the girl after looting her third chest.

'…'

'Let's keep looking.'

Soon they'd carved their way deep into a sea of lost manuscripts and kicked up a swell of bookish dust. There were books of all descriptions all around them, but none were marked with any kind of stone.

'I'm pretty sure I've seen this one before,' said the girl, lifting up a heavy red leather tome titled *The Banterbury Tales*. 'Yes. I have. We're doing this all wrong. We've mixed up the old books with the new books!'

'They all look old to me, miss?'

'No. I mean, we've mixed up the ones we've checked with the ones we haven't. Argh, this is a disaster.'

'…is it?'

'We'll have to start again, it's the only way to be sure we haven't missed it.'

'Shh! Wassat?'

'What's what?'

'Wait.' Niclas lifted his finger and pricked up his ears.

The girl waited.

'I don't hear anything,' she said at last.

But there was something. And now it was too late. The steps

had reached the bottom of the stairs, and the shimmering light from a freshly aflame lantern shivered into the cold, dark space.

'Quick!' The girl pulled back the lid of a chest and nodded to Niclas to jump in. Without question he leapt into the coffer, tucked his knees into his chest and squeezed down so that it could shut.

'Wot you gonna–'

'Shush,' the girl brought the lid down on him mid-sentence. She moved to the next chest. It was full of books. So was the one after that. The flickering lantern light was getting brighter, the steps louder.

Just before the lantern holder came within sight, she found a tattered portmanteau that stood out from the chests and crawled inside; shutting the lid just as the light shined over it.

At the end of the flickering lantern was a shaky, wrinkly hand. The librarian was a white bearded man, most librarians were. He glanced over the books and chests with old, prune-like eyes of suspicion and tut-tut-ed at the mess.

Those damn students had been at it again. They were supposed to carry things down the stairs and leave them in an orderly fashion, not trash the place. He shook his head and stroked his beard. He'd be sure to have words with the head librarian about it, maybe even write a nasty letter to the Academy.

But there was no one down there now, however; that was why he was there. From the stairs above, it sounded as if the rats had gotten in again. But everything was still and calm and there was absolutely nothing to worry about. Nothing at all. So the librarian turned, left, and took his bright light with him back up the stairs.

After a while longer, Niclas raised the lid on his chest and stuck his head out like a tortoise. 'Psst. They're gone,' he whispered.

The girl shot up from the portmanteau and stuttered out a dusty cough.

'You alright?'

'Yes. I'm fine,' she said, wiping the dirt from her dress.

'That was close. Reckon they heard us? Reckon they'll be back? Wot if they're coming back? There's only that stairs out? Wot if they're watching at the top... uh? 'Ello?' The girl wasn't listening, she had become absorbed by something near her feet. If Niclas had to guess by the look on her face and the cobwebs hanging from her right ear, it was a spider. A big hairy one at that. Girls were all afraid of spiders. He hoped she wouldn't scream.

'Is... is it... is it a spider?'

'Nope. Not a spider.' She lifted up a large tome and held it out to him as if it were some sort of trophy.

'Wot?'

'This is it isn't it?'

'Wot?'

'Your book? Big, leather bound, no title on it, and look, a black stone.'

She was right. The book cover had a shiny, marble sized obsidian shard melted into its centre. It was the blackest thing either of them had ever seen. The kind of black that makes ordinary black look like a rather pathetic shade of grey. It seemed to suck in all the light, what little light there was, like a dense black hole of the cosmos that could fit in your hand.

'Well. Let's see what this is all about shall we?'

'Pass it 'ere!' said Niclas, clambering over towards her.

'No. Not until I have first look.'

'But... I don't fink...'

Before he could stop her, she'd turned the first page. Then the second. Then the third. Then the tenth. Then the sixtieth. Then the three-hundred-and-fourth. Each time her face got that bit more flabbergasted.

'How strange.'

'Wot?'

'This writing... it's... what a weird language... it's not... it's not anything I've seen before...'

'Let's see.' Niclas wasn't sure why he was so keen to take a look, it's not like he'd be able to read it anyway. But when he looked at it, even he knew that it was written in a language from another time. Another place. Another world perhaps. The shapes and symbols looked like no drawings he had ever seen. They didn't even look... human, if words could look human.

'It's all just gibberish...' said the girl, an air of genuine disappointment in her tone. 'Who did you say it was for again?'

'No one, miss. I didn't say it was for anyone... did I?'

'Is this some sort of game?'

'No miss, it's very serious, 'and it over.' Niclas tried to snatch it, but she reeled it away. 'I fawt you was gonna 'elp me find it!'

'I said I'd help you find it, yes. I don't recall saying anything about letting you have it.'

'Wot! You can't do that. I needs it.'

'Why? Who's it for?'

'No one! I've told ya.' He tried to take it again, but the girl brought it up and out of reach.

'I should take this upstairs to the librarians and hand you in. It's a crime you know, stealing a book, even if you're stealing for someone else.'

'You wouldn't do that. You'd get in trouble 'n' all. Neiver o' us are allowed down 'ere.'

'Me, get into trouble. Ha! I don't get into trouble. I'm not the sort of person who gets into trouble. But you,' said the girl, with a haughty pointing finger, 'you'd get into all sorts of trouble.'

'Please, miss, you gotta give it t'me. It's me first job. Me first proper job. If I don't bring it back... me master might give me the sack!' Niclas begged, grabbing about the air, trying to snatch the book whilst the girl juggled it from hand to hand.

'Aha! So you are stealing it for someone!'

'…' Niclas sighed. He'd been betrayed by his own sorry self. It was tragic.

'Who?'

'I daren't say, miss.'

'Who is it?'

'Just some fella, you wouldn't know 'im. Pass it 'ere, please.'

'Is it a scholar? One of those Academy boys put you up to it?'

'Nah, I don'ts know no Academy boys.'

The girl touched the side of her face to think.

'Hmm…' She brightened. 'Someone who trades in antiques, I bet?'

'No miss, I don't fink so.'

At this, she stamped her foot the way someone usually does before they say "Oooh I give up!" Except she didn't say that, she said: '*Awgh moons!*'

Niclas didn't say anything. He'd given up trying to take the book and was now trying to give her his best puppy eyes. His expression was forlorn, hopeless, almost heartbreaking. It would have been slightly impressive had he been putting it on, but sadly, he wasn't. He really was that pathetic.

The girl stared at him with a dubious stare. Then, slowly, she let go of the doubt and sighed. He clearly was desperate for the book, and looked about as helpless as a hungry kitten left out on a cold night. Though, nowhere near as cute.

'Alright,' she said at last. 'It's yours.'

'Wot…' said Niclas. No one changed their mind that quickly, did they?

'But here.' The girl lifted her satchel bag off her shoulder and dropped the book inside. 'You'll need this bag. That way, no one will notice you walk out with it. Let's put a few more books in here too. They're probably highly valuable and I think your *master* will be pleased to know you've gone the extra mile.' She picked up a pile of old books that were falling apart, and dropped them inside the bag.

Niclas was struggling to find his tongue.

'Don't worry, you don't have to thank me,' she said, *in a tone that implied he did have to thank her*, and held out the bag to him.

He took it, hesitantly.

'Fanks…'

'But, if our paths cross again, I'll expect you to tell me what it was all about. Promise?'

'Sure, miss. That's very kind o' you. But… I don't get it. Why you being so nice all o' a sudden?'

'I don't want you to get into trouble now do I? What kind of person would that make me?'

'…'

'What did you say your name was?'

'I didn't.'

'Well, what is it?'

'Niclas… miss.'

'Nic-las? What a funny name. I'm Cassandra. With a C, the proper spelling. It's a pleasure to meet you Nic-las.'

'And you… miss.'

'Come… we should get out of here before he comes back.'

'…yeah…' said Niclas, a smile creeping onto his lips.

She smiled back. It was a strange smile. A little too smiley, perhaps. Maybe it was a trick, he thought. Maybe she was going to wait till they were upstairs, then let loose the pointed finger again and yell, "Guards!"

But she didn't. The two of them snuck back into the library. Cassandra went back to her table and Niclas, sweating like a lobster in a crockpot, shuffled his way to the exit and out into the street.

A while later, Cassandra left the library and was met by a horse and carriage at the bottom of the steps. It wasn't just any old horse and carriage. The tall, white horses were the kind trained in dressage. They were muscular giants, with magnificent manes and black feathered head dresses. The coach itself was made of the finest oak, and finished with intricate carvings made by a carpenter who clearly had too much time on his hands.

The driver didn't say a word, he touched the tip of his top hat and nodded. Out of the door came a man dressed a little on the threatening side. He was armed with a silver rapier and was padded and armoured from head to neck. His name was Rufus. Though his relationship with Cassandra was that of an unrelated uncle, he was much more than a close family friend, he was her loyal, sworn protector.

'Good day, M'Lady.' He held the door for her and helped her with a hovering wrist up the steps and into the back.

'Thank you, Rufus,' she said.

The door closed and the coach wheeled away.

'More homework from Mr Eccleston is it?' asked Rufus, noting the pile of books on Cassandra's lap. 'Want me to hold them?'

'No, no. I've got them,' replied Cassandra.

Indeed, she did have them. They were cradled in her lap by two over protective hands. At the top was *Professor Columbo's History of the Colonies*, at the bottom, *Holm Rhomsky's Tongues of the Natives*. And somewhere in the middle, a book with no name, no author and a mysterious black stone melted into its cover.

***

'One job! You had one job!' said a very angry Balthazar from the corner of the bed.

Niclas searched the empty bag as if it were bottomless and the book had fallen into another dimension within it.

'I can't believe this. None of these books are right. They're not even slightly right. I could understand if they looked similar to the one I described but they don't. Not at all. They're the least similar looking books you could possibly find. This one's clearly a recipe book and this one is… what is it? Ah! Poetry. I should have known you'd make a fluff of it.'

'I… I don't understand, sir. It was right 'ere, black stone like you said. Old dark leather. It was all funny scribbles inside too.'

'Well it's not here now is it! What do you suppose happened? It grew a pair of legs, hopped out of your bag and ran back to the dusty shelf from whence it came?'

'No… sir… I don'ts gets it, sir. I don'ts.'

'And this bag? Where did you steal that from?'

The bag was a luxurious bag, a little too luxurious for a bag as far as Balthazar was concerned. It was a plush, purple velour, lined with black silk; not the sort of bag you just found lying around.

'Some girl gave it me.'

Balthazar's green slit eyes widened. This was it. The missing piece of the jigsaw.

'*What girl?*'

'Just some girl… I didn't want t'tell ya, but I gots caught lookin' in the forbid bit. It's ok though. She didn't tell no one or do any-fing bad. She was quite 'elpful really.'

'Helpful? *How so?*'

'Well. If it weren't for 'er I'd never 'av' found it. And she gave me this bag, see, so I could get out without lookin' like I was robbin' the place.'

If Balthazar had had hands, he'd have slapped Niclas across the face and sunk his own head into his palms. But he didn't, he had paws, so he raised one to his nose and sunk into that instead.

'Wot? Wot is it, sir? Don't be like that. It ain't…'

There it was, like a bad smell the thought settled into Niclas' little pea brain.

'You don't fink she did one on me? Like, took the book for 'erself?'

Balthazar kept his eyes closed. He was bubbling with feline rage and if he looked at the boy just then, he'd probably have clawed him.

'She *was* proper interested in it...'

Balthazar held his miserable pose.

'...and, come to fink 'bout it, she did change 'er mind a bit quick...'

'Who is she?'

'I dunno, sir. But she was proper posh. From north ends for sure. She told me 'er name... but...' Niclas scratched his head.

Balthazar sighed and put distance between him and the boy. It was for the best.

'Don't be mad, sir. It ain't my fault. I bin hustled! Bin duped!'

'Not only did you fail to do your job, you've succeeded in making the situation worse.'

'Oh, sir, don't be like that. We can find 'er.'

'And how do you suggest we do that? It's lost. Forget it.'

Balthazar walked over to the window, jumped up and sat with his nose pressed against the cold glass. He liked to sit there. It was his thinking spot.

'I could go back. I reckons she visits the library a lot. She said she read a lot. She probs spends loads o' time there. I could wait around until I see 'er again and then... well... I dunno exactly, but... I could get it back.'

'Are you familiar with the Lunar Festival?' said the cat, eager to change the subject.

'Uhh... does that mean moons? Cause I know the moon festival. It's when the whole city gets drunk, there's dancin', 'n' games, 'n' drinkin' and all that sort o' fing. Us boys was never allowed to celebrate, but Mr K 'n' the grown ups used to leave us alone for the night. It's the one night o' t'year we could all 'av a bit o' fun... that was, until Smivy ruined a 'ole batch o' gin... Was proper bad that time... Never saw 'im again.' Niclas sighed ruefully.

'Hmmm, yes.'

'Sorry, sir. Wot woz you sayin'?'

'Do you know the history behind the festival?'

'Can't say I do, sir.'

'Allow me,' said Balthazar. 'Once a year the two moons crossover. Nei passes in front of Jah, and the two become one in the sky. In olden times, the First People thought the two moons were going to crash into one another and bring about the end of the world. Of course, they didn't. But it became tradition to celebrate it each year as if it were the last day of life. Such a tradition has survived the test of time, yet scholars and years of lunar studies have proven the old tale a myth.'

Niclas looked to be listening very intently. In reality, he was very much lost.

'It is now but a celebration of the passing of the old year and the coming of the new year. And that time again is fast approaching.'

'Sir… sorry… but… wot's this got to do wiv that book?' said Niclas, bravely.

'Everything. That book contains a certain knowledge that I require. And I only have until the night of the Lunar Festival to prepare for it. Else I'll have to wait another year.'

'Prepare for wot, sir?'

'I wasn't always like this you know. A cat. I was a man once.'

'Wot? Did'ya get sick or summin?'

'Yes, you could say that. If I am to be cured again, I need what's in that book.'

'…' Niclas squinted, frowned and looked around. 'Wait. Let me get this bent. So… you're a cat… but you ain't really a cat… you're a man who's now a cat… and you're wantin' to be a man again?'

'That's about right, yes.'

'Well…'

'Well?'

'Well…'

'Well what?'

'Well that's proper topsy turvy!'

'…' Balthazar let out a long hard sigh. He'd anticipated this. It was a difficult story to sell.

'So that's why you need this book then? I guess that sort o' makes sense,' said Niclas.

Balthazar looked up. He didn't speak. He almost did but he was a bit too surprised. Strangely, really, really stupid people could sometimes be very, very smart, precisely because they were so, so stupid.

'Soooo, wot you fink, sir, should I go back to the library? How long we got till the festival?'

Balthazar ignored Niclas. An idea had cropped into his head. Quite a decent idea too, evinced by the fresh glimmer of hope on his whiskered face. He leapt down from the windowsill and examined the purple bag which Niclas had dropped on the floor.

'Sir?'

The cat didn't reply. He pawed at the fabric. His exceptionally sharp eyes had spotted something important.

'Look. I feel proper bad 'bout it, sir. I was stoopid, I know. Taken for a right fool. Let me go back to the library now. I'll camp outside it until I see that posh bint and then I'll give 'er a piece o' the ol' souvern revenge and get your book back.'

'Shush.'

'Wot?'

'We're going to need candles. Candles and chalk. Pink chalk.'

'Sir? Wot for?'

Niclas wasn't sure why Balthazar's mood had changed, but he was sure the cat was now smiling. It had something to do, though he was even less sure why, with the single thread of long blonde hair beneath the cat's paw.

two

When darkness fell on the Guard's Square the lanterns kept it lit. Brightest were the ones on the eastern side, where the golden Palace gates shimmered below burning braziers. It was late in the night and all the Palace windows were washed in blackness. Even the servant quarters on the lower west wing were sleeping. But up high, in the centre of the Palace's facade, a small rectangle of illumination suggested that all was not still.

Someone was up, and way past their bedtime.

Cassandra had waited hours for the Palace to enter its slumber. When the day was done, she lay in bed beneath her duck down quilt, waiting for Martha, the maid, to tuck her in. The maid kissed her on the cheek, blew out the candle and backed out of the room closing the door behind her. Once the door clicked shut, and the muffled beat of the maid's footsteps had faded from earshot, Cassandra counted a minute.

She leapt up, threw off the quilt and struck a match over the still smoking candle wick. Then, from under her bed, she pulled out a pile of books, took up the untitled one and sat at her desk with it.

It was an odd book. The oddest she had ever seen perhaps.

It was made of a strange sort of leather that felt like frostbitten skin. The stone too was blacker now in the candle light than it had been when she first laid eyes on it. And the lack of any inscription on the cover excited her. Cassandra was a person who usually got excited by books, but none had ever kept her up so late.

It wasn't just the cover that intrigued her. As she flicked through the pages she frowned at the curious symbols. What were they? What did they mean? Was this a book from the Colonies? Yet she had studied the languages of the Five Isles and not come across anything quite like this. This was different. It was older and far more peculiar than any language that existed.

She had hoped there would be a section in the common tongue. A part of the book that explained itself.

There was no such section.

Soon her excitement fizzled out with a *poof,* like a very disappointing firecracker.

Maybe her private tutor Mr Eccleston would know. He was young for a professor but just as wise as the old, bearded ones. But could she really ask him? Questions would surely follow. The book was bound to be in the forbidden section for a reason; a section of the library only permitted to the highest echelons of the Academy.

Perhaps, she thought, she could take it back and say there'd been a mix up, then, slyly, inquire with the librarians as to the book's nature. But they probably wouldn't tell her. They'd probably just take it away. Or worse, get the Academy involved.

She was getting angry about it all, so she slammed the book shut. For all she knew it was probably just an old recipe book that had ended up in the wrong place.

She sulked into bed. Her head hit the pillow and she pulled the quilt over her shoulders.

From a sideways view, she could still see her desk, and couldn't quite lift her eyes from the tome. She started huffing and puffing. The more she looked at it the more frustrated she was getting. Her eyes clamped shut.

But the book wasn't finished with her yet. It played on her thoughts and whispered into her ears. And that's a little more than a metaphor. *Because something was whispering.* Though it was all too snake-like and ghostly to be understood. It sounded like the rustle of the leaves in the courtyard, like the seething of the melting candle wax, the breathing of the breeze creeping in from beneath the door. The breeze was more noticeable now than the whispering. It was oddly colder than it had been but ten seconds ago, and now colder still. A gentle bluster of air ruffled through the room, tickling the candle flame. This spooked Cassandra and she shot up. For the window was closed; and even if it had been open as wide as it could, there was no wind that night.

Yet now the breeze had stopped. The whispering too. The room was sleeping just as the rest of the Palace was.

She stared at the tome with scrupulous eyes.

'Hello?' she said softly, to no one in particular.

Without a mouth to speak, the book seemed to call back. The whisper was faint and barely noticeable, but it came directly from the dresser.

Cassandra rose again, walked over to the untitled tome, sat in the chair once more and turned the cover to the first page.

She nearly jumped. *Nearly fell off her chair.*

It couldn't be but it was. There, before her, the letters of her alphabet were arranged in the common tongue. What had once been a jumble of squiggles and symbols was now as readable as any of her other books. The word in the centre of that first page, though meaningless, seemed to strike a chord of recognition.

ZOLNOMICON.

She turned the page.

The writing was small. Etched in black ink that had lost none of its blackness over time. And there were more words there on a single page than there were in some entire books. They were crammed together and squashed into orderly lines, legible only to people with excellent eye sight or those with a spare eyeglass. But they were legible. Just.

This was the common tongue for sure.

Cassandra shrugged. What was that old saying? When you have eliminated the impossible, whatever remains, however improbable, must be the truth... something like that. It was no more possible for a book to change its words than for a leopard to change its spots; by that logic, though improbable, it was her eyes and imagination that had gotten away with her. Yes... that sounded... *reasonable.*

She ran her finger along the opening sentence and read the words to herself.

'*The eyes of the open mind belong to he who whispers in the astral plane.*'

The floorboards creaked and a breeze shuddered the candle's flame. Cassandra took no notice of it. Or at least, she tried not to.

She continued...

'*Herein lie the whispers of he who whispers, spoken by the tongues of eternals, interred on the flesh of their backs with the ink of their bones.*'

Something stirred in the room. The netting over the windows ruffled. The candle was burning just the same but the room was darker. There were corners of it that had disappeared entirely.

She continued...

'*This grimoire harnesseth the workings of the Zol. All that is, is the Zol. The All. The Source. The Fabric of the Universe. All space, time and energy are connected as one within the consciousness of the Zol. Open one's mind to the whisperings of he who whispers and the sapient shall have knowledge to bend the Zol to their will. It is all that was, is and will be. It is the gift of immortals. It is the instrument of* masters. *It is shadow and flame. It is the destroyer and the creator. There is nothing outside of it, there is only the Zol.*'

Cassandra stopped. She had heard about hairs standing up on the backs of people's necks and shivers shivering down spines. But it wasn't until just then, when she learned that hairs do actually stand up on the backs of necks and shivers do really shiver down spines.

She could have sworn too, that as she had been whispering, another voice had been whispering between her breaths. Something eldritch. Something which didn't belong.

Knock knock!

It was frightening enough to bring the girl to her feet. She slammed the book and turned to face her bedroom just as the door opened.

'Oh dear. Deary, dear, dear, dear. What are you doing up and out of bed Cassandra? You're just as bad as your brother you are.' It was only Martha, the house maid. 'Now is not the time to be studying, M'Lady. Now is the time to be resting. You needs to rest when you're tolds to. They call it beauty sleep they do. Now, I never had a chance o' been a beautiful maiden, but you M'Lady, you're a beautiful young girl, and one day I'm sure you'll be a beautiful Queen, just like your o'mam. But, if you go on like this, up all night, squinting under candlelight, not getting your beauty sleep then you'll be hiding from mirrors all o' your adult life. And you don't want that do ya?'

'No, Martha… of course not.'

Cassandra pushed the book aside and quickly placed the others on top of it.

'We've got visitors tomorrow and all. Got to look your best come rise and shine.'

'Visitors?' said Cassandra, crawling back into bed.

'Some of the Lords of Parliament, M'Lady. Coming for tea they are. An early tea. Around elevenses, if I'm not mistaken.'

'Oh.' Cassandra had about as much affection for Lords of Parliament as she did criminals. To her the two were one and the same. One lied and cheated because it was part of the job description, the other, because it was in its nature.

'What do they want?'

'Now, now, Princess. Don't fret. They're charming fellows every one of them, just awfully busy that's all, don't have much time for the younger generation like yourself.'

'Lord Waldor once asked mother to send me to my room. He said children should be seen and not heard. A child? I was thirteen!'

'Still, not an adult though, Princess. And if I remember correctly you were going on about the moons colliding into each other all through the meal.'

'And? I wasn't making it up… It's a very well documented theory, that given the orbits of the moons and the circumstances of their gravitational pull, eventually, not tomorrow, but in perhaps millions of years they will crash into each other. I was only remarking how enlightening it was that previous civilisations existing before the Realm of Logic had come to the same conclusion.'

'Yes… And you may have been right, my dear. But sometimes you need to know when to let go. Otherwise people get upset, that's all.'

'Well, he was a silly man, who shouldn't have let a *child* upset him.'

'That may be so, dear, that may be so.' Martha chuckled.

'What do they want?'

'I don't know the ins and outs, M'Lady. But they said it was urgent. Hence the last minute invitation.'

Lords of Parliament were the only creatures in the known world who officially invited themselves places. You didn't need to send them wedding or dinner invitations, if they were coming, they would likely have already invited themselves and let you know about it with as little notice as possible.

'I do hope they don't ruin the day, mother's always in a bad mood when they visit.'

'Oh, I'm sure they won't. Now come. No more reading. Give yourself the beauty sleep you deserve and I'll see you come rise and shine for some brekky.'

Cassandra knew that meant porridge. She didn't like porridge but had somehow kept it a secret from the maid for sixteen long years.

'Goodnight, Martha.'

'Night, night, m'dear.' Martha blew out the candle, plunging the room into darkness, and closed the door behind her for the second time in one evening.

Cassandra lay in the dark thinking about the next day, the Lords and salty rolled oats.

And she was thinking about something else as well.

A whisper in the corner of her ear.

***

That night a stranger arrived in Laburnum.

Little can be said to describe this man. His age was somewhere north of thirty and south of fifty. Where he came from remains a mystery; and if he had a name, there was not a living person who knew it. He kept to the shadows, wearing a dark greatcoat and a tattered slouch hat, which drooped its wide brim around his head and cast his face in darkness.

He'd not visited the capital for many years, but he was in no mood to reminisce. He had come for business.

Such surreptitious business will always find its way to the part of the city where questions are seldom asked: the Brewery Quarter. Where the only queries are to how much gin is left in the bottle and at what time last orders will be called.

At the ambiguous hour of four (a time both morning and night) the Quarter was filled with its usual crowd. The stranger passed through it, stopped outside one of the quieter pubs and looked up at the hanging sign. It read: "*The Medicine Tap*".

The door creaked open and a few drunken heads turned. Their drunken eyes fixed on the stranger. After a brief inspection, they arrived back at their drinks and each took a sullen sip. Or for some, a sullen gulp.

The stranger approached the barman, who had been watching him incredulously from the moment the bell above the door had chimed.

'Wot can I do you for, sir?'

'I'm meeting someone here,' said the stranger, his voice hoarse and deep, lingering just above a whisper. 'Name of Job Button.'

'Job. Aye, 'e's expectin' you. I understand you wanted some privacy, so we've got a room for you upstairs on the left.'

The stranger nodded and stepped away. But the barman, polishing a tankard so as to put something between him and the man, hesitantly called him back.

You saw all types of folk, working behind a bar, and the barman had developed a knack for sussing out the dangerous ones. They were usually quiet, shy individuals, who didn't like being stared at. The stranger looked the type.

'Uh… see… the fing is, sir… 'e said you'd fit the bill, that's all. For the room, see? Cuz, rooms cost money, even if you ain't stayin' the night… I could put one o' these 'ere gents–'

The stranger reached into his pocket and in doing so cast panic into the room, silencing the barman and nearly forcing him into an untimely bowel movement. The customers, the barman and one man's dog all sighed relief as they watched a handful of coins trickle onto the table.

The barman grinned. 'Ooo… Why fank you very much, sir. Erm… I'll 'av me wife bring up some drinks for ya. On the 'ouse, don't worry 'bout it.'

The stranger nodded then ventured up the stairs.

Conversations resumed and the barman counted his profits. His wife was standing arms folded at the corner of the bar.

''E looks like trouble!' came her vulgar voice.

'Shush woman! It'll be alright. No trouble. Job promist.'

'Job, promist did 'e? Dat's wot you sed last time. Last time, 'e damn near killed 'imself on ah bottle of dat dere medicine. I remember it like it woz yesterday - "one more bottle can't 'urt, I'll be no trouble", next fing we knows 'e's bent 'alf way over de bar given our glasses a good cleanin' wiv wot medicine 'e couldn't fit in 'is belly.'

'It's fine.'

'I 'ope so.'

'Pour two drinks and take 'em up will ye? And not a word you 'ere me woman? I knows wot yer like.'

'Wot sorta drinks?'

'Wot?'

'Well wot sorta drinks should I be pourin' for 'em?'

'I don't know. Gin?'

'Don't wanna waste good gin on 'em do we?'

'Suppose not. Whisky then. But the cheap stuff.'

Upstairs there were two doors marked with badly written signs. One "*vakent*". One "*occopyd*". The stranger gently rapped his fist on the former, pushing it open to a dull groan.

He was met with a dark room and the silhouette of a man sat in a cloud of smoke rising from his pipe and glowing in the moonlight.

Neither said hello.

The stranger closed the door behind him.

Job Button toked on his pipe.

'Evenin',' said Job.

The stranger didn't reply.

'I've got valuable information for you. Dangerous it is,' said Job. 'The kind of information that could get us sent to the gallows. I 'ope you know I value me life a lot, it 'as a 'igh price to be risked.'

The stranger, still ignoring him, searched the room for places someone could hide. He spied out the window, checked the door was properly shut and only then, when he was completely satisfied with their privacy, did he speak.

'Tell me and I will decide its worth.'

Job puffed on his pipe, feeding the unwelcome silence with a further pause.

Job was a part-time undertaker, full-time drinker, always on the lookout to earn a few extra bob. He wasn't a man people took seriously, but on this occasion it was vital that he be taken seriously. He'd had two less drinks to give him an edge of sobriety and bought a pipe, because he was sure gents with pipes looked more professional. And that was probably true, when they didn't splutter after every toke.

'I 'ears you're the man to speak to 'bout certain… unusual findings.'

'…'

'I does a lot o' work in Bloomhill Cemetery. You know it?'

'…'

Clearly the stranger wanted to keep things short. He hadn't even sat down.

'I suppose you've 'eard of grave robbers. Dem ones wot go round diggin' up the graves, robbin' the valuables wot get buried wiv loved ones.'

'…'

It was hard to gauge whether or not the stranger was following, his face was void of all expression, and his attention divided between the street out the window and Job.

'Dirty work it is.'

'I am not interested in grave robbers,' said the stranger.

'Ah! But these ain't regular grave robbers. Some of 'em are. But some of the graves I find... most queer they are... *most queer*.'

'...'

'Every now and then I come 'cross a grave that's bin robbed for summin else.'

'...'

'*The bodies*.'

Despite the extra care in dropping this punchline, Job was disappointed in the stranger's response. He'd expected a gasp, at the very least an eye widening or a nostril twitch. He got nothing.

'I've heard of this,' said the stranger. 'Men of science and students of anatomy digging up the dead to further their studies. It is not the sort of unusual I'm looking for.'

'Yes, but–'

There was a gentle tapping at the door and the barman's wife came creeping in with a tray of two drinks.

''Ere we are my sirs. Two on the 'ouse, courtesy of the 'usband.'

The stranger stared at Job. Job stared at the stranger. Both stared at the barman's wife who stared awkwardly at the drinks then set them down on the side table, bowed her head and retreated.

'Sorry to disturb ye. Beg me pardons.' It was obvious when a conversation wasn't meant for your ears, especially when it stopped dead as you came within earshot. The barman's wife backed out of the room and the stranger made sure the door was closed.

Job wasn't one to turn away a good drink. He picked up his glass and gave it an inquisitive sniff. It was whisky. An oak malt. 12 years old perhaps (actually this stuff was barely a few weeks, but he'd never know). He downed it in one and exhaled a bitter yet satisfied "*Ahhhh*".

''S'good that. You gonna 'av' yours?' asked Job, hovering his hand above the second glass.

'No.'

'Mind if I...?'

'No.'

'Very well.' The second one went down the hatch. '*Ahhhh*. Doubly good. Right… Where was I? Oh yeah. That's it. There's a bit more to this grave thing. A bit more wot makes it very unusual indeed.'

'Go on?'

'I knows when a grave's bin robbed by an academic. Body goes walkies. But a few of 'em 'av bin… different. *Illogical* some'd say.'

Job was a natural storyteller and it was beginning to get on the stranger's nerves.

'Yes?'

'You see, when it's smart folk wot rob the graves, they don't do it wiv their own 'ands. They employ people wiv experience. People wot rob graves for a livin'. And I ain't ever seen a grave robber miss up an opportunity to get their fingers on valuables.'

'Get to the point.'

'Wot I'm sayin' is: how many grave robbers do you know, wot would rob a grave of its body but leave the valuables behind.'

This was worth listening to and finally drew a curious brow furrowing from the stranger's face.

'That *is* interesting,' said the stranger at last.

Job replenished his pipe, struck a match to light it, toked it and coughed in a cloud of smoke.

'And you think this is evidence of the Black Science?' asked the stranger.

'There's more. See, when a grave's bin robbed for a body, it's usually fresh. It's usually dug up a night or two after it's bin put in the ground. Usually. But as I said, this ain't usual. Some of them graves wot's bin robbed… they're old. Weeks old. I saw one that was a month gone, I swear it.'

'And only the bodies taken?'

'Yep. All the shinies still there. Not bad for me own pocket, if you get wot I mean.' Job laughed. It was a horse's laugh and was immediately followed with choking and wheezing.

The stranger took a minute to reflect. It sounded suspicious enough to him, and that was exactly what he was hoping for.

It was exactly what Job was hoping for too.

'So? Worth a pretty penny I reckon? Wot you fink?'

'It's intriguing, yes. And worth a price, yes. I'll give you a twenty five percent down payment. The rest to be paid after.'

'After wot?'

'I can't take your word, you understand. I'd be a poor man if I went around handing out pounds for any old fool's gossip.'

Job's face sank.

It was soon revived. The stranger pulled out a red felt bag and emptied half of it into his hand. Job leant out of his seat for a closer look. What he saw made him grin. His teeth, what teeth he had, gleamed in the moonlight. As did the coins.

There was, however, another side to all this. A side that wasn't altogether private.

Mildred, the barman's wife, was a nosey woman. She needed to know who everyone in her tavern was, where they came from, what they were doing there, who they were involved with romantically and what they preferred on their toast in the morning. After leaving the two drinks behind, she had lingered in the hallway and pressed her ear to the keyhole.

She hadn't heard much but what she'd heard was enough. Something about bodies and grave robbers and that rarely uttered word that all citizens took particularly seriously. "*Illogical*". Not in her house, thought Mildred. There'd be none of that sort of thing.

She didn't hang about. At once, she darted down the stairs and snuck out into the street while her husband served his guests. There she found a thirsty boy, gave him a penny and whispered into his ear. The boy ran through the sleepless crowds of the Brewery Quarter and fetched the first Watchman he could find.

The guard had been quietly enjoying a pint at the end of his shift with his fellow Watchmen. But on hearing the gossip, the cohort left their drinks with near full heads of foam and rallied to the Medicine Tap. Normally the testimony of a young lad that early in the morning in the Brewery Quarter would have been laughed at. But this wasn't a laughing matter.

There are many crimes in the city of Laburnum. They are listed and ranked in the *Watchman's Law Book*, which every Watchman must carry on his persons at all times.

…No.423 Relieving oneself in a private doorway. No.365 Getting oneself too drunk to make it home. No.269 Feaguing a horse with a live eel in public. No.231 Napping whilst in command of a horse cart. No.190 Handling trout in a suspicious manner. No.155 Irresponsibly dying in the middle of the street. No.130 Unintentionally giving lost people awful directions…

And so on and so on until the more serious offences.

…No.22 Arson. No.7 Theft. No.3 Murder. No.2 Treason…

And finally, a crime worse than all put together. A crime so criminal that to even discuss it, is in itself, a crime.

…No.1 Logicide: thought, behaviour or dialogue, which is removed from reason and logic…

The stranger and Job Button had concluded their conversation and were about to go their separate ways when they heard it – the rising voices from below.

'No! You can't just go bargin' through… Stop! Come back 'ere–'

It was muffled but sounded like the barman for sure.

Then came the next muffled noise. The sound of boots. Boots clobbering their way up the wooden staircase. Job Button sprang into panic. He leapt up from his chair spilling his pipe on the floor.

'Wot do we do?' he said. 'Moons collide. We're doomed to spin!

76

They'll string us up, shoot us, torture us for weeks on end; or, be it worse… send us to the Hall–'

The stranger lifted his finger to his mouth and silenced the gibbering loon.

He exuded calm. He pulled the chair Job had been sitting on across the room and fixed it under the door handle – then he moved to the window.

Outside he saw the waggon and a guard on watch beside it. There were only two ways out of the room, the door and the window, and both it seemed would end in violence.

After a pause, which drove Job Button to the brink of madness, the guards began hammering on the door. The stranger turned to his anxious informant and said: 'Listen, this is what we're going to do.'

…

A few minutes passed.

…

The guard was hammering so furiously at the woodwork that when it opened at last, his fist remained dancing in the air.

A smiling Job Button curiously ushered him in. The guard, fooled by this nonchalant welcoming, lingered in the doorway for a few seconds before being thrust aside by another man, Laburnum's Chief Inspector.

The first thing people notice about Inspector Forsyth is the unfortunately long nose situated in the middle of his face. Wherever the word *logicide* is uttered, it can be seen poking its way in and weaving around like a shark fin. As a man of the law, the Inspector was richly decorated with all kinds of badges and medals for good service. They gleamed on his chest. Hundreds of people had been found guilty of logicide and other offences since he took the chief position in office. Who knew if they were actually guilty? Most were sent to the gallows without trial. That was the way he dealt with things. Swiftly.

'Having a nice evening to yourself were you?' asked the Inspector. Like everything he did, he spoke swiftly too, throwing out the words with such speed so as to make Job stutter.

'Ye-yes, sir.'

'Inspector, you are to call me Inspector, not sir. When I ask you a question, you give your answer followed by Inspector. Got it?'

'Yes,' Job said, rustily adding, 'Inspector.'

'And what's this?' The Inspector bent down and picked up the spilt pipe giving it a prolonged sniff with his elongated nose. 'Waste of good tobacco, don't you think?'

'I dropped it, Inspector, your man 'ere knocking gave me quite the fright.' No sooner had Job spoken than was Forsyth right up in his face with further questions.

'Frightened were you? Hiding something are you?'

'I ain't hidin' nuffin'. It's just a startlin' thing to 'appen. A man coming in the early hours like this, knockin' on your door as if the damn buildin's on fire.'

The Inspector vocalised his doubt with a long "Hmmm…".

'And just what were you doing awake at such an hour as this?'

Job Button froze. He hadn't crumbled yet. He was coping much better than he'd thought he would in the pointy nosed face of danger. But watching the Inspector search around the room, and draw near the bed, *beneath which the stranger was hiding*, caused a suspicious amount of perspiration.

At that very moment, the stranger, lying as still as he could, drew his pistol, ready to discharge a shot. The Inspector was about to pull the bed from the floor discovering the hidden man as well as a lead bullet right up his nostrils.

This tumultuous series of events came so very close to happening. But didn't.

The Inspector lurched away from the bed and stuck his nose right in Job's face once more.

'Answer my question, man!'

'Uhhh…'

'What are you doing up at this hour. All alone in here. Should be sleeping? Shouldn't you?'

'I'm not really a day person,' said Job, at last.

'Day person?' inquired the Inspector.

'I drink a lot and the day don't agree wiv me, see.'

The Inspector didn't back down. He stared into Job's eyes, searching for the truth. Then he stared at his hair and his brow and the droplets of sweat trickling down the side of his face.

'You're sweating an awful lot? Hiding something are you?'

'Let me in,' said the barman, storming through the Watchmen at the door. 'Now you've done it! Disturbin' my clientele – I ought to sue you in a court o' law. I said t'ya, there weren't nuffin' o' the sort goin' on in this 'ere establishment. Now, sling your 'ook, before I–'

The Inspector lunged from Job to the barman. 'Need I remind you, sir, I am the Chief Inspector of the City Watch. At the snap of my fingers I could have you shot for such lack of respect. I invite you to apologise.'

'Apologise?' asked the barman, infuriated.

'Yes, apologise,' repeated the Inspector.

Job Button stared at the two men, and out of the corner of his eye, the shadow beneath the bed.

The barman continued, 'I'll give you an apology alright. I'll shove it right up your–'

'Think, sir, I beg you, for your next words could be your last,' said the Inspector.

The barman calmed his temper, taking a few deep breaths to reason with himself.

He apologised, begrudgingly.

'Constable?'

'Yes, sir.' One of the Watchmen stepped forward.

'Have the license of this establishment checked. Every single detail. I want the log book of its guests scrutinised. I want its suppliers questioned. I want all the citizens drinking here remanded for interviews. And, I want it prohibited from serving alcohol and renting rooms until we've got to the bottom of this.'

'You can't do that! We'll go out of business. We've got rent that needs paying,' said the barman.

'We'll inform the landlord of our investigation. Be good to talk to him too whoever he is.'

'You'll put us out of business.'

'Perhaps we will. Perhaps in the future, you will better cooperate with the Watch. I shall expect your formal apology in writing tomorrow,' said the Inspector.

'Writing, sir?' asked the barman, clenching his fists.

'That's *Inspector* to you.'

There was a brief, tense pause and everyone in the room, except maybe the Inspector, saw the next bit coming.

'Well, Inspector, 'ow's about you inspect this—'

…

Mildred looked on whilst her husband was dragged from the Medicine Tap by three Watchmen and thrown in the back of a jail waggon. The Inspector followed, a bloody rag over his nose and a troop of guards at his back.

There was no sign of Job Button and the strange man that had come to visit. In the commotion they must have slipped out.

It was empty at the bar. All of the customers had slipped out too.

She poured herself a drink, a rather large drink, and took a sullen sip, a rather large one. Then she stared at her empty glass a bit, and poured herself another.

***

Earlier that night…

Niclas emptied the sack onto the bed.

'That's three black candles, one roll o' parchment, a stub o' pink chalk, a bag o' sea salts, a pencil and uhhh... I reckons that's all, sir. I didn't forget anyfing did I?'

'No, that's all I asked for,' said Balthazar.

'Them black candles woz proper spenny, sir. And I 'ad to go three different shops to find chalk this colour.'

'You've done very well, boy. Now, I'll need you to do some drawing.'

'Drawin', sir?' said Niclas, suddenly a little alarmed.

'Yes. Very easy. Don't worry. I just need you to draw a circle big enough to lie in.'

'Circle... that's the round one right?'

'...yes.'

'Just wanna be sure, sir.' Niclas picked up the pencil.

'No. Not with that. With the chalk.'

'Oh... Begs your pardon, sir.' He picked up the chalk instead.

'Roll back this rug first.'

Niclas rolled back the rug. Under it were old, unmarked floor-boards which hadn't been exposed for years.

'Big enough to lie in... right... 'ere goes.'

Needless to say, Niclas' first attempt at drawing a circle wasn't very circular. It was more potato shaped. Yet, he didn't think that was a problem and stood back, impressed with his work.

Balthazar really hadn't anticipated they'd run into trouble with this bit. He sighed and shook his head.

'Wot's wrong, sir? Too big?'

'Wet a cloth. Rub it out. Try again.'

Three attempts later and Niclas finally drew something circular enough to be called a circle. It certainly wasn't the ideal form of a circle. If there was an official board that went around judging circles, then this one would have got a very low mark. Though, top marks for effort.

'You'll need to draw a triangle inside it. That's the one with the three lines.'

'Wot kinda triangle, sir?'

'Pardon?'

'Well, there's lots of different types ain't there, sir. One which 'as got all sides wiv a different length. One which 'as got two sides wiv the same length. And one which 'as all sides the same like wot you get when you put your hands together like this.'

Balthazar stared curiously at Niclas' gesture.

'...an equilateral.'

'Which is that?'

'The last one.'

'All sides the same?'

'YES.'

'Ok, ok. No need to raise your voice, sir. Just checkin'. Wouldn't want to do a bodge job would I?'

Surprisingly, Niclas' triangle drawing was a lot better than his circle drawing. He stuck his tongue partially out of his mouth to one side, closed one eye and squinted with the other, making a face of utter concentration. Which also happened to look like the face of someone who's just had a very sour grape.

'Good. Now another circle, if you'd please, in the middle of that triangle.'

'Wot's this for, sir? If you don't mind me askin'?'

'Focus on drawing.'

'Yes, sir. Sorry, sir.'

Niclas knelt down and drew the final circle, taking care not to smudge the existing lines.

''Ow's that, sir?'

'It'll do.'

'Reckon I could get the 'ang of this drawin' business, sir.'

'No more drawing. I need you to place a black candle at each point of the triangle.'

'Ok, sir.'

'Good. Now place the parchment in the centre.'

'Any sorta way, sir?'

'That'll do. Tie the girl's hair, *carefully* – we don't want to break it – to the middle of the pencil. Good. Now put that on the parchment.'

'Like that?' Niclas stepped back like a chef putting the finishing touches on his pièce de résistance.

'Exactly.' Balthazar trotted into the centre next to the empty page. 'Step out.'

'Ok.'

'Now pour the salt sparingly around the outer circle.'

'Righto.' Niclas picked up the bag of salt, untied the string and began pouring.'

'*Sparingly.*'

'Right, sir. Sorry, sir!' The flow increased.

'*Stop, stop, stop.*'

'Yes, sir?'

'Do you know what sparingly means?'

'…not really, sir.' Niclas blinked.

Balthazar took a deep breath and said, 'less. Much less.'

'Right, sir. Sorry, sir.'

'It is vitally important that when this begins you do not enter the circle. Understood?'

'Don't enter the circle. Got it.'

'Under no circumstances must you enter it.'

'Yes, sir, I gets it.'

'No matter what happens, you will not cross into the circle.'

'…uhh…' Niclas was beginning to get the feeling he was missing something. He was used to that feeling. It occurred at least five times daily. 'I won't go in the circle sir, no matter wot.'

'You aren't to disturb me or interfere in any way. Understood?'

'Understood, sir…'

'Actually. It's probably best you stand quite far back.'

Niclas stood back. ''Ere ok, sir?'

'Let's try the other side of the bed.'

Niclas climbed over the bed. ''Ere ok, sir?'

'Hmmm… on second thought, how about you go into the bathroom and get into the bathtub.'

'I don't needs a balf, sir.'

'Do it.'

'Yes, sir.'

Niclas backed into the bathroom, climbed into the empty tub and sat, peering over the top through the door and across the bed. If it wasn't for the mirror on the other side of the room, he wouldn't have been able to see anything.

'That's a good spot, I think,' called Balthazar. 'Now, what's the time? Yes… I think it's late enough. Come back over here and light these candles.'

When the three black candles were burning, and the room's lanterns dark, Niclas returned to the bathtub.

'Boy?' called Balthazar.

'Yes, sir?'

'Could you shut the door?'

'This one, sir?'

'Are there any other open doors?'

'No, sir…'

'Then I suspect I mean that one, yes.'

'Ok, sir.'

'And, boy?' said Balthazar, the door a crack from closing.

'Yes, sir?'

'Stay in the bathtub.'

'Will do sir. I 'ears ye loud 'n' clear.'

Blackness.

Niclas twisted the nozzle on the bathroom lantern and lit the mantle with a long match. A flame was birthed, and the bathroom awoke in a low orange light.

He stepped into the bath and sat there. For a teenage boy who'd grown up in the slums without rule of law or those rarely sighted creatures called manners, he was remarkably well behaved. He just sat there, taking in his surroundings, not in the slightest bit moved about what was going on in the bedroom.

Anyone else would have been up on their feet, trying to peer through the keyhole, or listen through the slit at the bottom. But not Niclas.

***

Cassandra awoke. Sort of.

She sat up in bed as if pulled by strings. Her eyes remained shut, but her feet spun out of the covers and onto the floor. Then she stood. Her head sagged to her chest and bobbed there, her loose hair hanging down in front of her.

She didn't walk, more shuffled across her bedroom to her dresser. There, she slumped into the chair and reached out across the table. Her fingers ran over her hair brush, her clips, her jewellery, her quill. Her hands were like blind spiders, searching the table top.

Then they found what they were searching for.

Books.

It wasn't the top one. Not the second one either. Then… there it was. Its texture was familiar, and that icy black stone, what else could it be?

The hands pulled the book closer. They opened it and flittered through its pages.

One of Cassandra's hands held the page whilst the other moved to her face and parted her waterfall of hair. Its fingers grabbed either side of one eye and pulled the lids open. The eye underneath was white, her pupil dancing in the roof of her skull. It took a bit of work and focusing but soon the pupil dropped down, and her one eye, which looked oddly the same shape as a cat's eye, glanced over the page.

The other hand turned the pages, each time waiting for the eye's approval.

She was looking for something.

'Hello…'

The voice startled Cassandra's body. For a moment it sat up straight, one hand still on the book, the other clasping her face.

'Hello… Who are you?'

There it was again. The voice was ethereal, and sleepy, as if half spoken in a dream. But it was startling, *for it came from Cassandra's own lips.*

Her body returned to the book, rushing to find the right page. Time was short now. It wouldn't be long before Cassandra's mind caught her body out of bed. And that would take some serious explaining.

'Wait… Martha… Mummy… is that you?'

Cassandra's eye ran frantically over page after page after page…

'Who are you? This isn't… where am I?' Her voice was beginning to carry weight behind it. It was getting less and less mumbled and more and more grumbled.

Her left hand was turning the pages so quickly now, that her one open eye was struggling to keep up.

There!

That's the one!

Her right hand slammed down on the left to stop it. It returned to her face to open her eye. The dancing pupil focused once again and her body edged closer to study the page.

Niclas had noticed that the bath tap was dripping. It wasn't particularly urgent but he thought perhaps he should tell someone. He wasn't sure where the clean water came from, but it probably wasn't an infinite supply. If a tap like that dripped and dripped, all day and all night, there could come a time when all the water ran out. And that wouldn't be good. In the slums you had to boil the canal water when there wasn't any fresh. And it still tasted rancid. Gave you a funny tummy too, sometimes.

He'd not been paying any attention to what Balthazar was up to next door. Partly because it was so quiet. The dripping bath was the only thing making a noise.

That was… until he heard Balthazar say something.

He wasn't sure what it was but it sounded like a question. And this put him in an awkward predicament. Balthazar had specifically told him to stay put, no matter what. But what about when the cat was finished? How would he know?

Niclas climbed out of the tub, careful not to make a sound and crept over to the door to put his head against it.

'Hello… Where am I? I can't see… it's too… too dark…' The voice was Balthazar's for sure… but there was something odd about it, it sounded sleepy, half awake, and an octave or two higher than the cat's usual tone.

'Sir?' whispered Niclas. 'Everyfing ok?'

'What's that smell… candle wax… salt…am I dreaming?'

Whatever was going on, Balthazar was making some odd noises. There was a small chance, emphasis on the small, that he was in trouble, and what kind of employee would Niclas be, if he didn't at least check.

So he took a deep breath and opened the door a sliver.

Through the gap he saw into the darkness of the bedroom. The black candles were burning rapidly but they gave off little light. He could just make out over the bed and in the mirror's reflection, Balthazar, sitting still, chanting in a foreign tongue. And there was something else too.

The pencil with the thread of hair tied in a bow around its centre was upright against the parchment. It was scribbling. Writing without a master.

Niclas had never seen anything like it. It was as if the pencil had a mind of its own. *Or, had borrowed one.*

'Who are you? What do you want?' came the voice through Balthazar's whispering chant.

Niclas looked closer at the cat's reflection. His eyes were closed… no… they weren't closed… they were black.

'Sir… You alright?' he whispered. 'Psst, sir? Sir? It's me Niclas?' The cat's head twisted.

'*Niclas?* The library… The book?'

'Sir?'

'Niclas? *Niclas!*' the voice was getting louder.

'Wot is it, sir?'

'NICLAS!'

Cassandra's body shook. Hit by a supercharged bolt of reality, she fell backwards. Her right hand dropped from her face. Her left, slammed the book shut and pushed it away.

'NICLAS!' she was saying.

She tried to stand but her legs were still asleep. Her knees buckled and she collapsed in front of her bed.

Seconds later she awoke as if from a nightmare.

She sat up gasping, eyes wide, staring around at her empty, silent bedroom.

She looked up and saw the bed sheets overturned. She looked behind and saw the chair knocked over. She pulled herself to her feet and looked to the mess on her dresser; all her things muddled. And there, in the middle, the open Zolnomicon.

Back at the Queen's Garter, the pencil fell dead and the candles went out to a satisfying hiss.

Balthazar's eyes shut tight and reopened their usual green. He looked across the room at Niclas standing half in, half out of the room.

'What did I say?'

'Ugh… I don't know, sir. You woz callin' me name.'

'No! What did I say before? Did I, or did I not make it expressively clear you were not to disturb me!'

'I didn't, sir. But then you started calling me name and sayin' weird fings. I gots confoosed.'

Balthazar sighed.

'I'm really sorry, sir. Is everyfing alright?'

The cat trotted over to the parchment.

'Lights.'

'Yes, sir.' Niclas dashed across the room and relit the lanterns.

Balthazar examined the parchment.

Niclas craned his head for a look. There was a picture of a skeleton lying in a circle, and another picture of what could have been the moons eclipsing. The words didn't make sense to him, though he was sure they were written in the common tongue.

'That's common tongue ain't it?'

'Yes…' said Balthazar. He too was curious about that.

'Wot's it say?'

'It's a ritual. An important, highly complicated ritual.'

'…' Niclas took a minute to compute. 'Woz this a rit'wal, sir?' he said, referring to the pink drawings and dashed salt.

'Yes. But a relatively simple one. It's extraordinary what you can do with a piece of hair.'

'I didn't mess it up did I, sir?'

'No. Everything seems to be ok.'

'I'll do better next time, sir. No matter wot 'appens. I knows wot I'm doin' now.'

'Ah. Good.'

Balthazar took a closer look at the parchment. But something was bugging Niclas.

'Why were you callin' me name though, sir?' he asked.

'Your name? I wasn't.'

'But… you woz.'

'*I* wasn't.'

'Ok, sir… If you say so…'

Balthazar skimmed to the bottom of the page. His face showed all kinds of intrigue. As much as a cat's face can show.

'I'll need you to go shopping again. And some of the items on this list are going to be a little difficult to find.'

'That's alright, sir. I like shoppin'.'

***

The morning light filled Cassandra's bedroom. It wasn't dawn light. It was that bright late morning light, closer to afternoon than dawn.

She sat up. What a strange dream, she thought. There'd been a red room and a black cat and the cat had been chanting under its breath. It had seemed so real at the time. Even now it felt like a recent memory and not a dream. But it was definitely a dream, because cats can't talk.

The chair before her dresser was overturned and all her belongings scattered over the table. Except for the nameless tome. It lay there, mysterious and open.

Things were starting to come back to her. Visions were coming through a dense fog of *bleugh*. She vaguely remembered waking up with a mouth full of carpet and crawling back into bed like some creature from a swamp.

There was an urgent knock at the door and it opened.

'Cassandra! You're not even dressed, M'Lady. The Lords are arriving any minute and your mother is waiting for you in the dining room. It's not like you to sleep this late. Are you well? You look a little pale. Are you coming down with a fever?'

'No… I'm fine, Martha. Thank you for your concern. I haven't slept that well, that's all. I'll be down straight away.'

'Does M'Lady need help getting dressed? Come let's find you something.' Martha crossed the room to the wardrobe and walked right by the open Zolnomicon on Cassandra's dresser. The Princess woke up faster than if ice water had been splashed over her face. She leapt from bed and stood between the dresser and the maid.

'No, Martha. I can manage just fine on my own. I'll be down straight away I said.'

'Ok, M'Lady. No harm meant. Just trying to help.'

'I don't need your help,' Cassandra was so eager to hide the book that she practically pushed the maid out the door.

Martha looked a little hurt.

'Martha… I'm sorry. I didn't mean…'

'No, no. I know when I'm not needed. I'll help Agnes arrange the bourbons, she's always just dumping biscuits on a plate, has no thought to how they're presented.'

'Mar…'

Martha shut the door behind her.

Cassandra rubbed her head. It was sore. Maybe she'd hit it when she fell out of bed? Or was it off the chair? What had she been doing?

She'd read about this. A head injury, mild swelling, memory loss, foul mood. She was concussed, probably. But what had she been doing to get concussed?

She turned to look at the book. It was open halfway with an unsettling illustration on the right hand page. A grinning skeleton in a circle surrounded by other smaller circles with strange objects in each. *Lilith's Transmogrification*.

'Lilith's Transmogrification?'

It was a mouthful whatever it was.

Cassandra arrived in the dining room after having a transmogrification of herself, the kind that involves a hair brush, a box of talcum powder and a generous lashing of Violet Hamamelis perfume.

'Ah, Princess, nice of you to finally join us,' said Lord Darby.

The three Lords were sat at the dining table sipping on delicate porcelain cups. The ones with ducks on them. They were her mother's favourite and reserved only for the specialist of guests. Though, there was nothing special about these guests. Cassandra didn't think so anyway.

'Cassandra. Tea? Pot's still hot,' said her mother.

'Yes, please.' Cassandra sat and Martha fixed her a cup.

'Too early for cake, apparently. I always say you can't serve a pot of tea without something crumbly, sweet and slathered in icing. Shame the honourable lady disagrees,' said Lord Quincy, the oldest of the three.

'The rules of this household, as they should be in all households, are that there will be no cake served before lunch. You'll find the biscuits crumbly and sweet enough, Lord Quincy,' said the Queen.

'Oooh, I mustn't have biscuits. One can't ever stop once one's had a biscuit. Terrible for one's figure.'

Cassandra restrained a giggle. Lord Quincy was the oldest, the most smiley and probably the fattest of all the Lords in Parliament. He spooned four teaspoons of sugar into his tea, four heaped teaspoons, gave it a brisk stir and then a sip that sounded like a slug being peeled from a wet stone.

'Well, I'll have a biscuit,' said Lord Darby, reaching over. 'Biscuit, Princess?'

'Yes, please.' Cassandra took a bourbon and placed it on the side of her saucer. Lord Quincy smiled at her and tapped his belly.

'Where were we?' asked Lord Darby.

'The Plague,' said the Queen.

'Ah, tragic. So awfully tragic,' said Lord Quincy.

'It is spreading worryingly in the north,' said Lord Barton, the one with the curly moustache and rigid expression. He was Cassandra's least favourite of the special guests. 'No one knows what has caused it or how long it will last but the problem continues to worsen.'

'Boils I hear. Huge bulbous boils. They form all over the body, and they're filled with the most revolting puss and disease,' said Lord Quincy, taking another enjoyable sip of his tea.

'It may be time to consider a quarantine, M'Lady,' said Lord Darby.

'A quarantine?' asked the Queen.

'If the wretched thing does spread south, the city would be overrun in days, and not just Cheapside – the plague does not discriminate between squalor and cleanliness, rich and poor. It kills all households the same.'

'There have been illnesses before, my lords. They have their day and then they go.'

'Not like this M'Lady. It is most contagious. Doctors themselves are afraid to study it for fear of contracting it,' said Lord Barton.

'What about the other towns and villages outside of the capital? What will become of them?' asked the Queen.

'We must be realistic, Your Majesty. There are millions of people in this city, our port opens to the known world, an outbreak here could... well... it could spell the end of civilisation as we know it,' said Lord Darby.

Lord Quincy laughed, spilling a drop of tea down his front. 'Now, now. Let's not be rash. It wouldn't spell the end of anything. Lots of people will get sick. Lots of people will die. But the Queen's right, there have been plagues in the past, they are well documented and they all just up and disappear once they've had their fill.'

'But it would be irresponsible to keep the city gates open. Surely you agree?' said Lord Barton.

'Lord Barton, what kind of message would it send if by royal decree the city closed its doors to its people in a time of need?' asked the Queen.

'Well…'

'That wouldn't be responsible would it?'

'But…'

'Not to mention the angry mob that would quickly assemble outside,' added Lord Quincy.

'We must think of the bigger picture, Your Highness,' said Barton.

'I agree with Lord Barton on this one. The bigger picture is important,' said Lord Darby.

Lord Barton, as far as Cassandra was concerned, was a cruel man who had no interest in the people of the city. He was only interested, as most politicians were, in furthering his own career. And Lord Darby was no exception to this. The two often went hand in hand, agreeing and disagreeing with whatever her mother disagreed or agreed with.

The Queen pondered whilst the Lords sipped their tea and nibbled on biscuits.

'…' Cassandra hesitated to speak, but all eyes quickly fell on her and made her think twice about it.

'Cassandra?' said the Queen. 'Go on? What are your thoughts on the matter?'

'Really, Your Majesty? She's but a child–'

'I will have her thoughts, Lord Barton.'

Cassandra puckered her lips.

'Well… I was just thinking how awful it is…'

'And…'

'And wondered what we're doing to help the ones who are sick.'

'They're doomed, M'Lady. There is no cure,' said Lord Darby, darkly.

'No. She's right,' said the Queen. The three lords gave her the same flabbergasted look, one that said very loudly in the language of eyebrow raises: *"she is?"*

'While we're here eating bourbons, drinking tea and discussing the fate of the capital, the small towns in the far north are help-less. Forgotten. We should send supplies. Food and clean water. It's our duty.'

'Seems a waste to me,' said Lord Barton.

'Come now, Lord Barton, where's your heart, the women have the right of it!' said Lord Quincy.

'My heart has nothing to do with it. I, as should we all, am thinking with my head not my feelings. Sending aid to the north under the Queen's banner is tantamount to sending an open invitation or laying down a rather sizeable welcome mat. You would create a crisis of refugees fleeing to the protection of the capital – and diseased ones at that.'

'Lord Barton's right. We should all be thinking with our heads,' Darby agreed.

'But…' Cassandra began.

'Go on, dear? Spit it out!' said Lord Quincy beaming a bourbon encrusted smile across the table. He'd cracked, they were simply too irresistible.

'What happens when the plague passes. The people in the north, the ones who survive the epidemic, they'll be angry at us, don't you think? It wasn't so long ago that the northern cities were demanding independence from the Crown.'

'Ah. Now that's using your head.' Lord Quincy laughed, then grabbed another bourbon.

'You've been reading too much history, Princess,' said Lord Darby, 'the problem with history is it's all in the past. We have to think about the future,'

'Mr Eccleston tells me that history often repeats itself.'

'Does he now.'

'Enough of this,' said Barton. 'As with all things, it will be debated in the House and the House will decide. If it is the Queen's recommendation to send aid then so be it. We shall see what the Lords feel is right. And, we shall see whether we have any other options but to quarantine the capital.'

'It *is* my recommendation that we send aid,' said the Queen. 'And it is *also* my recommendation that we do not close the city gates. I feel strongly on this matter, and will make a speech about it.'

'M'Lady,' Lord Darby began. 'There's no need for a royal speech to the House. We barely have time to fit everyone else's speeches in and this matter is so black and white it's–'

'*I will have my say*, Lord Darby,' said the Queen, in a *putting-the-foot-down* sort of way.

'Very well,' said Lord Barton. 'Let's move on shall we?'

Lord Quincy quickly finished his fourth bourbon and lifted a monocle to his eye to read the document before him.

'Let's see here. The Bank of Varcia wants to know the progress of the Crown's repayment plan?'

'Have it deferred,' said the Queen.

'…Right, that's that. Then there's the arrangements for the Harvest Festival. The Moon Festival, M'Lady?'

'Everything going as planned?'

'I think so, nothing different from the last three hundred times we've done it.'

'Next,' said Lord Barton.

'Oh!' said Lord Quincy, rubbing his fingers on his thumbs excitedly. 'Spleeeendid! It's the Lords' Banquet coming up. That time of year again. Oh I do love it. You always put on such a good show, Your Majesty. I trust you've got it all prepared. It'd nearly skipped my diary.'

'Yes. We're well prepared for the Lords' Banquet. Aren't we, Martha?' asked the Queen.

'Yes, M'Lady. We're getting in the chefs and staff from a fancy restaurant called The Witz. Everything should go as planned providing this year the Lords turn up in the numbers they promise to,' said Martha, with just a touch of bitterness.

'Oh, yes, of course. Be about thirty of us this year. Thirty definites. And the usual plus ones,' said Lord Quincy.

'That's what you said last year, M'Lord. Forty five of you turned up and we had a right palaver with the seating arrangements,' added Martha. She was clearly still bitter about it.

'Won't happen this year. You have my word.'

'What else is there, Lord Quincy?' asked the Queen.

'Erm… Ah, yes. There's been the usual levels of unrest in the Colonies. The Chief Commander of Arkados insists that all is under control there, but that we should perhaps consider sending more soldiers to police the streets. They're a little short I gather.'

'I'll leave that matter to the House. But I will speak with the ambassadors; I think we can all agree that we need more talks and less guns involved in these negotiations.'

'Righto. Then there is a small matter here of… um… what does this say Lord Barton?'

'Security,' said Lord Barton.

'Ah, yes, see it now. Your s's look like c's and c's like s's.'

'It's the main reason for my visit, M'Lady,' said Lord Barton. 'I would suggest those who need not hear it, leave us.'

This didn't have the intended effect. Everyone stayed put. And in the silence Lord Quincy chomped down on another bourbon.

'My Lady?'

'Yes?'

'Might you ask for some privacy?' said Lord Barton.

'Oh. Right. It's one of those is it? Alright Martha, would you care to help in the kitchen, you can prepare something for Cassandra, I don't believe she's had breakfast this morning.'

'Oh dear! One must jentaculate. It's the most important meal of the morning,' said Lord Quincy. 'Terribly bad for the digestive system, having a tea like that on an empty stomach. It's the caffeine they tell me. Rotten stuff.'

'No problem, M'Lady. You want for anything just call.'

'Thank you, Martha. Close the door on your way out.'

Martha curtsied and left.

'And… perhaps the Princess would like to run along. Play with her dolls or something,' said Lord Barton.

'I don't have any dolls, sir.'

'Read a book then,' the Lord smiled, forcefully.

Cassandra rose.

'She stays,' said the Queen.

Cassandra sat.

'My Lady, the following gossip is not best suited to the Princess' ears.'

'If it is suited for my ears it is suited for hers.'

'It's quite sensitive that's all.'

'That's no bother.'

'…'

'Well? Go on?'

Cassandra's sore head was beginning to spin from all the back and forth dining-table-tennis she was watching.

'As you wish.' Lord Barton smiled. He was good at smiling. Not so good at making the smile look believable though. Lord Barton was the kind of person who smiled unconvincingly. To make him do so was like making a mirror smile, all the best intentions were there, but it was only ever a reflection of a smile.

'The Chief Inspector of the City Watch believes that there could be a plot to harm you.'

Cassandra looked at her mother and tried to read the seriousness of what had just been said.

'There's always a plot,' said Lord Quincy.

'Yes. But this time it's a bit more than the mumblings of a drunk in some Brewery Quarter tavern.'

Cassandra zoned out. The Brewery Quarter. Why was that familiar to her? And why could she see that crimson room clear as day in her head? And what was that name? She'd been dreaming of him. She remembered now. She'd been calling his name trying to get him to turn around. But he'd gone in the bathroom and locked the door and… it was all terribly confusing.

'I do hope I haven't frightened you, child?' said Lord Barton.

Cassandra stirred. 'No. Not at all.'

'Please, do continue, Lord Barton,' said the Queen.

'We, myself and a few other Lords have been talking and–'

'First I've heard of it!' said Lord Quincy.

'–and we've decided it would be in the Crown's best interest if we lent you guardsmen from the City Watch.'

'You want to put men with guns in my home to protect me?' said the Queen.

'They don't have to be armed, Your Majesty, but yes, we think that would be wise given the information we have.'

'I have my own guards. The Palace Guard and the Queen's Watch are enough to keep us safe. Have you informed Rufus about this?'

'We haven't yet spoken to the Queen's Watch, no. We're waiting for a couple of leads to come in.'

'Don't you think that the personnel who are tasked with my family's protection should be at the forefront of any *leads* you might have?'

'We don't have any particular evidence as of yet, and what the City Watch does have, Inspector Forsyth and his men are working around the clock to get to the bottom of.'

'There's always been danger with this job, Lord Barton, but if you are seriously suggesting that there could be a real threat to our safety, you should have informed Rufus immediately.'

'We aren't *certain*, Your Majesty, exactly the grander details of this plot. But, there is a minor issue in that potentially, one or two of the individuals in your household guard could be implemented in it. Of course, I'm not accusing anybody in particular, but it would be logical, you understand, to keep this conversation between us – at least until we know the full details.'

'Rufus is a loyal bodyguard. He's given his life to serve the Crown, my late husband and his father before him. I can certainly rest assured that he has no part at all in whatever you are suggesting.'

'I didn't say he did but precautions, Your Majesty, precautions.'

'We would offer you twenty Watchmen, they would work in shifts, be at your command of course and as Lord Barton said, they need not be armed. It's their presence we want more than anything,' added Lord Darby.

Lord Quincy had finished the plate of bourbons, and was looking sad about it.

'I think it's a good idea,' he said. 'Prevention is better than cure.'

The Queen looked at all three Lords carefully, then to the Princess. Cassandra didn't know what she was thinking, but knew how she would answer.

'And how will we explain this to Rufus? He's the head of the Queen's Watch and the Palace Guard, he manages all issues of security. He won't take lightly to City Watchmen being here. He'll want to know why?' she said.

'The Queen's word is final, My Lady, I suggest you use it,' said Lord Barton.

'He won't be happy.'

'He will be to know that you are safe once all this has blown over,' said Lord Darby.

There was a stiffening silence. Lord Quincy filled it, slurping the remainder of his tea, which was more of a caramelised sugary dessert.

'It will not be permanent. At my request you are to remove them,' said the Queen.

'Of course, My Lady, at your request.'

Cassandra didn't like the idea of secrets. She didn't like the idea of City Watchmen walking about her halls and chambers. But she even less liked the idea of danger, and part of her, as did part of the Queen, thought it was best.

***

Now we return to the stranger in the dead of night, just north of the river, a little west of the Brewery Quarter.

But he's not a stranger to us anymore. And from now on should really be known by his profession. A profession he shares with few others.

But first, a warning.

A city like Laburnum looks different to different people. A drunk will know it for its drink, its rough streets and for its banter. A pauper will know it for its cold nights, rat infested slums and cruel upper classes. A monarch will know it for its majesty, its history, its standing amongst other cities. And a pigeon, a pigeon will know all the best places to relieve itself mid-flight. These perspectives differ so much, that the city can appear a completely different place depending on what you have and haven't seen. But, know this: once you have been introduced to the dark, clandestine underworld that exists beneath its layers, you shall never quite see Laburnum the same again.

And so we continue. In the dewy mist of Bloomhill Cemetery, the stranger, or to those who know: the *Witchhunter*, followed his leads.

Bloomhill Cemetery was oddly named. There was more gloom than bloom, and there were no hills, except the mounds of dirt above the freshly dug graves.

The trees were the same shade of grey as the headstones. They were the kind of trees that moved their arms when they weren't being watched.

The Witchhunter found a spot beneath them where he could view both the ways in and out of the cemetery.

He had been there on a stakeout for the last few nights, taking note of the regulars: two owls, a stray dog and a rat.

The owls talked amongst themselves, filling the eerie quiet with eerie hoots. The dog wandered lost along the path with a flaccid tongue bouncing up and down, flicking its rabid drool from nose to ear. Only the rat paid him any attention, scuttling to a nearby tree and watching him with its beady eyes and wiggling nose. Rats knew when food was about. This one could sense that the man's being there was down to grave robbing. And that meant one thing. Leftovers.

The Witchhunter and the rat waited together each night. They didn't make each other's acquaintance but they became used to each other's company.

Each morning, when the sun started to rise, the Witchhunter would take his leave and check into a nearby public house. It would always be a different place so as to keep his nightly habits secret.

He was a patient man, but as each night past with nothing to show for itself, his doubt in Job Button grew. He was close to tracking down the informant and retracting his down payment.

But that night his patience was rewarded. That night, he and the rat were joined by a suspicious figure.

Suspicious in that only someone with motives that veered on the unorthodox side of things would be there at such a time. And if that didn't raise any alarms, he was also cloaked and armed with a shovel. His walk was curious too, a hobbling hunchbacked style.

The Witchhunter kept as still as a birdwatcher, cautious not to spook the grave robber. And a grave robber he was indeed. The figure teetered between the graves, stopping at one that seemed to hook his attention. Then in went the shovel and up came the dirt.

The robber was a cagey individual, darting looks over his shoulder between bouts of digging. Sometimes he paused for longer and listened to the owls and the stirring of branches in the wind.

Once a small mountain of dirt had been uprooted, he left and returned with a horse and cart.

The steed was old and sick and the cart was slipshod and rickety. The two as a combination made for the least efficient and most conspicuous mode of transport.

The robber stepped down into the grave with his shovel, and the thud of iron on wood rang out.

THUMP! THUMP! THUMP!

Then the sound of the coffin's lid being pried aside.

KEREEEEEEK! THUD!

The Witchhunter watched closely as the robber heaved something large out of the ground and onto his shoulder, then up into the cart. He unfurled a large brown sheet and wrapped his find tightly within.

Then he was up behind the reins – a lash of the whip and the horse fell into a lazy trot.

The Witchhunter didn't follow right away. The grave required inspection.

Inside, amongst broken soil and dead worms was a set of silverware. Obviously the kind that's best buried with loved ones because it just clogs up good cupboard space.

There was no corpse. That had been taken for sure. But there was something more chilling about this particular robbery. On the headstone, the name and a small message about what a lovely man the deceased had been. And there, etched below, the date he was born and the date he had passed. The body had been buried almost four weeks ago and was certainly decayed beyond an anatomist's use.

The Witchhunter caught up with the rickety cart. It was going slowly, keeping the noise of its creaking wood to a low. Mind you, it couldn't go much faster without falling apart.

The Witchhunter kept to the shadows, trailing behind. He followed it south, along the canals and across the water into Bog End. It kept to the quiet roads, the dark roads that weren't lit with lanterns.

If there was any dabbling in the Black Science he would find it south of the river. Those who dabbled valued their privacy. And there was no place more private than this, the poorest, dirtiest, most wretched of neighbourhoods. There were parts of Bog End not even criminals would go down. Areas that were known by name and rumour alone.

The horse stopped. It wouldn't move a hoof further. It was frightened, spooked by something peculiar in the air.

The cloaked robber stepped down from the cart.

He lifted the wrapped corpse onto his shoulder and left the horse standing in the road.

This was it. The Witchhunter was close. He moved in.

The streets were getting tighter. The buildings that lined them couldn't be inhabited, they were far too barren and wasted. Soon the moonlight couldn't reach the cobblestone and the streets turned to dark alleyways of shadow.

It was difficult to keep on the robber's tail and soon he vanished ahead, around the corners and into the blackness.

The Witchhunter reached into his coat. He pulled out a rusty old pocket watch by its chain and flicked open the little lid. At the centre there was no clock. Instead, behind the dusty glass, a diced piece of meat pulsed as if it were alive. As if a heartbeat possessed it. The black, congealed ink it was set in, was turning red. The colour of blood.

Whatever was here had a strong presence. Only the Black Science could make the Necrocardium beat.

The Witchhunter took in his surroundings.

He felt the uncanny chill in the air, the breeze that felt like whispers tempting him deeper into the alleyways.

His profession had certain skill sets. One such was survival. It was no good going around being a witchhunter if you were easily killed. In his time in the trade he had learned when to walk away and this was without a doubt one of those times.

He was in a dark, dark place and something evil was at work.

He pocketed the watch, and reluctantly, turned back.

three

Niclas didn't have much of a short term memory. He didn't have much of a long term memory either. He wouldn't have been able to read a shopping list let alone write one, so Balthazar figured it was best to go with him.

There were only a handful of items to find, fewer than last time, yet they were the most obscure things anyone had ever heard of. Who knew what a Salamander Stone was? Or where it was sold? Where did one even begin to look for Danga Root? And what in all the moons was an Egg White? Niclas imagined it to be some sort of luxury you got in toff restaurants – a kind of albino egg.

All cities tend to have a few of those shops that sell merchandise of a peculiar sort; emporiums for the weird and not really that wonderful. But in Laburnum, a logical city with logical shops selling only logical things, there's little room for bits and bobs that have no use in the logical world. In other words, it was going to be bloody hard to find those three things.

Yet there was one shop the cat knew of. It was in a shady part of town not far from the Brewery Quarter. The sign on the front read:

VERY VERY SPENNY POTS & PANS THAT'S ALL

Indeed, inside there were lots of shelves stocked with lots of pots and pans. They looked like ordinary pots and pans to Niclas, but the little paper tags on their handles suggested otherwise.

'Looking for a pot? Or is it a pan?' said a fat, foreign man from behind the counter.

'Sorry, gov?'

'I think you are in the wrong place, my boy, we have only very, very spenny pots and pans that's all,' came the accented voice of the shopkeeper.

Niclas looked to his feet for back up.

The cat seemed to think this was the right place.

'I ain't lookin' for pots and pans, sir, I begs your pardon. I's lookin' for some other fings. Uh, sort o' weird fings.'

'I don't know what you're talking about, boy. This is a pots and pans shop only. I not sell… weird things.'

'Oh… err… well, my mistake. Sorry to 'av' boverd you.' Niclas, who was always one to give up easy, turned and stepped towards the door. But Balthazar cut him off and with an insisting shake of the tail turned him back.

'Uh…' said Niclas, 'beggin' your pardon, sir, but you sure you ain't got anyfing else…'

The foreigner raised an eyebrow. Niclas had never seen anyone raise an eyebrow quite that high. Must have been a foreign thing.

'What is it you're looking for exactly?'

'Uhh…' Niclas lifted a finger to think and Balthazar watched with mild anticipation. 'Danga Root or summin like that. And, uhhh… Sal-ah-man-dar Stone?' he said, watching the cat's expression and gauging it to each syllable.

'Danga Root and Salamander Stone you say? Why you need these things?'

'It's not me who needs 'em, sir. It's me master.'

'And what does your master want these things for?'

'Uhh…' Niclas looked to his feet for answers once more. 'I don't know, sir, I guess I'm not bright nuff to be filled in on all the deeeetails just yet. But I gots to find 'em, else I'd 'av' done a bad job. I'm new in the business see and I ain't 'ad the best o' starts if I'm tellin' the troof.'

'And what makes you think you will find these things here. In this very expensive pots and pans shop?'

'To be honest, sir, I don't know wot I'm doin' 'ere. But me master is pretty sure this is the right place.'

The foreigner had picked up on the weird exchange of body language between the cat and the boy. The cat seemed to be watching and listening.

Balthazar caught him looking and meowed softly.

'You have money?'

'Yessir. This bag 'ere look.' Niclas held up the large purse of coins and gave it a jingle.

The shopkeeper licked his lips.

'Alright,' he said, 'come with me.'

Downstairs, behind a curtain of multicoloured beads (which Niclas nearly got stuck in), was an entirely different shop to the one above. It was a museum of strange odds and ends. There were jars of dirt and desert dust, corked bottles of all sizes and shades, crystal stones, some of which could be seen through, some were dull and foggy, some sparkled like a night sky full of stars. There were big plants, small plants. There were glass boxes of crickets and worms and next to those, glass boxes of black, velvety snakes that lay coiled on each other deep in sleep. There were books too. Lots of them. Though Niclas hadn't a clue what any of them said. Had he been able to read he might have browsed the spines. *Culpeper's Herbalis*, *The Secret of Spice*, *Healing with Flowers*, *How to: Acupuncture*, *Food for Health*, *Food for Wealth*, *The Encyclopaedia of Tonics*… to name a few.

'I have to be careful all the time,' said the shopkeeper. '*Very, very careful.* The Academy is always watching. *Always watching. Always!* They don't like the studies of my people. They think it old, barbaric, illogical. They don't understand that it works. One day, I beg to the fates that an inquisitor gets sick – *very, very sick* – on his deathbed almost. And I hope he stumbles down here for shop's help. Then maybe, who knows, they would change their minds about my people's traditions. Meh! Until then, it forbidden. So must be very, very careful. It is a science… Just not a recognised one.'

'Oh. I see,' said Niclas, in a way that suggested he really didn't see anything at all.

'Now, what do you need? Salamander Stone and Danga Root?'

'And an Egg White if you 'av' one.'

The shopkeeper raised his brow again.

'Salamander Stone. Very good for the blood.' He wandered around the shelves looking a bit lost, but soon returned with a crumbling yellow rock. 'Yes, very good for sick hearts this stone is. What else was it? Danga Root? Ah, *the whispering root*. A very rare nightshade that is. I think I have some around here somewhere. Yes. Here it is.' The root was fat and twisted like ginger, but lustrous, black and brittle like coal. It was flecked with dark purple specks, evocative of its rarely seen purple bell flower. 'Good remedy for sea sickness. But be careful. Very poisonous. Very dangerous. I trust your master knows what he's doing with it? Was there something else?'

'An Egg White, sir.'

'Hmm…' The shopkeeper stood for a moment, perplexed. Then he reached into an egg crate and handed Niclas an egg.

'Is that… an Egg White?' Niclas asked.

'It's egg. Egg white is inside.'

Niclas stared at the egg with curious eyes.

'Tell me, do you know which of the Five Isles your master calls home?'

'Five Isles?'

'Yes, the Five Isles. You know? Meh! Your people call them the Colonies.'

'Uhh, just… just down the road actually, sir.'

'Not from Five Isles then?'

Balthazar, who had been taking note of the shop's unusual stock for future reference, caught Niclas' eye and slowly shook his head from left to right.

Niclas shook his head from left to right too.

'I don't reckon so, sir,' he said.

The shopkeeper followed Niclas' gaze to where Balthazar was sitting. Then he squinted sceptically and looked back at the boy.

'*Very well trained this cat of yours.* Isn't it?'

'I guess so, sir.'

'*Belongs to your master, I suppose?*'

'Wot? Uhh… nah… just a street cat ain't it.'

'*Not sent here to keep eye on you?*'

'Nah, sir, just a stray like I said,' Niclas was beginning to feel very uncomfortable. He certainly looked very uncomfortable.

'So! A local then?'

'Wot?'

'Your master, a local you say. Very strange for Varcian to take interest in this medicine. I thought you were all as close-minded as your Academy. Meh! Each to their own I guess.'

'I guess… How much do I owes you, gov?'

'Let's think. Not much, not much… A sixpence for the stone. A threepence for the Danga Root. And call it a farthing for the egg.'

Niclas pulled out a handful of coins, stared at them nervously for a long time and then handed over a whole shilling.

The shopkeeper looked at the coin, knitted his brow and took it.

'A tip eh?' He smiled.

'Yes?'

'What?'

'You said a tip, sir?'

'Yes, a tip.'

'Well… Wot's the tip?'

'Well… it's…' The shopkeeper noticed it then, staring into Niclas' eyes, the thing Balthazar had come to learn already: that all the lights were on, but no one was at home.

The boy and the cat crossed through the top of Carrot Market on their way back to the Queen's Garter.

It was busy as usual with traders selling their wares and customers haggling down prices.

It was the first time Niclas had been amongst the market stalls since he'd been pinched for filching. It was also the first time he'd browsed them with money in a purse. It was a feeling he wasn't used to. Anything he wanted he could buy. A shabby, second hand top hat was a mere transaction away. But why settle for second hand, there were hats there from the haberdashery near Lords' Row and they were made of fine felt, some were even lined with silk.

There were all sorts of shinies too. Glimmering watches, twinkling rings, enough to make a magpie's head spin. For Niclas, the old slum boy urge to pocket things when no one was looking itched in the palm of his hands. But there was no need to steal when you had a purse as big as his.

Among the trinkets and jewels as big as rocks, he saw a silver pocket watch. It wasn't a particularly costly watch. It was scratched, discoloured and the hands ticked too fast. It reminded him of the watch that had got him locked up. The watch he'd promised to Mr K.

He looked down at Balthazar.

'Sir, is it alright if I…'

'Help yourself. There's no rush,' said Balthazar, making no attempt to disguise his speaking. The market was loud, busy and no one was really paying attention to small four legged creatures.

Niclas stepped closer to the stall and the lady in charge sprang up before him.

''Ello, 'ello. See something you like?' It was strange, Niclas thought, how people treated you differently when you dressed all respectable-like. Had he still been the dirty guttersnipe in torn, baggy rags, he'd have been shooed like a rat.

'I's just lookin', miss, that's all.'

'You like the watch?'

'Yes, miss.'

'It's a florin, my dear, on account of it being a little too fast.'

Niclas brightened. To have your very own pocket watch was a symbol of status. It made you look important, *or at least feel important.*

'A florin yeah?' he said. ''Av' you got one wot don't tick too fast?'

'Yes I do. But surely you don't want one of those,' replied the lady. 'This one's special, ain't it? And at a discount price.'

'Can it be fixed?'

'Why would you want to fix it, my dear?'

''Cause it tick too fast innit?'

'But that's what makes it special. You'll always be early. Never late. And things will always happen sooner than they is meant to! Just two of the many perks of it.'

'Righto.'

Niclas looked down at his feet and pulled a pleading face to ask the cat's permission.

Balthazar, mid bath, gave consent.

Niclas reached into the purse, counted out a couple of shillings and handed them over. It was a good purchase, something he'd actually use, and it'd help him serve his master that much better.

Better still if he could read the time.

He grabbed the watch and stared at the minute hand up close. It was ticking as fast as a second hand. Niclas didn't know much about watches, but he figured it made this one unique.

He was stood, watching the minutes tick by like seconds, literally, when out of the corner of his eye he saw a tiny pale hand snatch a ring from the stall. When he looked up, a small child was disappearing into the crowd.

He followed.

Balthazar, who hadn't been consulted on this sudden change of direction, interrupted his bath to follow after.

Niclas was sure he recognised the boy's ginger hair, pale skin and freckles. As he neared closer he recognised him even more. The boy, on the other hand, didn't recognise Niclas at all. And the closer Niclas got to him the faster he moved through the crowd, darting panicked looks over his shoulder.

'Hey!' said Niclas.

The small freckled boy moved away from the market and towards the buildings and alleyways.

'Hey, wait!' Niclas wasn't used to people running away from him. He wasn't even aware that the boy *was* running away from him.

'Hey–'

What happened next, happened fast.

Lightning fast.

A firm set of grubby hands seized Niclas by his armpits and rushed him off into the side street.

He was thrown against the wall, the bag of mysterious ingredients emptying out and the purse of coins scattering across the cobbles. Niclas cowered away from his attackers. A trickle of blood came down his brow.

At first, he was taken by surprise; he didn't know if he was being mugged or getting pinched. But when his senses came back to him and he looked up at the two towering thugs, he saw both had ugly, brutish, yet familiar faces.

'Well, well, well…' said Archie.

'This is a pleasant surprise, ain't it?' said Clyde.

'We fawt you woz done for, little Nick. We fawt them watchmen 'ad done you in. Locked you up and thrown away the key.'

'Didn't fink we'd see you again, that's for sure. Wot's all these shiny coins? A big steal is it?'

'And where'd you get this fancy look?' Archie bent down and caressed the green waistcoat between his fingers.

'I…'

'Wot? You wot?' Archie snarled. 'You know, Mr K is pretty peeved. Wait till 'e sees you again. 'E's gonna be overcome with joy.'

''E's gonna beat ya, that's wot'll 'appen. When 'e finds out you done a runner on us, *cor*, I wouldn't wanna be in your shoes,' said Clyde.

'Saaaay, where'd you get them fancy shoes?'

'Look, sirs, there's bin a proper bad misunderstandin'. I ain't done no runner, I promise, I–'

'Shut it you miserable creature!' said Archie. His breath reeked of gin, just one waft of it was enough to make Niclas drowsy. 'You can't lie your way out, little Nick, you're in the deep end now.'

'Yeah – and you're the one who can't swim, if me memory serves me right?' said Clyde.

Archie moved his oversized hand up onto Niclas' shoulder, then onto his throat. He squeezed him like an orange.

'Where'd you get the coin, boy?'

'*I found it*,' Niclas croaked, turning purple.

'Don't you be lyin' to me, little Nick, I'll snap you like a match stick.'

'Ha! Good one,' added Clyde.

'I swear! I swear it! I'm workin' for this gen'l'man wot busted me out o' the cells–'

'Oh yeah? Who is 'e?'

''E's… 'e's… 'e's a cat!'

'A wot now?' Archie squeezed tighter. It wasn't the most effective way to interrogate someone.

'*Ah… ah…*' The colour was draining from Niclas' face.

The thug loosened his grip and shook his head firmly from side to side.

'It's the troof, I swear it. I wouldn't lie to you, sir!'

'Club,' said Archie, holding out his hand the way surgeons do in the operating theatre.

Clyde's toothless grin expanded. He unbuckled a truncheon and placed it into Archie's hand.

'Now – I'm goin' t'ask you one more time – where'd you get the coin?'

'I swear it, Archie… It belongs to a cat.' Niclas' words had become messy and incomprehensible. It was the choking expectation of pain more than anything else.

'Clyde? Left or right?'

'That's a tricky one,' said Clyde. 'How about *you* bash in the left and let *me* bash in the right? We'll bash 'em in at the same time. Make it fair.'

Niclas had no escape, the two men stood around him like a fence.

His legs were pulled out, held down and the thugs took their positions with the clubs.

'You ain't ever gonna walk again, boy, unless you start tellin' me the troof,' said Archie.

Niclas closed his eyes. He decided it was for the best. Things always hurt twice as much when you watched them happen.

But as Archie and Clyde raised their clubs with eager and vicious expressions, they were stopped by a voice from downwind.

Balthazar's voice.

They turned, lowered their clubs, and looked straight past the cat.

'Who's there?' said Archie.

'I said I hope you don't intend to damage my property,' the cat said.

'That cat just spoke?' said Clyde.

'Don't be an eejit, cats can't talk,' said Archie, having seen no less than his counterpart.

'What business have you with this boy?' Balthazar stepped closer. Close enough for them to see his mouth moving below his bright green eyes.

'I've drank me own weight in gin and lost me bleedin' mind, Archie,' said Clyde.

Archie said nothing. He was still weighing up the situation.

'I only ask as I have employed him as my assistant, and I can't stress enough how useless he would be to me without those legs of his.'

Archie and Clyde looked at each other, then at Niclas, who was trying to mouth a warning to his master that these two gents were not to be messed with.

'I don't want any trouble, honestly. But I'd appreciate it if you would step away from my property.'

'...'

'...'

'You can have the money,' the cat continued. 'Take it as a symbol of my good will and be on your way.'

Clyde scanned the shillings around their feet. After a brief silence, he reached down to pick one up. Archie's boot came crunching down on top of it.

'Listen 'ere, gov, I dunno wot this is, or 'ow it's bein' done – but I ain't in the mood t'do business wiv no cat.'

If Niclas had been into gambling, he'd have placed a considerable bet on the two thugs. They were Mr K's lieutenants, part of the inner circle, part of the wolf pack. And wolves against a cat had to be the most one sided fight he'd ever heard of.

But Balthazar didn't look the slightest bit afraid.

And that made it worth watching.

'You would be wise to take my offer,' the cat insisted.

'Clyde. Sort it.'

Clyde wasn't sure what was meant by "sort it". He was the furthest from the cat and it made no sense as to why he should be the one to "sort it". But Archie was as serious as he could be, and knowing exactly what happened when Archie wasn't taken seriously enough, Clyde took a step forwards and started slapping the club against his open palm.

''Ere, kitty, kitty. 'Ere, kitty, kitty…'

Balthazar kept his eyes fixed on the eyes of the approaching thug.

He began whispering beneath his whiskers and little black nose. It was a ghostly whispering; a cryptic tongue that to untrained ears sounded like nothing more than gibberish – either that or a very unconvincing feline hiss.

After taking just two more steps, Clyde stopped and fell silent.

'Clyde?' shouted Archie. 'Oi?'

Clyde turned on the spot and stared coldly through his partner.

His face was blank, all expression and personality had fallen away.

'Wot you doin'?' said Archie. 'I told you to sort it? Don't tell me you've gone 'n' got the willies!'

Clyde said nothing. He just stood there – like a zombie.

'I'll sort it then!' said Archie, raising his club and rushing towards the cat.

Suddenly, and it really did happen suddenly, Clyde swung out his club and struck Archie in the head.

Archie grabbed his face and reeled into the wall. Niclas scuttled away, narrowly avoiding a trampling.

'Clyde, you friggin' moron!' blathered Archie. ''Av' you blummin' lo–'

Again, without remorse, Clyde struck him.

The blow came to the back of his head precisely as he was pronouncing the Luh in "lost it", and so his tongue was caught between a set of violently clenching jaws, severing its tip. He went with the force of the strike and landed in a mess on the floor.

The whispering stopped.

Clyde dropped the club and looked at his hands as if waking from a dream. He stared back fearfully at the cat.

'Now. Run along,' said Balthazar.

There was a brief hesitation, then Clyde legged it. His legs carried him away so fast that he tripped over his own feet at the end of the alley.

Archie spat blood into his palm. He was trying to work out whether he was lying on the floor or the *metaphorical* ceiling. He watched, dizzily as the cat came closer.

'You should have taken the money shouldn't you?' said Balthazar.

Archie did dare a reply but it was lost in his spittle and befuddlement.

'I trust I won't be seeing you again?' said Balthazar. 'Pick up the shopping, boy, and gather the coins.'

Niclas stood. Taking care not to stray too close to the groaning thug, he picked up the coins, filled the purse and collected the bag of mysterious ingredients. Then he followed his master out of the alley, looking back only once at the crippled Archie, who was still trying to discern what was who, who was where, and where why had run off to.

''Ow'd you do that, sir?' said Niclas, as they left the alley and entered the street.

'What?'

'Err… I dunno exactly, but you did summin right? You made 'em beat each other up back there?'

'Ah, yes, that.'

'Well? 'Ow'd you do it?'

'It's a trick.'

'A trick?'

'Yes. One of my many talents.'

Niclas stopped to think about this. Then raced after the cat.

'I don't get it, sir?'

'Remember what we've said about things you don't understand. There's no point in trying.'

'But… you didn't touch 'em or nuffin'. I never seen Archie and Clyde take a beatin' like that.'

'You know those men?'

'Sure I knows 'em, sir. They're the Bowler Gang. Me old employers before you, sir. 'S'ow I wound up gettin' pinched, sir.'

'I see.'

'Wot was all that mumbo jumbo I saw you mow'vin'?'

'Mumbo jumbo?'

'Yeah. You was sayin' summin? I just don't get it, sir. Them two great big men, and you, just a little black cat. No offence meant, sir.'

'None taken. I suppose you're not familiar with the expression *size doesn't matter*?'

'Oh I've 'eard that one, sir. The lady folk downstairs in the Garter were gigglin' to themselves 'bout it t'other day. Only they said it the other way round… I fink.'

'Right.'

'But how'd you do it, sir, whatever you did?'

'Look, it's not what you are that matters in this world, boy, it's what you know.'

'Know?'

'Knowledge.'

'O, I didn't get much of an education, sir…'

'No, I didn't think so. If there was a ladder representing all the intelligence of this world, I'd expect to find you somewhere at the bottom.'

'You're very kind, sir,' said Niclas, taking it as a compliment to even be on the ladder at all.

'I have a particular knowledge about certain things that I can use to my advantage. It's a science known by few people but a powerful one.'

'Eh?'

'There are those, like myself, who practice it. And there are those who condemn it. It is forbidden here, so it's best if we speak no more about it.'

'Could you teach me some stuff, sir?'

Balthazar stopped and looked up at Niclas. The boy's face was beaming with pathetic enthusiasm.

'No.'

Niclas frowned.

'Why not?'

'Well for a start you can't even read or write, you can hardly count, and…' Balthazar could see Niclas wasn't taking the criticism of his abilities very well. He looked like he was about to cry. Balthazar hated it when people cried, it was such a useless thing to do.

'Maybe, *and that's a big maybe*, if you perform your duties right, I could teach you a few things,' said the cat, changing his tone.

'Really! Wow! That's great, sir. I'd really like that! I won't let you down, sir. I'll get up extra early and do whatever, sir. T'fink, I might be able to give Archie 'n' Clyde a taste of their own good–'

'Don't get carried away. I think the alphabet would be a good place to start.'

'Wot's an alphabet?'

Sometimes in life, you regret things immediately after saying them. For Balthazar, this was one of those such moments.

Across town, in a part that didn't smell at all like horse dung, Cassandra was busy trying to make sense of her dreams.

While she would normally be roaming the Palace Gardens weaving among fountains with a book in hand, or sat in the private library making her way through a volume of *The Empire's Encyclopedia*, she was now cooped up in her room, and had been for hours, as if suffering some self inflicted case of the Rapunzels.

She'd looked over hundreds of pages, yet read hardly any of the words. The Zolnomicon was written in the most infinitesimal inkings. So small were they, that Cassandra doubted even a highly literate mouse would be able to read half of what was there.

It wasn't off the printing press either. The words were heavily cursive, written by someone who clearly didn't know how to hold a pen upright. And the bits she could read didn't exactly make much sense either. They were written like recipes, each with its own list of curious ingredients, and not the sort of ingredients that went into Martha's cooking. Though, Cassandra wouldn't have been surprised if frogspawn, badger eyes and snake scales had found their way into one of the maid's exotic stews at one point – *she was a bit of an experimenter.*

There seemed to be a dozen or so names that kept appearing and each recipe belonged to one. *Lyssa's Affliction, Caligula's Anguish, Cicero's Undying, Ophelia's Sorrow…*

The pages went on and on.

Cassandra had had about enough of the book's ramblings. She was due downstairs in the library at eleven for a lesson with her tutor Mr Eccleston, and she was still in her nightdress, which was hardly a ladylike way to present herself.

She went over to her wardrobe and navigated the endless rail of dresses. It was a time consuming job for a princess, deciding what to wear. She had silks and fine threaded garments from all over the known world.

She was in the process of making a shortlist when a gust of air blew into the room. It knocked bits off her dresser and sent the fabrics of her wardrobe billowing up into her face. The window had blown all the way open and the netting was flapping about. She rushed over to close it. It wasn't the first time she'd had blustering breezes sneaking up on her. There was something amiss about it.

There was something amiss about the Zolnomicon too. It had opened itself again, which is saying something, because the cover of the book was heavier than a paperweight.

It had opened to a recipe she hadn't yet seen, but one that was oddly familiar.

Kadrik's Eye.

There, in the centre of the page, was a circle within a triangle within a circle. She knew the mark. It was the one from her dream.

Mr Eccleston could wait.

Cassandra pulled up her chair and buried her nose in the book. Her eyes flicked from line to line.

Kadrik's Eye

One piece of the watch'ed's. Three black of candle. Two and a 1/2 pounds of salt. Pink of chalk. Quill or lead. Blank parchment.

Thee who casts Kadrik's Eye, into another they shall spy. As one lies sleeping, the other wakes, as one dreams the other rakes. What the eye of Kadrik sees, the quill shall scrawl on paper leaves. But keepeth thee mind as black as night, for in dreams the watch'ed hath sight. And should the watch'ed come to wake, the binding of the two shall break. Thee beware when two minds be paired, for Kadrik links are often shared.

Cassandra felt something over her shoulder. A feeling that she was being watched.

Nonsense, she thought.

But once her empirical, perfectly rational, sensibly minded brain had had its say, a troubling thought settled behind her thoughtful furrows. That thought went something a little like this…

"What if? What if such things were possible?"

In her dream, she had been in a red velvety room. The markings pictured in the book were chalked on the floor beneath her – pink chalk – and there had been black candles too, and the smell of salt hanging in the air.

She hadn't been alone. There had been a presence in the room. It was difficult to picture what it had been, but something had been in there with her. Something that made her afraid. She'd tried to ask who it was and then a door had opened, just a crack, and she saw and heard that boy… What was his name again? Niclas…

Dreams weren't the most logical things, but they always felt like dreams afterwards. This one felt real. A lucid dream's lucid dream…

Cassandra arrived late in the west wing library. Fancy places like the Purple Palace had three libraries. There was one in the east wing, one in the west wing and one next to the grand hall. The west wing library had all the best books, in Cassandra's opinion. Though all three libraries put together were no match for the City Library's collection.

Mr Eccleston didn't appear to notice the Princess come in. He was sat, leg over knee, enjoying a good book. He was usually enjoying a good book. He spent four fifths of his time reading, which didn't leave a great deal many fifths for much else. But it did make him very smart.

He was young for a tutor. Most tutors in Varcia had a lot in common with librarians. They were old, white bearded men, who spent most of their lives in-between book covers. But don't let his age fool you. Mr Eccleston was exceedingly bright, that's how he got the job of being the Royal Tutor.

'Cassandra, you're late,' he said, without looking up. 'Go on then? What's your excuse?'

'I don't really have one, Mr Eccleston.'

'You must have an excuse, Cassandra. One must always have a reason for doing something. Nothing can just be done willy-nilly. There's always a reason. So, let's have it.'

Cassandra paused to think.

'I got a little into my reading. The time just slipped away.'

'I see. Nothing wrong with that I suppose. Still reading *Professor Columbo's History of the Colonies*?'

'Yes,' said Cassandra.

'Remarkable, truly remarkable.'

'Yes,' lied Cassandra. She'd seen brickwork that was more re-markable.

'Remarkable that you're still reading it I mean. Does go on a bit in places, doesn't he? Perhaps one day you'll make a visit to the Five Isles in person. See the locals, hear the language, smell the smells, taste the foods. It's frightfully foreign. I've been twice and both times, I couldn't get enough of it.'

'I would like that very much. But, I'm not sure mother would allow it.'

'You're not a child anymore, Cassandra, you're becoming a smart young woman. I can picture you as a Varcian Ambassador, travelling the known world and speaking the many languages. Should you want it, there's a future in diplomacy for you.'

'Won't I be busy here. You know… being Queen.'

'Well, yes, of course you will. But your mother has many years left on the throne, *long may she reign,* there'll be plenty of time for you to see the world before you're swept up in all this domestic politics. And who knows? You might be a travelling monarch. It is not written that the Queen must be a permanent resident of the capital. If you think about it, the Queen should be the most travelled citizen. Going to the corners of her empire and beyond, waving a hand, smiling – it's probably quite exhausting actually.'

'I suppose.'

'Right, let's get stuck in shall we? Let's see what's in store for us today?'

Mr Eccleston ventured through his extremely organised notes. He was the type of man who wrote an agenda for everything. A man with whom spontaneity didn't stand a chance. The kind of man who pencilled in toilet trips.

'Ah! Today is Geography! And peat bogs too! I do love a good peat bog, don't you?'

'Mr Eccleston, may I ask you a question?'

'Is it about peat bogs?'

'Not exactly.'

'Well, we're running a little behind schedule but, go on?'

Cassandra wet her lips and pondered the best way to phrase it.

'What do you think dreams are?'

'Dreams?' The tutor pushed his glasses up his nose. He insisted on wearing ones that were too big for him and was constantly fighting a losing battle to keep them on. Martha had said it was something to do with his ego, that it made up for him not having a beard like all the other tutors. 'Hmm, dreams. Tricky dreams,' he began. 'There are many theories. Some scholars think their happening is something to do with our brains filing things away while we sleep. Some think they're a sort of situational gymnastics, preparing you for your worst fears and fondest hopes. The research done by one fellow, his name escapes me, is that they're to do with fulfilling wishes: the satisfying of unconscious desires.'

'But what if the dreams don't make any sense?'

'Most dreams don't make any sense. If we had dreams that made sense, we'd probably be able to make sense of them.' Mr Eccleston chuckled.

Cassandra was thinking about this very deeply. It was written on her face.

'Had an odd dream did we?' asked the tutor.

'No, no. Not at all. I was just curious.'

'I see…' Cassandra was hiding something. A man like Mr Eccleston knew when someone was hiding something. 'You have to be careful with dreams. Don't let them bother you too much. They're only dreams after all.'

'But surely odd dreams don't just happen, there must be a reason for them?' said Cassandra.

'Of course. There's a reason for everything.'

The doors flew open and Martha stormed the room armed with a feather duster.

'Oh. Mornin', M'Lady. Mr Eccleston.'

'Good morning,' said the tutor.

'I tell ya, there's people all over this palace these days. We got the florists in doing the new arrangements. We got extra cooks and staff downstairs prepping for the Lords' Banquet. We got all these blummin' City Watch fellows standing about in corridors like bad decorations. I was supposed to be doing the bedding, but Agnes has already done that on account o' bein' pushed out of the kitchen by all the new bodies we got in there. So I beg your pardon, I just thought I'd do a spot of dustin'. Library's needed one for some time now. I can come back if you're busy. But I could just be very quiet, going about the shelves and that.'

'That's fine, Martha,' said Cassandra.

'Dust away,' said Mr Eccleston.

'Good to see you up and out of bed Cassandra, I was beginning to think you were becoming an afternoon person. Remember what they say, the early bird catches the egg.'

'Worm, I believe,' said Mr Eccleston. 'The early bird catches the worm.'

'Yep, that's it. Silly me,' said Martha. 'I'll just go about me duties, you continue with your lesson.'

'We shall,' said Mr Eccleston, shuffling his papers awkwardly.

Cassandra smiled.

Whenever the maid and the tutor were in the same room, Mr Eccleston would turn a shade of pink and start acting out of sorts. Martha knew as well as Cassandra did exactly what was going on. She was especially good at milking it.

'Ah... Where were we? Ah yes, that's it. Peat bogs! Do you know which of the known world's three continents is most renowned for its peat bogs?'

***

Across town in a part that *did* smell like horse dung – and foamy beer, sweat, debauchery and poor people, Job Button was making his way through his ninth pint of ale aptly called Hoppy Endings. It was pretty strong stuff. He had managed it well up until about three sips ago, when he'd started swaying in his seat and sweating profusely like an onion in a pan.

'Aye tell ya... I've got a pair o' queens 'ere starin' at me, ya don't standy a chancy,' he was saying.

'Job, tellin' us yer cards ain't gonna 'elp you win back wot you lost,' said Tommy Woodcarp.

'Or is 'e now... I reckons 'e's bluffin',' said Jack Scrubbs.

'Bluffin'? 'E's too drunk to be bluffin'. Look at 'im. Drunk as a boiled owl.'

The three were engaged in a fearsome game of cards. And it was quite obvious who was losing.

'I... am... not... *hiccup*... drunk,' declared Job Button, to the tavern as a whole. 'Yer jussssst scared.'

'Yep, quakin' in me boots. I see your sixpence and raise you a threepence,' said Tommy.

'Weeeell, in that case, aye raise ya two bob.'

The men watched as Job threw two shillings onto the pile.

'Come on mate – Ouch!' Jack was about to talk Job down, but a foot swiftly kicked him in the shin.

'Didn't know the dead paid so well,' said Tommy, the owner of said foot.

'Oooh.' Job laughed. 'They paaays remark'bly well.'

Tommy Woodcarp was a seasoned gambler who'd had difficulty finding anyone to play cards with in the Brewery Quarter. That was until he'd met five-pints-in Job Button, who was now nine-pints-in and several shillings lighter. He laid his cards across the pile of coins with a delicate flourish and said, 'Pair o' kings.'

Job laid his two down. 'Two pretty little queens, as promisttt,' he declared, proudly, spitting a bit.

'Don't know why yer smilin',' said Tommy, 'kings trump queens.'

Job, still smiling, gave his head a confident shake. 'Ooh noo they don't,' he said.

'Oh yes they does,' replied Tommy. 'It goes queens, then kings.'

'Ushawally it does, but while there's a queen sittin' on the frone, it's queens beatin' kings.'

'No, no, no. That's not how it works. It's always kings over queens.'

'Really? Weeeell, say t'Queen were t'marry again,' Job looked around with a searching finger. 'The barman over there. Say he married the Queen. Woul…wouldn't make 'im king now, would it? Make 'im a duke? Or summin…'

'Wot's that got to do wiv it, Job?'

'I'll tell ya if you'd just let me finish! Fing is, while a queen is on the frone a king could come along and the queen still trump 'im.' Job picked up the cards and performed a visual demonstration of this. 'Seeee… clippty cloppty, "I'm the new king!" "I'm the queen!" "oh-noooo!".' The two gambling men watched as carefully as they could, they still didn't get it.

'This is a game o' cards. And in this game kings *always* trump queens. It's bin that way since the cards wos invented. It'll be that way till long after.'

'Bit sexist,' said Job.

''S'ow it is.'

'Well, 's'not fair,' said Job.

'Wot? Wot you mean it ain't fair?'

'Cheatin' you are.'

'You callin' me a cheat now?' said Tommy.

'Cool it, no one's callin' anyone a cheat,' said Jack.

'I didn't sign up fa'these rooooles,' Job slurred.

'Listen. The both o' ya,' said Jack. 'It don't matter. You're both out o' luck.' He threw his cards down. 'A pair o' wise men. Trumps the lot o' you.'

Job and Tommy blinked at the cards.

'Fair nuff,' they said.

Then Job screamed, 'ahnuva!' and slammed his half full pint down on the table.

'*How many times!* It ain't blummin' table service,' the barman shouted back.

'Should be… Let's go again,' said Job.

'You ain't got nuff coin for ahnuva game, 'av' ya?'

'Ooooo, 'aven't I? Job closed one eye and shook his purse of coin against his ear. 'Sounds full to me.'

'Where'd you get all that anyway, Job?' asked Jack.

'I sayed. The dead pays well.'

'Me late uncle was an undertaker, he said the money were tuppence, weren't worth it unless you 'ad a fing for diggin'. Left me a will 'n' all. Obvs weren't no fortune, otherwise I wouldn't be 'ere,' said Jack.

'Say, Job, if you're makin' so much moolah, why you wastin' it away in 'ere with us pair o' low-lives?' asked Tommy.

'That.. is ah… ex'lent… question,' said Job, zoning out to admire the rising bubbles in his drink.

'If I was loaded like that, I'd buy meself a 'ouse, get meself a woman, settle down.'

'Maybe I will. Maybe I could. Maybe I might.'

'Not me, nah, I'd be off t'Queen's Garter. 'av' meself a whale o' a time.'

'Ahhhh, yes… beauties…' said Job. 'Been a while since I ventured into that crimson palace. What's the name o' that music girl, you know, the one wot plays the 'arp.'

'Delilah?' said Jack.

'I fawt 'er name were Florence?' said Tommy.

'No… it was summin… summin wiv a Beeee.'

'Beatrice.'

'No.'

'Babs?'

'Nope.'

'Beth?'

'Uh-uh.'

'Bianca?'

'Nooo.'

'Hang on, weren't it Effel,' said Jack.

'Nah, that's the one wot runs the place. Effel Spriggs! Or *Madame Spriggs*. She's a dirty puzzle, she is.' Tommy sipped at his glass and lowered it to reveal a frothy moustache.

Just then a trapped blood vessel burst to life again in Job's wavering brain. His eyes sprang wide and he gasped as if he were about to keel over and die. 'Vera!' he said.

'That's not a b?'

'Ah Vera,' said Job, 'Vera, Vera, Vera. Wot a lovely, lovely gal. If ever I were t'marry, it'd be 'er.'

'You should pop along, mate, wiv that bag o' coins you might strike lucky.' The two men laughed.

'Ha! I wish. I'd 'av' to rob the Merchant Bank t'even be in wiv a chance.' Job laughed with them. Then he looked genuinely saddened. As if he'd come to realise that men like him were not meant for women like Vera... wotshername. Or any woman for that matter.

'Say, speakin' o' the ol'Garter,' said Tommy, 'I 'eard summin funny the other day.'

'Proper funny? Or just funny?' said Job.

'Just funny.'

'As funny as that time Sneebles fell off that horse?' said Jack.

'No.'

'Wot about when the baker on Timpson Street got so banana'd he jumpt in the canal starkers?' said Job.

'No... Not that kind of funny really...'

'Wot about when you got...'

'You know,' said Tommy, 'thinkin' 'bout it, it ain't really funny at all. Just weird.'

'Wot?'

'Well 'parrently, there's this little orphan lad wot's bin stayin' at t'Garter o' late. Practically livin' there I 'eard.'

Job had faded out again. His eyelids felt like they were being pulled shut by tiny invisible strings.

'Livin' at the Queen's Garter! Talk 'bout spenny!' said Jack.

'Yeah, but 'e don't mingle with the ladies. 'E don't drink neither. Boy likes 'is privacy see. He goes in 'n' outta t'place, always wiv candles, black ones, prob's 'as a fear o' the dark or summin. And he's got a pet cat too.'

'Didn't knows animals wos allowed in the Garter?'

'They ain't. But it's probs cos all the ladies 'av' got a sweet spot for the lad, 'im bein' an orphan 'n' all. They're *all* talkin' 'bout 'im.'

'Black candles...' Job murmured half asleep.

'Where'd you 'ear this then?' asked Jack.

'Uhhh... I got a friend,' said Tommy. 'A friend o' a friend really.

Actually, more like an acquaintance a couple times removed. 'E was there last night chattin' wiv the girls in the smokin' room. They're all goin' on about this little lad. Got a big in'eritance from 'is family or summin. They're all fascinated by it, as you can imagine.'

''Ere, 'ow old's this lad anyway?' said Jack.

'Dunno. But he's not a man yet. 'E's doin' better than the three of us all put together, Job and 'is purse included, and 'is tallywags probs ain't even dropped yet.'

'Lucky chap indeed.'

'Wot's lucky?' said Job, rousing.

Two men had stopped off at the Frothy Head for a drink. They had been sat at the bar, wallowing in their miseries, when their ears pricked up to listen in on the three gamblers.

They finished their gins, straightened their hats and strolled over to the table.

There was something menacing about them. Maybe it was the way they walked like they owned the place. Or maybe it was the clubs hanging from their belts.

'Evenin', gentsth,' said one, who had a swollen lip and a pair of black eyes. 'Me 'n' me pal 'ere couldn't 'elp over 'earin' your conversthaython.'

'Eavesdroppin' were you?' said Tommy.

'It ain't eavesdroppin' when yer talkin' loud nuff,' said the other hatted man.

'We didn't mean to disturb you,' said Jack.

'Wot'sth thisth you wosth justht thsayin'?'

'Sorry?' Tommy was too drunk for conversations with strangers. Especially ones with lisps.

'Thsummin 'bout a boy?'

'Wot's it got to do with you?' Unlike Jack, Tommy hadn't yet caught drift that these were two men you didn't talk back to.

'Call me curiousth.'

Tommy stared up at the man's bruised face. 'Just some rich boy.'

'Thisth boy, 'e hasth a cat wiv 'im you thsaid?'

'Yeah. Wot 'bout it?'

Job was looking through hazy eyes at the new encounter. He could just about make out the clubs under their moth-holed jackets. His drunk-sense was tingling. The sense that tells a man when he's had too much, or when he's had just enough not to be able to deal with the moment in hand.

'Wasth it a black cat? White patthch under itsth neck? Green eyesth?'

'Maybe. I don't know. I ain't seen it.'

'It's 'im Archie,' said the other hatted man. 'The talkin' cat.'

'Thshhhh.'

The two gamblers exchanged clueless looks at each other. Job straightened up.

'Wot d'you say?' he said.

'Thisth boy, thstayin' at the Queen'sth Garter you thsaid?'

'That's right. Wots it to you?' said Tommy.

'Hmmm. Thank you, gentsth, 'av' a nithe evenin'.' The lisping man turned and walked away. The other, doffed his bowler hat and followed after.

'Strange fellas,' said Tommy.

'Say, see 'is face, looked all smashed up.'

'Wonder wot they wanted. Job? 'ey, Job? You there?'

Job was staring into the bubbles again. Only this time he wasn't looking at the drink, he was staring into his head.

Boy likes his privacy, they said. Black candles, they said. *Talking cat, they said…*

'I've got to go.' Job rose so quickly he nearly took the table with him.

'Steady on, mate, you owe us ahnuva round.'

'Yeah, and I fawt we were gonna 'av' ahnuva game?'

'Uhhh… next time… Sorry. Sorry.'

Job departed, returned, finished his drink in one, then departed again.

Out of the mouths of babes oft times come gems. The same can be said about the mouths of drunks, though it's a great deal less common.

Job had a hunch. A feeling in his gut that wasn't just a bloated beer belly feeling. He knew there were certain kinds of gossip to listen out for. Some would net you a large sum of money, if you knew what to do.

But it's a rather difficult task finding a man who doesn't wish to be found. A man who has no fixed address or name or friends. Job had set up his first meeting with the strange man through a mutual connection. Another drunken rambling with a wealthy ending. But this time he was on his own. And unhelpfully, steaming.

So he did the very thing that no one ever did in the Brewery Quarter, he asked questions.

He walked from public house to public house, *a feat that wasn't new to him*, and in each gave a brief description of the Witchhunter's appearance.

He was served a collage of mixed reactions. Most threw him out at the door for being too woozy and everywhere else said they hadn't a clue what he was talking about.

Of all the places Job Button tried, only one seemed to have genuinely seen the mysterious man. The landlord told him that the man in question had stayed on one occasion, slept in the day and was out all evening.

''E kept 'imself t' 'imself, 'n' didn't even order a drink. Most strange, I tell ya.'

Job continued his inquiries, though it appeared to be in vain: how could he hope to find a man who only slept once wherever he stayed?

But that evening, which soon turned to morning, Job's search met an end, for let it be a lesson to all, that if you go about look-ing for troublesome things, they tend to find you before you find them.

And find Job Button they did, at the revelation of a pistol butt cracking against the back of his head.

A rough hand pulled in the fabric at his throat and pinned him to the wall. The barrel of the gun dug against the soft flesh be-neath his jaw.

'Are you an idiot? A malformed thinker? A fool on all rights?' said the Witchhunter in a voice that had all the aggression of a shout yet all the intimacy of a whisper.

Job stuttered incoherent sentences until his attacker retracted the gun a little.

'Did you think I had ripped you off? I had forgotten you? I pay my debts Mr Button. But to go about asking questions in such a manner that draws attention to my stay here, earns you your weight of gold in lead.' The hammer of the pistol clicked back and brought water to Job Button's pants. Literally.

'I cannot stay in a single place where you have painted my por-trait. You've made things very difficult for me.'

'I needed t'find you. I gots more news. More goss. More stuff 'bout… *the Black Science*,' said Job.

The Witchhunter stared into his informant's eyes, searching for any trace of deceit. Seeing nothing but a fool, he stood back, lowered his pistol and looked around to check no one was near.

'Speak it.'

'Right… There I was 'avin' meself a quiet game o' cards. I was havin' a stinker, but I was gonna win it back. I don't 'av' a gamb-lin' problem or nuffin'. And I ain't that drunk, I may look it, but it's cause I've been runnin' around for who knows 'ow many 'ours lookin' for you. You know, you'd probs get more leads if you 'ad a callin' card or summin. I know's a bloke who prints 'em–'

'I am not a patient man,' added the Witchhunter, accelerating

Job's tale to the point.

'Yeah, o' course, o' course. So, me gamblin' mates are talkin' and… word is, there's a suspicious fella stayin' at the Queen's Garter. Very suspicious. Likes candles. Black ones. That's Black Science stuff ain't it? I 'eard that once. No one uses black candles. No one.'

'If that's all you have then I should kill you dead just for wasting my time.'

'Black candles ain't good enough?'

'No, Mr Button. Black, red, blue I don't care what colour candles there were, that is not proof of anything. You're a fool if you think it is. Nothing but a drunken fool.'

'Look. That ain't all. We wos chattin' away 'bout this lad. Can't remember the ins and out exactly, I wos 'alfway through a good daydream… but then these two blokes come over. Mean lookin' blokes. Look like the sort that'd rob your nan. They started askin' questions. 'Bout the boy, see.'

The Witchhunter's finger tightened around the trigger of his pistol.

'Then… odd fing 'appens. One of em says summin 'bout a talkin' cat. The other tells 'im to thshhhh.'

The Witchhunter raised an eyebrow.

'He 'ad a lisp, see. But this all got me finkin', black candles, suspicious fella, a cat, which is weird enough cause we all know cats are dodgy. But he said summin 'bout it talkin'. I fawt to meself, cats can't talk. That's logicide that. But, if cats could talk and if this cat were talkin', it's either logicide or… it's…' Job paused for emphasis, '*the Black Science.*'

The Witchhunter stared blankly at the drunk.

'Is that all?' he said.

'Yeah… But that's good enough, ain't it? Good enough for another purse o' coins?'

'Mr Button,' said the Witchhunter, trying to keep his temper in, 'you've been drinking with other drunks and one of the drunks said he thought he heard a cat talk, and you thought that enough to come looking for me?'

'Don't forget 'bout 'em black candles.'

The pistol butt cracked Job over the head again.

'Owww!'

'Fool.'

'But ain't you gonna check it out?'

The Witchhunter clasped Job by his shirt and slammed him up against the wall.

'Stay away from me. Don't ever try to find me. Mention my existence to anyone and I shall come for you and do all the world a favour and put a bullet in your head.'

'…but.'

The Witchhunter had nothing more to say, he walked out of the alley and into the busy streets of the Brewery Quarter.

Job had never felt more sober. His pants were wet, his head was sore and last night's nine Hoppy Endings were churning in his stomach. But at least he could buy a drink with what money he had left…

Unless of course… he'd left it in the Frothy Head.

As for the Witchhunter, he had no reason to listen to the fool. But nor did he have a reason not to.

***

Later that day…

Niclas still hadn't quite got the knack of drawing. But, with constant assistance from Balthazar, he'd managed to draw the complicated sigil on the floor of the bedroom.

Two large circles, one just inside the other, chalked around a series of geometric lines crisscrossing through its centre like a spider's web. It almost looked like the one that had been sketched on the parchment. Almost.

Between the two circles, in a narrow ring around the edge, were glyphs which had taken literally hours for Niclas to get right. It had been a case of Balthazar placing his paw at one point, Niclas marking a dot, then again at another point, and Niclas joining them up.

Niclas wasn't sure at all if it was right, but he was impressed regardless.

'Pretty good that? Wot d'you fink, sir?'

'It's certainly an improvement,' said Balthazar. 'Lie in the middle of it with one of those candles would you?'

'Sure.'

Niclas lay so his head touched the top of the inner circle and his feet the bottom. It was just like old times, he thought, before he'd known about beds.

'This is just a rehearsal, so don't feel too under pressure,' said Balthazar.

'Ok…' Niclas suddenly felt under pressure, having not felt the need to feel under pressure before.

'Hold the candle against your chest.'

'Like this, sir?'

'No… pointed.'

'Like this?'

'No… pointed up.'

Niclas pointed the candle to the ceiling.

'Hold it like a… as you would a… a dagger.'

'A dagger, sir?' asked Niclas.

'A knife, you know.'

'Oh! I get you, sir,' said Niclas, laughing at himself. He must have looked pretty stupid. He adjusted his grip.

'The other way… With the pointy end against you.'

'Ohhhh,' said Niclas, finally getting it. 'I see, sir. Righto. Like this?'

'Yes. Perfect.'

'Wot 'bout all that stuff we got from that foreign geezer? Do we need that too?'

Balthazar was reading over the parchment, checking he'd got everything right.

'Uhh, yes,' he said, without lifting his eyes, 'but there's no need for it now. You'll have to drink something made from those things.'

'Drink summin? Wot's it taste like?' Niclas remembered all those days he and the boys had spent mixing Speckled Gin, the Bowler Gang's number one product. One of the boys would always have to taste a batch before it was bottled, that way they'd know if they'd made the semi-deadly stuff, or the straight-up lethal stuff. Neither tasted that good. It was like drinking dirty lantern oil, lantern oil that's on fire.

'It'll taste… very nice, don't you worry about that,' said Balthazar.

'Good. Bit parched now if I'm honest, sir.' Niclas licked his dry lips.

'Yes…' said Balthazar, not really paying attention.

'Reckon I could pop down for a glass o' water, sir?'

'Sorry, did you say something?' The cat looked up from the parchment.

'Just a bit firsty, that's all, sir.'

'Yes. Ok. But I need you to bring me something else.'

'Wot is it, sir?' asked Niclas, getting to his feet and dusting the chalk from his clothes. Whenever his new master asked for something, it was always something strange and odd.

'Milk,' said Balthazar.

'Milk, sir?' Niclas creased his brow and assumed the expression of deep, curious thought.

'Yes.'

'Wot's that for sir?'

The cat stared back ominously. Then he said, 'I'm thirsty, too.'

'Righto, sir, I'll be back in a jiffy.'

As Niclas approached the landing of the stairwell, a group of the Garter's maidens were all immersed in giggles and gossiping. He didn't know what they were laughing at. They lifted their hands to hide their snickering, and watched him go past with magnetic stares. He had an inkling they were laughing at him, but he couldn't explain why. He thought, perhaps, his new watch hanging from his waistcoat had something to do with it.

'Afternoon, ladies,' he said, confidently, tipping his hat where his hat would have been if he'd been wearing a hat.

Hehehe!

He walked into the lounge, past Vera the harpist who gave him a wink, and up to the main counter, where Madame Spriggs sat, painting her nails a shade of red that wasn't far off the decor.

''Ello, miss.'

''Ello, young master, wot can we do for you today.'

The girls by the stairs were still giggling.

'I just comes for a drink that's all.'

'Certainly, young master,' Madame Spriggs lit up and got to her feet. Her customers always spent a bit more when they'd had a drink or two, and she suspected this customer had quite a bit of money in his, *in-ear-ett-ence.* 'We 'av' whiskey, rum, gin, sacky, vodka–'

'Just a glass o' water will do me, miss,' said Niclas.

Madame Spriggs lost her shine.

'Right… o' course, anyfing 'is young master wants.'

To her surprise, Niclas began rooting for coins in his pocket. The water was free… but he didn't know that.

''Ow much is that?'

'…Uhh…' Madame Spriggs hesitated. 'A threepence, little sir,' she said.

'I also needs some milk, miss?'

'Milk?'

'Yeah… for me stomach. Always settles me uhh *in-der-gest-john*,' said Niclas.

'Right… whole or semi skimmed?'

'Sorry, miss?'

'The blue or the green, m'luv?'

'…' This perplexed Niclas even more, he didn't know that there were blue or green cows. 'Err… Which would you recommend?'

The girls could be heard laughing again.

Even Madame Spriggs looked as if she was about to laugh, but she kept her smile tight.

'Blue is best for a young lad like you.'

'Ok… some o' that please.'

'I'll just fetch it, little sir, we don't keep it in the warm.'

'Alright.'

Niclas turned smoothly and struck a lean against the counter doing his best to look cool. Some people, no matter how hard they try can't *look cool*, and the harder these people try to *look cool*, the *less cool* they look. Niclas was probably the most uncool cucumber in Laburnum.

He watched Vera like a charmed snake, unable to fathom how she moved her fingers up and down the harp to produce such delicate sounds.

The lounge of the Garter was never that busy, but nor was it empty, there were always a few old gentlemen puffing pipes and chatting to the girls. The Garter drew its own sort of customer, ones who had money, which in the Brewery Quarter was a very small slice of the pie. As such, you didn't get the usual rabble nor the smell and the noise that followed it.

In the corner of the room, there was a man with a slouch hat, smoking a pipe and like everyone else he was watching the harpist. But unlike the other men, he didn't have one of the maidens to keep him company. He was alone.

There was something about this fella, something Niclas couldn't quite put his finger on. Niclas was used to not being able to put his finger on things. He was cognitively fingerless.

He stared at the man for longer than he should have, and soon, through a cloud of tobacco smoke, the man stared back.

''Ere we are then, a pint o' whole milk. Do you want it in a glass?'

'No miss, in the bottle's fine. 'Ow much?'

'…' Madame Spriggs hesitated again, this time trying to work out how far she could push her luck. 'That's a sixpence altogether,' she said, awkwardly.

'Uh…' Niclas didn't have the right change. 'Is a shillin' alright, miss.'

'*A shillin'! For some water and milk*? Why uh, yes. That aught cover it.'

Niclas handed over the coin, gulped down the water with urgency and picked up the bottle of milk.

'You need anyfing else, young master, you just give us a bell. Still got those dancin' lessons if you want? And I reckon's we could give you a deal on 'em… 'alf price if you fancied it?' said Madame Spriggs.

'Oh! Uh, I'll fink 'bout it, miss,' said Niclas. Half price didn't sound bad, he'd have to run it past Balthazar.

As he was finishing up and on his way past the girls back up the stairs, the strange man had been watching him. Niclas had a habit of drawing attention to himself, but this was different. The stranger's eyes were fixed to the boy as he went up the stairs. It was nothing he'd said and nothing he'd done to pique the man's interests. It was the dusty chalk marks on the back of his clothes. Pink chalk marks.

Niclas got to the top of the stairs and took the key out of his pocket. Then he felt something. A presence lurking behind him. It was the same presence he'd felt downstairs. He gave a quick glance back and there, at the end of the corridor, stood the stranger in the greatcoat and slouch hat. The man was staring into his pocket watch with a look of mystified intrigue.

Niclas picked up the pace. He hurried to the bedroom door and fumbled the key against the lock. It dropped out of his sweaty hands and bounced on the floor. The man was walking faster too. The spurs on his boots chinking as he strode down the passage. Careful not to spill the milk, and peeking out of the corner of his eye at the approaching man, Niclas bent down, picked up the key and shoved it into the lock.

The door opened and he was but moments from slipping inside and locking it behind him, when the man, unveiling a pistol from within his coat, barged his way in.

Smash went the bottle, splash went the milk. Candles rolled across the floor towards the bed; where Niclas took refuge behind one of the four posts.

He couldn't draw his eyes from the flintlock. It was a fearsome design of the likes he had never seen; a chunky weapon of iron, with a screaming woman's face engraved down the barrel, and a revolving canister at its heart.

It's doubtful any intelligible thought entered the boy's mind from the moment he was muscled into the room. Why the man was there and who he was, were both questions for a sober mind. But Niclas, like most people, quickly turned drunk in the presence of a gun. Drunk on fear. His only thought, which, had the intruder pulled the trigger would have been noted as his last, was: *Balthazar?*

Granted, this thought wasn't the most useful to have at the current moment, but it was intriguing, for the cat was nowhere to be seen.

The Witchhunter said nothing. He held Niclas at gunpoint and cast his eyes over the room. He saw the sigil, chalked on the floor and surrounded by unlit black candles. On the table lay a bag overflowing with unusual items and a piece of parchment with penciled peculiar markings. And there, on the side table, a stale, half eaten croissant.

'P…p…pwease don't kill me… I'm sorry, gov… did Mr K send you? I've got money. You can take it for 'im. You can 'av' it all–'

'Quiet,' said the Witchhunter.

He stepped into the sigil and took a closer look at the glyphs chalked around it.

'What are you doing here?' he said.

'…Nuffin'… Just silly drawin's that's all.'

'You're a little young to be dabbling in this sort. Who else is here?' The Witchhunter crossed the room to check the bathroom. Niclas climbed over the bed, to keep distance between himself and the armed man.

'Wot do you want?' he asked.

'Where's the witch?' said the man, pointing the gun again.

'Which? Which wot?'

'*Witch*! Where is it?' the man demanded. His voice was cold, firm, the kind of voice that belongs to a man who'd have no trouble sleeping at night after killing a young boy.

'Listen, gov, I knows you fink you knows that I knows wot you're goin' on 'bout, but troof be told, I don't knows a fing 'bout wot you finks I know.'

The Witchhunter peered under the bed, then shot his attention back to Niclas.

'I won't ask again. Where's the witch?'

Niclas had picked up a pillow to defend himself. It wasn't doing him much good. He clasped it against his body in both arms, screwed up his face, closed his eyes and waited for the short, shrill, thud.

'*And which witch would you be looking for?*' said Balthazar.

Spooked, the Witchhunter drew his second gun and backed away from the bed.

Niclas pulled his face from the pillow and gingerly peered back at the man.

'It's just, there are many witches in this city. It helps to know whom you're looking for,' Balthazar continued, in a voice that could have greased axles.

'Avast, come at me, coward,' said the Witchhunter, exasperated. He searched the room with his pistols as eyes.

'I'd rather you didn't make assumptions. I'm certainly no coward.'

'Then why hide, witch? Face me!'

'I'm not hiding. I'm merely trying to avoid a nasty misunderstanding. If I show myself to you, you won't hesitate to shoot me. This way, I can explain a few things first, which might just have the weight to change your mind.'

Niclas too was puzzled as to where Balthazar was. His voice seemed to echo about the room as if called into a chasm.

'Firstly, I'm not what you think I am, as you'll understand when you look me in the eye. Secondly, the boy here knows nothing. *Absolutely nothing actually*. He is my assistant, that is all. Thirdly, my interest in the occult, as displayed by those curious pink markings goes only as far as curing my ailment, no further. And fourthly, I have no love for witches, and as we clearly share that attitude towards them, I believe I can help you. I can find every witch in Laburnum if you so wish. So, you see, it helps to know which witch you're looking for? Now, had you shot me dead, those four facts would have been lost to the void, wouldn't they?'

The Witchhunter was stunned and Balthazar took advantage of this, revealing his hiding place – the roof of the four poster bed. He hopped onto the top of the wardrobe, down onto the adjacent chest of draws, then across onto the mattress. The Witchhunter, startled, took aim.

The cat showed no fear, it purred behind green eyes.

'Are things a little clearer now?' At this, the hunter met the cat's eyes and was so bewildered he took a step back.

'What are you?' he asked.

'Ah, metaphysics. Am I a cat, or am I a man? Why, what are we both but not the same stuff arranged in a different way?'

Balthazar's nonchalant manner confused Niclas, and the silence that ensued made him wriggle in discomfort.

'Witch or no witch, there's witchcraft at play, and I will not stand for the Black Science.'

The man moved his fingers onto each of the triggers.

'Fine. Kill us if you must,' said Balthazar.

Niclas, who had started to believe things were on the up, tasted the appetiser to death once more.

'Of course, then you'd be just like those you hunt: a child killer,' Balthazar added, putting a hold on the Witchhunter's trigger finger and propping one of his eyebrows on end.

Niclas studied the man's expression. They held a stare: the boy frightened, the man dubious.

'Perhaps I'll let him live,' remarked the Witchhunter.

'Perhaps,' smirked the cat, 'but you'd be very foolish to kill me. I am no harm to anyone, except the odd mouse or fly. There's no logic in killing me, but there is reason to let me live. As I said, I know the whereabouts of every witch in this city. A man of your occupation could strike somewhat of a metaphorical gold mine, should you spare me.'

The Witchhunter, stubborn, kept his aim whilst Balthazar continued to ramble off this persuasive yarn. Eventually, after another painful and precarious silence, the man lowered his firearm, though refused to holster it.

'I am not a fool, how do I know you speak the truth?' he asked.

'You will have to trust me,' said the cat.

'I don't trust easy.'

'No, you certainly don't look like the type who does. But you must believe me when I say that I share the same hatred you have for the creatures you hunt. I was like you once, a man. It is because of them that I have become trapped in this fluffy existence. I want only to be free! To walk again on two legs and drink wine with a cup in my hand. I know that you and I can help each other and it would give me nothing but pleasure to see my curse avenged.'

'A witch made you this way?'

'Sadly, yes. It's a curse I have been trying to cure. Now, what say you lower the guns, you're frightening the boy.'

'Why would a witch want to make a man a cat?'

'Ah, if only I knew the motivations of those twisted and evil monsters.' Balthazar sighed. 'It's a rather long story. And one I don't wish to tell at gunpoint.'

The Witchhunter considered lowering his pistol, then reconsidered. 'How can you find them?' he said at last.

'I have a contact.'

The man and the cat tried to out stare one another, whilst Niclas did his best to hold Laburnum's most expensive glass of water in his quivering bladder.

'What contact?' said the man.

'We can go if you like. It's not far.'

The Witchhunter looked the cat up and down. There wasn't much to look up and down at.

'*Take me*,' he said.

'Splendid,' said Balthazar. 'See, boy, how much just talking can achieve. We could have had quite the upset, dead cat, dead child, that would lower the price for a room in this place quite considerably.'

'Enough,' snapped the Witchhunter, reinstating the gun. 'Right now, cat, I get the impression that you like to talk a lot. I also get the impression that you talk a lot of crap. I can't say I believe you can find witches any easier than I can, but I suggest you start moving – this gun intended to kill today, and right now it's struggling to trust you.'

The cat, offended at first, drew a caustic grin across his face. 'So be it, witch-killer.'

They left the Queen's Garter, crossed the Brewery Quarter and found themselves following the cat into an alley. Unlike Niclas, the Witchhunter was not used to following Balthazar into such inhospitable places. He kept his hands near his pistols and his eyes on every corner.

'Where are you taking me, cat?' he asked, browsing his necro-cardium.

'It's ok. Don't be scared witch-killer. We're going to visit the old-est, largest and most observant inhabitants of Laburnum. When it comes to finding anyone, they should be your first resort.'

'And who are they?' asked the Witchhunter.

Balthazar stopped in front of a drain grid, and nodded his head as a command for Niclas to remove it.

The boy crouched down and heaved at the drain's lid, but he was weak, and after frustrating the Witchhunter, and amusing Balthazar for a minute or so, the Witchhunter stepped in to help.

The cover slid aside and fumes of the sewer's stench escaped into their nostrils.

'The rats of course,' said Balthazar.

'Rats?' said the boy and the man as one.

'Yes, now Niclas, you run along back to the room, we should only be an hour or so.'

Niclas found the request odd, but did as he was told. Or at least he would have, had the Witchhunter not grabbed his waistcoat.

'The boy comes too,' he said.

Balthazar, for the first time since meeting the Witchhunter, showed an emotion that wasn't altogether nonchalant. For a rea-son Niclas couldn't grasp, he didn't want him to follow.

But the Witchhunter was an obstinate man, and he would have

his way or no way at all.

'Fine by me,' the cat said at last, as if laughing off a bad joke, and hopped down into the sewer.

The Witchhunter, poisoned with doubt, shoved his gun into Niclas' back.

'In,' he said.

'Easy, gov, easy.'

***

Niclas' nose was that of a stench connoisseur. It was accustomed to the damp, grime, rot and festering filth of Bog End. But below the city streets lived a far worse stink. For all things rancid soon find their way into Laburnum's sewers. There, they float in a putrid concoction, so toxic, that the slightest drop would give a seven-foot draught horse the trots for a year.

A dark, slimy river crawled through the tunnels; its viscosity nearer to curdled cream than water. Within it, Niclas could make out lost items from the upper world. Bits of broken toys, blanched newspapers, tattered clothes and ships of rotten food crewed by maggots. It made him ill watching the junk bob up and down on the surface, but it was also unpleasantly fascinating, for some of the stuff people flushed down their water closets was really quite extraordinary.

The side path was treacherously thin and the roof was arched, making it a death trap for the tall and the clumsy.

Fortunately for Niclas and the Witchhunter, there was just enough light to see where they were going. Every thirty feet along the ceiling was a drain, and from each of these drains poured a column of light. Like waypoints in the dark, they revealed the enormous length of the stream.

Niclas glanced back. The tunnel behind was now unrecognisable. There were no landmarks to guide them home, and it dawned on him that without Balthazar they could be lost traipsing in circles until the fumes strangled them.

He looked up at the nearest drain as the spores drifted into its shaft of light. It was impossible to see where they were beneath the streets. They could have been right below Poshside, under some Lord's toilet while he was making himself lighter. Or they might have been walking beneath the slums, right under the Bowler Gang's warehouse. It was mind boggling to think of all the hustle and bustle going on over their heads, while they were so close to it, yet so far removed.

Niclas was pondering just how mind boggling it was, when his foot caught a badly placed brick, sending him over the edge of the pathway – headfirst towards the sludge.

He froze in midair, his toes balancing on the edge, his body hovering over the living river.

The Witchhunter had caught him by the strap of his waistcoat. He yanked him back onto the path.

'Be careful you idiot,' yelled Balthazar from the front, 'that foulness will make you so sick that you'll wish you had King Cholera.'

'Fanks, gov,' said Niclas, looking up at his saviour with a beholden gaze.

The Witchhunter replied by raising his gun and pointing onwards. Niclas continued.

Balthazar led them through the labyrinth, round corner after corner until they came to a small iron bar gate, which he slipped through without problem.

'Almost there now,' he said.

Niclas tried to squeeze through the bars, but he was too big.

'Err… Got a problem, sir.'

The Witchhunter shook his head. He gave the handle a stiff push, the rust crumbled from its hinges and the gate whined open.

Niclas shrugged.

On the other side there were no more drains overhead and so the light faded quickly. This didn't seem to trouble Balthazar at all, he carried on walking into the darkness and out of sight.

'Sir? Sir?' called Niclas. 'Come back, sir, we can't see a fing.'

The Witchhunter holstered his gun and rummaged through his oversized pockets. Out came a small, intricate metal box. He flicked the lid open with his thumb and a smell of fishy blubber oil wafted into the air. With a strike of the flint, the wick caught alight, and a little flame sprouted up eagerly, pushing back the darkness.

Niclas was amazed. He'd never seen such a device. 'Nice one, gov,' he said.

And there was Balthazar, waiting for them just ahead, two eyes shimmering in the black.

'How very prepared you are,' he said.

The Witchhunter, with his pocket flame in one hand and his gun back in the other, ushered Niclas on.

'Blumin' 'eck,' said the boy, 'there's a 'ole world down 'ere.'

'Indeed,' said Balthazar. 'These are the maintenance tunnels. They built the network when they were building the sewers. You used to be able to get here from the street without having to go through the drainage but smugglers started using them so they bricked them up.'

'They run under the 'ole city?' said Niclas.

'Most of it.'

'How far?' said the Witchhunter.

'Nearly there,' said Balthazar. 'And I'd put that gun away if I were you. They won't like it.'

The Witchhunter dithered to obey.

'I'll keep it to hand,' he said.

'Suit yourself,' said the cat.

'I can't believe that this is all under 'ere. I've been walkin' round upstairs and didn't even know there was a downstairs,' said Niclas.

'You're not missing much,' said Balthazar.

'Yeah, but still, I didn't even know.'

'There's a lot you don't know, boy, plenty more to get excited about. Ah, here we are.'

Balthazar stopped at a dead end. A brick wall. He scratched his nails on its red brick surface and waited.

Nothing happened.

Still nothing.

Nope.

Not a thing.

Balthazar was well accustomed to the patience needed when dealing with rats. He took the opportunity to bathe himself and did so at the expense of the Witchhunter's nerves.

'I swear it, cat, I will shoot you both if this is your idea of a joke.'

Balthazar continued to bathe, unthreatened.

'Shoot me,' he said, 'I'm sure you can remember the way back?'

At this, the Witchhunter felt the tables turn. The power he held from the gun withered away from him.

'Only a fool would shoot the guide,' Balthazar teased.

'You…' The Witchhunter was about to embark on a train of thought that would test his rage against his reason, when the rats answered the door.

Two bricks receded from the wall. Head height for Balthazar. Shin height for the humans.

'Hello, only me,' said Balthazar.

Niclas leaned down and watched a rat stick its head out of the gap.

Its nose moved at a hundred twitches a minute and its beady eyes tried to see past the cat. It could smell something there but it couldn't see.

Rats can not only smell smells, but the very chemicals that make up the smells. They can recognise a change in atmosphere, and, even a change in emotions, so they can tell if other creatures are harmlessly passing them by, or set on having them as a rather unsavoury snack.

This rat was picking up a range of different chemical reactions and trying hard to read the olfactory language.

'I have come to seek council with the Chieftain,' said Balthazar.

Squeak, squeak, squeak.

'Don't worry, they're with me.'

Squeak, squeak. Squeak, squeak. Squeak?

'It's fine, really, I'll explain everything to the Chieftain.'

Squeak, squeak.

'Look. Listen here,' said Balthazar, taking a harsher tone, 'it's on my head, I'll take full responsibility. But, if you turn us away, then that's on your little head. And I don't know if the Chieftain will be pleased to hear that it was *you*, who turned *me* away.'

Niclas and the Witchhunter shared a look of mutual ignorance.

…Squeak…

'Thank you. I knew you'd see sense,' said Balthazar.

The rat disappeared back into the hole and the bricks ground back into place.

'Sir… did you just talk to that rat?' asked Niclas.

Balthazar stared into Niclas' gormless face, opened his mouth to explain, then thought better of it.

'You know those things I keep telling you not to waste time thinking about?' he said.

Niclas nodded.

'That's another one.'

That was enough to satisfy the boy.

It wasn't for the Witchhunter.

There was a loud grinding of brick against brick, the floor rumbled, and dirt and soil poured unsettlingly from the roof.

'Wot's 'appenin'!' said Niclas.

Just a little to the left, the floor had opened up and a stone stairway had been revealed. The opening exhaled a long, smelly breath.

'Wot's goin' on, sir? We goin' down there?'

'Yes. Come on,' said Balthazar, leading the way below.

If it weren't for the Witchhunter's flame, they would have been walking in complete darkness, yet, Niclas might have preferred it that way. What the darkness was there to hide were the open graves either side of them. In each lay a skeleton with its calcareous arms folded across its ribs. Niclas had never seen one before. Now he had seen many all at once.

'Is them skellies? Crikey! They're creepy as,' he said.

'What is this place?' asked the Witchhunter.

'The catacombs of Old Laburnum. Don't worry, they're very dead, they've been that way for hundreds of years.'

'Why're they all lyin' the same way, wiv arms crossed like that?' said Niclas.

'Who knows? Maybe they sleep better that way.'

'I don't like it… it gives me the herpes-jerpes.'

The Witchhunter and the cat looked askant at Niclas.

'Or is it… heebie-jeebies?' said the boy.

'Remarkable really,' said Balthazar, 'the crypts have been sealed since the city architects first discovered them. Must be lots of history buried down here, you'd think that would interest people. Apparently not.'

All the skeletons looked the same, but some had rusted daggers clasped against them and some had rusted cylinders with queer faded markings.

As they wandered through the tombs, more and more rats came into sight. They would scuttle out of hiding, and peer up at the humans. It wasn't every day a rat smelt a human, though it was squeaked, you were never more than six feet away from one.

''Ello,' said Niclas, waving, and sending a group of rats rushing back into cover. 'Can they understand me?'

'Doubt it,' said Balthazar.

'Where are you taking me, cat,' demanded the Witchhunter.

'Relax, witch-killer, it's the door just ahead.'

Out of the darkness, emerged a tall double door engraved with ancient markings. Light seemed to be coming from within, it seeped through the stone's cracks and edges.

'I don't like this. Not one bit,' said Niclas.

'After you,' said Balthazar.

Niclas looked to the Witchhunter.

'Errr... I fink 'e means you, gov.'

The Witchhunter braced himself for whatever lay beyond. He grit his teeth and pushed the doors open – the gun went first.

Light burned their eyes. It was more intense than the little flame, and washed it out completely.

Inside, was a sight so bewildering, Niclas vocalised his thoughts "what" and "how" at the very same time – thus discovering the word:

'WOW!'

It was a great hall, a mile long, wide and high. Stone pillars rose up and disappeared into the darkness above. From the middle of each hung lanterns of brightly burning oil. Their light poured below, to unveil an astounding sight.

Rats. More rats than Niclas had ever seen in his entire life. And that's saying something, Bog End was their holiday destination of choice. There were hundreds of them. Perhaps even thousands of them. They were crawling up the pillars, around the lanterns, across the floor, and in-between the open graves of skeletons that lay embedded wherever a flat wall could be seen.

It was a sea of fur and wormy tails and yellow toothy teeth.

The halls beneath the city had once many moons ago served a purpose for the people of Old Laburnum, but now they were abandoned, inhabited by a new kind of proletariat.

'There must be a 'undred of 'em,' said Niclas.

'Much more,' said Balthazar, 'much, much more.'

The Witchhunter was more used to unsettling things than the average person, but even he was troubled by the squirming furry floor. The rats were unsettled by him too. They seemed to be focusing their beady eyes and noses in his direction.

'It's the gun,' said Balthazar, 'they don't like it, I told you.'

The Witchhunter spun around, his gun hand reaching out ahead of him. The vermin ocean rippled away from it. But as he moved it left and right, the rats on either side closed in, scrabbling closer each time.

'This way.' Balthazar was unperturbed by the rats. He walked straight down the middle and the ocean parted before him.

The humans shuffled after.

Halfway through the great hall, steps rose up converging on a central point; a towering ziggurat of the underbelly. At its highest level lay a stone sarcophagus marked with the markings of an older world. All around it were golden treasures and glittering jewels, some the size of peaches. The coins had spilt down the steps and littered the floor in shiny metal puddles beneath their feet. Niclas had never seen so much loot. It was probably enough for Mr K to retire, he thought.

Some of the coins were recognisable, the Queen's head on one side and the seal of logic, an open book and a sitting owl, on the other. But some were older, much older. And some weren't coins at all, just pieces of silver and gold.

'This your bank, sir?' said Niclas.

'Yes,' said Balthazar, impressed that the boy was capable of remembering something.

When they got to the start of the steps, the rats refused to part. These were bigger, nastier rats, with battle scars, broken teeth and some with missing tails.

They hissed at the humans like a chorus of lizards.

'They're not going to let you pass. It's nothing personal, they're just a bit speciesist.'

'Oh. Wot do we do?'

'You're going to stay here. I'm going to speak with their king.'

'Their king?' said the Witchhunter, like a man who feels he's not part of the joke.

'Yes, their king – and you *will* need to put that weapon away. I can't guarantee your safety when I go up there.'

'What are you up to cat?' the Witchhunter snarled.

'I am a cat of my word. I'm going to get the list I promised. But I insist you put away your weapon.'

The Witchhunter considered this. The rats around them were huge, just a bit smaller than Balthazar, and they looked angry and hungry too.

He holstered the gun.

'Don't do anything until I return. Not a muscle.'

The Witchhunter nodded.

'Niclas?'

'Yes, sir?'

'Not a muscle.'

'Don't worry sir, I ain't got much muscles to move,' said the boy.

'Watch him,' said Balthazar, though not to Niclas, he was talking to the Witchhunter.

The man nodded.

The rats parted to let Balthazar pass, then closed behind him like two crashing tides.

'Don't worry, gov,' said Niclas, ''e knows wot 'e's doin'. 'E's got the gab o' the gift.'

At the top of the ziggurat, the rats were bigger still. They reluctantly stepped aside, allowing the cat to travel to the stone sarcophagus at the summit. Within it, lay a pile of bones with a crown of jewels at its feet.

'Your Uncleanliness,' said Balthazar, humbly.

Out of the skeleton rose a giant rodent, bigger than he, bigger than a small dog. Its teeth were splintered and one of its eyes was scarred. It was midway through a meal of the stinkiest blue cheese, and was being waited upon by tiny, fearful white mice. Slavery was still very much a thing down here.

'Balthazar. Back a little soon aren't you? Spent all your money have you?' said the Rat King, still chewing.

'Your Grossest, it always brightens my day to see you, perhaps I was just passing through.'

'*What do you want?*'

'I have come to ask a favour.'

'Not after more shiny coins then?'

'No, not this time.'

'You've not come alone I see,' said the Rat King, rearranging himself into a more comfortable position on his throne: the open rib cage of a corpse. 'You bring the two footed furless ones here. Why?'

'That's part of the favour,' said Balthazar. He was doing his best not to look too disgusted. Balthazar was not fond of disgusting things, he liked to be clean, and as far away from disgusting things as was possible. The Rat King was obese. A tub of lard that was probably more cheese and wart than fur and blood. Between its teeth were the remnants of food decades old. Rats weren't known for their hygiene standards, but their Chieftain was the king of squalor. Though, he did floss, and was currently doing so with a whisker between his two ratty incisors. It scraped in and out, a sound that was like nails on a blackboard to the cat.

'We don't owe you any more *favours*, Balthazar, you've still not lived up to your end of the bargain.'

'Soon Your Unpleasantness, but I can hardly do as I promised while I am still… stuck like this.'

'Hmmmm… What do you want?' the King spat, scaring a small mouse that had ventured in to replenish his cheese.

'I have a problem.'

'A problem?' asked the Rat King, tilting his head back and dropping a piece of the new brie down his gullet.

'You see the man down there.'

'Which one is the man?'

'The big one, Your Wretchedness.'

The Rat King leaned out of the sarcophagus to see. He squinted, and sniffed heavily at the air.

'The one with the musky odour. And, *sniff sniff,* is that gunpowder?'

'Yes… that'll be him.'

'What about him?'

'He's a witch hunter.'

'A witch hunter?' said the King. 'Interesting. I'd heard a rumour a witch hunter had been seen in Laburnum. I hear lots of things, don't always believe them. They're a dying breed witch hunters. Rarer than witches these days, funny that… *Ahahaha!*'

'Yes… most funny, Your Horridness.'

'What are *you* doing larking about with a witch hunter for?'

'It's bad luck, I'm afraid,' said Balthazar. 'He's under the impression that you know the whereabouts of all the witches in the capital.'

'*Ahaha…*' Again the Rat King laughed. It was a vile sound that echoed within the stone coffin and made Balthazar shudder. 'I know the whereabout of one right this minute.'

'Yes, very good, but he wants a list of them all.'

'Well… Where should we start? There's one in the industrial district, one in the slums, one that frequents the City Library, and one very generous woman that lives just off Hamford Common: always giving us rats a bit of the old cheese when we visit.' The King was startled by his own words, for they reminded him of cheese and his current lack of it. 'CHEESE!' he squeaked in a squeak of terror that was more the squawk of a vulture than the squeak of a rat.

Balthazar closed his eyes to keep the lashings of spit from entering them.

'I don't want a list,' he said.

The Rat King paused mid chew.

'Huh? But you just said–'

'No. *He* wants a list. *I* want something else.'

'Yeeesss?'

'I want you to kill him.'

'*Kill him?*'

'Yes. I want you to kill him for me.'

'Aha– kill him?' The Rat King was intrigued by this, so intrigued that he put his cheese down and edged closer. 'Why?'

'Isn't that obvious?'

'Yes. But why can't you be rid of him yourself?'

'I don't like to get my mitts dirty, and frankly, it would cause more of a problem if I were the one to do it.'

The Rat King pondered this over the delayed mouthful of cheese.

Balthazar watched.

It wasn't easy doing business with rodents, they were thoughtless creatures, ruled by their stomachs and wired with a propensity to spread disease. They only cared for gold or cheese. Though they had no use for gold as humans had use for it. And as for cheese, it was a mystery to Balthazar why all rats had that same insatiable appetite for the stuff, even the lactose intolerant ones, which was a high percentage of the rat population. He could only guess that it had something to do with its likeness to gold, in both colour and rarity.

Or perhaps it was just the smell.

'Ok,' said the Rat King, 'we'll get rid of these furless ones for you, but you owe us, remember?'

'Furless *one*.'

'What?'

'It's just the man I want dead. The boy is… important.'

The Rat King looked very closely into the cat's eyes. Then he looked to his nearby brutes, the warrior rats nearest him.

'No,' he said, firmly.

'I beg your pardon?'

'They both die.'

'You've misunderstood–'

'I have not, Balthazar. I am the Chieftain, my squeak is law. I have to be seen to be all powerful. What does it say about me if I take orders from you – a cat in the eyes of my brethren. They will be asking why I let the other go and what will I say? *Because you told me to?*'

'No, now listen here–'

'No. You listen here, Balthazar. It is the code of our city, that none of the furless ones shall step foot within. You know that, Balthazar. You knew when you brought them down here that they would be mine. You brought them both as gifts for me, yet now you take one away.'

'If I don't leave here with that boy,' said Balthazar, his claws itching to come out, 'then our bargain is off, understand.'

'This is different. This is above our bargain. This is the code. And the code must be obeyed.'

'Ah, yes, codes, precepts and rules – you have that in common with humans you know?'

'*Silence!*' the Rat King squawked. It was never a good idea to compare rats to humans. 'You forget your place.'

'My apologies, Your Purtidness,' said Balthazar, with an air of the sarcasm afforded to all cats.

'The code is there for a reason. If one of them leaves this place, what's to stop them from telling the other furless ones? We'd have the furless, two legged vermin infesting our homes with traps and poisons. Arsenic! Ever seen what arsenic does to the insides of a rodent?'

'With all due respect, Your Ugliness, you're very wrong. He won't say anything, and besides, the Academy has such a hold on this city now, that he'd be incarcerated for logicide if he so little as dreamed of you. The world above has changed.'

The Rat King abandoned his temper and became happily distracted by the cheese and grapes that had just arrived. The mice left the platter, and fled avidly.

He picked up a grape, sniffed it, and tossed it over his shoulder for the other rats to fight over. Balthazar watched them have off at each other like animals over the fruit, which in his view, really wasn't worth it.

Rats were a barbaric species of hordes. They were clan animals, always led by the strongest. There were few laws, but what laws there were, were sacred. Almost everything else was settled with violence, and the bigger, stronger rats were always the victors. It was the way of the wild. Not in the slightest bit kind.

It was whilst watching the way of the wild unfold before him, when Balthazar had one of his clever ideas.

'You don't have much sport down here do you?' he asked.

'Sport?' said the Rat King.

'Yes. You know, like dog fighting or something?'

'Dog fighting?'

'The humans like to pit hungry dogs against each other until they tear each other apart. It's entertaining. Apparently.'

'We don't have the traditions of the furless ones. Not down here. We wouldn't want them anyway.'

'Ah yes, but, the humans do it with dogs because dogs are their slaves.'

The Rat King crunched a red grape between his jaws, it squelched, and was chewed up into the oozy cheesy bile. Balthazar tried not to vomit.

'Where are you going with this?'

'You could have a contest of your own,' said Balthazar. 'You could make the humans fight each other, to the death, it would be most entertaining for your kin. And it would be within keeping with the rat code, for the strong walk over the weak, no? I'm sure your kin would understand if you had to let the victor go, he would be the strongest after all.'

The Rat King didn't look sold just yet, but he was warming to the idea.

'They would eat each other for our entertainment?'

'Humans don't eat one another, not these ones anyway. The man has gunpowder, two guns I believe. I would suggest a duel by pistol. You don't want them to stoop down to your honourable level and fight like rats now do you.'

'No. They are not rat kind, they are furless scum.'

'Exactly. I must say, you've out done yourself with this idea, Your Most Rotteness. You get to be remembered as the Chieftain who made humans fight like dogs. I get to have this witch hunter chap killed. Your fellow rats get the thrill of the sport and the spoils to feast on. And the boy gets to leave, all within the rat code.'

The Rat King stopped his open-mouthed chewing to contemplate. Then he stuck another piece of cheese into the mix.

'What makes you so certain yours will win. The big one smells, *sniff sniff*, big.'

'The rat code isn't very precise, I'm sure the rats of old wouldn't mind if we twisted the situation to our advantage.'

'Huh?'

'Just speak and I shall arrange it.'

'A duel?'

'Yes. A duel.'

The Rat King swallowed and reached for another snack to find he had no more cheese or grapes to bide his time with. He sat up, as well as a lardy rat can sit up, stared Balthazar in the face and grinned a yellow ratty smile.

***

Above the catacombs and sewers night had fallen on Laburnum. The Brewery Quarter was very much alive, but north, in the splendid part of town, households were quiet and the streets were emptying.

Except at the Palace. The huge golden gates were wide open and a procession of Lords, Ladies, magistrates and other charming nobles were arriving in golden encrusted carriages.

The Lords' Banquet was an evening of extravagance. It happened once a year to mark the union between Parliament and the Monarch, and it was always the most talked about affair.

Cassandra didn't care for traditions. Now that she was older, a space had been reserved for her next to her mother at the head of the table. But she wasn't there.

Instead, she was lost between the pages of the Zolnomicon, reading it like someone obsessed.

Before the Realm of Logic, poetry and fiction were popular pastimes. Men and women of the past would write nonsensical things and tell nonsensical stories. It was all a bit nonsensical, and as with everything as such, went out of fashion horrendously. Cassandra thought that perhaps this text was from that bygone era, when things hadn't had to make much sense.

But though the book was senseless, she felt shackled to it, unable to eat properly or sleep properly until she had finished it and found some sort of purpose for it. For all things must have a purpose, books most of all. It was part of the Academy's teachings in the *Codex of Logic*: *All that exists must have reason to.*

It seemed to be a collection of absurd formulas and unscientific experiments written by at least nine individuals. There was a substantial amount, enough to rival a volume of *The Empire's Encyclopaedia*. It made no sense whatsoever that so many people would have sat down to put together a book of its design for no reason at all.

She was determined to get to the bottom of it. But then the door knocked. It was a gentle knock – not Martha then.

'Come in,' said Cassandra, hiding the book beneath her pillow.

'Princess. Your mother requests you downstairs,' said Rufus, the royal bodyguard.

'She sent you? She is eager.'

'Martha is preoccupied, there are a lot of guests to look after.'

'Do I have to, Rufus.'

Rufus opened and closed his mouth a few times. He entered the room and shut the door behind him.

'You don't want to?'

'No. I hate this banquet, it's just a bunch of silly old men stuffing their faces, drinking their fill and chatting about nonsense for hours on end. I don't know why mother puts up with it. If I were Queen, the first thing I'd do is put an end to this stupid night.'

'Hmm…' Rufus mused. 'It is important for the Queen and the Lords, this banquet. It marks a peace between Parliament and the Monarchy. You're too young to remember the civil war. The horror it brought to this great nation. Father against son, brother against brother. The fighting in the streets. The blood running through the canals. The unrest. The mob. The constant lynchings in the Guard's Square. Every day. Every night.'

'Rufus, forgive me, but I don't think lavish food and exotic wine ended the war.'

'No. Your grandfather did,' said Rufus, sagely. 'Even though he didn't want to, he sat down with the Lords and agreed a truce: that the Empire would be governed not by one but many – by working together. That's what this evening symbolises: the Great Peace.'

'Hmph.'

'As a future queen, an heir to a great family line, you have to be seen there, at the table, breaking bread with them, though you may not like to do it.'

'It's just…' Cassandra tried, then said, 'I know…'

'What are you doing in here anyway? Just sitting around, staring out the window?'

'Yes… something like that.'

'Reading again then?'

'Yes…' said Cassandra, hastily adding, 'but nothing unusual.'

The bodyguard smiled.

'You will be a great queen Cassandra. Even greater than your mother I think, though, let's keep that between us.'

'Hmm!'

'Always reading. I can't remember the last time I saw your mother read a book. Then again, she has little time for it.'

'Mother says I shouldn't get caught up in my reading. That the real world is about getting experience.'

'Well. She's right in that respect.'

'Maybe…' Cassandra sighed. She really didn't want to go downstairs, especially now that she was late. Everyone would notice her arrive at the table. Somebody would probably draw attention to it. It was going to be embarrassing.

'What say tomorrow, in the morning, I let you ride Cornelius?'

Cassandra brightened.

'Really?'

The Princess didn't have a horse of her own yet and always had to practice on the Royal Stable's ponies when she had a riding lesson. She had insisted time and time again that she was ready for a real horse, but her mother wasn't fond of them. The Queen had broken her arm in a fall when she was a girl, and grossly overprotected Cassandra because of it. But occasionally, without her mother's knowing, Rufus would let her ride his noble steed, Cornelius. The black stallion powered up and down the Palace Gardens like a monster, but was passive in temperament and never got too riled up like the other stallions in the stables.

'We won't tell your mother about it either?' Rufus winked and put his hand gently on the Princess' shoulder.

'Ok,' said Cassandra, beaming.

'Come on, up you get. Such a lovely dress too, be a shame to waste it up here with your books.'

Cassandra rose, adjusted her dress and checked her hair in the mirror. The book would be safe under the pillow, Martha was too busy to be making beds and tidying rooms.

'I have to dash off. There's all these City Watchmen around the Palace tonight. They've been here for days, presumably to oversee the preparations. I've told your mother they will just get in the way but she doesn't want to talk about it.'

'Oh... yes... I've noticed them.'

Rufus hesitated at the door.

'You don't know anything about it do you?'

'What, the City Watch? No. Not the foggiest,' Cassandra lied.

'Strange.'

The Palace was the grandest building in the city. It wouldn't have been much of a palace if it wasn't. You couldn't go around calling any old place a palace, even if the Queen lived there, it had to have a certain amount of panache.

But though the Palace had enough panache to deck its halls and rooms ten times over, it was rarely used to its full potential. Martha and her brigade of maids had enough on their hands just fighting back the plagues of dust and moths. There wasn't time to light every candle, burn every gas lamp, polish every piece of silver and shine every face of wood.

It was as if the Palace was a flagship of the navy, running on a skeleton crew who could barely keep it in order, let alone afloat.

Only when important visitors came was there a glimmering of its true magnificence.

The Lords' Banquet was probably the grandest event in the Queen's Diary. Every Lord, magistrate, chancellor and generally anyone with a title before their name, was invited. Though, it was mainly just the Lords who attended. And only about half of them ever turned up on the night. The ones who didn't show were sure to give as little notice as possible, which in most cases was no notice at all.

But this year, more Lords than ever had made the trip to the royal dining room, and the Palace was in full swing in all its glory and panache.

There was a long table that ran down the centre of the room. Each side sat over a dozen pompous gentleman, wittering on about taxes, foreigners, political philosophies and *pheasants*. One end of the table was entirely set on remembering a lost recipe for pheasant soup. The wine wasn't helping.

Down the blistering white table cloth, across the scraping plates and chinking glasses, over the extravagant flower arrangements, the freshly lit candelabrum, platters of bread and forgotten napkins, at the heart of the organised chaos sat the Queen, in a royal plum dress. She was surrounded by chattering Lords all engrossed in their own conversations and in no hurry to include her in their ramblings. Beside her, the only empty seat at the table, where Cassandra quietly slipped in.

'Ah, Princess, so lovely of you to finally join us,' said Lord Darby, drawing as much attention as he could.

'We've saved you a seat,' said Lord Marston.

'Come for the pudding have you?' said Lord Quincy.

'Or is it the wine, she's after? Trust me, she'll need it,' said Lord Everett, setting off a bout of laughter around him.

'We are a boring lot aren't we?' said Lord Quincy, 'I for one don't blame her.'

'No, Lord Quincy. I don't think that,' said Cassandra, 'I was just very busy studying that's all.'

'Ah! Get thee to the Academy!' said Lord Everett, looking down either end of the table. 'Where are those clever fellows when you need them.'

'Oh they don't come to these things,' said Lord Quincy, 'too busy.'

'Precisely. Too busy like our Princess here, we should sign her up.'

'The Academy doesn't take women as scholars,' said Cassandra.

'No of course not, but you're the Princess, I'm sure they could make an exception,' said Lord Everett.

'Don't you have to have your… you know… chop chop,' said Lord Quincy.

'Well, M'Lady has made a head-start in that department, *ha-ha*,' Lord Everett said, again setting off a bout of laughter around him, though, this time, it was shorter lived.

'Lord Everett. You are a guest in my household, and I do not want such foul talk spoken at my dining table, least of all when it concerns my daughter.'

'I was just having a joke, Your Majesty,' said Lord Everett taking a reserved sip of his guarded pinot noir.

'I like jokes. I do not like your jokes. They are not amusing,' said the Queen.

'Each to their own…'

The conversation at the centre of the table died a cold death.

'I know a joke,' said Lord Quincy, at the volume of someone who can't hear his own voice.

'Oh must we?' said Lord Marston.

'Yes! Yes! There was a dinner party, much like this one, and everyone was having a spectacular time, and then one of the guests calls over the cook and says "See here, cook, I believe I've found a button in my salad." And the cook says, "That's alright, sir, it's part of the dressing."'

There was a raucous of laughter. Some a little more enthusiastic than others. Cassandra too found herself laughing, though more at Lord Quincy's snorting than anything else.

'Very good,' said the Queen, dryly.

'Oh I've got plenty more where that came from!'

'No, Lord Quincy, please, your talents are best observed in small quantities.'

'I second that,' said Lord Marston.

Conversations sprung up around the centre of the table, while Cassandra was brought out a speedy main to catch up with everyone else.

Spiced duck with apricots, cherries and polenta medallions, served in a rich, red wine jus, that looked a little like... pigs blood. She quickly regretted coming down.

'Don't worry, Princess,' said Lord Quincy, 'the starter wasn't anything to talk about. But this dish, this is simply exquisite.'

'Call me old fashioned, but I prefer a more Varcian palette, if I could choose,' said Lord Darby.

'There's nothing wrong with Five Isles cuisine,' said Lord Quincy, turning to the Queen, 'quite a treat, Your Majesty.'

'It's the spices. They spice everything and it does give my tummy an ache,' continued Lord Darby.

'But it's so exciting, not bland like our own foods. We have to cover everything in gravy just to keep from choking.'

'You know, they only use the spices to preserve the food, it's awfully hot in the Colonies, stops the meat from rotting. *And*, should it rot, *stops* it from tasting foul.' said Lord Darby.

'Is that so? What do you think Queeny?' came the slurred voice of Lord Everett.

The Queen raised an eyebrow. She wasn't accustomed to being asked her opinion on food, nor was she at being referred to as *Queeny*.

'This isn't strictly colonial food,' said the Queen. 'It's a fusion, I believe. The Witz are very good at mixing traditional Varcian dishes with flavours from the Five Isles. Personally, I am very fond of it. Though, if I said I wasn't fond of it, I fear the restaurant would close down and the chefs there would never see the inside of a kitchen again.'

'Haha. All too true, Your Majesty,' Lord Quincy chuckled.

Cassandra wasn't afraid to speak her mind.

'The duck's too chewy for me, and the cherries too sweet, and… this sauce… what is it? It's very sour, very sweet, very salty and very spicy. They all cancel each other out so that it doesn't taste of anything really.'

'Ah! There we go. An honest review,' said Lord Darby. 'If I may be excused, Your Majesty, I might just pop out for some air. As I said, these spices are not well received by my stomach.'

'You may, Lord Darby.'

'Thank you, Your Majesty.' Lord Darby rose and was immediately pounced upon by a waiter, who helped him out, tucked in his chair and folded his napkin for him.

'Your Majesty,' said Lord Marston, who was sat to the Queen's right, 'I had hoped to discuss matters of finance during this meal. I'm afraid all the conversation has swept it under the rug.'

'Yes, where it belongs I should think. Well go on, Lord Marston, you've got me trapped. I suppose you bring word from the Chancellor?'

'From the Bank directly, Your Majesty. They are most displeased with your… efforts of evasion.'

'Evasion? I am not evading them, Lord Marston. I am right here if they wish to talk.'

'Yes, well… they say they've tried on numerous occasions to discuss the crown's debt with you and–'

'No, Lord Marston, I believe they are mistaken and so you too are mistaken. They have tried on numerous occasions to talk to me through my House of Lords, such as they are doing now, and I will not speak about the crown's finances, except to the Treasury's Chancellor and to the officials in the Varcian Bank. I do not need every Lord in my Parliament bickering on about the country's money and how best to spend it. Certain things are best kept between those whose job it is to discuss. You can tell them, as I have told them before, should they wish to discuss the crown's finances, then they are always welcome at my door.'

'Right… Certainly…'

'Trust you, Lord Marston,' said Lord Quincy, 'to bring up money during the grand meal. We've got better things to talk about anyway. Like what's for dessert? Anyone know?'

'And wine? Could we get some more wine?' said Lord Everett waving over one of the staff. '*Yoohoo*, hallo there, could we get another bottle of red.'

'Lord Everett, I think you've had enough for one evening,' said the Queen.

'Enough for one evening? Moons collide, I haven't had enough for an aperitif!'

'Perhaps you ought to step outside, Lord Everett,' said Lord Barton from two seats down.

'Barton, come now my man.'

'Perhaps you should,' said the Queen, icily.

Lord Everett hesitated, and rounded his gaze back at the Queen. He was getting that feeling, the one when your sober self taps your drunk self on the shoulder and says "psst, I've got to deal with this in the morning." He finished his glass defiantly.

'Come now,' said Barton, appearing over his other shoulder, 'I shall go out for a pipe, you should come too, air would be good for you.'

'Air. I've got enough air. I'm breathing aren't I.'

'Come, Lord Everett, there's no need to make a scene.'

'Certainly not. What I meant was that I was just thinking I might go out for a good pipe myself. Care to join me ol' chum?'

'Of course.'

Lord Barton smiled to the Queen, helped Lord Everett out of his chair and guided him out of the dining room.

'I heard a rumour it's something in the domain of custard,' Lord Quincy continued.

'Why do men drink so much?' Cassandra said softly to her mother.

'Because some of them are fools. And you can always trust a fool to make a fool of himself.'

'Shame to see a man unable to hold his drink, and a Lord at that,' said Lord Marston, 'I shall have a word tomorrow, Your Majesty.'

'No, no. No need for that,' said the Queen. 'He'll have a word with himself I'm sure.'

The remaining Lords laughed politely.

'May I?' asked a waiter, gesturing for Cassandra's plate.

She'd barely touched it. She'd stabbed the duck, prodded the polenta and eaten one of the cherries, which had left her with a tart pinch in each of her inner cheeks.

'Yes, thank you. I'm finished.'

'Have you thought to visit the Colonies, my dear?' said Lord Quincy. 'Extraordinary food and an interesting culture for your studies I'm sure.'

'My tutor does go on a bit about the Colonies. But mother…' She stopped, she didn't want to look like a child, the Lords already thought little of her as it was. '…I mean, I'm not too sure I'd like it.'

'You should go, Cassandra, you are a young woman now. It is important for a young woman to see the world. Especially a young woman who will one day command fleets and ambassadors,' said the Queen.

'Oh… But mother I thought–'

'You are older now.'

Cassandra lit up. She'd wanted to go to the Colonies for years, but had reasoned with herself that it wasn't going to happen, not while her mother was Queen. She'd heard of the enclosed markets and the camels and the white sand beaches and tropical plants and the languages of the Five Isles, and the strange practices that went on on the fringes of the Realm of Logic.

'We'll have to arrange a trip, perhaps in the sun season? The waters are far choppier in the moon season, not the best way to travel, I've done it once or twice.'

'You've been to the Colonies, Lord Quincy?' asked the Princess.

'Oh once or twice. They do an absolutely splendid nut cake. Made with honey, if I recall.'

Cassandra had noticed out of the corner of her eye, over Lord Quincy's shoulder, that Rufus had come into the dining room.

She wouldn't have thought anything of it. She was used to seeing him roaming around the Palace, speaking to Palace Guards and running his secretive errands. But this wasn't the same. He looked unwell. Pale and distracted. His eyes seemed to be staring straight ahead, as if looking at nothing in particular, and he was walking with an urgent, yet staggered pace.

Then she saw the gun. He was holding the pistol in his right hand.

Of course, Rufus went about the Palace armed with sword and pistol, but she had never seen them out. The scene looked so out of place, that there, in the midst of dining, conversing, laughing, drinking and cheersing, he would enter the room gun in hand.

He was walking right at her. Or was it her mother?

Before anyone could stop him to ask if he was alright, his arm raised the gun and pointed it straight at the Queen.

No one had even noticed yet.

Except the Queen, who rose from her chair in dismay. And Lord Quincy, who had seen the fear on the faces of Cassandra and her mother. And two City Watchmen, who had been standing by the door, and were now running to the table, in what had become a sort of slow, steady motion.

Cassandra couldn't move. She was rooted to the chair, squeezing the table cloth in each of her hands. She stared into the body-guard's eyes. Those eyes she knew well, yet, these ones she had never seen before. They were stone cold. The face of a murderer.

'Rufus!' gasped the Queen.

CLICK went the gun.

The shot misfired.

The City Watchman clasped Rufus by his arms and tore him back and to the ground.

'Goodness gracious me!' said Lord Quincy.

'What is the meaning of this!' shouted Lord Marston.

The conversation in the room had jumped off a cliff. No one dared breathe. The only noise came from the guards grappling to get Rufus under control.

Cassandra rose to get a better look and her mother shielded her away.

'Get off me! What in the name of Logic are you doing?' said Rufus. 'Unhand me!'

'What is going on?' said Lord Darby rushing in.

'The Queen's bodyguard… he… he's just tried to have one off at Her Majesty…' said a very solemn Lord Quincy.

'Have one off?' said Lord Darby.

'A shot!' said Lord Marston.

'An assassin!' said another Lord.

'Treachery!' cried another.

'Treason!' another.

'Unhand me! What are you doing?' Rufus fought free, struggled to his feet and pulled his sword. The two guards pulled theirs in return. The steel screeched coldly.

'Your Majesty? Are you ok? Are you harmed?' said Lord Darby.

'I…'

'It misfired. Most lucky, at that range you would be quite dead, Your Majesty,' said Lord Marston.

Rufus looked confused, he stared around at the eyes that were gazing back at him.

'Take this man to the Guard's Tower at once,' said Lord Darby.

The guards took a step forward and Rufus raised his sword, directing it at their throats.

'You take a step further and I shall have you,' said Rufus.

Cassandra must have been the only one who found it odd that Rufus, the man who had moments ago been about to murder his Queen in cold blood, was now puzzled, and, by the looks of the glint in his eye, a little afraid.

'Rufus… Why?' said the Queen.

'Your Majesty?'

'Now is not the time for questions, Your Majesty, there will be plenty of time for that,' said Lord Darby.

'I will not hesitate to defend myself,' said Rufus, to the advancing guards.

More guards flooded in through the doors. At least eight of them, some with muskets, some with rapiers.

'You will surrender your arms and go quietly with these men to the Guard's Tower,' said Lord Darby, firmly.

'I do not take orders from you, sir, I am sworn only to the Queen,' said Rufus, raising his blade again.

'Rufus,' said the Queen, 'sheath your sword.'

'But, Your Majesty…'

'*Sheath your sword.*'

There was a moment's hesitation.

Sweat dripped down the faces of the guards.

Cassandra clenched her fists.

Then Rufus dropped his blade and it clattered weightily on the blue carpet. The guards leapt at him, restraining his arms behind his back and pushing his head down.

'Take him away,' ordered Lord Darby.

'There's been a mistake,' said Rufus. 'This is a mistake!' He carried on all down the hall, until the front door of the Palace slammed behind him.

The room was shaken. Shellshocked. A hundred appetites spoiled in a flash.

'What in the world has happened?' asked Lord Barton, coming in with a dizzy Lord Everett at his back.

'An attempt on the Queen's life! All is well, but I think it's best if we call upon the coaches to take everyone home,' said Lord Darby.

'Of course, of course,' said Lord Marston. 'You there, call the coachmen.'

'An attempt? Who?' asked Barton.

'The Royal Bodyguard.'

'The Royal Bodyguard?' Lord Everett hiccuped. 'Some bodyguard. I do hope someone's going to fire him.'

'Goodness, this is most distressing, Your Majesty. Are you well?' asked Lord Barton.

'…'

'Your Majesty?' again.

The Queen was startled, stunned like a deer in the road. It wasn't everyday your most trusted protector tried to murder you in front of your dinner guests.

'Everyone outside, come on, give the Queen her space,' said Lord Darby.

'We should call for extra guards,' said Lord Barton.

'I agree,' said Lord Darby.

The other Lords began leaving, talking amongst themselves and shaking their heads.

'Most horrid… most horrid. I can't believe it,' said Lord Quincy.

'Your Majesty?' said Lord Barton, still trying to get through to the shaken Queen.

'It's not right,' said Cassandra. 'Something isn't right. I saw him come in. He looked… strange.'

'Strange, M'Lady?' asked Lord Quincy.

'His eyes, they were glazed. He looked drunk.'

'Drunk?' said Lord Marston.

'That would help explain it,' said Lord Quincy.

'But Rufus doesn't drink… he frowns upon it…'

'Sounds like a madman to me,' snickered Lord Everett.

'Oh, Lord Everett, do go home,' said Lord Darby.

'It's not right, mother. You didn't see his face… he wasn't himself. He didn't know what was happening.'

'Silence, Cassandra,' said the Queen.

'But, mother, it's Rufus… he couldn't have–'

'*I said silence*,' said the Queen. 'Martha. Take the Princess to her room and see the rest of the Lords out.'

'Yes M'Lady, right away. Come now Princess, you come with me.'

'It's not right. I won't believe it, I won't,' said Cassandra. She didn't intend to, but had started crying. Her eyes began to feel heavy and pained, tears formed in the creases and had started to stream down her blushed cheeks. She fought to control her breathing, to keep her composure, lest her mother thought she was weak.

'Now, now, child, run along to your room. This isn't the place for tantrums,' said Lord Barton.

Cassandra clenched her fists tighter. She wanted to run right up to Lord Barton and punch him in the groin. And she would have, if it didn't defy her well-bred nature.

'Come, Princess,' said Martha, coaxing the Princess away.

'Your Majesty, we'll lend you as many guards as we can spare. They'll watch over the Palace until we know exactly what has occurred here. Is there anything else we can do for you?' said Lord Darby.

'Leave,' said the Queen.

'Your Majesty, perhaps we should stay too, just so it's–'

The Queen had given her order and said enough. She walked out of the room.

'Righto, you heard the Royal Highness, out, everybody out,' said Lord Quincy.

The remaining Lords made a hesitant exit. Their coaches came one after the other and took each of them back to their houses on Lords' Row. The restaurant too was sent home with the extra staff that had accompanied them.

The golden gates shut and a troop of City Watchmen took up posts at every corner, doorway and stairwell on the grounds.

Soon the Palace was as quiet and empty as it had always been. And the tick tock of the grandfather clock was audible once again.

***

Rats are known to live in darkness. Yet here, under the city streets, beneath even the sewers, their halls were lit with oil lanterns. Niclas had been watching them leap along the ropes above like acrobats. When a lantern would go out, a rat would soon be there to refill it with an oil jug no bigger than a gravy boat. As he looked closely, he was sure the lantern rats were wearing little brown belts with matches tucked in like swords.

Perhaps, thought Niclas, everyone was wrong about rats. Perhaps the darkness scared them as much as it did people.

The Witchhunter wasn't concerned with the fears or smarts of rats. He stared up the steps to where Balthazar had gone. The cat was taking his time, and the man didn't like it one bit.

There was a scuffling at the top of the stone steps, and the sea of rats parted for Balthazar's return.

'What's goin' on, sir?' said Niclas.

Balthazar sighed, dramatically.

'What is it, cat?' said the Witchhunter.

'I'm afraid they haven't taken too well to your being here.'

'My list?'

'Yes… we'll come to that.'

'This is trickery,' cried the Witchhunter, reaching for his pistol.

As he did the circle of rats pulsed, closing on them by half a metre; a ring of gnashing rodent teeth.

The Witchhunter lifted his hand away from his belt and the rats eased back.

'We have,' continued Balthazar, 'somewhat of a dilemma.'

'Die wot?' asked Niclas.

'It's nothing to worry about. Really. It's just, only one of you will be allowed to leave this place.'

Niclas knitted his brows and scratched his head. That sure sounded like something to worry about.

'Nonsense,' said the Witchhunter.

'I'm afraid not. They've been talking and they've come to the conclusion that you must duel one another.'

'*Ah-aha!*' Niclas wasn't sure why he found it funny, but he soon didn't find it funny. 'You're joking, sir? Right? Sir?'

'No.'

Two large rats appeared at either side of Balthazar.

'They want your guns. Both of them.'

'Do you take me for a fool?' said the Witchhunter.

'No. But, you can either play this out how they want it, or…'

'Or?' said Niclas.

'Or, they'll kill us all. It's not nice getting killed by rats. It's ghastly. They'll eat the flesh from your bones, the eyeballs from your face, the tongue from your mouth, everything, and you'll be alive for most of it.'

The Witchhunter looked over the shifting horizon of hungry rats. Niclas stared, mouth open at Balthazar.

'Can't you do anyfing, sir?'

'Believe me, I've tried. If it was up to them, they'd eat both of you.'

'This is your doing, cat. You brought us down here,' said the

Witchhunter.

'Funny that. I didn't think you'd let me come alone. And you were the one who insisted that both you, and the boy came.'

The Witchhunter daggered his eyes.

'If this is a game you will lose. Do not think I'm afraid to kill this boy.'

'Wot?' said Niclas. The ground didn't quite break away beneath his feet and swallow him, but his bowels moved up and down ever so slightly, and he did, nearly, soil himself. 'B…but, I don't knows 'ow to duel.'

'Quite simple really,' said Balthazar, 'you point and shoot.'

The Witchhunter placed his guns on the floor, watching the rats cautiously.

The two largest ones screeched at the smaller ones, and they swarmed around the firearms, lifting them the way rainforest ants carry leaves. The guns floated atop the swarm, up the steps to the Rat King.

'Where are they taking them?'

'Their Chieftain wants to inspect them I imagine.'

'Wot if we don't do it?' said Niclas.

'Then they'll eat you.'

'Wot if we both miss?' said Niclas

'They'll eat you.'

'Wot if one of us misses, and the other only injures 'im. Shoots 'im in the knee or summin?'

'…In that case, they'd probably give the win to the one of you who wasn't injured. And eat the other one.'

'*GULP.*'

'You look very relaxed about this, cat?' said the Witchhunter.

'Oh trust me, I am greatly distressed. But I find panicking only exasperates things like this.'

The Rat King screeched from above. It was a terrifying noise and didn't sound like a rat at all.

The rats around them parted to form two paths, and the two big rats ushered the humans towards them.

'I think that means they want you to follow them,' said Balthazar.

The Witchhunter went down his path.

Niclas hesitated.

'Can't do it, sir… I ain't ever 'eld a gun before, let alone fired one. I don't knows wot I'm doin'. I'm gonna die, sir. You gots to do summin…'

'…Niclas…'

'…I don't wanna die, sir. I ain't ready for it. Not like this, sir, please, please…'

'…Niclas…'

'…Please, sir, do summin. Like you done before. You know that mumbo jumbo malarky…'

'*Niclas.*'

'Sir?'

'Get your head in it. *Do not* miss.'

With that, Balthazar headed up the ziggurat and Niclas was shepherded to his spot, some ten paces from the Witchhunter's spot.

Back up top…

'Everything alright?' said the Rat King.

'Oh, yes,' said Balthazar, arriving back at the foot of the sarcophagus.

'Odd guns these.'

'May I have a look?'

'Be my guest.'

Balthazar stalked over to the guns.

They were extravagant pistols, made of iron that had been shaped with great detail. A banshee howled down the length of each barrel. The centre of each gun was different from other pistols Balthazar was used to. It could be opened and inside were three chambers of wadding. Most guns were loaded down the muzzle, these were loaded above the trigger. The load was the same as normal though. A ball of lead, paper wadding and a sprinkling of gunpowder.

'This is exciting isn't it,' said the Rat King, watching the spectacle unfold below.

In rat tongue, rats were shouting out betting odds and passing between them thimbles, earrings, pegs and other types of human junk that had worth in their culture.

'I wonder which will win. I would have put my cheese on the big one. But, you never know with these things. Toss of a coin, really.'

'Yes, Your Foulness, *toss of a coin*,' said Balthazar. But whilst the Chieftain was gazing below, Balthazar had taken fate into his own paws. He'd squatted over the chamber of one of the guns and managed to stir up just enough pee to wet it. It wasn't something he was proud of, but sometimes you had to do things you weren't proud of.

'Come over here, Balthazar, you'll get a much better view of it all. Oh, and send those guns below.'

'Certainly, Your Hideousness,' said the cat.

The swarm of rats approached and wrapped themselves around the guns. Balthazar placed a claw on the damp one.

'*This* is for the big human,' he said.

Squeak, squeak.

The rats didn't look like they understood, but nodded anyway and carried off the guns.

Balthazar would have crossed his fingers, but it's not something cats can do.

Below, on the outskirts of the hall, an orchestra of makeshift percussion instruments had started to play. Empty jam jars with grease paper lids, wooden bowls and metal pans, hollow bones and upside down chamber pots. As one, the rats slapped their tails against their drums and the beat beat out. None was particularly big enough for a loud sound on its own, but together they filled the hall with a thunderous measure.

Each thud brought Niclas that much closer to soiling himself.

One of the guns arrived at his foot.

He bent down and picked it up. It was heavier than he'd thought. He'd anticipated it being heavy, it was made of solid iron, but it strained his arm and shoulder to lift it. He looked across at the Witchhunter. The man had picked his gun up and was inspecting to see that it was loaded. Niclas thought he'd best look over the gun too, to check everything was in order. Not that he would have known what to look for.

The Witchhunter's eyes looked focused. They stared across the ten paces into the boy's, ignoring the scurrying rats below and the flickering oil wicks above.

Niclas tried to stare back with the same cold hearted expression, but his hand was shaking, the gun slipping, and sweat was running into his eyes.

The drums were beating faster, building to their crescendo.

I'm going to die, thought Niclas, this is it, kaput, finito, the end.

Then he saw something he didn't expect. A flutter in the Witchhunter's gaze. A drifting of the man's firm emotionless eyes that went up and to the right. Niclas tried to follow it, but he couldn't see anything there. Just a hanging lantern and rats crowding round the ropes above.

The drums ceased.

Silence.

The sound of Niclas' breath drawing shakily through his open mouth.

The sound of the Witchhunter taking a deep, calm breath.

The man raised his gun out straight.

The boy lifted his and pointed it blindly, closing both his eyes and then opening one because he decided he'd probably need it.

Balthazar had anticipated the boy would need to grieve, but figured it would be a learning curve that would make him stronger. Or, if not stronger, he would be scarred for life and remain the silent type from that day forth. Either way, the cat wouldn't mind.

What he hadn't foreseen was what actually happened, which, when it happened, happened far too fast for the rats to keep up with.

The Witchhunter lifted his gaze from the boy and landed it upwards to the top of the ziggurat. His gun arm followed, finding the Rat King in the iron-sight. He squeezed the trigger.

The gun misfired.

Niclas blinked. He touched his chest softly, to check he was still alive. His finger hovered over the trigger, hesitantly. It took him a few seconds to work it out, which was just about all they had.

He turned his gun towards the ziggurat. Then aimed up, to the nearest lantern, and let fly a shot.

Nothing could have prepared him for the kick. He landed on his rear and the gun flew from his hand.

The shot glided towards the lantern of oil, missed it, and obliterated one of the rodents balancing on a rope.

The rat didn't squeal. It died instantly. Its corpse, what was left of it, *not much to be honest*, swung through the air and landed splat on the stones below.

Balthazar raised a paw to catch his sinking head.

'Outrage!' screamed the Rat King. 'Betrayal!'

And so, hysteria ensued.

There were headless chickens with more sense than the panicked swarm of rats. They ran to and fro over each other fighting to get through. Though they out numbered the humans ten thousand to one, this thought was somewhere at the back of their minds. The one currently at the helm and directing their squabbling feet was: *I'm next! I'm next.* And so it quickly became every rat for itself.

The Witchhunter slapped his gun and tried the trigger again. When it still didn't fire, he opened the chamber and rubbed the powder between his fingers. It was damp and smelt like…

…he scowled.

Niclas was scrambling across the floor trying to get to the fallen pistol. But the rats, at the screeching commands of the larger warrior rats – the generals of the horde – were starting to rally together.

The Witchhunter strode towards the boy, squashing rodents below his feet, he recovered the fallen pistol and held the swarm of rats back by casting an aiming arm.

The smaller rats were afraid. The larger ones, not so much. They knew the workings of human weapons, and they knew the gun had had its shot.

But they didn't know this gun.

The Witchhunter pulled a vial of gun powder from his coat, popped out the cork with his thumb and scattered it in front of him. The warrior rats sneezed and he fired the gun's second shot. The powder flashed and the blast blew the rats to smithereens. The hysteria returned, and any rats with all limbs still intact routed.

'Up!' said the Witchhunter pulling Niclas to his feet.

Above, at the sarcophagus, the Rat King had turned on Balthazar. His giant warrior rats circled the cat, barring his escape.

'Balthazar,' said the Chieftain, 'what is the meaning of this? You planned this, didn't you? Think you can outsmart me do you? Think I don't know what's going on? You've come for the gold! You greedy betrayer. I shall have you dead! I shall have you tortured! I shall make an example of you! In the name of the rat code I shall…'

He was clearly very angry. His whiskers were wriggling like spider legs, his nose throbbing with rage, and he was spitting with every word he squawked.

Balthazar had had enough.

He lifted his right paw and sprung his claws one by one.

'You know,' he said, 'I never really liked you anyway.'

The cat dug his claws into the fat rat and tossed him off the ziggurat. He screamed all the way down, bouncing and splashing over jewels, coins and fearful rats.

The warrior rats watched their king fall. Then they turned slowly to face the cat, teeth coming out, tails coiling up, furry backs arching, noses twitching. *They charged.*

But they were little trouble. They were dealt with deftly – necks broken, bellies sliced open, tails and limbs torn off.

'Eugh… how unpleasant,' said Balthazar, trying to flick the blood from his paws.

Niclas and the Witchhunter had clambered up the first few steps. They were kicking the rats away, holding them back. Well, the Witchhunter was, Niclas was just being useless.

Balthazar soon arrived next to them, skinning several rats as he did so.

'Balfazar, wot do we do?'

'I'm thinking,' said Balthazar. And he was, but the only solution that presented itself to him, was to push the Witchhunter into the swarm of tail and teeth and make off whilst they fed.

Time was short, and the swarm was *quite literally* pulling itself together, climbing up the steps at all sides.

''URRY!' screamed Niclas.

'I'm thinking,' replied the cat.

They didn't have much longer. The Witchhunter knew what to do. He had one last shot to make.

He raised his gun.

'What are you going to do,' said Balthazar, 'shoot them all?'

The man declined to reply. He squeezed the trigger.

The cat and the boy watched the shot exit the barrel and strike a lantern in the distance.

It burst into flames, dropped and sprayed burning oil across the floor, scalding the rats nearest and sending the others back into writhing panic.

'Cor, nice one gov,' said Niclas.

Balthazar was not amused. The smell of melting rat flesh just made everything worse.

Still, the fire broke apart the swarm and allowed the two humans and the cat to make it halfway down the hall. But the diversion didn't last. Soon, the swarm was back, moving as one great big flesh eating cloud once more.

It surrounded them.

'They're all round!' said Niclas. 'We'll be et for sure. Sir, oh, sir, 'elp us, do summin.'

Balthazar hissed at the approaching rats, but couldn't stop them all from leaping past. Two made their way up the Witchhunter's legs, over his back and up to his throat. He snatched them up and broke each of their skulls with two fierce clenches.

'I don't suppose you have another shot in that thing?' said Balthazar.

The Witchhunter looked up. There was another lantern hanging above them a little towards the exit, but his guns were empty.

'Not for that,' added the cat, 'for me.'

Niclas screamed.

A rat had crawled through his waistcoat, out onto his shoulder and sunk its teeth into his ear lobe. He grasped hold of it and tried to yank it loose, but it was as good as trying to yank free an earring. Its jaws were tightly clamped. The pain was intense. And so Niclas gave it more than a yank – a great big two handed wrench – and the rat came off tearing a chunk of his ear with it.

He glowered back at the vermin, squeezed its squirming, wriggling body, said: 'Piss off will ya!' and launched the critter up through the air and into a distant lantern.

The lantern wobbled, fell, shattered, and burned the rats beneath it viciously, creating a perfect path through to the exit.

Balthazar and the Witchhunter shared a look of bemusement.

'Crikey!' said Niclas. 'Wot're the chances o' that?'

One by one, they leapt over the flames, through the rodent chaos and out of the great hall.

The rats assembled behind them. In the flickering light, six foot shadows with six foot tails chased them out into the passageway.

The Witchhunter stopped.

'Gov, wot you doin'?'

'Come, boy,' said Balthazar, running on.

The man had remembered the darkness. He put away his gun and made ready his pocket flame.

'They're gainin', they're gainin'.'

'Hold this,' he said, handing Niclas the little firebox. 'I'll be right behind you.'

Niclas stalled, dithered, then saw the vicious vermin shadows and fled after his master.

The Witchhunter wasn't afraid. He emptied vials of gunpowder from his pocket, plucked out a match and struck it against the wall.

Just then, the giant shadows gave way and the army of ravenous rats came dashing around the corner.

The match dropped. The gunpowder caught, flashed – exploded.

A cloud of dust and dirt and bones and bricks blew through the tunnel.

At the exit where the wall opened, Balthazar was waiting for Niclas.

'Quick boy, run!'

'I am, sir! I am!' Niclas skidded through the opening and bent over to catch his breath. 'Don't worry, sir, 'e's comin', 'e's just behind me.'

Looking back, Balthazar could just make out the Witchhunter

sprinting away from the dust cloud.

'Go on, boy. I'll wait,' he said.

'...'

'Go!'

'Yessir!' Niclas ran up the steps, out of the catacombs and into the sewer tunnels, the pocket flame providing just enough light for him to see the way.

Balthazar stayed for the Witchhunter. He pushed a loose brick back into the wall beside him and watched as the stone ground together and the doorway began to close.

The Witchhunter slowed – stopped. He wasn't going to make it.

The two stood facing each other, until the wall sealed shut between them.

Back above on the streets of Laburnum, in an alley somewhere west of the Brewery Quarter, a drain was pushed aside and to the astonishment of one stray dog, a boy and a cat surfaced gasping for air.

They lay there breathless for a while, adjusting their eyes to the morning light and taking in the city air. Laburnum wasn't known for clean air. When people went away and returned, their first nostalgic reminder was usually how difficult it was to breathe. In this case, Balthazar and Niclas had gone away somewhere with a far worse climate, a place that quite literally smelt like every toilet in the capital.

Niclas lay watching the open drain. Waiting.

''E's not right behind us is 'e?' he said.

'No,' said Balthazar. 'I tried to…*cough*…hol…*coughcough*… holdoor…*cough*… sorry, furball.'

'Should we go back, sir?'

'Go back? *Are you well?* We can never go back there. Never.'

'...'

'I'm sure he can take care of himself, boy, he's a grown man.'

'But the rats…'

'Yes, I know.'

'And I've got 'is box fingy…'

'Unfortunate.'

'I should 'av' waited… It's my fault.'

'He wasn't our friend, you know, he would have killed you.'

'But why?'

'One of those things, Niclas, one of those things.'

'Oh…'

'There are people, as I've said before, who condemn the things we practice. For no reason at all, they seek to harm us and in some cases – murder us…'

'But you made a deal with 'im?'

'He's a madman. You can't make a deal with a madman. They'll stab you the moment you turn your back on them. Trust me, it's better this way.'

'…Alright, sir, if you says so…' said Niclas, ruefully.

'If you must worry about something, worry about us. That little incident has cost me dearly, I'm not even sure we'll have enough in the purse to last the week. That's right, no more trips to the bakery, no more detours to the market, no more gifts or luxuries…'

Niclas looked like someone who'd had a death in the family. No more croissants, no more cinnamon buns, no more chocolate pretzels.

At least he had his priorities right.

'Now do come on,' said Balthazar. 'You need a bath. We both need a bath.'

When Niclas and Balthazar returned to the Queen's Garter that morning, someone was waiting for them.

Little Ron had been camped up outside, across the street, on a stakeout. He wasn't allowed to sleep until the next guttersnipe relieved him of his duty, and by this point, he'd been up all night and was beginning to feel it. He'd been biting his finger nails to keep awake, but he'd run out of nail to bite and was now resorting to his dirty finger tips.

You'd think a small boy sitting on the street with a flat cap over-turned in front of him would get at least a few pence to help him on his way. Or perhaps a rich family would take him in, save him from a life of crime and he'd turn out to be related to them or something nice like that. Alas, things like that don't happen in Laburnum.

Children on the street are normally moved on in much the same manner rats on the street are moved on. With a firm boot.

The Brewery Quarter is one of the worst places to beg. No one has any money to spare, everyone's too busy getting drunk and the sort of folk who congregate in such a place, frankly, don't give half a damn.

But Little Ron wasn't there to beg. He was there to watch. He'd waited hours for this glance of Niclas and the black cat with the white patch under its neck. And seeing them woke him up faster than a cupful of espresso liqueur. He snatched up his flat cap and picked up his painted sign which read:

Me leggs dante wrok. spar ah farvin

…and ran full pelt out of the Brewery Quarter heading south.

'Mornin' young sir,' said Madame Spriggs, powdering her nose.
'Mornin' miss,' said Niclas.
'Blimey! Wot's that smell!'
'Uhh… smell? Wot smell, miss?'
'That stink. It reeks!'
'Dunno, miss, me nose ain't so good these days.'
'Wot 'appened to your 'ead 'n' all?'

'Sorry miss?'

Niclas felt the side of his head, his ear was sore, a raw gash weeping at the bottom of his lobe. Blood came away on his fingers. It had dried into his neck and down his waistcoat. A dark, rusty crimson.

'Crikey, uh…' Niclas remembered the psychotic rat that had taken the piece out of his ear. 'Not sure how that 'appened, miss,' he lied. 'I 'ad a rough night see.'

'On the drink were you, young master?'

'No, miss, never touch the stuff. I'd like to go up to me room now, if that's alright.'

'Certainly, little sir, I never meant to keep you. But, you did 'av' some family in 'ere earlier, lookin' for ya.'

Niclas stopped at the stairs. Balthazar, didn't hear this, and continued up to the room, eager for a bath.

'Family?'

'Yeah… two uncles, one had a funny lisp. We've got a no questions, no answers policy, so I didn't say you woz 'ere. But they said they knew you woz, and that they'd be back another time.'

'Ok… Fanks, miss.'

'If they come again wot shall I say?'

Niclas didn't have any family as far as he knew. And how could he have an uncle. He didn't have a mother or a father or a brother or a sister. Actually, it occurred to Niclas, he didn't know what relation an uncle was. Maybe it was just another term for a friend… he'd heard that somewhere.

'Probs best say I'm not in, miss. Don't fink I gots any uncles…'

'As you wish, little sir. Don't suppose you fancy some refreshments? Or how about them dancing lessons? Scarlet'll give you the first one gratis?'

'Not just now, miss. But fanks. I'll let you know.'

four

Cassandra was lying in bed. It was a big bed, but she'd curled up into the smallest ball in the middle of it. It was made with the finest cottons and threads, fabrics that soothed young princesses to sleep, yet she had pushed them all to the floor. No better sleep could ever be had in any other bed, but she hadn't slept. She'd spent the night watching the darkness and had spent the morning watching the sun chase it away.

It had been a night of little consequence. The first noise came at about five, that was when the gardeners started work, clipping the perfectly clipped hedgerows and pruning the perfectly pruned redbud trees. A little later she heard the stables. The clip clop of horses being taken around the Palace grounds. She thought of Cornelius, Rufus' horse, she wondered if he'd noticed that his master had not come in to see him.

Around about seven, the Palace came to life. The servants could be heard going about the rooms, getting everything in order for the day. Cassandra could hear the guards too, marching up and down the staircases, through the corridors and out in the court-yard. They were clearly not Palace Guards. Palace Guards were taught to be respectful. These were the common guards of the City Watch. And they were a noisy bunch.

All the while, the Princess had been lying there thinking about what had happened. Thinking about how that one event had now turned her world inside out. She had been replaying it in her mind, the moving pictures going round like the disc of a zoopraxiscope running at half speed. The Lords were laughing, the table was being cleared, the glasses refilled, dessert had been called for and everything had felt perfectly ordinary.

Then everything changed.

She saw Rufus; no more than a shadowy figure stepping into the room. A look of stone was cut on his face and there was a gun in his hand. She watched it rise, cock, click, then click again without shot. She could remember everyone's expressions: her mother's widening eyes, Lord Marston's gasp, Lord Quincy's flinch, the servant to her left who had dropped a platter and let it clang against the floor with no effort to catch it. She remembered everything about that moment. Especially Rufus' face.

He was the sort of man who always looked switched on; wide eyed, jittery, craning his head about the room like a bird of prey looking for the slightest movement out of turn. But in that moment, his eyes had been fixed on only the Queen. He had strode down the room with such determination that even if the floor had been made of burning coals it wouldn't have deterred him.

She remembered the shot. *Or the lack of shot.* Any reasonable assassin would have frowned at the gun when it didn't fire as it should. He hadn't even noticed. His stony, cold blooded, pale faced, dazed expression hadn't moved a muscle. Not an eyelash, not a dimple, not even the smallest flickering of his irises.

And she remembered the confusion that followed. She remembered how he looked scared, troubled, like a man who'd woken from sleepwalking, naked, in the middle of a fancy ball without a clue as to how he got there.

It wasn't right, she thought. She didn't know why it wasn't right, but it wasn't. And she was determined to get to the very logical bottom of it.

At that moment, Rufus was chained up in a cell somewhere inside the tower. They all still thought he did it. Martha, her mother, the Lords, the servants, the cooks, the City Watch, even the Royal Guards who'd worked as closely with Rufus as thread through a needle. All of them, pointing the finger and shaking their heads calling shame. She was the only one who had heard him scream "*this is a mistake*," and she was the only one who believed it.

It was up to her.

There was no time to shed tears about how awful it was. She wasn't that sort of person anyway. Cassandra was a thinker and she was deeply, profoundly stuck into it, searching for a logical solution.

The clue was in the way he looked, she reasoned. His body language had been at odds with its usual tone. He'd looked unwell almost. Drunk? He couldn't have been. Drunkards stumbled and slurred their words. She remembered Lord Everett, and how Rufus had been nothing like him. And besides, Rufus didn't exactly have a good view on drinking. It had to be something else. A poison perhaps? She couldn't stop thinking about how he'd looked when he realised what had happened. It was as if he'd been sleeping…

…a small bug crawled over the pillow next to her.

Cassandra studied it closely. She wasn't afraid of bugs. Martha had once run out of her brother's room, down the hall and out into the courtyard screaming because of a spider. It hadn't been a particularly big spider. Cassandra had rescued it, placing a glass over it, sliding an envelope underneath and setting it free to start a new life at the back of the garden.

This wasn't a spider. It didn't have eight legs. It had a lot more than eight legs. It was long and spiky, and crawled like a snake, slaloming across the white cotton sheet. A myriapod, thought Cassandra. Of course what she really meant was *a centipede*, but the Princess was pretentious like that.

It was the first time she'd ever seen a centipede inside. They usually liked it outdoors under a log somewhere. This one had obviously become misplaced.

And it wasn't alone.

She felt something tickling her knee. She sat up and looked down as two more blackish red centipedes crawled over her bed.

I like bugs, I'm fine with bugs, she thought to herself. But then she saw another one. It was crawling across the carpet. Its legs scurrying about in a way that made her skin start to itch.

The ones on the bed scrabbled to its edge and fell on the floor. They were all going the same way, and there were even more of them further ahead. She could count at least eight of them, crawling across her floor, up her dresser's legs and onto the desk.

And she knew just where they were going.

She stood and followed them. There were nine in all. Nine blackish red centipedes crawling around the leather cover of the Zolnomicon.

She watched, partly astonished, partly disgusted as one seemed to force its head into the heavy pages and slither inside. The others began to follow. It was like watching earthworms dig into soil.

Cassandra hadn't looked at the book since Rufus had come to get her. Last time she checked it was still hidden beneath her pillows. Martha had taken her to her room, and come back a few times in the night and asked if she was ok through the door. Cassandra hadn't slept and no one had been in the room. It made no sense whatsoever why the book was out.

But all this was just a passing thought. What made even less sense and captivated the Princess' attention, were the wriggling centipedes forcing themselves in-between the pages of the tome that looked as though it should crush them.

'Strange,' she said.

She watched until the last of the nine had crawled inside, then walked over to take a closer look.

There was nothing wrong with arthropods, *or insects to everyone else*, except when they got together and jumped out on you all legs and antennae jiggling. Cassandra stared at the tome's ominous black stone. She told herself to stop being silly. They couldn't hurt her. They were tiny.

One of the centipedes was still struggling to get all the way in, so she reached out and levered the book open to the page it was on.

She had braced for the worst, expecting nine mischievous little beasties to be wriggling about inside. But there was nothing there. Nothing at all. Not even the one that was halfway in. When the book slumped open, there were no creatures at all.

The Princess blinked a few times. She rubbed her eyes. Sleep deprivation can do some odd things, but this was madness.

Nero's Charm.

It was the picture that caught her attention. The illustration was of a skeleton, they were always of skeletons, but this one was kneeling before a cloaked figure. A hand was outstretched over the skull and strings from each finger fell to each joint as if over a puppet.

She read…

He who whispers bestows on thee a gift. To speaketh the tongue of another's mind. To harnesseth their thread. To shapeth their will. The weaker the mind, the stronger the claim. Maketh thou bind through open eyes. Dust of whispering root will giveth sway. Speaketh in the colour of he who whispers into the other's ears. Command it to listen and it shall obey. Give it instruction and it shall heed. Whisper in the whispered chants and teach its body howeth its body shall dance.

Cassandra had sat down and leaned right into the book so that her eyes were but an inch from each word. It had had a magnetising effect on her. She felt charged, enlightened and dreadfully afraid. She was having one of those Newtonian realisations.

It wasn't as foolish as it sounded. She'd read about this kind of thing before in a psychology text. *Hypnosis*, that's what they called it. Swinging a pendulum to and fro in front of someone's face and sending them into a trance like state.

A trance like state just like the one Rufus had been in.

Of course, we know it was something a bit more sinister than a mild case of hypnosis. But Cassandra didn't know that. She didn't know anything about *that* at all.

There was a noise in the courtyard.

She leapt up from the chair and rushed to the window. Perhaps they'd brought him back; if not, perhaps there was something new, something important going on.

The gate had opened for a carriage. The guards had rushed out to meet it.

Mr Eccleston stepped out and adjusted his spectacles.

They were saying something. He said something back. She couldn't hear through the glass.

Then she heard Martha. Martha's voice was shrill and penetrated even the brickwork.

'Sorry, Mr Eccleston, she's not feeling up to it…'

Cassandra shouldn't have been in the mood for tutoring. She should have been swept up in the morbid cycles of grief like everyone else. But she wasn't. She was very much eager to meet someone like her, someone capable of thinking things through.

And Mr Eccleston was precisely that person.

Cassandra hurried out into the courtyard just as Mr Eccleston was entering his coach.

'Wait,' she said, 'Mr Eccleston!'

'Cassandra, what is it?' said Martha.

'Mr Eccleston, stop, don't go.'

'Cassandra, it's ok, I've told him you aren't in the mood for tutoring.'

'But, Martha, I am. Mr Eccleston, won't you stay?'

'You don't have to Cassandra, not after everything that's happened,' said Martha.

'Perhaps we can reschedule, Cassandra,' said Mr Eccleston.

'No. There's no need for that. We'll have the lesson as planned.'

'Cassandra, are you sure?' asked the maid. Cassandra was usually an ardent pupil, but this level of enthusiasm was unheard of. The Princess hadn't been down for breakfast, she hadn't even changed her clothes from the night before.

'Yes. Everything should carry on as normal, don't you think?'

'Well…'

'It's ok, Martha, it'll do her good. A pleasant distraction is most called for I think,' said the tutor.

'Alright, Mr Eccleston, should I put a pot on?'

'Yes, splendid, Earl Grey please, no–'

'–No sugar, no milk, extra strong just how you like, Mr Eccleston. I know.'

'Splendid.'

Mr Eccleston unloaded his suitcase onto the library table, took off his glasses and gave each of the panes a blow and a wipe with his handkerchief.

He cleared his throat and looked through the day's agenda.

'Right, today we're to engage in some mathematics. How's your trigonometry?'

'My trigonometry is just fine, Mr Eccleston.'

Martha entered with a tray. She placed it down on the table, poured the black tea through the strainer into the tutor's cup and left the pot alongside.

'Want anything, my dear?'

'No, that's alright. You can go now.'

Martha wasn't used to being bossed around by Cassandra. She curtsied uncertainly.

'Alright, you need anything just–'

'I will, Martha, that's all.'

Cassandra could get rid of the maid, but the two City Watchmen standing like statues on either side of the door would be much harder to disperse. It would be ok, she thought, they looked like they weren't listening to anything anyway, and besides, Watchmen weren't intellectuals, they probably wouldn't understand half of what was going to be said.

Martha left.

'I shall show you some angles to begin with, and I'll ask you to work out the missing one–'

'Mr Eccleston, before we get into triangles, I'd like to ask you something about psychology if I may?'

Mr Eccleston pushed his glasses up his nose.

'Hmm, you're full of questions these days but you've got the timings all mixed up. Our schedule says we should be doing maths.'

'Yes, but, it's just a question and we don't always have to follow the schedule by the book. I mean, who writes these things?'

'I write them,' said the tutor, with haughty offence. 'And they're very precise. They're intended to give you a wide range of study without cramping a subject or neglecting one. I spend a lot of my time perfecting these schedules, Cassandra.'

'Yes, but…'

'Is it dreams again? You were curious about them last time too.'

'No, not dreams.'

'Well, what is it?'

'Do you know much about hypnosis?'

'Hypnosis?' The tutor frowned curiously. 'Well, yes, a little, what do you want to know?'

'I was just wondering, Mr Eccleston, just curious that's all, if perhaps it were possible to hypnotise someone? Make them do something they wouldn't normally do. Something that maybe they didn't want to do.'

The tutor thought for a bit.

'There was a chap, Dr William Laurence, whose writings were about this sort of thing. The conscious and subconscious mind.'

'The subconscious mind?'

'The part of your brain that's working behind the scenes. If I ask you to think of a blue chair… there you are, you just thought of a blue chair. That was your conscious mind working. It's the mind we're aware of; the thought after thought pattern of our working brains. The subconscious is everything that happens off that track. If I remember correctly, some of the doctor's work suggested that the subconscious mind can indeed influence the conscious one.'

'So… is it possible? I mean… in your opinion.'

'Hmm,' said Mr Eccleston. He liked a good hmm, and started most of his sentences this way. 'I believe that certainly most of what we think is inspired by our unconscious mind in some way. There is, without doubt, a connection. But for someone to hypnotise another person, in a sense take hold of their conscious thoughts and presumably their actions, well there's little empirical evidence to support it. Not in the sense I believe you are alluding to. For example, a psychologist can make someone feel a certain way towards things. That's a good trick. I read about a man once who was scared of dogs. Hypnosis helped him replace that fear with overjoyed love. It went a bit too far apparently, and the poor chap cried tears of happiness every time he saw a pooch.'

Cassandra didn't see the intended humour.

'I read recently that it *was* possible to control someone's actions.

To shape their will.'

'Shape their will? That sounds a bit fishy. Not any work I'm familiar with? What book is this?'

'It said that you could speak to someone's mind and convince and control their actions, at least I think that's what it said. It mentioned something about a whispering root...'

'Cassandra?' Mr Eccleston's tone had changed. His head was tilted and he was showing the Princess two concerned eyebrows. 'That sounds like alchemy?'

'Alchemy?'

'What is this book?'

'I can't remember it was in the City Library,' Cassandra lied, badly, shakily. 'What's alchemy?'

'Cassandra. Alchemy is outlawed. The stuff of pseudo science. Backwards colonial stuff. It has no place in your head or the logical realm.'

'Yes but, Mr Eccleston, Rufus didn't do what everyone's saying. I was there, I saw it, he wasn't acting himself. He was–'

'Ah, so this is what it's about is it?'

'You don't understand, Mr Eccleston. It makes no logical sense that Rufus would try to harm my mother. It is more reasonable to believe that someone poisoned him or hypnotised him or–'

'Cassandra, enough.'

'But–'

'No. I don't want to have this conversation. We are here to do mathematics.'

'I don't want to do mathematics.'

'Then I shall leave.'

'*You can't leave.* I demand you to stay.'

'Cassandra, what's gotten into you? I understand you must be shaken about what happened. You must be confused and over-whelmed with lots of emotions, but you must think clearly at all times and not jump to unfounded conclusions from something you've read in a… alchemy book by the sounds of it.'

'It's not an alchemy book. And if it makes sense why shouldn't I believe it? Surely it would be illogical to ignore something just because it's forbidden.'

'Are you justifying alchemy?'

'No. I'm saying that what happened doesn't make sense and that we should explore all the possibilities before we rule anything out. Isn't that scientific method?'

'Cassandra, you're speaking dangerously.'

'They'll hang him you know. Rufus. He'll be hung. It's high treason.'

'Princess, there will be a trial and the best minds of the Empire will debate and pass verdict. If Rufus is innocent as you so claim, then he has nothing to hide.'

'You think he did it don't you?'

'Come now, Cassandra, it doesn't matter what I think.'

'Everyone thinks he did it. Well I was there. I was in front of him. I could see his eyes. I spoke to him less than an hour before. I know he didn't do it, I feel it.'

'You *feel* it?'

'Yes.'

'Right, I've had enough of this. I'm going.' Mr Eccleston stood, his tea hardly touched.

'*Sit down.*'

'No, Cassandra. I am going to the City Library to find out what book you've been reading. It's clearly had a negative effect on your ability to reason.'

'Sit down, *now.*'

'Good day.'

Mr Eccleston packed his suitcase and left the library in a hurry. Cassandra chased after him.

'Stop, come back.'

'Everything ok?' said Martha coming to see what all the fuss was about.

'Martha,' said Mr Eccleston. 'I'm afraid you were right, she's not up to it. The girl needs to rest. She's clearly very shaken. I shall cancel this week's lessons and return in a fortnight.'

'Very well, Mr Eccleston, I'll get your coat.'

'Don't you dare get his coat. He's not going anywhere,' Cassandra shouted.

'Is her mother about?' asked the tutor.

'She's out with the Lords and the Chief Inspector, sir. Not due back till the evening.'

'I shall like to speak to her. Perhaps I could stop by in the morning.'

'Of course, sir, I'll let the Queen know you're coming.'

'I think it wise that we let the girl calm down a bit.'

'I'm right here. Stop talking about me like I'm not here. I'm right here.'

'Cassandra dear,' said Martha, 'why don't you go and wait in your room, I'll be up–'

'You're not my mother, Martha. You cannot send me to my room.'

'Come now, dear, you're causing a scene.'

Indeed she was. The other servants were poking their heads out of the kitchen and the guards were shuffling their feet, trying to blend in like they weren't there.

'Rufus is innocent. He'd never hurt mother, you know it, Martha.'

'I do, dear, but please, quiet down, you're shouting.'

'Good day, Cassandra, Martha.' Mr Eccleston slipped into his coat, and went out the door.

'You're all mad. All of you. Everyone's gone mad. *Logicide*. I want to see Rufus.'

'Now, dear, that's not going to happen we both know that.'

'Why not?'

'Because it's not, dear, they won't let you near him for your own safety.'

'Safety? *Safety?*' Cassandra couldn't take it anymore, she bubbled over with frustration, let out a shrill cry and stormed off upstairs.

Martha watched her go with a worried frown. She heard the stamping along the corridor, then the door slam. Then the door slammed again, louder, just in case no one had heard it the first time.

The maid looked around at all the pale faces looking back at her.

'What are you all looking at? Back to work the lot o' you!'

***

Every Cause has its Effect. Every Effect has its Cause. Everything happens according to law. Nothing merely happens, there is no such thing as chance, only law unseen.

***

The clock struck six.

The Palace gates, mechanical in their design, rattled and ticked, huge golden cogs twirling around pulling the golden, engraved doors aside.

A coach pulled by four black horses wheeled into the courtyard.

Out stepped a man dressed in a crimson robe that draped all the way to the floor. At his neck was a tight fitting white slanted collar, and behind it hung a baggy crimson hood. His sleeves were long and hung in funnels from his hands, which were clasped together in front of his waist. His fingers were lustred with golden rings and sparkling rubies. His hair was greyed, textured like straw and simply cut, sitting over his lined forehead. His lips were thin and pale and his eye bags creased like prunes and his nose narrow and bony.

Normally the Queen's bodyguard would meet guests like this.

In his absence, Martha was left to do the greeting.

She stepped out into evening air and came to the steps as he was coming up.

'Good evening,' he said, charmingly.

'Evening, sir,' said Martha. 'The Queen's not here I'm afraid.'

'That's quite all right, it isn't her I've come to see.'

'Oh, and what's your business here, sir, late in the evening like this?'

The crimson man gave the maid a smug look: a look that said he didn't have to explain.

She wasn't taking nothing for an answer.

'May I inquire as to your name?' he asked.

'Martha, I'm the housekeeper.'

'Martha, if I were you, I'd run along like a good dog and do the dishes.'

Martha was trying to be brave. The man's presence was one that struck fear into all people. He could make birds fall from trees just by looking at them.

'There's no need to be rude, sir. Now, I've told you, your business here can wait till the Queen returns.'

'And when shall that be?'

'You could come back in the morning, that's to be expected of you.'

The man took a moment to reflect on the hour, and the guards that stood around the courtyard.

'No,' he said, smiling, 'I think I shall carry on. I do not require the Queen.'

Martha stepped in his way.

'I must refuse you, sir.'

'Sorry?'

'You can't come in.'

'Can't I? You see this ring?' he held up his bejewelled hand and out stretched his index finger. The signet ring was golden and engraved with the seal of logic: an owl perched upon an open book, enveloped by a laurel wreath.

'This seal gives me the right of passage in all domains. No lord, no queen, least of all a servant shall stand in my way. Please, step aside.'

Martha looked for help from the guards standing at their posts around her. They were Watchmen not Royal Guards and that meant that they were more inclined to take his side than hers.

'Upon my honour, sir, you aren't coming in.'

'Your honour?' asked the man, 'or your freedom?'

Suddenly Martha didn't feel so brave.

'To deny me the right of passage would be... *illogical.*'

There it was. The buzzword. He may as well have said: "Open Sesame."

Martha stepped to one side.

'There's a good dog,' said the man, bowing his head with a courteous smile.

Cassandra was hiding in her room. She was too embarrassed to show herself. She was going to have to explain everything to her mother, and was working on how she'd start.

She hadn't been in the mood for the Zolnomicon. It sat on her desk, open to the page on *Nero's Charm*. She wasn't in the mood to read anything. She wasn't even in the mood to eat. And she doubted she'd be able to get to sleep again, even though she'd been up far longer than she'd ever been up before. But it didn't matter. What was that thing they said? There was plenty of time to sleep when you were dead. She'd have plenty of time to sleep when Rufus was proven innocent. But she had to think carefully. She was dealing with subjects that weren't considered science. She'd have to make her case as clearly and as logically as she could.

The last thing she wanted was a moth tapping against her window.

It was a large moth and an unusual shade of grey. It pattered against the glass trying to get out.

She opened the window and ushered it through. But it came flapping back, around her head, into her face and against the glass again.

'Silly creature,' she said. For some reason, whenever people tried to save things like moths, they'd always put up a fuss about it. You could open every window and doorway in a house and still the fly, or bee, or moth would flutter about helplessly trapped.

'Go! Get out!' she said.

The moth flew across the room, over to the dresser, hovered above the Zolnomicon and then found a resting place in the desk's candle flame.

Cassandra lifted her hand to her mouth.

Its wings burned instantly and the creature fell onto its back, its legs kicking frantically at the air. Then it stopped.

Dead.

The door knocked.

Cassandra jumped.

It wasn't a Martha knock. It was hard, firm, someone who didn't knock on doors regularly and didn't quite understand the etiquette of it.

'Martha?'

The door opened.

Cassandra would have rushed to cover the Zolnomicon or cast it under her bed, but she couldn't move. The sight of the visitor had stiffened her joints and sent her heart racing.

Her back pressed against the open window.

An assassin? No. Her logical mind knew who he was and why he was there.

The saliva in her mouth had been stripped away. She couldn't speak.

'Good evening, child,' said the haunting man.

She identified him by his crimson attire as a man of logic, one of the Academy's inquisitors.

If in all the Empire there is one thing that people fear more than cutthroats, highwaymen, diseased rats and the torturer in the basement of the Guard's Tower, it is the Inquisition. To be face to face with one of them in her own room was more horrific than any nightmare she could imagine, especially as, across the room, nearer him than her, lay a book of a most forbidden sort.

Her eyes tore away from it, but they had already betrayed her. The Inquisitor glanced over at the dresser.

'Little birds tell me little things. And the little birds have been chirping about you today, Princess. Do you know what they've been chirping about?'

'...'

'Don't be afraid, I mean you no harm,' he said, darkly.

'Martha,' the Princess called.

'Oh, the maid is quite busy, I'm afraid.'

'Where's my mother.'

'Out, it seems.'

'What do you want?'

The Inquisitor stepped closer. Cassandra had nowhere to back up to, except out the window.

'The little birds tell me you've had quite an upset today. It's to be understood, you're under a lot of stress, emotions run high in such cases and sometimes they get the better of us.'

The man constantly smiled. It was a forced smile. Cassandra knew a forced smile when she saw one.

'And what's this I see?'

'Nothing...' Cassandra flinched towards the dresser.

It was too late.

His hands browsed through the old, tea-stained pages.

'Interesting. Most interesting.'

'It's a bit late for visitors don't you think?' said Cassandra.

'Ah, but my visit is a matter of urgency.'

'Urgency?'

'Tell me, what is all this nonsense?'

'I don't know.'

'Then why is it here, open?'

'I was reading it, of course – only browsing. I was going to take it back to the library.'

'You found it in the library?' The man furrowed his silver brows.

'Yes.'

'Most interesting. Tell me, what does it say?'

'I don't really understand it… sort of like recipes and strange things. I think it could be alchemy maybe… or some old colonial text.'

'Recipes you say?'

'Yes?'

'Strange how you got all that from this. It's not written in any language I know of. Looks like a child's scribblings to me.'

Cassandra leaned closer and looked at the pages. They were as they had been when she first found the book. A strange, runic language that wasn't the slightest bit decipherable. All the titles and pictures were gone too. It was just gibberish now.

'No… it was…'

'It was what, Princess?'

'It was… nothing.'

The Inquisitor slammed the book shut. The thud shivered the candle and made Cassandra jolt.

'I would recommend you come with me tonight.'

'No,' said Cassandra.

'No? But Princess Cassandra, I don't believe you're very well. I believe you need our help.'

'Help? I don't need help? I'm perfectly fine, thank you very much.'

'Fine? If you are fine, then come. We shall see how fine you are.

And, if you are *fine* as you say, you will be back in time for supper tomorrow. What say you?'

Cassandra thought about it. She didn't think about it very long or hard. 'I'm sorry, sir, I will decline your offer. It's very kind of you to check in on me. But I think I'd like to speak to my mother.'

'She will be informed of what has transpired here when she returns.'

'I told you, sir, I am not going with you, and I told you in a polite and dignified fashion. I am the Princess, and no means no.'

'No one is above the Realm of Logic, child. You mistake my tone. If you are not able to make this choice yourself, I must commit you to my care.'

'Get out.'

'Let's not do it that way. You wouldn't want to do it that way. Would you?'

'I'll call the guards.'

'Guards? Which ones. The same ones who pledge allegiance to the Realm of Logic? Or some other ones?'

'Get out of my room.' Cassandra was trying desperately not to show the man how frightened she was.

The Inquisitor remained calm, like an ominous ocean, darkening before a storm. 'Be logical, child,' he said. 'Think. Come with me and dispel the doubt in your reason. Any other choice is surely *illogical*.'

Martha watched from the steps as Cassandra entered the Inquisitor's coach.

The Princess sat and looked around her at the claustrophobic design. The coach wasn't like the ones she was used to travelling in. It was split into two compartments. Her side had no handle on the door. It was cramped, and the wooden interior was scratched with markings that looked like the claw marks of a wild animal. She ran her fingers over the scrapes and grooves, and saw that they more or less lined up with the shape and size of her fingernails.

The dividing wall had a window, but it was barred with black iron rods.

This is the right thing to do, she told herself. Once he sees that I'm perfectly normal, he'll let me go as he's promised.

But as the coach pulled away, the uneasy feeling in her stomach turned into a maelstrom.

'I'm sorry about the appearance of your transportation, child, they don't make these things for royals you understand,' said the Inquisitor, speaking through the bars.

'Where are we going? The Academy?'

'Correct.'

Cassandra had only ever seen the Academy from the outside. It was a grand stone building at the heart of the Scholar Quarter. It was the centre of the logical world, where the Empire's most revered scholars received their degrees and where all the laws, sciences and great ideas of intellectualism were established. If she hadn't have been so afraid, she would have been excited to see inside it. Women were not permitted to enter, unless committed. It was one of the laws she had on the top of her list to change.

'Princess, you say you found this book in the City Library?' said the Inquisitor, whisking through the Zolnomicon on his lap.

'Yes.'

'And the librarians were aware that you borrowed it?'

'…Not exactly.'

'What do you mean?'

'I… There was a…' She had to be careful. She knew she shouldn't. She had to lie. But something about the man's presence made it awfully hard to lie. His eyes sought out truth like magnifying glasses, and burnt away lies like ants.

'Child, the more able you are to cooperate with us, the sooner you will be able to go back to your palace and forget about all this.'

'. . .'

'Is there something you want to tell me?'

***

Balthazar awoke.

He leapt up from the damp towel on the end of the bed, bounded across the room and landed in a frantic skid on the windowsill.

Niclas snored from the floor. He hadn't yet mastered the bed and had developed the unfortunate habit of rolling out of it.

'Wake up, boy. Boy, wake up!'

'*Fglfh. . .*'

'Niclas!'

'Wot?' Niclas awoke startled and hit his head on his way up.

'Pack everything. Now.'

'Wot? Wot time is it?'

'I don't have time to explain. Quickly. Wipe away the chalk, pack the reagents in the bag, the candles, everything.'

Niclas rubbed his hypnopompic head and stood to his feet.

'Quick!'

'Alright, alright. Wot's goin' on?'

'We're in danger here, it's time to go.'

'Danger?' Niclas looked around. The room wasn't on fire, it hadn't flooded whilst he'd been sleeping and there were no rats coming through the door. The way Balthazar was acting, you'd think the world was going to end.

'Is it the rats, sir?'

'No.'

'Then wot?'

'*Would you just pack.*'

'Sorry, sir.'

Balthazar was fixed to the window staring out into the street. Looking for something. Waiting for something.

'Wot's goin' on, sir.'

'It's the girl. She knows you're here.'

'...' Niclas rubbed his head again, he'd hit it pretty hard. 'What girl?'

'The girl from the library.'

'Wot libra– Oooooh... 'er. Wot 'bout 'er?'

'She knows you're here.'

''Ow'd she know that?'

'Well I suspect it's because you told her you were here.'

'No I never.'

'Well you must have, how else would she know where to find you?'

'I don't get it, sir? Is she comin' 'ere? 'Ow'd you know?'

Balthazar hissed.

'Steady on, sir.'

'I don't have time for your brainlessness.'

Niclas looked out into the street.

'Eh, sir, ain't that?'

'*WHAT*?' Balthazar turned to follow Niclas' gaze out the window. In the street below a man in a long coat and a slouch hat was pushing his way through the drunkards, his eyes fixed up on their window.

'Cor! 'E made it out,' said Niclas, brightening.

'You've got to be kidding me,' said Balthazar.

The cat jumped to the floor and started running in circles.

'Put something against the door. Barricade it. No... that won't work. Why aren't you packing! Pack!'

'Sorry, sir. Doing it, sir.'

'We'll head out of the Brewery Quarter, maybe leave town for a few days. We don't need to be here anymore. We could leave, go into the country, be ready for when the moons cross.'

'We ain't got much money, sir,' said Niclas, pouring the last three coins into his hand. A shilling, a penny and a little dirty farthing. 'We's broke.'

'BLAST!'

'Sir, you gots to calm down, no good getting yourself into a tizzy.'

'You really are stupid aren't you. Thick. Slow headed. A moron. Of all the people I choose, I choose a complete and utter halfwit. Not even a halfwit, a quarterwit. An eighthwit! *A sixteenthwit!*'

'Sorry, sir.'

The doorknob began to turn. The door was locked from the inside. It rattled, shook, began to thud.

'I'll let 'im in,' Niclas went to the door.

'No!'

Niclas stopped.

'No?'

'Are you mad?'

'But…'

Niclas didn't have time to answer this. There was an enormous crash and the door smashed open taking half the frame with it.

The Witchhunter bundled in, both guns drawn, the stink of the sewer still clinging to his clothes.

'You!' he said, taking aim at Balthazar.

'Easy, gov. We didn't mean to leave you, honest.'

'Listen to me,' said Balthazar, 'we are all in danger. We have to leave this place right now.'

'You think I'm going to listen to you again, cat?' The Witchhunter raised his thumbs and cocked each hammer back.

'You really should listen to me.'

Just then, Vera the harpist arrived at the tattered doorframe.

'I do apologise, little sir,' she said, ''e just barged past, I tried to stop 'im but…' She paused, noticed the Witchhunter had guns and was pointing them at the cat, then noticed that the cat was speaking, and promptly fainted on the spot.

'Please, sir, you ain't gonna shoot 'im.'

One of the guns found Niclas in its sights.

'Nah, gov, I'll stay outta it!'

'*They are coming*,' said Balthazar, 'the City Watch and *the Inquisition*.'

'What?'

'Eh?'

'They'll be here any minute.'

On street level, in the drunken disorder of the Brewery Quarter, Little Ron had returned with two men in toe.

They both had bowler hats and they were both beating a studded club into the palm of their hand.

'You thsure 'e'sth back?'

'Pos'tiv, sirs.'

'Wot we gonna do? That woman weren't so friendly last time,' said Clyde.

'We're gonna thsmasth the placth up, good 'n' proper,' said Archie, starting on a menacing stride down the street.

Clyde followed.

They got five paces before they stopped like a pair of spooked alley cats.

Two six horse guard waggons came clattering down the road towards them and reeled in right outside the Queen's Garter. City Watchmen armed with muskets began to empty from their rears.

The two thugs had a sudden change of heart. They turned swiftly and walked the other way, keeping their heads low and hiding their clubs in their overcoats.

Balthazar was back up at the window pane, Niclas and the Witchhunter leaning over him and pressing their faces to the glass.

'They're 'ere for us?' Niclas shrieked.

'They're here for you,' remarked the cat.

'Why? Wot I done?'

'Shh, listen,' said Balthazar.

They tried to listen but they couldn't hear with their human ears what he could hear.

Below them, through the flea infested floorboards, an altercation was taking place. Inspector Forsyth was demanding a room number and Madame Spriggs was playing stupid.

Their words escalated into noise as the Inspector snatched the guest book and read through the list of names.

No one gave their real name at the Garter.

Only an idiot would give their real name.

'We need to leave now,' said Balthazar.

The Witchhunter stuck his head into the corridor. He signalled the coast was clear, stepped over Vera the harpist and knocked on the door opposite. There was no answer. He knocked louder.

The cat and Niclas entered the hall and stood at his back. Niclas tried to wrestle the sack into a better grip.

The door opened a crack and a freshly shaven gentleman peered out at them.

'Ella, is that you…' he said, excitedly. This excitement evaporated when he gazed upon three of the most peculiar guests: an armed and rugged man, a frightened, scruffy boy, and a very vigilant looking cat. 'Can I help you?'

With a bash, the Witchhunter broke the chain off the door and sent the man toppling backwards onto the bed, where he grabbed his top hat just in time to cover his jewels.

'Wh…wh…wh… what's the meaning of this?' he stammered.

The Witchhunter went straight to the window whilst Balthazar kept the naked man in place by hissing at him. Niclas shut the door behind them, and apologised on behalf of his friends.

'Help!' squealed the man. Hurting their ears and alerting a few other ears downstairs.

'Shut up you miserable fool or we'll cut your throat,' said Balthazar.

The man shut up and gave the cat an anxious gawk.

'It… it spoke…' he said, stabbing at the air with his finger.

'Don't worry, gov, you ain't nuts, it's a complicated science that's all.'

The window opened stiffly, the breeze swept in and the Witchhunter leaned out. It was a cheaper room, one with a lovely view of red brick wall. Three floors below, an empty alley ran between the back streets of the Brewery Quarter.

The Witchhunter snatched the sack from Niclas and dropped it out.

'You first, boy,' he said.

Niclas poked his head into the draft just in time to watch the sack thud on the ground below.

'You're 'avin' a laugh, gov, I'll break me bloomin' neck.'

'Put your feet on the far wall and your back against this one,' said the Witchhunter.

'Blimey,' said Niclas, taking another look at the drop. 'Wot 'bout Balfazar?' he asked.

'Carry him.'

'What?' said Balthazar, provoking the stark naked man to stagger backwards, trip on his trousers and crawl into the corner like pitiful prey.

'Come on, sir, I'll take you down on me chest.' Niclas got into position.

'What's the matter, cat, afraid of heights?' said the Witchhunter.

'No. I… I will not be touched.'

The boy and the Witchhunter didn't understand what this meant, but Balthazar was serious.

'I'll meet you in the alley,' said the cat.

The guards would hardly notice him sneaking between their feet. But it wasn't going to work like that, because on hearing the cat talk again, the pale buttocked man was driven into madness. He placed his hands over his ears and made a dash out the door and into a troop of Watchmen.

The Witchhunter picked Balthazar up by the scruff of his neck and dropped him onto Niclas' chest.

'Ow! Yer nails, sir!'

The guards entered the doorway, and the Witchhunter took aim.

He fired a shot

The first guard took the lead bullet in his chest and fell back into the corridor.

The blast above scared Niclas and he missed his footing and slid down the wall a couple of feet.

'Be careful you idiot!' shouted Balthazar.

''S'alright, sir,' said the boy, easing himself into a more comfortable descent. More shots fired above and smoke curled out of the window and into the air.

'Hurry, you fool!' said Balthazar, backing up into Niclas' face.

Niclas got a mouthful of fluff. In particular, bottom fluff, which even on a cat is not desirable.

'I can't see, sir,' he said, spluttering.

'You don't need to see,' cried Balthazar. 'You don't want to see. Stop spitting – down, down, steady…'

The Witchhunter looked out to check on their progress and a shot shattered the glass pane above him. He turned and fired back.

Shards of glass showered the cat and the boy. Balthazar wriggled the pieces from his back, unbalancing Niclas; who, in an attempt to restrain the cat, reached with one hand and met the pointed ends of his master's claws.

'Don't touch me,' snapped the cat.

'Sorry, sir. Nearly there.'

The Witchhunter moved towards the door. Out in the hallway,

guards were filling up all the space. A shot splintered the wood-work beside him, an inch more to the left and his brains would have splattered everywhere.

He slammed the door shut.

Both his guns were dry.

He tossed the duvet onto the floor and pulled the sheet from the bed.

Was it long enough?

He wrapped one end of it around the near bedpost and spun the rest into a makeshift rope.

Niclas felt his feet touch the bottom and opened his eyes. Balthazar jumped down.

'I'm glad that's over,' he said, returning to his usual calm and collected demeanour, and bathing the boy's germs from his paws.

Niclas looked up. The shots had stopped.

What was going on? Where was the Witchhunter?

'Let's go!'

'Ain't we gonna wait?'

'Don't you learn anything? No, leave him,' said the cat.

They were just about to flee, when he saw the Witchhunter above. The man bungee jumped – or *sheet jumped* from the win-dow, and fell through the air like a stone.

Upstairs, a Watchman had made it into the room, and had rushed to the window with his musket in hand. At that moment, the sheet pulled taut, ripped the bed from its spot, across the floor and slammed it into the window.

SMACK

Balthazar stepped aside to avoid the falling rifle and the Witch-hunter, who landed with birdlike elegance.

'Impressive,' he said.

They darted through the back streets of the Brewery Quarter. But they were not out of trouble yet. Rifles fired at them from down the street and as they came close to the next corner, a coach carrying a fresh batch of Watchmen rolled to a stop and unloaded before them.

'This way,' said the Witchhunter, slipping off into a small passage.

Down a treacherous flight of narrow steps and across a tight cobblestone street, the yeasty pong of the canal came into smell – and then view.

The Witchhunter leapt off the wharf and landed in a small rowing boat captained by a lone gondolier. He grabbed hold of the boatman's oar, gave him a stiff shove into the canal then turned the oar over in his hands and eased the vessel out.

Balthazar paused over the edge of the wharf. 'What are you doing?' he said.

The Witchhunter didn't answer back. There wasn't time for detailed escape plans.

Balthazar inspected the water. He looked for the crossings. The nearest bridge was three hundred yards away. The guards wouldn't be able to follow if they could cross. He leapt and briefly flew, limbs akimbo like a flying squirrel, and landed neatly into the stern of the boat.

Niclas' descent wasn't as graceful. He tripped, scattering the reagents and candles from the sack.

He recovered himself and as quick as he could, gathered the things up and raced to the end of the wharf. But he'd lost valuable time. The boat was drifting further away. Maybe even too far.

'Jump, boy,' cried Balthazar.

Niclas hated water. He'd gone all his life without ever crossing the canal on a boat. He stared fearfully at the gloopy, green algae infested surface. It was like a patch of grass, with bottles and papers and twigs and leaves half submerged within it.

'What is he doing?' said the Witchhunter.

'*What are you doing?*' called Balthazar.

The guards were coming up behind him. He could hear their boots on the cobbled steps.

If the sack could make it he could make it. That was the extent of his reasoning. He tossed the bag through the air and into the boat.

Right, I can do this, he thought. He took a few deep breaths and swung his arms to and fro, psyching himself up.

Balthazar and the Witchhunter looked on with puzzled expressions.

He needed a run up. It wouldn't be a big one, the City Watch were nearly on him. He took a few paces back, held his breath and broke into a fierce sprint to the edge of the wharf. Then he leapt.

In mid air, about halfway between the ground and the boat, he regained his smile.

He was going to make it!

Then he fell straight down and the water went *splash*.

The boat knocked against the wharf on the other side of the canal and Balthazar and the Witchhunter fled to cover.

'We have to go back!' said Balthazar. 'We can't leave him.'

The Witchhunter peered from behind the wall and looked across the canal. There were at least ten Watchmen in sight, all with muskets.

'We can't leave him, he's just a poor boy, he–'

'What do you want from him?' said the Witchhunter, bluntly. He was a man who liked to get straight to the point of things.

'He's my helper… carries things… brings me milk… opens doors…'

'Bull.'

'What?'

'You're lying.'

'How *dare* you… I am not.'

The Witchhunter pulled a gun from its holster and confirmed it was empty. He opened the clockwork centre, poured a vial of gunpowder into each of the three cylinders, inserted three pinches of wadding after them, then popped in three lead balls the size of marbles. He closed the mechanism and unhinged the ramrod from the underside, then pushed down the barrel and twisted the centre three times so each shot was loaded.

Balthazar watched carefully.

'What are you doing?'

The man pointed the gun at the cat's head.

'Wait.'

'Why should I?'

'Why would you? I'm no harm to you. It'd be murder.'

'I can live with it.'

'But...'

The Witchhunter's finger lifted from the trigger guard and onto the iron ring.

'You're serious?' said Balthazar, realising his life now hung in the balance of the man's index finger.

'I know what you are, witch. I know what those markings in the room meant. I'm well read in the Black Science and I know what you're planning to do with that boy. He's better off with them than he is with you.'

'I told you... I'm not a witch. I'm merely a man seeking a cure. You've misread it. It's not–'

'It's not what?'

'*It's not what you think.*'

The Witchhunter was about to squeeze the trigger but Balthazar managed to get one last word in.

'*Logicide.*'

'What?'

'They'll have the boy for logicide. You must know what they do to people in that building of theirs. He'll be broken, physically and mentally. They'll take their time with him. Atone him for his madness. They'll crush every last bit of him. And then, only when he has one last breath of life to give, they'll kill him.'

The Witchhunter considered this.

'So,' he said, 'nothing I can do about it.'

'But there is. There is something *we* can do about it.'

'We? There's no we, cat.'

'Of course there is. I have talents. You have… muscles… and guns.'

The Witchhunter shook his head.

'Fine. Shoot me. Be done with it. But you will remember this day for as long as you shall live. It will burn your conscience forever. You'll wonder what would have happened had you listened to the cat that could talk.'

The Witchhunter flexed his finger.

He stared into the cat's eyes.

Balthazar stared back.

The two were locked in a vicious stare off.

It's a fools game to play, trying to outstare a cat, they've got the eyes for it. But Balthazar didn't have the self confidence he usually had. This man was cold. There was none of the jolly naivety behind his eyes that ordinary people tended to have. And so the cat wet its lips and was about to utter the beginnings of a reptilian chant.

But he didn't need it.

The Witchhunter had no qualms murdering a cat, least of all one enveloped in the Black Science. He did, however, have issue with the boy. Leaving him there was as good as shooting him in the stomach and leaving him to die.

'Blast you, witch,' the Witchhunter shouldered the pistol. 'I swear it, I will be the one to kill you and end your diabolical ways. Whether tonight, tomorrow, the next day, mine will be the last face you see.'

Balthazar smiled. Then withdrew it immediately.

Probably best not to get carried away, he thought.

***

Niclas was wet through, dripping and shivering in the nipping breeze. The canal wasn't like the bath in the Queen's Garter. It was cold and smelly and had made his eyes red.

He was fished out and thrown into the back of a black coach.

Through the barred window he could see Inspector Forsyth talking to a bald man in a red dress.

In the seat opposite him, the naked man from the Queen's Garter curled up away from him.

'Don't hurt me, please… I beg of you…' The man was a quivering wreck. At first Niclas thought he was just cold, being naked in the night air would do that to you. But he wasn't shaking from cold.

''S'appenin'?' said Niclas.

'It spoke… I know it spoke… I saw it speak… No one believes me… Why don't they believe me?'

'Calm down, gov, it's alright. It ain't so bad.'

'Alright! How is it alright?'

'I figures it could be worse. Still alive ain't you. I'm sure they've got a…' Niclas tried to avert his eyes '…a towel or summin somewhere.'

'It's logicide… Moons collide… Reason forbid… Bedlam incarnate… It's logicide…' The man's eyes were streaming. Niclas had seen a lot of people cry, but he'd never seen anyone cry like this. Alongside the tears, the man was squealing like a straining pig. He wished he had a handkerchief to offer the poor chap.

'Logiwot?' asked the boy.

The whip cracked and the coach pulled off.

Niclas looked out the window and managed to catch a glimpse of the boat on the other side of the canal.

It was empty.

'I can't go there… *P-p-please… H-h-elp. HELLLLP!'*

'Go where, gov?'

'The Academy you fool!' said the man, wide eyed and loony. '*The Academy!'*

***

It was a jail cell, but not the sort of jail cell found in the Guard's Tower. This one had a carpet, a sink, a toilet and a red frosted window that couldn't be seen through. Cassandra lay on a small, stained mattress in the corner. Princesses are known for their heightened mattress sensitivity, peas and so on, and she could feel every coil digging through it. She may as well have been sleeping on a sack of potatoes.

She dozed.

That was all there was to do.

Time moved differently there. There were no sign posts to break up the day. No clocks, no visitors, even the light coming through the window always stayed the same.

She had a lot of time to think. That was what rooms like this were for, to lock people away with only their thoughts.

The silence didn't help either. It made her thoughts feel louder and all the little noises people phase out daily, played like drums in her ears. Her breath, her heartbeat, the sappy sound of her lips coming unstuck.

It was enough to drive a person mad…

Maybe that was the point.

'Hello?' she cried out, hoping her voice could be heard through the thick iron door. 'Is there anybody there?'

No one answered.

She drifted in and out of sleep, hoping each time she woke there'd be something to see. But nothing happened.

Then, hours later, the portal under her door opened and a bowl of food slid into the cell.

She fumbled onto her hands and knees and rushed to the portal. It slammed in her face.

'Wait! Come back! Hello? Hello?'

And just like that, they were gone.

The food was a porridge-like gruel. It made Martha's porridge seem a hundred times more appetising. It looked like lumpy grey sick and it smelt like damp wool. They'd obviously forgotten the cutlery. She tried a dab on her finger. It tasted like damp wool too. She pushed the bowl away and sat back, hungry.

She wondered what was happening outside. Her mother had surely heard by now. She was probably already there, in the Academy, demanding her daughter's release. Any minute now they were going to open the door, apologise unreservedly and let her go home.

Any minute now.

Any minute now.

Any minute now…

Any minute…

A horrid thought dawned on the Princess as she lay counting the grey bricks that made up her four walls. *They might not be coming for her.*

It had been hours. Maybe even days. There was no way to tell.

A while later, she was awoken by a cacophony of locks sliding across, unlatching, unhinging; the rattle of keys. When the door opened, she came face to face with the Inquisitor who had brought her there. He stood over her, silent, greeting her with a pleasant, distrustful smile and a bending hooked finger that told her to come hither.

She'd had a bag over her head last time, so this was her first look at the innards of the Academy. It was dark, crimson, a building with stone walls that had seen many generations of witless folk.

Her corridor was just like all the other corridors, lined with iron doors and red, glowing lanterns. She wondered how many of the rooms were occupied. Then she wondered how many of the corridors were full. Then she wondered how many corridors of rooms there were, above her, below her. It was a troubling thought she'd never once thought to have, wondering just how many of her citizens were of unsound mind.

The Inquisitor's chamber welcomed her with a warm crackling fire and a cosy leather chair. She sat. The Inquisitor sat opposite. A hefty mahogany table sat between them. The contents of the table were ordered neatly, not a paper lay out of place. There was a golden globe, a set of golden scales, a golden inkwell and a quill with golden feathers. Clearly, an inquisitor was a job that paid well.

But Cassandra wasn't interested in golden possessions. She was interested in the books. One was bound in red leather and lay open in front of the Inquisitor. It was some sort of log book, a register with names and dates scribbled down in columns similar to the Palace's Guest Book, but much busier.

The other book lay to the side. It was closed now, but the Inquisitor had likely been looking through it. Cassandra's eyes were drawn to it.

'Child. You are very quiet. There's much to admire in that. Citizens often bang on the doors during their first days here. Screaming. Shouting. Some have been known to injure themselves. But you've been very calm.'

'What's your name?' said Cassandra. It was best to get the details now, she thought, so she knew who to hang later.

'I am Inquisitor Sinclair, I shall be responsible for you during your stay here.'

'My stay? You said I would be home tomorrow?'

'Cassandra... It's been three days since then.'

'Three! No… It can't have been…'

'We extract all patients from the notion of time. It happens in the first three days. Helps them adjust to their new surroundings.'

'Patients? Is that what I am?' Cassandra's stomach turned.

'Do you know what an inquisitor does?'

'Yes. You ask questions.'

'Precisely. I want to ask you some questions, Cassandra. Do you know what they're about?'

Cassandra's eyes fell on the Zolnomicon again.

'Yes,' said the Inquisitor, 'most clever.' He lifted the tome and opened it partway.

Cassandra shuddered. She'd forgotten about the writing. She'd forgotten that it had changed.

'You said you were reading this book? What language is this, I wonder?'

'I don't know…'

'You don't know? But you can read it?'

'No…'

'So you can't read it? Yet, you were reading it, didn't you say that?'

'It…' Cassandra had to think very carefully about this. The truth sounded completely mad, but inquisitors could tell when people were lying.

'Yes?' he said, expectantly.

'I was trying to read it. That's what I've been doing. I couldn't find any books about the language that it's written in, so I thought I could use the pictures and compare it to colonial languages and maybe…'

'But, child, this is gibberish. It's hieroglyphic. And there are no *known* hieroglyphic languages.' The Inquisitor cast his eye over his papers. Or *her* papers, her name was inked in the corner of each page.

'Our report here tells me that you told one Mr Eccleston you believed the Royal Protector had been hypnotised and made to attack your mother by someone else. Is that correct?'

So there it was, the name of her betrayer: Mr Eccleston. Cassandra would add his name to the hangman's list too.

'Cassandra?'

'Yes. That's right,' she said, bitterly.

'And you still believe this?'

'…I don't know.'

'Why Cassandra, who would do such a thing, if such a thing were possible?'

'I don't know…'

'You haven't a suspect?'

'No.'

'Nor a motive then, I suppose.'

'…'

'Not a shred of evidence besides your overactive imagination?'

Cassandra's case was falling away from her fast.

'He was in a trance,' she said, 'and he didn't remember what he did afterwards.'

'Perhaps so, child. Affected by madness no doubt. Who knows the thoughts of a madman, their actions are mad so their thoughts must equally be so. But it is no longer disputed, I believe the Chief Inspector of the City Watch has already taken a full confession.'

'What?'

'Oh, of course, you wouldn't know.'

'What do you mean confession? But he didn't do it? He was screaming that he didn't do it, why would he confess?'

'Madness comes and goes. But please, we're not here to talk about Rufus Atwell. I want to talk about you. You said that you'd stopped a boy from the Queen's Garter stealing this book?'

'Yes.'

'Why didn't you report it to the librarians? Or the authorities?'

'Pardon?'

'Well, you saw a crime didn't you? Why not report it?'

'...I–'

'And then... it was you who ended up stealing the book, no?'

'Only so the thief wouldn't get it.'

'I see.' The Inquisitor steepled his hands and sat in a moment of thoughtful silence.

It was a torturous silence. The sort of silence that hurts.

'Inquisitor, may I ask you a question?'

'Of course,' the man smiled.

'Why does the Academy, the source of all the Empire's knowledge, forbid certain books?'

'Like this one?'

'Yes.' She wasn't sure how he would react to this and waited nervously.

'It is a good question, child. Sometimes, you see, it can be difficult to tell what's real apart from what's not. Of course, an educated young girl like yourself should have no difficulty deducing one from the other. But there are many citizens throughout the Empire who would struggle: the more *fragile* minds of our society. All illogical thought breeds suffering, and the first pillar of madness is belief. So you see, we are protecting the realm when we prohibit a book such as this. For they cause unfounded beliefs in unrealities. And those unfounded beliefs cause needless suffering.' The Inquisitor spoke in quotes, likely because he was reciting the Academy's maxims.

'I see.'

'I'm glad. It is for the greater good after all.'

Cassandra pondered how many terrible things had been done in the name of the Greater Good. She wondered what the Greater Good would think about it. Whether it was alright with people going about doing bad things in its name all the time. And she thought, what if all those terrible things out weighed the Greater Good a million to one.

'What will happen to it?' she said, pulling her eyes from the Zolnomicon's magnetic hold.

'What do *you* think should happen to it?'

This was her moment to prove her loyalty and clearness of mind. She knew exactly what needed to be said.

'We need to destroy it.' She played her hand confidently.

'Yes. We ought to. It shan't be missed I don't think, a book not written in Varcian isn't worth remembering. But, the real question will be: are you devoted enough to destroy it yourself?' said the Inquisitor.

Cassandra could see the burning fire twisting in his perverted smile. She felt its heat flushing against the side of her face. She knew what had to be done but doing so went against every moral bone in her body. Books weren't just pages and inkings, to her, they were living creatures, alive with ideas.

The more she thought about it the harder it became and the Inquisitor was watching her every thought, as if she were an ape putting shapes into holes.

It's best to do things like this quickly, without thinking about it.

She stood up, snatched the Zolnomicon from the desk, marched over to the log fire and held it there above the flames.

'Yes. An excellent idea, Cassandra,' said the Inquisitor, studying her intently.

She let go.

The book thudded onto the logs and sat there, immortal for a second or two. Then the leather cover began to curl and the pages began to char. The fire raged happily, its dancing flames wrapping themselves around the tome. She stood watching, hiding her horrified face from the Inquisitor. Hot, orange cracks of fire were spreading like burning veins through the leather. The face of the book slid off into the white hot logs and shrivelled like a withering leaf. The stone melted away like a shard of black ice. Pages began to burn loose and rise up in the heat, as if trying to escape it. She watched the inked illustrations bubble and the words turn to ash. Within minutes, the book was dead. The lingering smell was pungent, stifling and filled the room.

Cassandra bit down on her lip to hold back her tears.

'It's done,' she said.

The Inquisitor had stood up and was now behind her, smiling proudly at her good work. He placed his grey, bejewelled hands on her shoulders.

'Marvellous. You've taken a very important step. Now come, there is something I want to show you.'

The Inquisitor took the Princess deeper into the building; down into its foundations, where the air was colder and the corridors far, far darker. There were no more lanterns, instead, flickering torches on the walls. It was medieval in its appearance, and, as Cassandra was about to see, in its purpose too.

'All students of the Academy are given a tour once they have passed their induction. You are a very special internee here. I believe, for that reason, it is fitting that you see some of the work we do.'

Cassandra was familiar with the workings of the Academy, but no more than everyone else. She knew there were Philosophers and Logicians who were said to sit about all day in plain rooms, debating and writing the rulebook of the Empire.

She knew about the professors and scholars who studied the sciences in depth, and brought the teachings of The Curriculum to the fringes of the Empire.

Then there was the bit everyone knew about, but no one *really* knew about. The Inquisitors and the Justiciars. The enforcers of logic, order and reason. Everyone knew what happened to people guilty of logicide. The Academy came for them and took them away. What happened next was the foggy bit. No one knew anyone who knew anyone who had even heard of anyone who had heard about what happened next. That's because people who were committed to the Academy were never seen again.

'This is where we begin to rehabilitate offenders,' said Inquisitor Sinclair. 'Their cells are shrouded in darkness and sound proofed from the outside world. Their senses are postponed, if you understand.'

The doors here were different. They were iron like the ones above, but thicker, bulkier, with spinning wheels at their centre.

'We keep them unfed and unwatered for as long as is necessary.'

'You starve them?'

'For as long as is necessary.'

'How long is that?'

'Until their minds are simplified. You must first destroy all trace of a person's unreality before showing them the path to true reality.'

Cassandra was feeling faint. It could have been the air. It was stuffy and dark, and not meant for Princess lungs. Or perhaps it was the thought that she would end up in one of these rooms. It was probably a bit of both.

'I don't mean to scare you,' said the Inquisitor, in a tone that suggested that that was precisely his intention. 'I only want to show you the fragility of the human mind. It is the best lesson I can offer.'

They stopped at one of the doors.

'This offender is early on in his re-education. Any further in and it would be damaging to disturb him, but at this stage we may be allowed to take a peek.' He opened the small letterbox sized viewing window and beckoned her to look.

Cassandra didn't want to, she was quite fine where she was, but the Inquisitor insisted.

She stood on her toes and peered into the room…

In the single beam of light, she saw a gaunt, naked man, rocking to and fro cradling his body with his arms. He was absorbed within himself, so much so that though his eyes were open he wasn't the slightest bit aware of her…

And he was chanting…

The word rolled off his tongue as though it were the only word he knew.

'*Logicide-logicide-logicide-logicide-logicide.*'

She fell away from the window in terror.

The Inquisitor slid it shut.

'It's horrid, just horrid, how can you do such a thing to a man?'

'It is necessary. We must cleanse his mind in order to heal it.'

'And starve him?' she gasped.

'Food, Cassandra, is a distraction of the mind. Its taste, its texture and its appearance all distract us from what it truly is: sustenance. He will eat not when he wants to eat, but when he needs to.'

'You think *he's* mad? Can you see yourself? This is madness defined!' Cassandra swayed a little, putting her hands on the wall to steady herself.

'Cassandra, please, your compassion gets the better of you. We wouldn't do it if it didn't work.'

'No. It's horrid. I want to go home. Right now, you hear me, sir.'

'I don't think you are ready just yet.'

'I demand it. I am the Princess. My mother will be looking for me–'

'Your mother understands the good work we do here. She understands it is in your interest.'

'You're lying. I command you to release me.'

'Hmmm… You are very much like your father, child. He too tried to assert his power in this place. He was not capable of understanding that the Realm of Logic stands above all.'

'My father was a good man.'

'Your father was a sick man.'

'You dare, sir.'

'Are you questioning our judgment of the matter? I was one of many who over saw his detention. He was gravely ill and in his latter days he grew only worse.'

'You kept my father down here?' Cassandra's voice was faltering.

'For a time. But he was soon transferred. His mind required a firmer discipline.'

The feeling of vertigo was rising in the Princess. She felt sick. Literally sick. Like she was going to throw up at any moment.

'There is a train of thought, Cassandra, that certain illnesses of the mind can be passed down, inherited from our parents. I personally do not think that you are of the same degree that your father was, but you will understand our caution to release you. It is best for all if we keep you here a while longer, so we are able to better observe you.'

Cassandra threw up a bit in her mouth. The Inquisitor's words were disorientating. He was speaking slowly, articulating every single word. Teasing her.

'Cassandra? Are you alright?' His words spiralled around in a kaleidoscopic echo. 'You are not sick, yet you feel sick. It is in your mind only. Do you not control your mind? Are you not queen of your thoughts?' The Inquisitor's words span Cassandra round and round like a wheel within a wheel. 'Cassandra, are you well? Cassandra?'

It was the voice of Rufus. The voice of her mother. The voice of Mr Eccleston. The voice of Martha. And she saw them all, all the Lords of Parliament, crowded around the dining hall table, eating and drinking and laughing at her. They were tearing the duck meat from the bone with their razor sharp teeth. The red wine looked like blood. They were drunk. They were all drunk and laughing at her. And her mother was laughing at her too. She felt like she was shrinking, then she fell off her chair and was in a dark hole looking up. She saw their faces circling the light above.

They were faces one minute then skulls the next. Laughing skulls right out of the pages of the Zolnomicon.

The hall span…

The torches span…

The doors span…

Her knees buckled and the Princess fainted.

She awoke back in her cell with an itchy blanket thrown over her. She was wet through in sweat.

Still here, she thought and was briefly grateful. For a moment she could have been certain she would wake up in one of the lower cells.

She could still see him. The feeble man behind the door, quaking back and forth, chanting that word over and over.

She could see his skinny, tortured face…

She didn't know him…

But we know him…

For that man, locked away deep within the Academy, used to go by a name before he was branded nameless and insane…

And that name, was Job Button.

***

Abe Goodfellow came from a wealthy background. His father, like his father before him and his father before that, had long served the Academy as an inquisitor. Abe had joined at the age of fifteen in order to follow in his family's footsteps. After six years, his father was still one of the leading inquisitors in the Empire, but Abe was not the brightest of students and had hardly progressed through the Academy's ranks. Whilst his friends went on to become inquisitors and justiciars in the unreasonable world, he stayed within the Academy, cleaning the halls, preparing the rooms, and doing whatever was asked of him. In this respect, he had the same attitude towards life as a dog: as long as he was given some praise and not beaten too much, he remained a loyal companion; though in all other eyes but his, he was a slave.

Among his duties was the upkeep of the cells, and the delivery of food to the inmates. It was a fairly easy job with little room for error. All he had to do day in and day out, was push a trolley through the corridor, stopping at each cell to slide a portion of soup or bread through the portal. Then, at another time in the day, he came back around and reached through the portal to reclaim the plates and bowls. Occasionally, an inmate would forget to put the bowl back and he would have to bang on the door and request it.

'Bowl, please,' he said, rapping his fist against a door.

After waiting a reasonable amount of time, he asked again.

'Excuse me, bowl.'

When still there was no reply, he squatted down, put his face to the floor and looked through the tiny opening. From what he could see the room was empty, except for the soup bowl, which lay just out of reach.

'Hey, wake up in there,' he said, exasperated.

The retrieval of bowls was never usually this troublesome.

When still no reply came, he took it upon himself to reach in with his arm. His hand slapped about blindly, then he withdrew and took another look. The bowl seemed to have moved an inch or two further away. Odd, he thought.

He stood and unhooked the keys from his belt.

He wasn't allowed to open the cells, but figured if the inmate was able to sleep through his knocking and frolicking about they would sleep through a quick intrusion.

What didn't occur to Abe Goodfellow, was that the inmate wasn't sleeping at all.

Upon opening the door, he was met with a mighty strike to his nose from the elusive soup bowl.

The blow sent cartilage into his throat and tears out of his eyes.

In the confusion, the inmate grabbed him, pulled him in and struck him again on the back of the head. The force was hard enough to dent the bowl, but not enough to send him to sleep; and so another clout was needed, and this time, Cassandra put every fibre of muscle into it, so that when he hit the floor, she thought she'd killed him.

'That should do it,' said Balthazar, pawing the student's drooling face to check for life.

'Is he dead?' asked Cassandra, staring at the weapon in her hand and considering what an odd way to go it was.

'No, still breathing, unfortunately. Take his keys.'

'Goodness… This is really happening isn't it?'

Cassandra was not acquainted with danger. She wasn't sure exactly how one was supposed to act in these kinds of situations. So, she thought, it was best to do whatever the talking cat asked. She pried the keys from the student's hand and locked him inside her cell.

That was a little too *in medias res*. But don't worry, we'll go back a bit.

She had been sleeping when the cat came to her, slipping himself through the portal at the bottom of her door. When she woke, she was startled to see its green eyes staring back at her; and when it spoke, she leapt up from the biting blanket and flattened her back to the wall.

'You've caused me quite the upset,' it said.

'You're a cat?'

'Well observed.'

'But cats can't talk?'

Balthazar rolled his eyes. He hated that almost all his conversations began this way.

'Listen to me, girl–'

'How did you get in here?'

'No time for–'

'How are you doing that? You're not real, you can't be.'

'I assure you I am.'

'Well you would say that wouldn't you.'

'I beg your pardon?'

'I'm dreaming. And you're part of my dream, so of course you'd say you were real, else I'd wake up.'

'Yes… that does sound plausible… but this isn't a dream.'

'Of course it is. Cats can't talk. It's impossible.'

'Highly unlikely, I would say. Impossible, no. We share a connection you and I. Our threads have been wound together.'

'Stop talking, it's not right.'

'Perfect.'

'What?'

'Just my luck. A smart arse. To think! I actually prefer the stupid ones.'

'I'm not stupid.'

'Supposedly not. Though, sometimes girl, you can be so educated that you are indeed completely stupid.'

'What are you trying to say? In fact, no. Stop talking. Go away. I need to wake up.' Cassandra lay down and closed her eyes.

'You are awake.'

'Not listening.'

Balthazar wasn't patient. He sauntered up to the Princess' face, went down to her feet and dug a claw into her little toe.

'*OUCH!*'

'Oh, sorry, did that hurt?'

'YES!'

'But if you were dreaming, it wouldn't hurt, would it?'

'Well… it depends.'

'Depends? Depends on what?'

'How deeply I'm dreaming.'

'This is ridiculous.'

'Tell me about it, it's logicide.'

'There we go. Logicide. That'll explain it for sure.'

The Princess rubbed her toe and sat staring at the cat. He'd drawn blood.

'Well, what do you want?'

'Coming round are we?'

'No. But you must have a purpose. Is it to frighten me? Make me go mad?'

'My servant,' Balthazar rephrased, '*associate*, is imprisoned somewhere in here. I cannot find him, but I was able to find you – and you are going to help me find him.'

'This is preposterous. Bedlam incarnate. What if I don't want a part in this dream. I'd like to wake up thank you very much.'

'You could stay here forever. That's the alternative.'

'Fine.'

'Fine?'

'I don't do silly dreams, I'm a logical, reasonable, perfectly ordinary member of society.'

'Ok. Let me put it this way, girl. You can stay here – forever. Or you can come with me and escape this place. Now, if this turns out to be a dream, you'll wake up just as you are, but if by some chance this is real, then you'll get out of here. Let's have a little wager on the pensées shall we? Do you feel lucky?'

'. . .'

'Well, do you?'

Cassandra did feel lucky; and so they waited for Abe Goodfellow to do his rounds, and when he did, began their escape.

All the corridors looked the same. Getting lost was easy. But Cassandra remembered virtually everything she read. Her memory was faultless. You might say it was her greatest gift. It was times like this, that she could really show off. Using the door numbers alone, she steered them through the labyrinth, this way and that way, until they came to Inquisitor Sinclair's office.

'This is very dangerous,' she said, 'but a little exciting too.'

Balthazar looked askance at her; he failed to see anything exciting about it, and found her enthusiasm disconcerting.

She spied through the keyhole and saw the table furnished with golden ornaments. There was no one sat behind it. She tried various keys in the lock until one clicked.

Inside, the smell of the burning Zolnomicon was still lingering in the air. She stared mournfully at the flames.

'What are you doing?' asked the cat.

'Nothing.'

She searched the table.

'It was here, I swear it was here. A big red book,' she said, sweeping papers onto the floor.

'A drawer perhaps?'

She opened one of the table's drawers. Two books were hidden within: the Codex of Logic, and the big red book titled: *Committal Register*. In her rush the Codex of Logic was flung onto the floor.

Balthazar began to browse the open pages. They detailed various methods a person could use to test their own mind for traits of insanity. It was mildly entertaining.

Cassandra browsed the register. There were many names; at least five people a day were taken to the Academy, sometimes as many as ten.

Along the column of names she saw her own; next to it, the date of her committal, a marking of her assessment, and a column titled treatment, which read: *Re-education*. But the word was crossed out in red and replaced with: *The Hall of Atonement*.

'The Hall of Atonement?' she said aloud, pricking Balthazar's ears.

'Pardon?'

'That's my treatment...' said Cassandra.

It was odd that they would send her there, he thought. But there was no time to reflect on it, because at any moment Inquisitor Sinclair could have entered his office, or Abe Goodfellow could have woken from his nap; and Balthazar had a plan that required strict timing, a plan with no room for dawdling.

'Need I remind you we have a time frame, girl.'

'I've been here *four* days,' she said, 'it feels like four weeks!'

'Trust me, it's been a very long four days for me too,' said Balthazar, broodingly, lending the girl a look that said: "hurry up".

The Princess nodded.

Her finger drew down the list of names around the date she was arrested.

'What name am I looking for?'

'Nicholas… or Niclas… something like that.'

Cassandra looked up.

'Niclas?' she whispered.

'Yes? What's wrong?'

'The boy from the City Library?'

'That's the one. Can you see him?'

'Erm… Yes. Here we are, *Niclas*. Treatment: *re-education.*'

'Mmmm,' Balthazar groaned, 'I hope we're not too late. Does it say where he is now?'

'Twenty six thirteen,' she said.

'Right.' Balthazar sighed. The Princess had been in room seven one seven, but the Academy was a vast building and it could take hours to find Niclas' cell. Hours they didn't have.

'I'll let you in on a secret, girl, I only have an hour, less now, until your way out of here closes. So we best move quickly.'

Cassandra pondered the time. She could see their predicament. Then she brightened and began raiding the drawers.

'I doubt he's in there,' said Balthazar, 'too big…'

The Princess pulled out the small blade of a letter opener.

Balthazar couldn't see where she was going with this, but she was adamant that he follow her, so he did.

His confidence in the girl improved substantially when they returned to her cell and began to rouse Abe Goodfellow by slapping him in the face.

He stirred, opening his eyes one by one in a drunken daze and reaching for his sore head. He focused on the Princess, remembered everything all of a sudden, and woke fully with all the grace of an electric shock. He would have let out a shrieking scream, had Cassandra not brought the letter opener to his throat.

'Please don't make any loud sounds,' she said with a firm, yet polite tone, 'I won't hesitate to use this in an undesirable way.'

'You wouldn't…' mumbled Abe.

'Oh yes I would – I'm crazy, remember, and therefore highly unpredictable.'

Abe went quiet.

'What's your name?' asked the Princess.

'Abe. Abe Goodfellow.'

'Well, Abe, I want you to take me to room twenty six thirteen. Will you do that for me?' she said, insisting with the blade.

'Yep,' said Abe.

Balthazar kept quiet. The boy was already ruffled enough. He didn't need talking cats too. And he was already intrigued by the cat's presence…

…and why was it staring at him like that?

As Abe lead them through the corridors to the cell marked twenty six thirteen, he became more and more wary of the cat's eyes, but he dared not ask.

'This is illogical you know,' he said.

'I know,' said Cassandra. 'Tell me, Abe, do you know what the Hall of Atonement is?' Balthazar's eyes stuck to the student.

'Yes…' said Abe.

'Well? What is it?'

'It's an asylum off the mainland. Reserved for only the worst cases of logicide.'

Cassandra felt a cold rush come over her.

'Why would they send me there?'

'Send you?' replied Abe, confused. 'They won't send you there.'

'It says in the register. That's how I'm to be treated.'

'No. Probably a mistake then. It's for complete lunatics – the highest degree of logicide. It's more a prison if anything. Once crazies are sent there, they don't ever come back.'

'That doesn't make sense,' she said.

Abe turned his head to examine the blade at his back and the cat at his side. There was a lot that didn't make sense.

'It's here,' said Abe.

They had arrived at Niclas' cell without quarrel.

'Face the wall, Abe, and don't move. There's a... good fellow.'

Cassandra jingled through the keys one by one. None worked.

'Ahem,' said Balthazar, nodding towards Abe.

'Which is it?' asked the Princess.

'The square headed one for this floor...'

'Thank you. Very kind.'

'D...don't mention it.'

The door opened and the Princess, the cat and Abe glancing over his shoulder, came face to face with Niclas.

Or at least, they would have, had his face not been halfway down the toilet and his legs hovering in the air.

'What's he doing?' asked Cassandra.

Niclas pulled out and fell down.

'Woah... It ain't wot it looks like... I... *Balfazar*?' A smile as round as a banana and almost as yellow shone from Niclas' face. Then he saw the Princess.

'You!'

'You!' she said.

'Wot's goin' on, Balfazar?' he addressed the cat.

Abe Goodfellow frowned. Clearly these were very damaged people.

'What were you doing?' asked Cassandra.

'Oh, I was finkin' yeah, that this 'ere loo must be joined up wiv the sewer, so if I could break it off I might be able to squeeze meself down the pipe to where the rats live 'n' that 'n' then make me way back to the street.'

'I see,' said Cassandra.

Balthazar smiled. It was good to have him back, he thought.

Then he opened his mouth to speak. 'We don't have a lot of time left—'

'*Moons collide!* That cat just spoke,' said Abe. 'Did you hear that?'

'No, I think it's only you, Abe,' said the cat.

'Luh-luh-logic defied!' The student fell over, as if winded. '*When my experience deceives me, my reason will guide me…*' Abe plunged full flow into one of the Academy's many mantras.

Balthazar rolled his eyes.

Cassandra raised the letter opener.

'Abe, get a hold of yourself,' she said.

The student yelped, backed away and ran as fast as he could, shouting the mantra down the corridor.

'I guess we have even less time now,' said Balthazar.

'Wot's the plan, sir?'

'We may have to run.'

''S'alright, sir, I bin walkin' up 'n' down in circles round this room 'ere for ages – be good to 'av' a bit o' the old eggsysize.'

They ran in the opposite direction to Abe Goodfellow, cutting through the corridors and back down the stairs. Cassandra was doubtful, but Balthazar never once made an error and guided them back past her cell in no time at all.

'Through here,' Balthazar nodded to the door, 'across the hall, and down into the aqueducts.'

'Will we 'av' to swim?' asked Niclas.

'The water gate will close at any moment. Come!'

Cassandra opened the door, let Balthazar slip through first, then followed after with Niclas.

They arrived on a balcony overlooking a magnificent nave of red stained glass windows, black iron chandeliers and huge stone arches of gothic design. The cat led them over the edge, onto the top of the nearest arch. To Balthazar, it was a simple bridge to the balcony on the other side. But for Cassandra and Niclas, this bridge was but a mere beam of stone, hovering above a dizzying drop in the middle of a hall so grand that rays of light could not cross it without fading through the atmospheric clouds of dust. All they had to do was cross to the other side. But the other side was a long way off. And the height wasn't the worst of it. Below them, there were at least thirty students dressed in the red, cere-monial robes of the Academy. They were all versed deep in some sort of initiation, all looking towards the altar; and there were a dozen inquisitors dotted around them.

'*Logic will govern my thoughts,*' said the leading Inquisitor.

'*Logic will govern my thoughts,*' the crowd repeated, in a harmo-ny that reverberated up the stone columns, through the arch and into Niclas and Cassandra's legs.

'Come on,' mouthed Balthazar, prancing across the beam with all the dexterity belonging to a cat.

'*Reason will be my weapon.*'

'*Reason will be my weapon.*'

Cassandra and Niclas began to make their way across as slowly as possible.

'Why couldn't there just be a door?' murmured Niclas. 'Why's it always gotta be heights.'

'Shh!' said Cassandra.

'*I will seek to rid the world of the unreasonable.*'

249

'*I will seek to rid the world of the unreasonable.*'

Niclas could feel his sweat dripping off his body and raining on the students below.

They were halfway, edging across the beam.

'*I will spread the word of law…*'

'*I will spread the word of law…*'

Just a bit further.

'*…And bring light to where there is darkness.*'

'*…And bring light to where there is darkness.*'

A little bit further…

'*By the hammer and the scales.*'

'*By the hammer and the scales.*'

A little bit more…

'*By the book of the realm.*'

'*By the book of the realm.*'

Almost there…

'*I swear this oath.*'

'*I swear this oath.*'

Almost… Almost…

'*I, Inquisitor Harrow, welcome you scholars into the Order of Logic. May you go on to be the greatest of logicians, teachers, inquisitors and enforcers of reason–*'

The main doors to the front of the hall banged open. All faces turned to look. In came an out of breath, sweaty, red-faced Abe Goodfellow.

'Logicide! Logicide! Help! Help!' he screamed.

The students fell into whispers, whilst three inquisitors rushed to meet with Abe to calm him down.

Niclas stared below, dividing his concentration, which for someone like Niclas, whose concentration is pretty thin to begin with, is not ideal.

Cassandra, who was coming up behind him, could see him drifting over the edge.

'Niclas!' she said.

Her warning had an adverse effect. The boy, startled, swung around and knocked Cassandra with his shoulder. She fought to regain her balance, and the letter opener fell from her hand. It cut through the air like a… well… letter opener, and clattered on the floor below.

There was a moment of confusion, as people questioned the likelihood of letter openers materialising in thin air. Then, suddenly, the students began looking up and pointing, uncertain of what they were seeing.

Inquisitor Sinclair followed their fingers, shot his eyes upon Cassandra, and made haste out the door with Abe Goodfellow.

Niclas reached the end of the arch. He climbed over onto the balcony and tried the door. It was locked. Cassandra soon followed, sticking one key after another into the lock.

'Faster, faster!' said Balthazar.

''Urry!' said Niclas.

'Look!' snapped the Princess. 'Both of you! Can't you see I'm doing it! Shouting certainly doesn't help. Be patient!'

They calmed.

The correct key slid in, turned and the three of them fell through the door.

They continued through the passageway, until they came to a spiral of stone steps.

At the bottom of the steps was a large room, filled with crates and sacks of various supplies: mostly food stores for the Academy's kitchen. There was a cold breeze in the air too, and the sound of lapping water nearby.

Two men were unloading the last box from their boat onto the dock. They had been working all day and were rushing to get the job finished so they could go home. Despite the warning printed on the last box: *fragile*, they tossed it carelessly onto a sack of coal and started untying the boat.

'Don't forget to close the water gate,' said one.

'Aye, I won't make that mistake again. I got no pay last month, because the Academy complained to the management. They said I had caused them a whole heap of worry. Don't see why, it's not like anyone would want to steal from them.'

'It's not to keep people out, it's to keep people in.'

'Wot?'

'Like a precaution, there's all sorts of crazies in 'ere, imagine if one day, one escaped and made it down 'ere. They could swim out and be free to roam about the city!'

The other reflected on this. 'Still, I don't think it was worth a month's salary; you know what I mean?' he said. 'A man's got to put food on the table.'

'If I were you, I'd shut up about it and forget it ever happened. Don't want to be upsetting the Academy of all people.'

'Ah, I don't care, I'm out of this job in three months – can't be dealing with lifting all this cargo off and on boats all day long, it's done me back in proper.'

'And what will you do in this day and age that don't require a good working back or at least a set of brains?'

'Might leave the city, get out of the stench, find myself a bit of land – that's the life see, growing your own food and living free.'

'And just how are you gonna afford your own land? It's expensive business, land business, not easy to come by. And even if you get it, these days Government can make a compulsive purchase.'

'A what now?'

'A compulsive purchase. It means they buy your land off you, and there ain't nothing you can do to refuse it.'

'That's practically theft!'

'It sure is…'

The two men continued in this way of conversation, whilst the cat, the boy and the girl watched and listened behind a large barrel of malt.

'What are we waiting for?' said Cassandra.

'Phase two.'

'Face wot?' said Niclas.

The two men had finished untying their vessel and were about to push it out and lock the gate with a large iron key the size of a forearm, when a third man rose up out of the boat's bow.

'Eh!' cried the first.

'Who the?' cried the second.

The Witchhunter pulled both his guns and kept them trained on each of the men.

'Hey, no trouble, gov,' said the first, raising his hands.

'You want the food? The boat? Take it for all I care – it ain't worth a bullet,' said the second.

The three escapees emerged from behind the men and hopped onto the boat one by one.

'What's going on?' asked the first.

'If you'd kindly alight here,' said Balthazar, 'oh, and mind the gap.'

The first man stepped from the boat to the dock, fearing that he'd be shot at any moment. The second followed, eyes fixed to the talking cat.

'Thank you,' said Balthazar.

'Fanks, gents,' said Niclas.

'Much obliged,' said Cassandra.

The Witchhunter, one gun still aimed, put one hand on the iron gate and pulled the boat along the fence and out of the dock.

'Wait! Stop them! Stop them! Logicide! Logicide!' Abe Goodfellow ran out onto the dock pointing and screaming. The two couriers stared at him then at each other – apathetic.

'Aren't you going to stop them! They're escaping!'

'Pardon me, gov, I don't believe this is anything to do with us this time.'

'Nope, nothing we could do. And it ain't our remit to be stopping looneys.'

The student, infuriated, and overcome with *madness* raced to the edge of the dock and leapt into the water.

'The boy is adamant, I'll give him that,' said Balthazar.

The Witchhunter took aim.

'No!' shouted Cassandra, pushing the gun down.

She picked up an oar and tried to raise it over her shoulder like a spear. Like most oars, it was surprisingly heavily; so she gripped it with two hands and clumsily brought it hammering down on Abe's head.

The Witchhunter frowned. He failed to see how that was any kinder.

And so it was. The escape was a success.

The four of them made off down the canals and were too far gone to be chased by the time the Inquisition had informed the City Watch.

The two men delivering the cargo were banned from all future visits to the Academy and docked a month's wages each. But it wasn't so bad. They'd succeeded in keeping what they'd seen concerning a certain talking feline to themselves.

Abe Goodfellow, however, had not.

He insisted that the talking cat had orchestrated the entire thing. The two men didn't back up his story (not that it would have helped), and Abe was convicted of logicide.

He was committed and scheduled for immediate re-education.

***

The six bells in the six towers of the Academy rang out for hours. Soon, Laburnum was crawling with more guards than rats. The City Watch, commanded by inquisitors and justiciars, tore through the capital's establishments from roof to cellar. They searched the canal network and put up blockades at every bridge.

There hadn't been such a force of gun and sword on the streets for nearly a decade. It would only be a matter of time before the escapees were found. Nowhere was safe to hide.

But there was one place they could hide.

One place the City Watch didn't go. Some called it Bog End. Others, The Rags. Rat Bottom was a popular choice too. Most called it the slums.

Niclas called it home.

They travelled by canal. It was the safest way to travel unseen. And they had to do so, because Niclas and Cassandra were dressed in matching grey tunics, the kind only found in the Academy.

'What a horrid place that was,' said the Princess. 'I must speak to mother about it. If she knew… what they do there… what they've done there… '

'It weren't so bad, miss,' said Niclas.

'What? How can you say that? It was awful.'

'I dunno, it 'ad a bed, a water closet which flushed funny but worked all the same. There was a window… the view weren't great but you can't 'av' everyfing.'

'Then you must be mad,' said Cassandra.

'I just ain't picky, miss. Though, I'm glad you came when you did… I was startin' to get a bit bored… and the food weren't great.'

'Didn't they interrogate you?'

'Interrorwot?'

'Question you?'

'No, miss, didn't speak to no one. Just got a bag over me 'ead, got shown me room, then they left me. I did fink they might 'av' forgotten 'bout me. Easy fing to do I guess. I gots one o' 'em faces.'

Cassandra couldn't believe it. Here was the boy who had started all of this. It was because of him she had been taken – him and that book; and they hadn't even questioned him.

'Say, Balfazar, how'd you get in that place anyway? How'd you know where to find me?'

'Another one of those things, boy.'

'What things?' said Cassandra.

'You wouldn't understand,' said Balthazar.

'Try me. I understand most things rather well.'

'Trust me. This, you wouldn't.'

The Witchhunter appeared detached, but he was listening – even whilst he steered the boat into an open lock, and set upon the mechanism to close one gate, lower the water level, and open the next – even then, over the clanking of rusty cogs and gushing of falling water, he listened. And intently…

'Have you always been able to talk like that? How did you learn?' asked Cassandra.

'I learnt the same way you did, I suspect. I was not always a cat.'

'No?'

'No miss,' said Niclas, about to proudly do a bit of mansplaining. 'Balfazar 'ere was a person once. But someone turned 'im into a cat see. Ain't that right, sir?'

'Yes. Exactly.'

'That's impossible,' said the Princess.

'I suppose most things are impossible to a closed mind,' said Balthazar.

Cassandra lit up. She had the face of a person who had put two and two together to make five, but was happy about it.

'What do you know of hypnosis?' she asked.

'I'm sorry, I don't follow?'

'I read that a person could control another person, make them do things against their will?'

'Where did you read that, in the book you stole from us?'

'I did no such thing. It didn't belong to you in the first place. He was going to steal it from the library… I was protecting it.'

'Wait a minute,' said Niclas, 'you robbed me, I just remembered.'

'I didn't rob you. I–'

'Where is the book now?' asked Balthazar.

'…'

'Girl?'

'They burnt it. The Inquisitors,' she lied.

'Burnt it,' said Balthazar, with a look of genuine displeasure.

'Yes. Burnt it. Right in front of me…'

'A shame.'

The Witchhunter, still listening, sat down and guided them out of the lowered lock, pushing off the wall with an oar.

'What was it, the book?' asked Cassandra.

'A grimoire.'

'What's that?'

'A spell book.'

'A spell book?'

'A philosophy of olden times. A measure of the universe, the only one of its kind, older than all of us put together. And now it's gone.'

'*I'm sorry,*' said Cassandra, but only she knew what for.

'It's no bother. I've got all I need from the Zolnomicon. I think.'

'You didn't answer my question.'

'Your question?'

'Can people… control other people? By means of hypnosis?'

'I don't know if you'd call it hypnosis. But for those with a particular knowledge, it is not impossible to control the thoughts, words and *actions* of another. They call it charming the thread.'

'Charming?' said Cassandra.

'Because it's a bit like charming snakes – I gather.'

Balthazar watched the Witchhunter carefully. He knew that underneath the man's distant demeanour, he was listening.

'That would explain everything,' the Princess said to herself.

Niclas and Balthazar looked at each other and for the first time found themselves equally puzzled.

'Wot miss?'

'The Royal Protector tried to kill my mother, except it wasn't him, he was under some sort of… some sort of…'

'Trance?' said Balthazar.

Cassandra nodded.

'Who's this Royal Protector again?' asked Niclas.

'My family's bodyguard.'

'Don't sound much of a bodyguard to me. Why'd they call 'im royal?'

'Because he protects the Royal Family…'

'But that would make your family the…' It wasn't everyday Niclas had an epiphany, but when they came along they usually walloped him on the head. 'Moons collide!' He reached for his metaphorical hat and removed it charmingly. 'I didn't know you woz royalty, miss. I shoulda, shoulda washed me 'ands or summin.'

'That's quite alright,' said Cassandra.

Balthazar was less surprised. He was more curious about the other bit.

'Are you telling us that a witch has tried to kill the Queen?'

'Witch?'

'That's what they call them. The ones who use the world in a different way.'

'Well I don't know. But I do know that something unexplainable has happened and the only thing that can possibly explain it, is something… illogical.'

'I highly doubt your suspicions. Witches are hardly concerned with the workings of mortal folk. They have far more *meaningful* things to be doing.'

'There's nothing else that will explain it. And I would have come round to my senses, but now I've met you. A talking cat! If you can talk… then… We have to do something,' said Cassandra.

'*We?*' said Balthazar.

'We?' said Niclas.

We, said the Witchhunter, somehow with his eyes alone.

'Yes. You have to help me. If people see you talking the way you are, it will defy the Realm of Logic. It will unwrite The Curriculum. Everything would have to change. Everything! The laws, the way we write the laws, our very understanding of the laws. Your ability to talk is magnificent. It's revolutionary – extraordinary. And it's proof that Rufus is innocent.'

''Ang on,' said Niclas, who had been following remarkably well, 'who's Roofas?'

'You want me to do what exactly, walk into the Academy and say "how'd you do?"'

'Yes. Something like that.'

'Well, I'm not going to do that,' said Balthazar, grinning.

'Why not?'

'Because, girl, I'm not an idiot. Besides, politics doesn't concern me. I find the whole thing quite unpleasant and unattractive.'

'That's outrageous. You have a duty to your Queen?'

'She's not my Queen,' said the cat.

'But… you have to help me… you're the only ones who understand?'

'Look,' said Balthazar, 'if I were you, Princess, I'd want to get as far away from this city as I could. Something is rotten in Laburnum. If they were planning on sending you to the Halls of Atonement, then something is very rotten indeed.'

'I command you to help,' said Cassandra, firming up.

'You cannot command me.'

'I just did.'

'No you didn't.'

'I'll expunge your crimes. Have you made heroes of the Empire.'

'Thank you, but no thank you.'

'Is it gold you want?'

'Not a penny.'

'What is it then?'

'I've told you. I want no part in your trouble. As soon as we've docked, you will go your way and we shall go ours.'

Silence.

Then…

'Who's Roofas, again?' said Niclas.

'This is ridiculous. Absolutely ridiculous.' It's difficult to storm off when you're on a boat, so Cassandra just turned her back, folded her arms and gave a very dissatisfied "HMPH!".

'I knows this bit,' said Niclas. 'I grew up round 'ere.' He brightened; glowing with excitement, nostalgia, and probably a bit of *anaemia*.

The others couldn't see why he was suddenly so chuffed.

The water was murkier and dirtier, similar to the river in the sewers. The buildings were worn out, under siege from dust and dirt with broken windows, collapsed walls, and roofs of malicious tiles threatening anyone passing under them.

It was a canvas of destitution; as if an artist had captured all the depression and poverty of the slums in pastel shades of grey and brown…

…then used it as toilet paper…

…stood on it a few times…

…then a dog had come along and peed on it.

'Ah, 'ome sweet 'ome.'

'*You're a slum boy?*' remarked the Princess, a touch insulted

'Yes miss. Bred and born.'

'Well that explains a lot.'

'Whatchya mean that explains a lot?'

'Never mind.'

The boat floated into a wide expanse of water; one of those little lakes where canals come to meet and trade their grotty secrets. It floated on the dead surface, as still as stillness; a harmony of boat

and water. Then the bow struck the stone wall and scraped painfully along its port side for a good four feet.

KERRRRRRRRRRECHHH!

THUD!

'At last. I was beginning to get sick,' said Balthazar.

The cat proceeded to disembark but the cold muzzle of the
Witchhunter's gun stopped him.

'What are you doing?' said the cat, half laughing, half fretting.

'Keeping my promise,' replied the man.

''Ey, gov?' said Niclas

'Get out of the boat, boy. And you girl.' The Witchhunter kept
his unyielding stare on the cat, waiting for him to make any sudden move that would justify pulling the trigger.

Cassandra was first to go. She stood, gained her balance on the
rocking water and stepped onto the land.

'Boy,' said the Witchhunter, in the kind of way that only needed
to be said the once.

Niclas didn't move.

'Get off.'

'You wouldn't kill me like this would you, in front of them?'
said Balthazar.

'Why?' asked Niclas. 'Wot you doin' gov? We're all in this togever? Ain't we?'

'He's a witch, boy. Don't think he's your friend. He's got plans
for you. For your body.'

Cassandra was quiet for the first time since leaving the Academy, she didn't know the Witchhunter, and didn't know if he
might shoot them all if the wind changed.

'*Boy–*'

'No, gov, I ain't gonna get off the boat. If you wanna shoot me
master, then… well… you're gonna 'av' t'shoot me too.' This surprised everyone, especially Niclas, who, fearing his shaky words
wouldn't be taken seriously without some sort of action, moved

himself between the cat and the gun.

The Witchhunter cocked the pistol.

Whether the boy knew something the others didn't or was just plain stupid, he didn't move and wasn't going to until Balthazar said:

'Get off the boat, Niclas.'

'Wot?'

'Just get off the boat.'

'But, sir, this gen'l'man means to shoot you.'

'Do as I say, boy,' said the cat.

Like most instructions on route to Niclas' frontal lobe, this took a few moments to sink in. When it did, Niclas nodded, and stepped out of the boat to join Cassandra on the side.

The cat and the Witchhunter stared each other down.

Of course, Balthazar could handle this, or at least he would have been able to if he'd been alone. It was important, he knew, for Niclas to have complete trust in him, otherwise the ritual wouldn't work. So there could be no tricks.

It was a fair fight.

Except it wasn't.

Because the Witchhunter had a gun.

'I guess you were right,' said the cat. 'You would be the one to do it.'

Many a philosopher has endeavoured to answer what makes humans, human. Here, as witnessed by three pairs of eyes and countless rats, lay one of those baffling moments. An unexplainable moment. A human moment. They are the moments when morality is placed above logic and when madness is justified. For the Witchhunter had been desperate to prove Balthazar was a witch, and now that he was sure of it, he was set on doing as he did to all witches he encountered. Yet now, faced with no obstacle in his path but the strength to pull a trigger, he was stopped. Not by a Black Science, nor reason, but by the swelling tears of a young boy.

'...*Please, mister... don't do it,*' said Niclas, in a breaking voice. '*'E's me friend... And I only gots the one see...*'

Who knows what went through the Witchhunter's mind at that precise moment. But something moved him.

He looked to Niclas then to Balthazar; angry, mostly with himself. He stood, gun still pointed at the cat, and backed out of the boat.

'Come on, let's stop this childish behaviour shall we? You're not going to shoot me,' said Balthazar, provoking the last of the Witchhunter's blood lust.

But no blood was shed.

With a weighty push of his boot, the Witchhunter sent the boat floating away.

'No! Sir! Sir!' cried Niclas, rushing to the edge of the water to catch the rope.

But it was too late.

The boat drifted out and its bow rope slithered into the murky canal.

'Why'd you do that, gov?' asked the boy. ''E never 'urt no one. 'E was only ever good to me. Why'd you do it? Wot's wrong wiv ya. Ain't you got a 'eart–'

'Do you know the way to the Narrows?' asked the Witchhunter.

'Balfazar! Balfazar!' Niclas ran along the path after his master, but no reply came back, and soon, the cat and the boat were swallowed by the misty miasma of filth and fog that clung to the top of the water.

'*Balfazaaaaar!*'

'The Narrows, boy?'

'I don't care 'bout yer stinkin' Narrows. You're cold, gov, cold. Proper cold. Never known someone so cold. Wot 'e ever do to you anyway? Nuffin' – 'e did nuffin'.'

Niclas delivered a barrage of insults and when they failed to work on the emotionless man, resorted to violence, kicking and beating at the man's body, with blows that looked to Cassandra as vicious as a rabid dog's wrath, but to the Witchhunter were nothing more than prods and pokes. But everyone soon gets frustrated by incessant prods and pokes no matter how trivial they are. The Witchhunter twirled his pistol around in his hand so that he gripped the barrel and cracked Niclas over the head with the butt. The boy fell on his arse. Blood ran from his hair and into his eye, and the vein in his forehead throbbed like a second heart.

'*Stop*,' the Witchhunter said, shaking the gun threateningly. 'You are a fool. A great fool. He was using you, boy! You don't have to believe me. You don't have to understand it. I hope one day you will, but I don't give a rat's hole what you think now. I need you to show me to the Narrows. You will take me there, boy, or moons collide, I'll beat the directions out of you.'

Niclas stood, holding his head, his eyes fearfully watching the Witchhunter's hands. He was used to beatings, and had completely forgotten this fact until just then. He remembered the Bowler Gang, Mr K, and his life before meeting Balthazar, the life he was now destined to return to.

He said nothing, turned and dragged his feet towards the shabby buildings.

The Witchhunter followed.

'Wait! Where are you going?' said Cassandra chasing after them. 'Excuse me? Excuse me? *I said excuse me!*'

The Princess had never seen the slums, only heard of it. She knew nothing of poverty, of day by day suffering, of the crippling power hunger has over its victims; but she did know that a young girl wandering alone in that miserable place, was a question of *when* rather than *if* she would have an unfortunate encounter.

And so she trailed on behind them, deeper into the slums, until its filth and stench consumed her.

five

It is common knowledge among slum dwellers to keep well away from the Narrows. Every guttersnipe, street wench, vagrant and rat knows the tales associated with that twisted place. Some say they've heard the singing; a child's song echoing throughout the cobblestone alleys. Some tell tales of folk they once knew, who ventured down the narrow lanes and did not come back. Some say the place is a labyrinth, impossible to find your way out of. Some say Laburnum's most dangerous convicts and murders have taken up home there and murder anyone who trespasses. But there are some locals who believe a simpler truth: that the Bowler Gang spread the rumours to keep their stores of gin hidden. Niclas, of course, knew that wasn't so. For the Bowler Gang feared that dark and eerie place just as much as everyone else. The gang's thugs were the meanest and toughest of men, capable of the cruellest crimes, but they seldom mentioned the Narrows in conversation. They ignored the frequent disappearances and strange sightings, and not one of them dared walk down its streets.

Niclas hadn't thought much about the Narrows. Like most

things, it wasn't worth thinking about. The slum boys liked to whisper and gossip and make up stories. But stories like that troubled him, so, as with most things that troubled him, he ignored them. Life was simpler that way. But now he was having to face those stories.

He led the Witchhunter and the Princess deeper into the slums, to where the streets began to shrink, to where they were darker, tighter and quieter. Soon there was only the sound of their steps, and the sound of the ghostly wind, and the sound of dripping gutter drains…

…and of course, the sound of…

'If I may, I'd like to clarify something,' said Cassandra, 'after you've done whatever it is that you're going to do, what is it you plan to do with us?'

The Witchhunter paid no attention to the girl. He focused ahead, watching Niclas.

'If it's gold you require, I'm sure my mother will pay a great sum should you take me to the Royal Palace.'

'I'm not holding you here, girl, you're free to go. Stop pestering me.'

Cassandra looked around at the broken windows, the damp festered walls and the debris and garbage that littered the floor.

'The thing is: I don't really know where here is, and I think it would be rather foolish of me to go around this part of the city by myself.'

'If it's company you're after, girl, you best be quiet,' the Witchhunter said, increasing his pace and leaving the Princess shunned.

'*Girl?*' she said, exasperated, standing on the spot in the hope they wouldn't leave her behind.

But they would have, so she ran after them.

'What's so special about this Narrows place?' she asked.

'Ain't nuffin' special 'bout it, miss,' said Niclas, broodingly. It was the first time he'd said anything in a long time.

'Then why are we going there?'

No one deigned to answer. This infuriated Cassandra who was beginning to get frustrated by the lack of respect some people could show a member of the Royal Family. She was quite ready to grab Niclas by the collar and shake him from his melancholy, when, suddenly, he stopped walking.

He just stood there, staring down the twisted alleyways that led into the Narrows. His bowels loosened, his stomach twisted, his knees rattled.

At that moment he would have traded anything to see Mr K and his fellow thugs again; for beat him they would, but it would be a lot better than this.

'What is it?' asked Cassandra, not quite seeing what all the fuss was about.

''Ere you are, gov. That down there is wot you's looking for,' said Niclas.

The Witchhunter reached into his coat and grasped his pocket watch; the same watch Niclas had seen him studying at the Queen's Garter.

'What time is it?' asked Cassandra.

The Witchhunter raised an eye to the Princess. He tossed her the watch. She fought at the air to catch it, pulled back the lid and both she and Niclas stared into its chamber. Animated expressions of intrigue and disgust appeared on their faces. Behind the glass was a tiny lump of flesh, which looked like a piece of diced kidney from one of Martha's stews. It was dry and had the appearance of death. But there was something else – it had started to bleed.

'How grim,' said Cassandra, holding it away from view. Niclas grabbed the timepiece for further examination.

'Wot is it?' he asked.

'A *necrocardium*,' said the Witchhunter, pulling out his guns to check they were loaded and untampered with.

'A necrowotium?'

'A dead heart.'

'That's a heart?' said Cassandra.

'A piece of one,' said the man.

'How monstrously grim!'

'Wot's it for?' asked Niclas.

'It tells me the Black Science is near.'

'How?' said Cassandra.

'Black Science makes it bleed.'

Niclas remembered his first encounter with the Witchhunter at the Queen's Garter. He had been looking at his watch and holding it up just like people did with compasses.

'Its range is limited,' said the man.

His adjustments made, the Witchhunter held out his hand for the watch, received it from the boy's sweaty palms and studied it closely.

'What is this Black Science?' said Cassandra.

'Means there's a witch. At least one.'

'Round 'ere? 'Ow you gonna find it?' Niclas asked, an air of concern lingering in his voice. He was beginning to wise up about these sorts of things.

'I'm not. You are.'

Niclas frowned.

'I need you to go in. The necrocardium will guide you.'

'Oh I see,' said Cassandra, working it out, 'you want to use him as bait.'

The Witchhunter ignored her and held the rusty pocket watch up to Niclas' chest.

Niclas took his time to think. Which was odd, because he didn't normally think about anything. But this occasion demanded some thought.

He turned his head to take in the sight of the alley. It seemed to twist and stretch further away as he looked at it. There was a breeze too, a sucking wind that pulled him in and whispered into his ears.

'Mister, I begs ya, don't make me go down there.'

The Witchhunter reached into his coat and pulled out a firearm. Niclas flinched. The gun spun around so the handle was facing the boy.

'I'll be close by,' said the man.

Niclas looked at the gun and the necrocardium. Part of him wanted to snatch the weapon and shoot the horrible man dead, but he wasn't a killer. He stood frozen, his thoughts jostling with each other.

It was Cassandra who snatched it.

'Don't be such a coward, Niclas, it's frightfully unattractive.'

Niclas stuttered. He felt like a chick, prematurely pushed from the treetops and hurtling down towards the ground. It was now or never, which probably meant splat.

He grabbed the necrocardium.

'Best let me 'av' the gun, miss.'

'Why?' said Cassandra.

'Well... Coz... I'm...'

'You're what? Have you ever fired a gun?'

'Uh...'

'Do you know how to use one?'

'Err...'

'Hmm, I think I'll hold onto it if it's all the same to you. You can hold onto that dead thing. I'm not going anywhere near that.'

Niclas agreed and gestured into the Narrows with an outstretched hand.

'Ladies first then,' he said.

'Thank you. Very polite,' said Cassandra.

As the two walked into the shadows, the Witchhunter pulled his remaining gun and tipped his hat down over his face. He knew what he was doing. It was the only thing to be done. But still, he hoped he'd not sent the two children to their deaths.

The buildings either side had faces made of doors, windows, bars and cracks. They watched the two children as they ventured deeper. It would have been silent, had the wind not crept through the winding alleys, creaking the rotten wood and slamming the open shutters. The sky above began to shrink away as the roofs closed in and the light faded to grey. There were no rats, no roaches, no lice; not a soul breathed in that foul place.

'I'm most curious to actually meet a witch,' said Cassandra, doing her excited thing again. 'I mean… I guess the cat was a witch… but he was also a cat… so not a real witch.'

'He weren't no witch, miss.'

'Well he was something. He said himself that a witch is someone who uses the world differently. He was able to talk. And he was able to find me in the Academy. Sounds like a witch to me.'

'Wot you know 'bout it?' said Niclas, bitterly.

'More than you do, I can tell you that. I've been reading up on the subject since we crossed paths in the library.'

'Wiv that book you stole?'

'Yes. That one.'

'That one you gots burned.'

Cassandra hurt a little bit.

'Look, cheer up, he's not dead. You don't have to look so glum. We'll find him. Once we've done as this gentleman wants, we'll go looking and we'll find him. We have to. Rufus' life depends upon it.'

'I'll be as glum as I like, miss, and don't you go acting like you cares, you didn't knows 'im like I did.'

'On the contrary, I do care. I care a great deal. It would be difficult for Inquisitor Sinclair to argue logicide with a talking cat, don't you think? Once we make all this public, lots of things will have to change.'

'Wot makes you fink they'll believe you?'

'Evidence. Proof. The laws of logic dictate that proof is stronger than testimony. If I can find something illogical and bring it before the Academy, it would be illogical of them to denounce it...'

Cassandra continued to ramble on about justice, logic, conspiracy, treason and other words Niclas had no understanding of until his head began to ache.

'Shush will ya!' he said.

'I beg your pardon?' Cassandra stopped, turned and raised the gun at him, shaking it like a rebuking finger. 'Don't you speak to me like that, sir.'

'I'm sorry. I meant no offence. It's just, I've come to notice, miss, that you like to talk a lot, a bit too much if you don't mind me sayin', and 'ere o' all places you shouldn't be makin' so much noise. It ain't smart.'

Cassandra's eyes inflated. There was something up ahead, lurking in the shadows, barely visible but certainly moving.

And moving towards them.

'Wot?' said Niclas. Then he noticed something else. The necrocardium that hung around his neck was now warm and a weird, black nimbus was beating out of it. His fingers picked open the lid. Inside, the glass was black with blood, the little piece of heart twitching unpleasantly within.

'Wot does that mean?' he said.

'Shh! There's something over there.'

Niclas narrowed his eyes into a stare down the alley. He couldn't really make out anything in particular. Probably because he'd never had his eyes checked, and, truth be told, was seriously in need of a pair of glasses. But what he could see, were two glowing slits of blue that seemed to be getting nearer.

Something scuttled behind them.

They spun around.

There was nothing there.

Cassandra held up the gun and wrenched the hammer back with an arduous pull.

'Mister?' Niclas called out, his voice bouncing off the empty buildings and silent cobbles.

Cassandra looked back.

The thing, whatever it was, was still there only nearer, and she could just about see that it wasn't human.

It looked like a dog.

'It's a dog. I think,' she said.

Niclas didn't reply. He didn't even move to look. His eyes were stuck on the other thing. The other thing that had come the other way.

It too was a dog, the growling from the shadows confirmed as much.

'Oh! Another one…' said Cassandra, turning.

Before they could realise just how much danger they were in, the nearest dog bared its teeth and leapt towards them.

Cassandra froze.

Niclas snatched the gun and pulled the trigger.

The shot struck the canine in its upper body sending it crumbling into a whimpering heap on the floor.

The gun's mechanism ticked bringing the next shot into line with the barrel.

'It's alright,' said Niclas, 'we gots two left.'

Cassandra didn't notice the mechanism. Her eyes were fixed on the dying dog squealing before them like a stuck pig.

'Sorry, miss, but… but it was gonna get us.'

She pushed him aside, snatched the gun, pointed it and pulled the trigger.

The second shot entered the dog's head and tore its ear off, acquainting them with its maggoty brain.

They shuddered in a cloud of gun smoke.

'It's dead,' said Cassandra.

'No, it ain't,' said Niclas.

'Yes, it is.'

The dog *was* dead. But it was also alive. Its flesh was somewhere betwixt and between, with patches of rank decay growing all over its body. The jelly in its eyes had long ago rotted away, and its ribs and organs could be seen pulsing beneath its belly. Yet, it still moved. With a shot in its body and another lodged in its skull, it got back to its feet and growled.

Cassandra raised the gun to fire the final shot. But there wasn't really any point. And now the second dog was growling down their backs.

In such situations, when faced with a pair of immortal hounds set on tearing one's throat from one's neck, there's only one thing you can do. That is to scream. Or piss your pants. But Niclas and Cassandra were both too scared for either, and so, using the last deafening shot to stagger the nearest dog, made like a pair of jackrabbits and bolted for their lives.

Niclas was faster, and not knowing the meaning of the word chivalrous, was prepared to leave Cassandra behind. He didn't know which way to run. He couldn't remember the way out. But that was the least of his worries.

The shark-like jaws were snapping at the Princess' heels, closer – closer – until their breath and spittle were beating down on her. The gun was heavy. It slowed her. She discarded it with a wild toss and the first dog tripped over it and sent the second dog rolling. The fall bought her a metre, perhaps two, but just like that they were both up and galloping down on her once again.

To outrun a pair of dogs takes some legwork. But these weren't just dogs, they were greyhounds, and as anyone who's ever been to the races knows, you can no more outpace a greyhound than you can the wind. The dogs reached their full speed, pounding over the cobblestone, legs over legs, jaws up, noses pointed.

Niclas was running as fast as he'd ever run in his life. So fast, that his feet couldn't keep up with his legs. Was it this way? Was it that way? His clunky boots caught on the cobbles, he floundered, fell and tore his knees across the floor.

He expected to see Cassandra overtake him. But she didn't. She stopped, pulled him to his feet and urged him on.

She immediately regretted this.

The first dog rounded them and blocked off the way ahead. The second dog came up behind, cutting off their retreat. They were trapped.

There was more light in this part of the Narrows. Only a fraction more, but it was enough to see the dogs clearer. The second dog was more skeletal than the first. Its rotten flesh clung to its bones like wet newspaper, and its calcareous tail twisted behind it.

Niclas and Cassandra cradled each other in their arms and faced the panting, slavering, growling sets of jaws. Cassandra imagined what her bones would sound like, crunching in the dog's salivating chops. Niclas wondered how the dog facing him would swallow him, there was almost nothing around its throat, only bone.

'Where is he?' said Cassandra, clutching tighter at Niclas' arm.

'Miss… We's done for…'

Then…

'*Castor. Pollux. There.*' The dogs stopped advancing and growled from the spot.

A man's shadow had stepped out into the alley further down.

'*That'll do,*' he said, easing the dogs into calm, and they sauntered past the children, tails wagging, to be at his side.

Now that consternation wasn't blurring their senses, they both clearly saw that the dogs were grotesquely decayed; one more so than the other. They stood panting at their master's feet. A ghostly blue nimbus seeped from their mouths and eyes.

'*GULP…*' said Niclas.

'Who are you?' demanded the Princess.

The dogs answered with a growl.

But they were growling at something else.

Something at the other end of the alley.

It was the scent of the Witchhunter. He stepped into view, his pistol held up and aiming downwind at the shadowy figure.

The children scarpered to safety behind his back.

He wasn't much of a talker. He cocked the gun with his thumb and let fly a shot.

The gun began to tick.

Niclas peered round the side of the Witchhunter's greatcoat to see where the shot had landed. When the smoke cleared he saw the figure, unhindered, take a step forward in front of his dogs.

The gun clicked…

…cocked…

…fired again.

This time Niclas saw the shot dash the shadowy man's shoulder, staggering him back a step.

He regained his stride and continued forward.

The dogs were barking.

The gun was ticking.

The shadowy man was nearing.

Cassandra, too, curious as to where the shots were going, poked her head round the other side of the Witchhunter's coat, just in time to watch the third shot flick the man's head to the side. But it didn't stop him; he snapped it back into place and began to laugh. It started as a snicker and grew into a chuckle, a sound that echoed throughout the Narrows. Then his laughter ceased abruptly and he stepped out of the shadows.

Cassandra looked away. Niclas couldn't.

The Witchhunter reloaded urgently.

He didn't have time to load three shots, just the one and rushing to do so spilt the gunpowder over his hand and onto the floor.

'Mister!' said Niclas tugging at his coat. 'Mister!'

The man was getting closer and the very sight of him was too much for Niclas to take.

His clothes were old and torn. His leathery flesh much the same. His skin, where he still had it, was a pale blue. His feet were bone, and Niclas would have guessed that his legs were too, but hidden behind baggy trousers. From his stomach to his throat, there was no skin or muscle, just the sight of rotting organs throbbing away like organic clockwork. But it was his face that was the worst of it. The upper half, hairless, had the pallor appearance of a drowned corpse. The lower half had no fabric to it at all, but for a few strands of tissue-thin flesh stretched over the throat and cheeks. And where his mouth should have been, a permanent skeletal smile housed a putrid green tongue.

Clanging in his hands was a long chain, which split at the end into two separate leads. Collars for the dogs, thought Niclas.

'*She expects you,*' said the undead man, in a splintered, inhuman voice.

The Witchhunter gave up on the gun and reached for his short sword. The two dogs barked loudly as his fingers touched the blade's handle, and calmed to a growl as he removed them.

The undead man rasped wordlessly and tossed the chain at the feet of the Witchhunter.

'*For them,*' he croaked.

It was then Niclas realised, after the usual delay, that the chain wasn't for the dogs at all.

Canal water isn't drinkable. You'd have to boil it at least three times to be safe and even then, it's still a risk. But the canal water of the slums is worse. If bottled, it can be passed off as a dark, bitter ale, until of course it's been sampled and induced an episode of the most violent vomiting imaginable. It smells pungent, *repugnant* – stagnant, like sewage, and in areas of Bog End not frequented with the passing of boats, a gelatinous skin clings to its surface.

The boat had floated to such a part of the network. It found a home underneath one of the many arched bridges and came to rest out of reach of the cobbled path on either side. Balthazar could swim. It was the germs he had a problem with. Water like that was crawling with them. Whole universes of organisms and parasites looking for their next big gig. He had discussed his options with himself and decided it was much better to stay put than to try and swim for it. Even if he was in the water for ten seconds, who knew what he could catch. King Cholera, typhoid, syphilis. No, it would only be a matter of time, he reasoned, before someone further up the canal opened a lock and got things moving again.

Or, until someone found the boat. It was a small boat. A merchant rowboat. The kind of boat that drew attention in a place like this.

He just had to wait…

…he didn't have to wait long.

'This little bugger's 'eavy considerin' 'e ain't eaten for weeks.'

'It'sth justht that you're not as thstrong asth you fink you are.'

'Funny. If you fink you're so strong, why don't you carry 'im by yourself.'

There was a pause, followed by a thud.

'I thsaid nuffin' 'bout me bein' thstrong, Clyde, you got to learn to thstop comin' to conclusthionsth. Now, 'ere, 'elp me pick 'im up.'

Balthazar peered out of the boat and observed two familiar faces on the bridge above. They were carrying what looked like a small body wrapped in linen.

'One. Two. Three. Heave.'

It splashed into the water.

'Glad that'sth done wiv,' said Archie, rubbing his hands.

''Ey look!' said Clyde.

The body that had moments before splashed into the water,

rose in a secondary splash to the surface, where it floated, face down, the linen cloth pulled away.

Archie slapped his hand over his eyes and took a deep breath. 'We've only gone 'n' forgotten the blummin' weightsth,' he said.

'I did fink that, right 'fore we tossed the little bugger in, I fawt "summin's missin' 'ere".'

'Too late now. Ah well, no one ever comesth down 'ere, and even if they did, who caresth? Just anuver dead gutterthsnipe.'

'Yeah, just anuver one innit.'

'Exthactly – but to be on the thsafe thside, we bethst not tell the bossth 'bout thisth, 'e'sth proper paranoid asth it isth. You know how he likesth to thsend them into the Narrowsth before they expiresth.'

'Never understood it meself,' said Clyde.

'Thsimple really. If you thsendsth them there, you ain't gotsth to disposthe of their bodiesth. Imagine 'ow many corpsesth would be in thisth 'ere canal, if the bossth didn't 'av' a thstrict policthy 'bout thsending the thsick onesth into the Narrowsth. It would be outrageousth. You'd 'av' damsth o' 'em – a problem like that could attract plenty o' unwanted attenthion. People don't mind it thso much when bratsth disthappear, but if they thstart piling up in the water worksth, then questionsth 'av' got be asthked.'

Clyde nodded, uncertainly. 'You know Archie, you'd be best off avoiding words with too many esses…'

'Thshut up.'

Balthazar heard them walk away above him. Then the steps came back.

'That's strange,' said Clyde.

'Huh?'

'This 'ere boat – it's a merchant one. Funny place to park. Got some stuff in it by the looks o' fings,' said Clyde, noting the sacks and boxes. 'Probably summin valuable.'

Archie perked up at the word "valuable".

'Valuable,' he repeated.

The two headed down to the path and began searching for something they could use to bring the boat nearer. Amongst the furry green stone at the water's edge, Archie found a rope. He lifted it from the water. It surfaced, covered in algaeous icicles. He pulled it through his hands, loosened a bit off and tossed it at the boat's stern.

It missed.

He tried again.

'Go on, Archie! You can do it! 'av' another go! This time for sure... no, you missed it. 'Ere, let's get a go. Oh! Oh! Bravo!'

They pulled the boat in together.

'Wonder wot's in these boxes,' said Clyde, clambering aboard and landing his hands on the nearest crate.

Archie was busy fastening the boat, when he heard his companion scream and topple over against its decking.

'Wot isth it?' said Archie.

'Get it away from me! Get it away! It ain't real!'

'Wot ain't real?' Not being quenched with an answer, Archie climbed aboard the boat and saw Clyde trembling against the stern in the tiny, insignificant shadow of a black cat.

'Gentlemen,' said Balthazar.

'I don'ths believe it,' said Archie, rubbing his jagged tongue across the roof of his mouth.

'Get it away from me!' Clyde scurried away.

'Pull yersthelf togever Clyde. Wot a coincthidencthe thisth isth. We bin lookin' for you, 'n' 'ere you are. Not talkin' now are ya, eh? Wot'sth the matter, cat got your tongue.'

'There's nothing wrong with *my* tongue,' said Balthazar, scaring the life into Clyde. 'Your tongue, maybe, but not mine.'

'Kill it, Archie, moons collide, just kill it...'

'Thssshhhh. I don't know 'ow you did wot you did. Our bossth didn't 'alf believe usth when we toldsth 'im. Gave usth a right clobberin'. Thsaid we mustht 'av' bin drinkin' the merchandis-the. Thsaid we were mad. But I knowsth we weren't mad.' Archie unbuckled his club, and gave it three firm swings into the palm of his hand. 'Catsth thshouldn't be able to talk. It'sth againstht the nature o' fingsth. I'm gonna thsort you out kitty. I'm gonna thsort you out proper.'

'I don't believe you'll do any sorting of the sort,' said Balthazar.

'Oh yeah, why'sth that?'

'Don't let it talk, Archie!' said Clyde.

'It's a matter of money.'

'Wot money?'

'I want to make you a mutually beneficial proposition.'

'A wot now?'

Balthazar rolled his eyes; he had forgotten who he was talking to.

'A deal.'

'Wot kinda deal?' said Archie.

'I need to find someone – and you… you look like you could do with some new clothes.' Archie lowered his gaze to his garments, poisoned by vanity. 'Fresh, clean, lacking in moth holes.' The thug lifted his foot and stared through the loose sole at his toes. 'I can make all this a possibility.'

'Don't listen to it, Archie, 'ow many weal'fy cats do you know?'

'I suspect just as many as you know can talk,' added Balthazar.

''Oo you lookin' for?' said Archie.

Balthazar smiled, he'd felt the tug on the end of the line.

'I couldn't help but overhear you gentlemen talking about a place called… What was it now? The Narrows?'

'Wot of it?'

'Forgive me, I may not have heard you correctly, but did you say your employer is in the habit of sending dying children there?'

'You 'eard right.'

'What do you think happens to them?'

'Wot kinda questhion isth that? They die, innit.'

Again, Balthazar had forgotten how stupid people could be; and though Niclas wasn't a genius, he would have won a Nobel prize had he been competing against these two thugs.

'I think I'd like to talk to the man in charge.'

'The bossth?'

'Yes.'

'Why?'

'Because I believe he may be of use to me, and if he turns out to be even remotely useful, I shall reward you with the location of a hidden fortune.'

As dubious as they were, both Archie and Clyde couldn't resist the exciting prospect of hidden fortune; though the only fortune they would get, would be the misfortune of being eaten alive. But they didn't know that.

'It's a trick,' added Clyde.

'Please, haven't you anything constructive to say?' said Balthazar.

Archie remained silent for a moment, ruminating on the situation the way a gambler ruminates on a roulette wheel. In the end, he saw nothing bad about taking the cat to see his boss: for what harm could come of it? If the cat proved honest they would all be rich, and if it didn't then Mr K would deal with it; but either way, Mr K would see that the talking cat was indeed real – and that was reason alone to take it to him.

'Alright, you want to thspeak to the bossth, you can thspeak to the bossth.'

'Splendid,' said Balthazar, presenting Clyde with an imperious grin.

***

There are two moons in Laburnum's sky. Jarh, the closest, is so bright that it's sometimes easy to mistake for a small sun. Though not as glaring as the sun, if Jarh is full on a clear night in an open park, scholars can read their books without the need for lanterns.

The furthest moon is called Nei. Often referred to as Jarh's shadow, it is dark and harder to notice. But Nei is not altogether black, it has a unique blue glow to its celestial body; a ghostly sapphirine light.

The old saying, "moons collide", comes from the early days when people were unable to understand the passing of the moons and bi-lunar eclipses. People would gather to say their goodbyes, have a last meal and sing long into the night in the belief that they wouldn't see the morning.

This was found to be utter nonsense after a few hundred years of the same thing happening without an actual doomsday.

In modern times, most people in the Varcian Empire celebrate the day just as it was celebrated back then – though, without the animal sacrifices and a little less of the *dancing au naturel.*

During the night of the festival, people from all over the capital pour into the Brewery Quarter and its surrounding streets to drink their weight in booze. The only doomsday that comes to them, as with the ancient people, is the doom of a horrible, head thumping hangover the morning after.

Like Alchemy, Astrology and Astronomy are an unsavoury subject in the Realm of Logic. The Academy welcomes all empirical knowledge, but when things start to get a bit, out of this world, literally speaking, evidence becomes a little harder to find. Without evidence, grand theories quickly become little logical heresies. And we know what happens to people who believe illogical things.

It's extremely hard to be an academic searching for newfound knowledge in an environment that prides *THE CURRICULUM* above all.

Laars Copernicus, a philosopher of the Empire, once wrote a paper about how Jarh was spinning away from Ebb (the world) at a faster rate than Nei. He theorised that because of this, the moons would, in fact, one day, several millions of years into the future, collide. There was little empirical evidence to support his claim, but he stubbornly went around showing the paper to anyone who would read it.

Soon after, Mr Copernicus disappeared, and all trace of his life's work vanished.

Probably in a fireplace somewhere.

The moons above were approaching each other. Their glowing light began to dance in a swirl of blue aurora. The crows, ravens and pigeons of the city took flight in all directions. Below in the streets, people were rushing out to see the annual phenomenon. Most had made it to the Brewery Quarter. It was packed, rammed full of people each with a drink in hand. The Lunar Festival was in full swing and the city was in full celebration – and that meant well and truly getting smashed.

But nowhere was more sombre, quieter and felt further away from the festivities than the tight, eerie streets of the Narrows. It was through these that Niclas, Cassandra and the Witchhunter were marched; through the twisting alleys of lifeless, empty buildings.

The children didn't worry about where the dead man was leading them, they were far more concerned with the decomposing dogs, and the man's juicy organs. The Witchhunter followed obediently. He didn't know if he could take on the dead man and his dead dogs, but he knew he was being taken exactly where he wanted to be.

They came to a door and stopped. It was an oddly inviting door. It was well kept, lacquered with a fresh coat of dark blue paint.

The dead man drew from his pocket a key, unlocked and pushed the door open. He ushered his three captives inside. Cassandra didn't want to, but the growling dogs insisted.

The room beyond the door was near empty, with only a small table to fill the space. Crooked bookshelves leant slanted against each wall, like dominos that hadn't quite committed to the fall.

There were few books on their shelves. Instead, tiny glass vials of a clear, blue liquid sat upright in wooden racks. There was only a drop's worth in each vial but it glowed a bright, ghostly blue, which glistened on the floating dust particles and vacant spider webs.

Niclas was drawn towards them.

Up close the liquid didn't look like a liquid at all. It was moving, as if evaporating and condensing all at once; and as he looked even closer, he saw something which very much looked like the shape of the cosmos within the gaseous liquid. Or, as he would later describe it: the centre of a spiralled marble.

His curiosity was short lived. The dead man yanked his chain and grunted towards an open wooden stairs at the back of the room.

It was a good job Niclas was an idiot, because the stairs, and the lingering darkness above, was a terrifying thing to face. Only an idiot could have walked up it so nonchalantly.

Each step creaked like the discordant keys of a haunted piano. At the top of the noisy steps, on the next floor, an eerie blackness loomed over the boy. And in it, an abominable smell. A miasma of the same kin as the dead man, but here at the source it was almost suffocating. It was the sweet, sickly smell of death.

'What *coughcough* is that smell?' said Cassandra, fanning air over her face and doing her best to cover her mouth and nose. She knew the poorer districts of Laburnum were notorious for their stench, but this was something different altogether.

Candles were dotted around the upper room. There were tall skinny ones, fat chunky ones, some that had never been lit, some that had melted down to the bases of their holders. Only one was burning, the others were cold. Niclas noticed they all had one thing in common, that they were made from black wax.

When they were done taking note of the number of candles, they focused on the wonky wooden construction, that emerged through the dim, sparse light. Neither of them had ever seen anything like it. Had they spent more time in the Guard's Tower, or learning about torturous tools, they might have recognised it. It was a pillory – a set of stocks – a wooden frame meant to shackle a man.

The dead man moved towards it, lifted its top and grunted for the Witchhunter to come closer. There was no point in resisting, so the Witchhunter rested each of his wrists on the grooves and lowered his neck. The top was slammed down and fastened with locks and a rusty old key that hung at the living corpse's belt.

As soon as the Witchhunter was locked in, the two dogs tamely entered their cages at opposite sides of the room. The dead man unshackled Niclas from the chafing collar and manoeuvred him into one.

Castor welcomed him with a hospitable growl.

The bars were pulled across.

'I am not getting in there. You can do what you like, but I am not–' Cassandra objected, but the dead man, not being at all considerate, yanked her towards him by the chain, clipped it loose, and, clutching the back of her neck, shoved her into the cage with Pollux.

'Where's your handler?' said the Witchhunter.

The dead man pretended not to hear. Or perhaps he didn't hear? Both his ears were rotten, just holes in the side of his decaying head.

Then the witch came to play.

Music began to sound from above and the floorboards creaked. It wasn't the music of an instrument, it was the music of a humming woman. Her song was melodic and innocuous, the kind of innocent tune that sounds just like pure evil.

Two withered shoes danced down another set of creaky wooden steps at the back of the room. A moth-eaten dress followed. Above it, a bird's nest of unnaturally pink, frizzy hair. The nonchalance of the song matched the woman's mood: cheerful and distracted.

They had all expected an old woman. A hag. A crone. A long, twisted nose, a pair of purple prune lips, razor sharp teeth, monstrous red eyes, hands with fingernails the length of knives. They had thought she'd be taller, bulkier, or perhaps a hunchback, grotesquely deformed. She wasn't the slightest bit of any of those things. She was scrawny, hollow cheeked, but she was beautifully human, full of colour and life. Her hair was pink and her smiling lips lipstick red. It was only her song that was warped and odd. And the way she moved. The way she danced right up to Niclas' cage and gave it a theatrical sniff.

She ain't bad lookin', he thought. Her features were all in order, her complexion flawless, her eyes bright and ripe with colour and her figure, young and buxom. There was definitely something about the way she looked, something that almost didn't look real.

She spun away, twirling over to the other cage to examine Cassandra, and did so with another eccentric sniff.

After she'd smelt both the children, she skipped to the centre of the room to stroke the Witchhunter's face.

Niclas and Cassandra met eyes. Neither dared speak.

'You're handsome,' said the witch. 'I wasn't expecting handsome. I don't know if I can do handsome. I wanted ugly, fat, bald – something natural. I mean, you're no prince. You could do with a shave – maybe a trim – and these clothes are so out of fashion. You could… no – nevermind. Or maybe if I… no – that won't work. Here to kill me? Don't answer that – I know – The Whisperer told me you'd come. I've been waiting – looking forward to you – and you've brought me two little gifts – how kind.'

She cackled. It was a rotten laugh, loud and sharp with an air of falseness to it, as if the person laughing had forgotten how to do so.

'Oh,' she said, noticing the Princess' startled face. 'How rude of me. There should be introductions of course. Well go on – what's your name then girl?'

'I'm the Princess, don't you recognise–'

'Funny name that,' pondered the witch, 'sorry, go on.'

'Don't…' Cassandra continued with added caution, 'don't you recognise me?'

The witch squinted at her, searching and searching, and looked as though she was about to get it, then said: 'No!'

'I'm royalty – the whole city is looking for me right now, it's only a matter of time before they send guards here and then you'll be in all types of trouble. You should probably let us go: if you do so now, I promise I won't speak a word of this.'

The witch stared at her, aloof. 'Trouble?' Her infectious smile returned. 'I like trouble. Toil and bubble; how goes it? You're cute. I like you. I like your fleshy tongue even more.' This was perhaps one of the oddest compliments Cassandra had ever received. The witch, keeping her eyes on the girl's mouth, spoke over her shoulder to the dead man: 'Greg, do we need another tongue?'

'*Mine works just fine, mistress,*' he rasped.

She turned back and sighed. 'Guess we don't need another tongue. Shame. I like yours. I might just take it anyway – got some pliers round here somewhere – can always use a spare. Do it again. Go on, say something, *Princess.*'

Cassandra, for the first time ever, was left utterly speechless. She stared across the room at Niclas.

'Why are you looking at him? Does he have a lease on the tongue? If so I'm sure he'd be open to negotiation.' The witch appeared at Niclas' cage so quickly that it made him jump back against the bars.

The dog didn't move, it was used to her capricious nature.

'And you are?' she said.

'Name's Niclas, miss.'

'Niclas. What a lovely name. How old are you Niclas?'

'Dunno, miss, I reckons five and ten years. Got told that once.'

'Five and ten years you say – I like 'em younger – usually… but there are two of you – a special gift indeed. Tell me, Niclas, do you know what night it is tonight?'

'No, miss.'

'Please, call me Susie – it's not my name, but I'd like that.'

'Sorry, miss.'

'Sorry, Susie,' said the witch.

'Sorry, Susie.'

'Hmm, actually it doesn't sound so nice now you've said it…' The witch stared around the room as if trying to recall something. Then she snapped back to the bars. 'You probably haven't noticed that I get easily distracted.'

'No, miss… Susie… not really.'

'Tonight! Tonight is special. A special, special night! Tonight's the night the moons collide. Very important. Very special. Very good. Very – significant. To celebrate this spectacular event, we're going to have a tea party. Do you like tea parties? You know – with games, and dancing, and cake – a party isn't a party without cake. Do you like cake?' A stiff silence filled the room whilst Niclas determined whether the question was rhetorical or not.

It wasn't.

'I fink so, miss Susie…'

'Think so? You don't know so? How so? Why so? Surely you've had cake before so?' said the witch.

'Uhh… not that I knows about, miss Susie…'

'Oh! You poor, poor, poor, little insignificant speck of life,' said the witch, reaching into his cage and stroking him as though he were one of the dogs. 'I'll bake up something nice, just you see. No soggy bottoms here.'

The witch was noticeably neurotic, and she was only getting

worse. She began opening cupboards and drawers and knocking bits and pieces off shelves, spouting the odd, 'nope,' and 'not here,' as she did so. Her eyes seemed to dart about the room as if unconnected to her thoughts. She scratched her head frequently, sometimes pulling out whole clumps of hair, and Cassandra reasoned that the crimson nail polish was probably not nail polish at all but blood.

'Oh where is it! Where is it! ARGH!' Suddenly she didn't seem so ditsy. She was angry. Enraged. She reached for the nearest jar – full of badly preserved eyeballs – held it close to her chest for a tranquil moment, then rattled it up and down vigorously before smashing it into the wall.

She stood, post tantrum, looking down and breathing deeply through her teeth. Greg knew just what to do. He picked up a broom and swept the rolling eyes, broken glass and amniotic fluid into a pile. The children didn't blink.

'I guess cake's off the menu!' She perked up. 'Ah well – maybe another time – of course there won't be another time because you're all going to die. Now, how about some dancing.'

At once, she began twirling anticlockwise around the Witchhunter, singing to herself and laughing mercurially.

Cassandra had never actually seen a mad person. This was certainly one. The epitome of madness.

The witch danced for a good few minutes, grabbing Greg by the hand and spinning herself around. 'Oh, you're still a gen'l'man,' she said, wiping a spurious tear from her eye.

Then she came to a sudden standstill.

'Bored,' she said. 'Bored of dancing. Some tea party this is turning out to be. No cake. No tea. No one to dance with… Ok then – on to games,' she said. 'Do you know what our first game is going to be, Niclas?'

Niclas shook his head, he couldn't remember being more scared in all his life. Not by the rotting man nor by the fleshless dog in his cage. There was simply no way of knowing what she was going to do next, and that petrified him.

'We're going to play piñata. Do you know how to play piñata?'

'…No… miss… I mean… Susie.'

'You smack the piñata over and over and over and over and over and over again. Until its insides become its outsides and its outsides become its insides. Then you get to eat all the delicious sweets inside.'

'…'

'All we need is a piñata… Hmmm, let's see… ah! There we are. You, sir,' she said, approaching the Witchhunter in the stocks. 'You look like a fine piñata to me, if you don't mind me saying. And the insides will be sweet so sweet to taste. Greg, let us show our guests how fun games can be – they're looking a bit bored if you ask me – must impress.'

The dead man walked slowly up to the Witchhunter and stood in front of him. He tightened his bony fist with a joint crackling sound, raised it and punched him square in the nose.

Then he drew back and punched him again…

Niclas and Cassandra couldn't watch, but both dogs growled until they looked up.

The third blow split his eyebrow.

They thought it would stop, but it didn't. The hard, wet, thudding sounds continued.

Over and over and over.

The streets of Bog End were a sad and miserable place. There weren't many people, and the few that could be seen were sat wrapped in lice infested blankets, spluttering and wheezing. They could easily be mistaken for beggars, but they weren't beggars. These were a people stripped of everything, but most of all they were stripped of hope – and hope, is pretty important when it comes to begging.

The hopeless vagrants just sat there, staring at the two thugs and the cat. Some of the blighted slum dwellers made efforts to cross to the other side of the street or head inside the dilapidated buildings. The Bowler Gang hats had a reputation here. Archie and Clyde wore them like crowns, their heads held high, their chests puffed out. Here they weren't just thugs or common criminals. They were kings.

There were more rats nearer the warehouse than people. The worm tailed creatures piled over each other to watch the thugs arrive with their feline guest.

Balthazar shuddered. He wasn't welcome, and the people as well as the rats were all thinking the same thing. Which was: "Cor, blimey! There's a lot of meat on that cat.".

Archie rapped his knuckles on the warehouses' rusty, metal door.

''Oo is it?' asked a child from the other side.

'Open up,' said Archie.

The rusty latch slid across and the door opened, revealing a scrawny looking boy whose blistered feet produced a smell that was so potent, it drowned out all the other wretched smells.

Balthazar scowled at the stench.

'Move asthide, Montsth, we got busthinessth to attend to,' said Archie, pushing past. 'Where'sth Mr K at?'

The boy gave the cat a curious stare. It wasn't like Archie and Clyde to have a pet; and even so, he'd always took them for dog people, big scary dog people, certainly not cat people.

'Dealin' wiv a client just this minute.'

'Righto,' said Archie hanging his moth-eaten jacket on a broom.

The boy couldn't take his eyes from the cat's, he tilted his head left to right and watched as it mirrored his movements.

'Wot's wiv the cat, sir?' he asked.

'None o' your beesthwax, now, clear off 'fore I thset Clyde on you.'

Clyde, who normally relished such opportunities to beat children, evinced that he wasn't himself, remaining quiet – troubled by Balthazar's presence.

'Sorry, sirs,' said Monts, running away to join the other children, who had all risen from their beds on the floor to see what was going on.

'Thisth way,' said Archie, gesturing that Balthazar follow him, which of course he did, igniting a curious bout of whispering and giggling among the children.

On the outside, the warehouse was an uninhabitable, shabby building, made of rotten bricks and broken windows. But within its high walls, it sheltered at least two dozen dirty faced boys – each and every one of them doomed to a life of hardship and misery, a life which mercifully wouldn't be long.

They huddled behind the crates and barrels of gin, watching Balthazar as he was led deeper into the building, ducking when either one of the thugs looked round, and creeping on when they looked back.

Balthazar wondered what kind of clients Mr K would have. When he saw, he realised that such a horrible man could only have one kind of client: the desperate. For the client alluded to by the child with the smelly feet, was the most desperate of men. He was a thin, twig shaped man, whose every sentence was accompanied by a cough and whose only wish in all of life was for a small bottle of Speckled Gin to help him on his way. So desperate was he for the bottle in Mr K's hands, that he had brought his own son to exchange.

'This skinny runt ain't worth the bottle it's in,' Mr K was saying.

'I begs you *cough*, I begs you, Mr K, please take 'im in, show 'im a good life – 'e's a strong boy – looks small but 'e's strong *coughcough*.'

'Are you quick boy? Quick wiv yer 'ands?' said Mr K.

The trembling boy didn't know what to say, he looked to his decrepit father for an answer and was given an eager nod.

'I fink so...'

'Fink so?' Mr K, not impressed by the conferring going on, snorted, filled his mouth with spit, then spat at the father's raw feet.

He tossed the bottle to the boy.

The boy's hands fumbled in the air. His father's face twisted. The bottle fell and was caught.

'Good reflex, boy,' said Mr K.

The boy smiled. He couldn't believe his catch.

'See *cough*, 'e's useful *coughcough*.'

'Quick 'e might be, but useful, let's not push it. Go on boy, give yer father the bottle 'n' go 'n' join the others.'

The boy was sad to go, but knew it was for the best. It was a blessing to be brought into the company of the Bowler Gang. He held out the bottle to his elated father, who snatched it without giving him the slightest thank you or goodbye.

'Get out o' 'ere, 'fore I change my mind,' said Mr K; and with that, the transaction was done; the child joined the others, the desperate man's thirst was quenched, and Mr K turned his attention to the patient Archie and Clyde.

'Wot is it? Why you just standin' there?'

'Bossth, we've got you a visthitor,' said Archie.

'A wot now?'

'A visthitor.'

'It's... it's...' Clyde tried.

'Thshut it, Clyde. Remember the talkin' cat we toldsth you 'bout? The one thshacked up with little Nick? Well, thisth 'ere'sth it.' Archie stepped aside to reveal the black cat. ''E wantsth to talk thsome busthinessth with ya.'

Mr K sharpened his eyes and scrunched up his brow, if just one more second of silence had gone by, he would have snatched Clyde's club and beaten the two of them dead.

But the cat spoke.

'Good evening,' said Balthazar.

The children gasped behind the barrels, giving their position away.

Archie and Clyde looked at one another, uncertain of what was going to happen next.

Balthazar waited.

What ensued was unexpected by all.

Mr K didn't lose his temper, nor his mind, he remained perfectly composed – a manner which Balthazar found most suspicious.

'Archie, Clyde,' said the cruel man at last.

'Yes bossth?' Archie stuttered.

'I want them kids beaten, beaten till their backsides run red.'

At this, the scampering of a dozen terrified children sounded from behind the barrels and crates.

'Yes, boss,' said the two thugs.

'You best come into my office,' said Mr K, and he turned and walked away.

Balthazar wasn't one to be afraid, he'd encountered much worse men and women in his life than the Bowler Gang's boss. But something about this man was unsettling.

He followed.

Mr K's office lay behind a red brick archway. It was a small room, littered with bags of juniper berries, oranges and empty barrels piled up on their sides. At one end, there was a tall dusty window of little glass squares; it was fragmented and most of its glass panes were missing. Just before it, facing into the room was Mr K's ragged leather chair, and before that, his cluttered desk.

Mr K's desk was not equipped with much paper. There wasn't a book in sight and not a pen or pencil to be found. It looked instead very much like an armoury, and a menacing one at that. It was armed with two brass knuckledusters, one iron truncheon embellished with wonky nails and knobbly studs, and there was a frightful collection of knives including one butcher's cleaver that was lodged upright in the wood – and that was just a glance. Bottles were strewn amongst the deadly objects, some empty, some full, most in between. Evidently, thought Balthazar, this was a man who liked to drink, but despite the amount of booze around him, he hardly seemed intoxicated at all. To the boss of the Bowler Gang, Speckled Gin was nothing but water.

Mr K slumped into his chair, reached down and slid the footrest out from under it and through the gap between the desk.

'Take a seat,' he said.

Balthazar hopped up onto the leather cushion and sat, his head just high enough to gaze over the weapons; but not the forest of bottles, so Mr K moved a few of them to the side, clearing a path to the cat's face. Then he reached for the nearest bottle and pulled the cork out with a very satisfying PLOMP. He poured the poison down his throat, swallowed, then extended the bottle across the table.

'Drink?'

'I don't drink,' said Balthazar.

'That's unfortunate.' Mr K took another swig, completely unaffected by the gin's notoriously crippling, sour taste. He leaned back and threw his boots up. They weren't particularly nice boots, like everything in this part of town they were old and dirty. But there was very little mud on their underside. This suggested to Balthazar that either Mr K was very thorough on the welcoming mat or that he simply just didn't get out that much.

'To wot do I owe the pleasure then?'

Balthazar peered round the boots.

'You don't seem particularly bothered by my talents.'

'Wot talents?'

'My talking talents.'

'I've seen many fings, trust me, you ain't nuffin' compared.'

'And what sort of things have you seen, I wonder?'

Mr K sat studying the cat and stroking his scar. He wasn't in the mood to elaborate.

'Interesting fashion statement,' said Balthazar. 'M for murderer. T for thief. I wonder, what does K stand for?'

'You wonder too much. You wanna talk business, let's talk business.'

'Very well. What's your business with the Narrows.'

Mr K gave no answer, but his eyes widened ever so slightly, so slightly anyone else would have missed it, but not Balthazar.

The thug resisted the urge to look out the window behind.

'Why?' he asked.

'Just wondered, that's all.'

'Be careful cat. I can't be swindled and I ain't no gen'l'man.'

'Believe me, I never took you for one.'

'Don't fink yous a guest 'ere either. You're gonna speak what you've gotta speak, then I'm gonna cut your paws off, skin ya and turn ya into a soup.'

'What a lovely idea,' said Balthazar, 'I hope you'll use a lot of salt and pepper, I'm probably quite chewy.'

Mr K swung his boots from the table and lurched forward.

'You know,' continued the cat, 'you shouldn't assume I'm clueless to what's going on here. I find it strange that you would set up your enterprise so close to such a place as this Narrows place seems to be. I've heard about you sending children into it, that's also a source of great wonder. But what's got me wondering even more is that in this day and age, in this city, a man can talk face to face with a cat without the faintest glint of trepidation in his eye.'

'You've a lot to say, ain't ya?'

'Funny that, I don't think you're saying enough.'

Mr K took another protracted gulp from the bottle, and let the gin slide down his throat to warm his insides.

''Ow's Nicky? Lyin' dead in a gutter somewhere?'

Balthazar certainly hoped not, but didn't want to play all his cards just yet.

'I didn't believe 'em 'bout you,' said the thug. 'I fawt the lad 'ad done a runner 'n' them two was too scared to tell me the troof. Told me you beat 'em up. Ha! So I beat them up. You cost me one o' my employees. More than that. *One o' my boys*. I put a roof over 'is bleedin' 'ead for a good ten years. And he repays me by eloping with some furry animal. He best be dead, I tell ya.'

'You talk as if you were doing him a favour,' said Balthazar, finding the idea that a man like Mr K could care about the little creatures he worked to death night and day just a tad amusing.

'Same story. Mother didn't want 'im. A little hungry mouth is a dear expense. I don't know where you're from but round 'ere they chuck 'em out on the street like chamberpots. O' course they try 'n' silence 'em before they come into this world. My gin's good for that. Mother's Ruin they call it. But some o' 'em always get through. And wot a world they come into eh? A nasty, spittin' world. I'm an opportunist. I gives 'em opportunities.'

Balthazar listened, then gave a slow nod. 'If you say so,' he said.

But Mr K was tiring of the chit chat. He put down the bottle and ran his hands over the weapons on his desk, drawing them close to the cleaver.

'I don't fink me and you are on the same page of fawt. I've been more than reasonable and given you a chance to talk your business wiv me. Now I'm–'

'I want you to tell me everything you know about the Narrows. In exchange, I will divulge the location of a rather large stash of gold,' said Balthazar.

For some reason unknown to the cat, this amused Mr K and set him off leaning backwards, quietly laughing to himself.

'Gold is it?' he said. 'And wot will you suppose I spend it on?'

'Whatever you want. Whatever a man of your taste desires.'

Mr K paused. Smiled. Stopped smiling. He took another swig of his poison.

'Let me give you an education. 'Ere in the slums, people ain't livin' on the breadline – we live far below it – on a line that exists somewhere above dead and somewhere below livin' – sufferin' with every breath we take. Now I like a bit o' shiny just as much as the next man, but I'm curious as to why I'd need gold – when right here, I gots a livin', breathin', speakin' fortune right in front o' me.'

'I don't follow,' said Balthazar, watching like a fearful pigeon as the thug rose out of his chair and walked around the desk.

'I 'ad to work me way up in this city I did. I was one o' 'em boys once. No hope. No future. No one to look out for me. I gave poor buggers like meself a chance to make summin o' 'emselves. I gave 'em summin to live for. And you know how I was repaid?'

Balthazar shrugged.

'To the gallows they said. So I's exiled. I ain't been norf o' the river for sixteen stinkin' years. Sixteen stinkin' years I been rottin' away in this 'ole.'

Mr K had a brooding expression drawn across his scarred face. He lifted a sack of juniper berries and poured them through his open hand.

'It was 'ard, makin' a name for meself at first – gettin' the business up 'n' runnin'. But when I 'eard 'bout the Narrows and 'eard the stories, I knew it was meant for me. See I feared it, I feared it just like all them other buggers. But I knew if I was ever gunna be anyfin', ever gunna establish meself proper, I'd 'av' to show I 'ad guts.'

The bag had run empty, and Mr K was now fluffing it out with both his hands.

'I remember it well, the day I went there to see for me own eyes wot was causin' all the upset; wot was going on there; wot was the source of all 'em rumours.'

'What?'

Balthazar didn't see it coming. He had been lulled into a false sense of security listening to the thug speak, and when it happened, it happened fast. One moment, he was listening intently to the thug's every word, trying to see where the conversation was going. The next, he was struggling for air, plucked at the neck by Mr K's rough hands.

The thug's grip was tight enough to stiffen his whole body.

'She's gonna like you,' he said. He held the cat out in the air, tilting him like a specimen and admiring his liveliness. 'Oh yes, she's gonna like you lots.'

Then, just like that, Balthazar was stuffed into the sack.

Jarh began to move over the face of Nei.
The street dogs howled.
The alley cats yowled.
The night brightened in a blue, iridescent glow.
A midnight sun was beginning to show.

By now the Witchhunter's face was hideously bruised. Both his eyes were black and one was swollen up like a raisin. The skin over the bridge of his nose was cut. Blood had run from each nostril and from his mouth, and it was matted in his stubble, smeared over his cheeks, down his neck and the collar of his shirt. Though, it was likely the blood was not all his. Greg had been hitting him without respite and with such ferocity that it was hard to see whose blood was whose.

The witch had been laughing to herself all the while, giggling and snickering, with the occasional outburst of laughter that was sudden enough to make the children jump.

The Witchhunter had tried to hold his nerve. He was a man who was used to holding his nerve. But there came a point where the pain was too much, and at that point, fearing he would lose consciousness if he did nothing, he let out a long protracted scream. It was an angry sound. A manly groan that made Niclas shudder and Cassandra close her eyes.

'Oh,' said the witch, 'how beautiful. What a lovely thing it is. Your pain. Your hate. Your impotence to do anything about it. I find it greatly satisfying.'

The witch moved between the dead man and the Witchhunter and leaned in in the hope to look into his eyes. But the Witchhunter wouldn't look at her. He looked anywhere but. So she grabbed his face by its chin and wrenched it up so she could peer into his swollen, blood encrusted eyes.

'Such a pity. So weak. So helpless.'

The Witchhunter spat his bloody spittle at her face, but it fell short and landed on her shoulder. She grinned, and turned her head to appreciate it; and he looked past her, to the keys dangling at Greg's waist.

'Oh, did you hear that?' she said, pulling away and putting her hand to her ear. Niclas hadn't heard anything, but he hoped it was someone who had come to save them.

It wasn't.

'It's the Whisperer. Yes, I heard the Whisperer. The Whisperer whispers.'

Cassandra remembered something. She thought hard about it. The Whisperer. The one who whispers. It was written in the Zolnomicon but when she tried to remember, she found she couldn't.

The witch rambled on.

'Ah yes! The Whisperer whispers! He whispers to us now. Can you hear him? Do you hear the messenger of Kaos? Can you hear his whispers?' She moved from one part of the room to another, listening to the walls and ceiling as if there was something there too quiet for the others to hear. Then she rushed over to the Witchhunter and cackled right into his ear. Then she ran her slippery tongue over her lips, brought them closer, so they touched his lobe and whispered something to him.

'I'm going to kill you,' the Witchhunter whispered back, loud enough for the children to hear.

'Oh?' said the witch, stepping back. 'You've had your chance, I'm afraid. But I saw it coming. Because I can see more than eyes can see. The Whisperer sees for me, and he whispers sweet whispers to me. He told me you'd come. He said you'd bring gifts. Oh, when I heard the news I was so ecstatic, I got this old set of stocks just for you – well, Greg got it, I couldn't possibly carry it, haven't got the strength in me these days. But never mind that – the point is – I said to Greg, I said, "he'll have so much fun in this," and you are right? You're having the best time, aren't you? We're all having such a wonderful tea party, aren't we? And to think! We don't even have any cake.'

No one dared speak.

'No? No one enjoying themselves?' the witch gave a last grin at each of the children, then turned her smile into a sour glare. 'Fun bunch.'

She rummaged through the pouch at the front of her dress. Out came a hammer, which she threw aside, a pair of pliers, which she displayed to Cassandra, a mouldy piece of bread, which she tried to sneak back in, and a box of matches, which she shook with excitement.

'It's almost time for rituals. We need the candles to be lit. Greg, candles.' The matches landed on the floor beside Greg, who bent down to collect them and set about lighting each wick in the room.

'Excuse me…' the Princess started.

The witch pounced on her cage and set Pollux off barking.

'Woof! Woof! Woof!' the witch barked back, rattling the bars. '*Oh do shut up you silly mutt.* Yes my dear?'

'I just want to know what you're planning to do with us, that's all.'

'Yes? You would wouldn't you? I guess we'll have to see which of you the Whisperer wants the most… *Take your time Gregory the moons last forever I hear.'*

The witch seemed to have two voices and two faces as if two personalities were tightly wrapped around one another within her. Cassandra guessed the snappier, angrier voice was the true voice.

Greg moved quicker, lighting the candles twice as fast.

Now there was some more light, it drew Niclas' attention to the chalk circle and the black candles surrounding it, and the slab of stone that lay at the centre. It was a similar design to the ones Balthazar had asked him to chalk out on the floorboards of the Queen's Garter. There was something else too. Within it, a long, bronze needle with a thick, engraved end. It looked like a snake with a tongue that narrowed into a blade. It was more a dagger than a sewing needle.

'Let's see who's the ripest, shall we?' The witch snatched up the blade and closed in on Cassandra. She tried to scurry out of reach, but Pollux was there, jaws drooling.

The witch reached through the bars, grabbed the girl's neck and pulled her face to the cold steel. Then, to the Princess' horror, she brought the needle to her hand, then her thumb, and pricked it.

'OW!'

'Good blood this. Very red. Much haemoglobin,' said the witch, carrying the crimson droplet to a bowl of water. She let it fall in.

Then she was at Niclas' cage.

'Come here, boy – come on – don't be shy.'

Niclas didn't want to move, and wouldn't have if Castor hadn't have barked.

'Hand,' demanded the witch.

He stuck it through the bars and closed his eyes, hoping that she'd do no worse than what she'd done to the Princess. And she didn't. She took a delicate prick at his thumb and carried the blood carefully, on the tip of the blade, across the room and into the bowl.

Then she stood watching as the two bloods spread like smoke in water.

'Hmm,' she pondered. 'That's most astonishing, two lives from two sides and who do we find has the thicker thread? Not what I expected at all, I have to say.'

The two children caught eyes, selfishly hoping against one another.

The witch fixed her glare on Niclas.

'Wot? Wot does it mean. Wot does that mean?'

'Ah, boy, you are most lucky. Most lucky. Alas our little tea party here has come to an end. *Now you must serve your purpose.*'

Greg lit the last candle and moved to the boy's cage to open it. Castor growled Niclas out the door and into the dead man's cold, bony hands. They manoeuvred him into the circle and onto the stone slab and pushed down on Niclas' shoulders until he collapsed.

The witch reached into her dress pocket and made a series of thoughtful expressions until her fingers found what she was searching for. An empty glass vial. She twisted off its ornate silver stopper.

'The Whisperer, who is that?' said Cassandra, abruptly.

The witch turned to notice her. 'Never you mind child. Your time will come to meet him.'

'I've read it you know, the Zolnomicon. Not all of it, but a lot. That's what this is, isn't it? Some sort of alchemy.'

'The Zolnomicon?' said the witch, pausing thoughtfully. 'Never heard of it.'

'But you're a witch, aren't you? You know things… You understand the universe better than anyone else… You're probably very smart. I wish I was smart like you. I want to know more. Would you teach me? I'm bright, logically educated. I can–'

'Hush, hush… Want to learn do you?' said the witch. 'It takes years, girl, lifetimes to master any of the craft. It's not like catering

– it's not a career – more of a life choice.'

'I'm ready. Believe me, I'm ready! Would you have me as your student?'

'There are no *students*. There aren't teachers. There's no school for it... Ha! Imagine that. Hogwash!'

'Then how?' asked Cassandra, 'how did you learn?'

The witch reflected on this. She stroked the Witchhunter's face as if he were part of the room's decor and brooded for a moment. Then quickened, and slammed the blade to rest in the woodwork – inches from his throat. She picked up an unusual purple flower, and, caressing it, moved to Cassandra's cage, frightening the girl away as she drew nearer.

'Stories. I do love a good story. I long for the nostalgia that clings to them.'

Niclas had been watching Greg feed Castor a dead rat. The dog chewed it as if it were made of rubber and then, when it came to swallow, the sticky masticated carcass fell out of its throat and onto the floor, where it was eaten again and then again, getting sloppier with each cycle. It was such a disgusting sight, that it was all he could look at.

But now he was back, and the witch was talking, and Cassandra was listening, and the needle was within his reach.

'It is said that when the time is right, it chooses you,' the witch began. 'That the Whisperer sends for you, sets you down a path. That time came for me many moon crossings ago. I was wife to a man. You wouldn't know this. Too young perhaps. But I was in love once. Have you ever known what it is to love?'

Cassandra hinted with her eyes, trying to get Niclas' attention, trying to nudge him towards the blade.

The witch tried to follow her stare.

'NO!' said Cassandra, drawing her back. 'I mean... no... I can't say...'

'Oh. Well if you did, you'd know. It's something you don't forget. Mine was called… John, or Joseph… Or was it Jack? It began with J, but… Ah, it doesn't matter. He was a caring man. Very caring. He cared for me… and I cared for him. Then, one moon season he fell sick. A disease of the body. I tried everything to save him. Everything. I even found the things I wasn't meant to find. The herbs, the candles, the chants. The path of the tree peoples and those in faraway lands. I read every page of every text, tried every ointment, every medicine. Alas, he died. One day his heart stopped. Just like that. Alive one second, dead the next, and not a goodbye to be had between us. But, I was not afraid, I was not disheartened. Lots of the ways to save him, could only be tried once he was in the in-between. That's how I found his thread and stitched him back together – piece by piece, until he was my lovely, lovely Jason again.'

Cassandra looked at the standing corpse in the corner of the room.

'Is he…,' she said, watching as Greg's organs pulsed and oozed beneath his ribs. She dared not speak it, in case it be true.

And…

…out of the corner of her eye…

…she saw Niclas snatch the needle, unseen.

'No,' said the witch. 'That was long ago. Long, long, long ago. Greg here is the latest in a long series of… progress… he and his dogs that is.'

'What happened to…?'

'My fella?'

'…'

'Oh, we had some problems. Some differences. Life together soon became unbearable and I had to divorce the so and so. I learned an important lesson about men and dead things. Men are useless. And the dead don't get the same souls. The same habits maybe… but not the same souls.'

Cassandra watched Greg feeding Pollux the same chewed up rat

Castor had moments before been trying to eat. The creature-man patted the dog affectionately on the head as if they had known each other for years.

'They get the same brain chemistry,' said the witch. 'But they're not the same people. You'll be surprised how much difference a life thread makes.'

'A *life thread*?'

'A life thread. We are all but the Zol. And there is nothing but the Zol. And within the blanket of the Zol are threads stitched and woven here and there and everywhere. Threads of essence. Threads of the Zol. Threads of you and me. Each of us has one running through us, stitching us to this tapestry. You can take one's thread and wind it through another, if you know what to do.'

'So... he has... another person's thread inside him?'

'Not exactly. It's a difficult practice, extracting the threads of others. The young are preferred. But you can take from all. Greg here has the stitchings of a hundred different threads within him. Who knows, a bit of Jacob might be in there too...'

'Why is he... rotting?'

'You can't fix people, dear. Only keep them here. Put a stop to the eternal clock, their entropy. His body doesn't know it's dead, so it works. But it doesn't know it's alive, so it has no reason to sort itself out.'

'So, he's... dead?'

'Betwixt and between. *The dead who breathe.*'

Whilst the witch had been speaking, Niclas had found a place to hide the blade against his clothes. And now she had her back to him.

The Witchhunter had been watching the whole thing and gave him the same look he had given in the rat city. That throw away now's-our-chance look.

'Enough, enough... we must continue... the eternal clock

is running away and the power of the midnight sun will soon wane...'

It was now or never. Niclas had to strike.

He went for it.

The needle cut through the air, its tip homing in on the witch's spine like an arrowhead. But it did not find it's intended target. Because as if she had known, as if she had always known, she lifted her hand and caught his wrist, stopping it dead in the air.

She shook it from his grasp and slapped him with her other hand.

And then the dead man was on him, ripping him away.

'Feisty one aren't you,' said the witch.

Niclas tried to fight back, punching at the dead man's intestines and kidneys. He didn't mind the sticky, wet residue that came off onto his fists, he had to stop them, he had to do something. But he'd had his chance. As though he were just a fly, pitching on dead meat, Greg carried him unperturbed to the circle, where he dropped him down and tightened the chain. He bolted the end of this chain to a ring pull on the floor. It was so tight now that Niclas couldn't move from the ring of candles without breaking his neck.

Cassandra tried to act normal, disappointment twitching in the corner of her eye.

The Witchhunter wasn't disappointed. He had seen what the boy had done.

Missed the stab.

Punched the zombie.

Snatched the keys.

'What a troublesome two you are,' said the witch, turning her attention back to Cassandra. 'Want to learn do you? Think you can fool me do you? Think I'm stupid do you?'

'I'll have you hung! I'll have you tortured and hung! I'm the future Queen of the Empire!'

'Enough of your wail you hideous girl.'

The witch turned to the dog in Cassandra's cage.

'One more word from this little rabbit and you have my permission to gouge out her throat!'

What was more terrifying than these words was Pollux's understanding of them, and the smile that seemed to stretch across his diseased face.

'Lie on your back, Niclas,' said the witch.

Niclas didn't lie down. Or at least, he thought he didn't, but his body seemed out of his control and he lay without the slightest resistance.

'Let's see some flesh, shall we?'

The witch slipped the needle, which was now back, clasped firmly in her hand, vertically up his abdomen, cutting away only the fabric of his tunic so easily it was as if the steel were made of fire.

The grey Academy tunic fell away and his stomach and chest were revealed.

They were pounding like a startled animal.

The knife hovered about his skin like a spider spinning a web. It dithered here, then there, up and down, side to side, round and round, dancing, prancing, searching for a place to bite.

'Do you know the best place to make the incision,' said the witch to the Princess. '…No? neither do I.'

Then the crazed woman slipped into a serpent chant and began to draw on the boy's stomach with the needle's tip. It didn't cut. It tickled. But that didn't make him feel any better about it. A wrong move from him or a right move from her and his belly would open, spilling whatever was left of his last meal out before him.

He lifted his head to look down his chest.

The tickling sensation was starting to itch, now burn.

Was she cutting into him?

Was this what it felt like, to be sheared open on a stone slab, like a cold cadaver on the anatomist's operating table?

No, not yet.

She was drawing strange patterns across his stomach and chest. A trail of glowing blue flesh was left behind the blade. It was searing his skin. Particles of his body were blowing up like embers above a fire. A soft, blue, flickering light.

He started to shake left to right. Or at least he tried. He had barely enough strength in him to wiggle his little finger.

'Stop!' he cried out. 'Please don't, miss!'

But the witch, though physically present, was somewhere else entirely. Her voice was a chanting whisper, her body was moving mechanically, and her eyes were solid black marbles of obsidian stone. The kind of black that makes ordinary black look like a shade of grey.

His head shot back and his mouth sprang open.

He resisted at first, clamping his jaw shut, but an overwhelming force seemed to be prying it apart. The more he fought it, the stronger it became and soon his mouth stretched wide open.

He tried to scream.

It felt like his tongue was a hundred feet long and was being reeled up from the bellows deep inside him. And indeed something was being reeled up from within, but it wasn't his tongue. He could see it now. A blue and ghostly nimbus, that rose higher and higher out of his mouth and spread out in the air above as if it did not know gravity.

Cassandra saw it too and shrieked at the sight of it. It was utterly terrifying but also the most unnaturally beautiful thing she had ever seen.

The Witchhunter saw it too, and he rocked in his stocks, trying with all his might to break free of them.

Niclas was fading. He was turning pale and his pupils were shrinking into two tiny specs of black. The more of the blue that came out of him, the more he hollowed out and sank into his bones.

The witch reached for her silver topped glass vial. She pulled out the stopper once more. She raised it up to meet the blue cloud above and all around her.

Then the dogs turned vicious...

They began to bark and howl against their master's command. Greg smacked at the cages, but they wouldn't shut up. Their noise became unignorable and soon the witch couldn't hold her chant.

The ritual collapsed...

...and the blue essence spiralled back into Niclas' throat, like water down a plug hole.

His pupils popped back to their usual size and the colour in his face returned. He took a deep, gasping breath.

The witch too awoke back in the room; the burning writing fading from the boy's flesh, and the candles flickering from blue back to amber.

'WHAAAT?' she groaned.

The dogs only barked in reply. Something was troubling them. Something near. Something yet to be seen by anyone without a canine's appetite for smell.

The witch sniffed the air and followed the direction of the barking. It was aimed at the stairs leading down.

'Visitors? At this time? Gregory, see to it – and quickly – quickly. The moons close. Time is wasting. I can feel it.'

Greg, failing to silence his dogs, set off down the stairs to take a look outside.

The moons above sat firmly over one another.

A ring of blue celestial light shone from the cosmos onto Ebb.

Laburnum bathed in the astral rays.

The pigeons had gone into hiding, but the crows were out, flapping through the sky above like a plague of locust.

The witch waited for Greg's return, restlessly tapping her fingernails against the needle.

When she had grown tired of the barking dogs and her silent captives, she stuck the blade in the stocks, threw her arms into the air and traipsed down the stairs.

'Enough is enough, Gregory,' she said. 'Who the blummin' 'eck wants to call on a young girl at a time like this anyway – I say – chivalry is dead.' Her voice dwindled away until it was nothing more than a muffled blur passing through the rotten floorboards.

The children tried to listen to the scene below in hope of figuring out what was going on.

Then the Witchhunter caught Niclas' eye, and imparted that this would be their final chance.

The witch strode to her front door, accosting her butler, and was about to pull him in from the street when who should barge past but that cruel and disreputable man known as Mr K.

Overwhelmed by a scuffle of sentences trying to escape her mouth at the same instant, she stuttered out an incomprehensible garble.

'Your doorman 'ere tells me you're too busy to take me call, but I tells him it's urgent and cannot wait.'

'Mr K, what an unpleasant surprise,' said the witch, 'have you lost your way?'

'I ain't lost me way, not at all, I'm right where I wants to be. I gots summin 'ere which I fink you'll find interestin'.'

Mr K, sensing he was about to be tossed back into the street by an exasperated corpse, shook a brown juniper sack in the witch's face.

'Mr K, this unannounced intrusion is remarkably rude. It's definitely not part of our arrangement. I dare say you know what night it is: a night I'll not get for another passing!'

'You've still got time to do wot takes minutes. I know 'ow it works.'

'Mr K, do not think that we are friends and that I will excuse such beastly behaviour. I could have your mortality stripped from you, and set the dogs to feast on your entrails, and send for the crows to pick out your eyes for all eternity. I shall make you suffer a thou–'

Mr K was not warded off by the witch's threats. He slammed the door and pushed his way into the room where he emptied the contents of his sack onto the table.

Greg tried to make an expression, he didn't have the muscles for it.

The witch raised an eyebrow.

She presumed the only possession Mr K could possibly have which would excuse him of his eagerness, would be a newborn child. For newborns were rare in the slums, they often died moments after birth and Mr K knew that she desired them greatly; especially during the crossing of the moons. However, what rolled out of his sack, along with a sprinkling of juniper berries, was something she would never have anticipated.

'A cat, Mr K?'

'This ain't no cat – least no ordinary cat. I ain't ever 'eard a cat speak, 'av' you?'

'Speak?'

'It talks.'

Mr K, the witch and Greg studied Balthazar expectantly.

'Go on – *speak*,' said Mr K, pushing the cat over.

Meow

'Mr K, I think the fumes from your gin stores have finally burned away your mind,' said the witch.

'It talks! I swears it!'

The witch sighed. 'I don't know, Mr K,' she said, 'but this looks like an ordinary cat to me, and contrary to popular belief, us witches aren't too fond of 'em. In fact, I swear I have allergies with 'em.'

'But… it can… it can talk,' insisted Mr K, angrily grabbing the cat's tail and squeezing the cartilage until it crunched.

Balthazar let out a screech and slashed the thug's hand, drawing blood.

'You'll talk cat – I swear you'll talk – If you don't talk – I'm gunna break every bone in your body startin' wiv your tail.' The infuriated villain drew from his side a frightening club, and pinned the cat to the table.

'Mr K! I've seen some things in my life, but this is… mad. Exceptionally mad. And it's wasting my precious time.'

But Mr K would not be defeated, and, putting Balthazar's silence to the test, brought the club down on the tip of his tail.

The weighty truncheon slammed with such vehemence that it splintered the table's legs and cracked its top.

The witch blinked surprised.

The thug panted viciously through his mouth.

And Balthazar spoke: revealing to all not only that he could speak, but that his vocabulary was extensive, and, when need be, damn right disgraceful.

The witch staggered back from the table – at first shocked – then amused – then delighted. She laughed.

'I told ya, didn't I?' continued Mr K.

'Well I never… A talking cat – how does it work?' she prodded Balthazar to check he was real.

'Now you see why I come 'ere – it's witchcraft this, ain't it?'

'Oh, Mr K, it must be – it must be – but not any kind I know of. This is most unreal. I've never seen anything like it.'

The two gaped and prodded; Balthazar winced, and shot fleeting glances at his mutilated tail.

'Are you pleased?' asked Mr K.

'Oh, pleased, Mr K, pleased? I'm exhilarated. Do you have a name, kitty cat?'

Crippled from pain, there was no coherence to Balthazar's thoughts, his head spun.

'Don't be rude! Answer her!' said the savage.

Balthazar looked daggers at Mr K; eyes that, even being as brutal as he was, inspired a small amount of uncertainty within the thug's mind.

'Don't look at me!' he said, making ready the club for another devastating blow.

The witch seized his wrist.

'Now, now, Mr K, you don't give someone a gift only to pulverise it in front of them.'

'Gift?' inquired the thug, wrenching his arm free, 'who said any fing 'bout a gift. I'm 'ere for business.'

'Business?'

'*Business.*'

'And what kind of business would that be, Mr K?'

Mr K dropped the club to his side and took a short stroll around the perimeter of the room, his eyes gazing up at the dusty shelves and the vials of gaseous liquid.

'One or two of these ought be fair,' said the thug.

'One or two of what?' asked the witch, for the idea that Mr K would want one of her precious vials was so far at the back of her mind that she failed to regard it as a serious possibility. A possibility that became a reality, as the thug's stubby, coarse fingers picked a vial for closer study.

'Oh, Mr K, why would you want that? It's useless to you.'

The thug glowered.

'It's not happening, Mr K, you can take your foul mouthed animal and go back from whence you came.'

'Look 'ow many you have, you can't spare two?'

'Put it back you brainless oaf, before you break it!'

Mr K took a small amount of pleasure watching the witch reach out as he tossed the vial from one hand to the other.

'Mis-ter K!'

'Wot? I brought you summin special, I want summin special in return; and I reckons this is the most special fing you got.'

'Too special, Mr K, it's not a fair trade,' said the witch.

'I fink it is. I fink it's the fairest trade there is.'

'It really isn't,' said Balthazar, entering the conversation. 'What use am I to her? She already seems to have someone to talk to, and he's probably a little less opinionated than I.' Greg grunted. 'I suppose I could help keep the vermin out of the house, but then, it appears she's done a good job of that herself. No, I'm afraid I'm useless to her. But that? That offers her so much more. Power. Youth. Immortality.'

Mr K would have lunged for the cat, ripping off the first limb his clutching hands could grab, but the witch, intrigued, raised her finger and brought the two hundred and forty pound beast to a halt.

'What did you say?' she asked.

'I do hate repeating myself,' replied the cat.

'Do you know what that is?' asked the witch, pointing in the direction of the vial grasped tightly in Mr K's hand.

'Of course I know what it is. But what does that matter? It's not worth the trade, we both know that, so you can show Mr K the door and he can take his *knowledgeable* animal back from whence he came.'

As if spellbound, the witch couldn't shake her eyes. The cat had succeeded in piquing her interest, and whilst she stared at him, Mr K stared at her.

'I'll be on my way then, is it?' he said.

'No, Mr K, wait. This creature marvels me – but I will not hand over a single vial of essence for it. What I am prepared to do, however, is let you take from here one of the prizes I've got upstairs.'

This was not what Mr K wanted to hear, but he was curious to know what kind of prizes she had.

'Gregory.'

'*Yes, mistress?*'

'The girl.'

'*Yes, mistress.*'

Now to lend our attentions to the scene occurring above.

With the witch and her undead minion below, Niclas had managed to unlock his collar and had moved upon the stocks with the rusty keys. The dogs were not oblivious to this. They barked and growled and pushed their sickening bodies against the bars. Such a din should have brought everyone racing back up the stairs, had it not appeared to them as a continuation of the earlier racket.

'Come on,' said Cassandra.

'The lock's stiff, it ain't me fault.'

The key didn't turn easily – it had to be jiggled, bashed and pulled out by a hair's width before any movement could be had. By the time the boy had unlocked the first bolt it was too late. For the stairs were creaking, and the walking corpse was coming.

Greg arrived at the top of the stairs and stood to examine the three prisoners. The Princess cowering in her cage, the Witch-hunter with his head down slumped in the stocks, and Niclas, lying still with the collar back around his neck.

Niclas could feel the sweat running down the corner of his brow. Had he left something unturned? Had the monster heard their voices or the fiddling with the lock? It was only when Greg's dead eyes settled on Cassandra, that Niclas sighed relief. A relief that wasn't altogether the relief he had thought it to be, because the corpse marched over to her, opened the bars and grabbed hold of her ankle.

She kicked away his rotten hand and retreated towards the vicious dog – it welcomed her with a snap of its putrid jaws, and then again came the rotten hand, only this time with the dog hungry for blood, Cassandra was helpless to avoid the bony fingers.

She was dragged from the cage.

'Get off me! Get off me, I say!'

Pollux couldn't control himself, he bolted for the entrance, clanging into the closing bars. Consumed by bloodlust, he went for his master's hand.

Greg, insulted, riled up and punched the dog on the nose.

'*That'll do*,' he rasped.

Pollux backed away, and growled vengefully.

'*Don't lose your manners, 'sonly a mouser.*'

Mouser? thought Niclas.

'Ah, here she is,' said the witch, delighted.

Cassandra was wriggling in Greg's arms, repulsed by his stench and sticky texture.

When he put her down, she glared back at him, then across at the witch, then across at Mr K. She gave the thug a wary stare and backed up into Greg's fierce grip.

She was frightened so much by the three of them, that she hadn't spotted the black cat on the table. Not until it moved to look over its damaged tail.

Balthazar held her stare, slowly shaking his head from side to side.

She said nothing.

'I don't want 'er,' said Mr K.

'Oh, but Mr K, she's very special this one. Very special,' said the witch, rushing over and stroking the girl's hair.

''Ow so?' asked the thug.

'This little madam is your future queen.'

'Nah she ain't.'

'Yes she is, Mr K.'

Mr K snarled. 'You may fink me a fool, but I ain't. It's a vial o' this stuff or nuffin' at all.'

The Princess eyed the vial in Mr K's hand.

'Got any coin, Mr K?' asked the witch.

'Coin?'

'You know. Shiny. Round.'

'Course I know. Wot's coin got to do wiv' it?'

Cassandra couldn't stop her eyes wandering back to Balthazar. What was he doing here? How had he got off that boat? *What was he planning?*

'If you look upon your coins you will see the face of her mother – the spitting image no doubt of this young Princess,' said the witch.

Mr K hesitated stubbornly. He foraged a coin from his pocket. He held it up in front of the girl's face and focused his eyes between both.

'You can't deny that it's her, the Princess, my trade to you,' said the witch.

'Wot's she doin' 'ere?'

'Do you want her or not, Mr K?' The witch was beginning to get impatient.

Cassandra shuddered as the cruel man approached her, sniffing her neck and running his fingers through her hair. Despite not bathing since the night of her abduction, she smelt… *well she didn't exactly smell of lilies*, but it was pleasant – proof to the thug that she was indeed royalty.

'You could do whatever you wanted with her. Work her, ransom her, sell her. I'm sure there are those in the city who would pay a great deal for such a treasure as she – people that may even be able to overturn your unsavoury record, Mr K.'

'Why don't you want 'er? If she's a princess ain't she special to you?'

'No, apparently not – I've consulted he who whispers and she's spoiled goods I'm afraid.'

'Spoiled?'

'Yes, not much more to her thread than a fly's perhaps.'

'Why's that?'

'Who knows these things but the Whisperer? I am but a listener.'

Mr K contemplated both the girl and the vial in his hand. He studied the witch, the corpse and the cat. He was known for his lack of trust and for his obstinacy, but something in the witch's voice and words told him to take the girl and leave the vial.

He placed the soul essence back on the shelf and grabbed Cassandra by the wrist.

Greg held on as the thug tugged at her arm.

Cassandra screeched.

'Let go, Gregory, she belongs to Mr K now.'

The corpse released the girl and Mr K jerked her closer.

Then the witch said, 'I'm glad we were able to settle our little problem.'

Just then the dogs upstairs broke into the meanest barking fit yet. But they were further ignored. Except perhaps by Greg, who recognised something different about the noise.

Mr K grunted.

'Are you not happy?' asked the witch.

The dogs were howling like wolves and the witch had to raise her voice to be heard over them. 'Gregory, shut those hounds up, before I rip out their vocals. They don't need them after all,' she said, smiling amicably at her guest.

'*Yes, mistress.*' Greg went up.

An ugly awareness fell upon the Princess as Mr K pulled her towards him. She tried to break free but in one mighty swoop the thug swung her up onto his shoulder.

'Wait… Stop… Put me down! Stop it! You can't do this! Help me… Help me! Baltha–'

'If I may,' said Balthazar, speaking over the girl's cries, 'a suggestion. You might consider gagging her – she might scream a lot on her way out. You wouldn't want to attract any attention now would you, running around with a princess over your shoulder?'

Mr K grunted at the cat, retrieved the sack from the floor and stuffed it into the girl's gob.

'Bal…' she stifled.

'Night,' said Mr K.

'Good evening, Mr K,' said the witch.

With these goodbyes, Mr K went out into the street, the door slamming behind him.

The witch gave a loud sigh, turned to Balthazar and said: 'I'm glad that's over. He is most unpleasant that man.'

Then, like a punctured leather football, Greg's severed head came bouncing down the stairs…

…and rolled across the floor…

…and came to a stop right by the witch's foot.

'Gregoreeeeeeey!' she wailed.

She hoiked up her tattered dress and rushed up the steps.

Balthazar examined the twitching facial expressions on the corpse's face.

Then he sniffed at the air.

Something was burning.

The witch arrived on the floor above to a blurry phantasmagoria. She saw her headless minion grappling blindly with the boy. There was fire too. The curtains were thick with it, knocked over candles burning beneath them. The dogs were going savage. The stocks were thrown open, a set of keys dangling in the lock. And there, in the midst of it all, was the Witchhunter, his short sword in one hand, and her ceremonial needle in the other.

He was about to charge her and would have probably caught her by complete surprise, if Niclas hadn't have let out a high pitched squeal. The headless corpse had hold of him against the wall, and was feeling his face, working its thumbs into his eye sockets, pushing hard against his gummy eyeballs.

''Elp me! Mister, MISTER!'

At once, the Witchhunter sped across the room in a sweeping stride and cut the corpse down by its legs. As it fell it lost hold of Niclas, and knocked the boy back against the cage – bringing him within inches of Castor's snapping jaws.

The Witchhunter turned to look back at the witch. *She was gone.* There was only the billowing black smoke and the flames catching on the roof. He raised his sleeve over his nose and mouth, searching the room with flickering, fire-lit eyes.

Where was she?

Where?

Suddenly, a sharp jolt grabbed his arm and his whole body went stiff.

She was behind him. He tried to turn and drive one of the blades into her, but instead caught her gaze. And that was about the worst thing you could do with a witch. She leered into his eyes with black, lightless mirrors of darkness. He felt her voice reach down vertebra by vertebra, travelling the length of his spine and penetrating deep into the marrow of his bones. It was as if a thousand needles had been inserted at once into his every joint and tendon.

'*Yes! Fight it,*' she said '*fight it with every fibre of your thread.*'

Across the room was a headless Greg trying to stand. He reached blindly for the cage release and pulled it down.

The bars shot open. Castor shot out.

Niclas was sure that that would be the last sight he would ever see – a demon dog leaping for his face. But the dog was set on another smell. It leapt past him and galloped down the stairs.

The boy wiped the sweat from his eyes and took a moment to breathe. It was then that he noticed just how hot the room had become. The fire was raging out of control all around them.

And through the smoke he spotted the Witchhunter falling to his knees, the mad witch standing over him, clinging to his arm like a crab.

'Just let it go… let it go… there… there… it'll be over soon…' she was saying.

The Witchhunter was defenceless. His arms were no longer his to command. He turned his hand towards his chest and angled the blade inwards.

He's gonna do 'imself in, thought Niclas.

The witch felt the boy's fearful stare and craned her head to look at him. She grinned a demonic grin; her eyes black and fire raging all around her; a vista of pure, undiluted malevolence.

She twisted so the boy could watch. And now the Witchhunter was staring at him too. Pleading through his swollen eyes. But Niclas couldn't move and the blade had started easing into the man's chest. He'd stiffened up, made a statue by fear. The fear had gripped hold of him so much so, that he didn't notice Castor run back up the stairs and into his cage whimpering like a spooked pup.

The man's arm shook violently.

The witch cackled viciously

The boy trembled cowardly.

And the blade sunk a quarter of an inch into the flesh. Then a quarter of an inch more. Niclas expected blood to pour out, to burst and spray like a fountain. But it didn't. The blade just travelled deeper, determined to find his heart.

Then, seemingly for no reason at all, the tide changed.

The man's arm grew strong against the witch's spell. His other hand dropped the needle and joined with the short sword. Together, his arms pulled the blade out of his breast and away from his chest. Then, slowly, it tilted back towards the witch.

'Impossible!' cried the crone. *'Your will is broken! Your might is shred! Impossible… How do you defy me so?'*

The Witchhunter didn't understand what was going on either – not until his eyes fell upon the top of the stairs. The witch followed his bewildered gaze, and Niclas followed hers.

There stood Balthazar, black eyed and chanting under his breath.

'How?' demanded the witch in an eldritch cry.

The blade stuck her in the belly.

She gasped and it drove further in.

Niclas, overcome with courage, shuffled across the floor and snatched up the fallen needle before the witch could reach for it. He looked up into her fading eyes.

'Don't think!' said the Witchhunter.

So he didn't. He looked away, squeezed the needle in his hand and slipped it into the witch's side.

Balthazar gave an exhausted sigh and lost hold, but the spell was already broken.

The Witchhunter ripped out the blade. He stuck the witch again. She bellowed out with an ear-splitting banshee wail and her darkening eyes flooded black. He stabbed her again and she fell to her knees snatching for Niclas' shoulders, trying with all her strength to get a grip around his throat. In squeamish panic, Niclas withdrew the needle and stuck her with it again, and she groaned a noise that seemed to come from the bottom of her stomach.

Her arms fell limp.

Niclas jumped back. He stared at his hands. They were red and the blood had got underneath his fingernails. He'd never seen so much of it. Bright red like scarlet milk up to his wrists.

'Niclas, time to leave,' said Balthazar.

In the drama of the fight, they had forgotten the fire, and the flames were now dancing on the ceiling and the building was creaking and moaning as if alive and in agony.

Niclas didn't have to be told twice, he got up and ran for the stairs.

The Witchhunter pushed himself up. A bloody sword in hand. The witch coughing blood at his feet.

'Well? What will it be, witch-killer?' asked Balthazar.

The two stared at each other for a moment, whilst a maelstrom of fiery mayhem raged around them.

Then, a flash of blue light startled them.

Greg, Pollux and Castor had burst into sapphirine flames. The light flickered much faster than the orange fire, and within its quivering heat, hundreds of screaming faces climbed upwards and vanished into the air. The threads of a hundred souls were sizzling free into the black smoke.

Whilst the monstrous manifestations burned away to nothing but dust, Balthazar turned his back on the man and fled.

The Witchhunter stared down at the dying witch. She was no longer so youthful. An old woman with cratered skin, liver spots and sagged eyes looked up at him. Her teeth were like rat teeth. Her hair thin and white. And she was getting older by the second, wasting away under her gown.

He always watched them die, just to make sure. But there was no time to watch her die, if he hung about he would likely follow her.

So he began to make a move.

And there it was again…

One last, final mercurial cackle.

'Ahahahaha! Can't you hear him? The Whisperer! The Whisperer whispers. He whispers to me now…Nothing matters! This. You. I. All of it. 'Tis but the tapestry of his design. The answer's in the blood… watch the needle, see the spindle… for the end cometh… and all will be as if all never was… As above, so below… Yes! As above, so below…'

She would perhaps, have continued on like that until her last breath. But her hysterical cries were cut short. Under fierce assault by the fire, the roof above gave up and a falling load of flaming rubble crushed the witch in a shower of smoking ash and burning embers.

The flames too, would have continued to roar until that whole horrid district was reduced to a smouldering rubble. But they soon reached the vials of essence below, and, on exposure to their heat, a ghostly, obsidian flare burst into existence and devoured the witch's lair. Then, just as soon as it had appeared it vanished, and everything with it.

All that remained was the burnt out shell of a house. A house that had once been, but was no more, the fountainhead of nightmares.

Mr K had only made it two hundred yards down the street. The Princess hadn't made it easy. With every step, Cassandra's kicks, punches and pinches became more ferocious.

The thug slung her from his shoulder and she spat the gag from her mouth; screaming as soon as she caught breath.

'Shut it, wench!' He slapped her across the face. It was a hard slap. The kind that echoes.

'Let me go. Let me go!'

Mr K looked back at the plume of black smoke rising up over the buildings, and caught a glimpse of the dark, otherworldly flash. He checked his pockets to see if it was still there.

It was.

A single vial of extracted thread.

Cassandra snatched it.

'Give me that!'

She raised it above her head and spun away from him.

'I'll break it – touch me and I'll break it!'

'I'll kill you.'

'Princess!' came a voice, accompanied by the patter of running feet. 'Princess!'

Niclas had heard the screams the moment he'd reached the street, and had chased after them while fresh heroism still flowed through him.

But the heroic euphoria had had its day.

He skidded to the floor having not expected to see the scarred face of Mr K; and on seeing it, was crippled by nostalgic terror.

'Nicky-boy?' said Mr K, who too was taken aback.

'Mister K?'

'Fate's too kind.' Mr K reached for his club and began advancing towards the boy – forgetting the Princess in an instant.

Niclas crawled backwards, but it wasn't something he could do very fast.

'Hey!' cried Cassandra.

Mr K stopped. Turned.

She gave only a moment's notice before tossing the vial of essence into the air. It spun up, wringing Mr K's face like a dirty rag. Its glass chimed above and shattered in a crystal splash on the cobbled stones below.

She'd done it.

Now she'd done it.

And she hadn't thought about what to do next.

At once Mr K turned his wrath on the girl, moving for her with brutal intent, the way a hound rips and roars after a fox.

The Princess back peddled – tripped – and landed with a thud on her rear, right smack in a puddle.

Mr K was far past threats, insults or scares; like an enraged bull, he had seen red and was only concerned with violence.

And who knows what violent end the Princess would have met in that one fatal blow, had Balthazar not leapt between the thug and the girl.

The cat let out a sour hiss.

Mr K paused.

Considered this.

Then a tar drenched laugh surfaced from the deepest crevices of the thug's lungs.

A laugh that was brought to an abrupt end, for something strangled Mr K and wet him with fear. All Cassandra saw was the tormented expression on the brute's face.

Balthazar's eyes washed black...

The children watched the Bowler Gang boss drop his club, stagger backwards and run.

He ran down the cobbled street, turned off into an alley and disappeared from view without even looking back.

Niclas couldn't believe what he had seen. Mr K, the most frightening man in all the city, had run away from a small black cat. Such things ruined a man's reputation, and put an end to a boy's nightmares.

Cassandra offered her dirty hand to Niclas' bloody hand and said: 'Are you ok? Niclas?'

'Yes, miss?'

'Are you ok?' she asked.

'Yes, miss. Are you ok, miss?'

'Well, I'm not hurt, if that's what you mean.'

Niclas looked around them. Someone was missing.

'Where's...'

'Gone,' said Balthazar. 'Perhaps he felt his task was done. He got what he came for after all.'

'Won't he come after you, sir?'

'Perhaps. Let's hope not.'

Niclas looked back at the black smoke melting away over the buildings. Those narrow streets were no longer as threatening as they had once been. And above, the blue shimmer in the sky was fading to dark and the moons were coming apart.

Balthazar looked up and watched mournfully as the two celestial bodies pulled away from each other. It would be another year before he'd see the midnight sun again. Another year spent in his whiskered existence.

He decided to be stoic about it.

'I'm hungry,' he said. 'Anyone else hungry?'

Niclas licked his dry, cracked lips.

'A little thirsty, sir…'

'Yes, well, we could all use a drink.'

six

Pete's was a shabby looking tavern on the other side of the canal to Bog End. It was the nearest place to buy a drink, and Niclas was at the bar getting a round in.

'So, you want two tap waters and a saucer o' milk wiv some liquor in it?' said the barkeep, looking across suspiciously at the table in the corner, where the Princess and the cat were waiting.

'Baileys, sir.'

'We ain't got nuffin' called Baileys 'ere lad. Plenty o' gin? Gin alright?'

'Errr… I reckons that's alright, sir.'

'Alright…'

Niclas cradled the two glasses between his hands, clasped the saucer between his fingers, and journeyed cautiously to the table.

Balthazar sniffed at the milk.

'Didn't 'av' that Baileys stuff, sir.'

'Gin?'

'Yessir, is that alright?'

'It'll have to do.' Balthazar took a moment, then pushed his tongue into the milky beverage and began to lap it up.

Cassandra wasn't impressed with her glass. It was dusty and stained with watermarks and fingerprints, as if it had never been washed. She gave the rim a squeaky wipe with her sleeve, but it didn't make it much cleaner.

Niclas had no problem with his glass. It was just as dirty, and his water even had little hairs and particles of dust floating in it, but he gulped it down none the less. Then he thought to try the bread that had been served in the middle of the table. It was common courtesy in some of Laburnum's establishments to serve a piece of bread with a drink. It helped keep things down, the noise and the booze. He broke off a piece of the stale bloomer and crunched it between his tawny teeth.

'Sorry 'bout your rit'wal, sir,' he said, when his mouth was completely full.

'Don't look at me when you talk, look at her or look down. We're in public you fool,' said the cat.

Niclas apologised to the table.

'Wot 'appens now then?'

'Now? As in, as of now? Or right now? Right now, I'm going to drink this and then you're going to get me another and then perhaps another and then I'll begin to come to terms with our circumstances. That's what people do in these places, isn't it?'

'Guess so, sir.'

'It'll be another year before the moons crossover. Another year of licking my fur until I throw it back up. Another year of being unexplainably excited by birds. Another year of being chased by uncontrollable dogs. Another year of fleas, this intolerable stench, and having insolent morons blow kisses at me for reasons I couldn't care to understand. I've a lot to look forward to, as of now.'

'Err...' Niclas tried to gauge whether this was a good moment to ask about his employment... it probably wasn't, but then, there probably wasn't going to be one. 'Will you, errr... be keepin' me on, sir?'

'Keeping you on?' said Balthazar, pausing to think about it. Then he said, 'Unfortunately.' But for Niclas that didn't seem to be clear enough, so he added a, 'Yes,' which had to be further hammered home with a, 'Yes, I shall be keeping you on.'

Niclas showed off his despicable grin. 'Awh! I'm so happy to hear that!'

'Well, I'm glad someone is.'

Niclas was smiling so hard that his face hurt. He hadn't had much practice using those particular muscles before, and so looked a little like a deranged psychopath.

This unnerved Balthazar.

'Stop it,' he said.

'Sir?'

'Stop smiling.'

'Yessir.' Niclas ironed out his expression.

Cassandra was detached from their conversation.

Niclas took note of this and asked, 'You alright, miss?'

'I cannot unsee what I have seen,' she mumbled to herself.

'Sorry, miss?'

Cassandra met Niclas' clueless eyes across the table. How could he just carry on like that? As if nothing had happened. Didn't he see it too? The dogs. The dead man. The witch. And there was the thing that stuck with her most, the sight that made her sure she could believe anything. She had seen a piece of Niclas. Something that even now, even as they sat there drinking and talking, still lived within him.

'It came out of you. A blue… smokey… living thing… it came right out of your mouth… as if it were a… a part of you?'

'You saw his thread,' said Balthazar.

'And what is that?'

'Ah yes. Oblivious. Totally oblivious aren't you?' said the cat, and he lapped away at his milky beverage until the two blinking blank faces forced him to elaborate. 'His life force, you know life thread, soul thingamajig. His essence of being. Call it whatever you want. No doubt the witch tried to extract it, and no doubt she failed… else he wouldn't be sitting here now.'

'Wot's me wot-fred?' said Niclas, holding his chest uncomfortably. It wasn't as if he'd forgotten about it, it's just, Niclas had a remarkable gift of not dwelling on things.

'It's a complicated science. I'll need a few more drinks in me if you want it explained.'

'You shouldn't drink so much, sir, it's a slippery slope… So I 'ear…'

Balthazar looked up at Niclas. He didn't say anything, not with words, but his eyes said enough.

'I mean… you can drink as much as you like, sir. I ain't gonna stop you.'

'What is this thread you speak of?' said the Princess.

'Ugh,' said Balthazar, 'did you learn nothing from that book you stole?'

'I didn't steal it!'

'Calm it you two, people's lookin'.'

The three returned to their drinks while the wandering eyes in the tavern settled down.

'We are mere mortals, child,' said Balthazar, eventually. 'Mere shadows and dust. We are all just floating specks of nothingness. Then we are bound. We are stitched together, piece by piece with a single thread. That thread is made of a pure unrelenting energy and each of us living things has one. Without it, you cannot exist. The universe itself is a fabric made of such threads. They can be cut, they can be stitched, they can be borrowed and they can be consumed, but they cannot be destroyed. Only the forms they create can be destroyed. Do you understand all that?'

'But… there are no teachings in The Curriculum about this… thread…'

'Of course there aren't. They don't call it the Black Science for nothing girl. Niclas, another round if you'd please.'

Niclas took the saucer to the bar.

'How can the Academy be so ill-informed? The greatest minds of the rational world and not one has ever written a thing on–'

'Ill-informed?' said Balthazar.

'Well, they can't possibly know. If this living energy is real, which it must be because I have seen it with my own eyes, then it changes all our understanding of the world. Everything.'

'*Hiccup,* yep.'

'Yep?'

'Look my dear, sweet, naive, heavily sheltered girl, I'm going to pull the veil from your eyes. You won't like it.'

'What?'

'It will be a hard fact for you to understand that the Academy is not the founder of all knowledge,' said Balthazar. 'That it is an organisation, like all before it and all after it, designed primarily to control. It does so by choosing to teach what it believes should be taught. No one dares question its logic because no one dares question the law. Anyone who goes widdershins is dubbed a criminal, convicted of logicide and dealt with as swiftly as an itch.'

'Widdershins?'

'It means to go against the grain.'

'What you're saying is a travesty: that all our knowledge is taught by liars? That's the most absurd thing I think I've ever heard.'

'Believe what you've been indoctrinated to believe, I'm not trying to convince you otherwise. I'm just telling you how it is. How it really is… Ah, Niclas, excellent.' Balthazar sunk his head to the freshly filled saucer.

Niclas took a seat.

''Sup wiv 'er?' he asked. The Princess' face was pale and fixed elsewhere.

'She's having a reverie, best not disturb her. Say, boy, you should have a drink too. We should get drunk together. It's no good drinking on my own. Get yourself an ale or something.'

'I'm alright, sir. I don't really touch the stuff.'

'No? Odd that a slum boy refuses a drink? What's the matter with you?'

'I just seen wot it does to people that's all. No one that ever came lookin' for gin from Mr K was 'appy 'bout it.'

'Ah, yes. Probably because they were out of gin! It's not the drink that makes you sad. It's the lack of it. Now get yourself a half ale. I insist. Put it on the tab.'

Niclas wavered, but his now milky-nosed master was insistent, so he went and got his ale.

'I can't believe it...' said Cassandra. 'I just can't...'

'Ah, but you've seen it. And seeing is believing. You've seen more than just a talking cat. You've seen it up close. The other side of the coin. The upside down, inside out, the in-between. The widdershins way.'

Niclas returned.

'Sir, you are talkin' a bit loud... Probs best to keep it down.'

'Shush.'

'Yessir.'

'Why hasn't anyone done anything about it? Exposed them for the liars they are?' said Cassandra.

'Oh... there's plenty of those. People are always trying to out the truth. No longer with us, I'm afraid,' said Balthazar.

'Well, we have to do something about it.'

'Do summin 'bout wot?' said Niclas, feeling he'd missed a key bit of the conversation.

'No, Princess, there'll be no doing anything of the sort.'

'But people should know.'

'Why?'

'Because... because it's the truth.'

'Ah... truth...'

'Yes. Truth!'

'There is no truth in this world, girl, only the truth we choose. And it is better to choose a truth that you can live with, rather than one you can't.'

'You're intoxicated.'

'Truth is intoxicated.'

'I will not sit here and watch the two of you get drunk.'

'Get a drink then.'

'No. We are going to the Palace. The three of us. Right now. I'm going to show you to my mother, you're going to explain everything, and then we shall tackle the Academy together.'

Balthazar laughed.

'Tackle them will we? The Academy is more than a thing like you and I. It is a thought. A truth if you will. It is above the City Watch, beyond Parliament, the Monarchy and the High Court. Every fibre of this city's fabric is at its most basic level founded on the principles of the Academy. I'm afraid, Princess, there is no stopping the wind from blowing, nor the waves from rolling.'

'No. You listen here, I'm going to change things in this city. I will be Queen one day, in a position of immense power. If anyone can change things it's me.'

Balthazar, feeling content with his state of merriment, ruminated on this for a second and had a thought that had not yet presented itself to him before. He entertained it a while.

'Ok,' he said at last, 'then we have to leave Laburnum.'

'Leave? No, I can't…'

'You must. We must all leave the city right now. It's not safe for you here.'

'I cannot run away, I have a duty.'

'Maybe you do, but trust me, the people who go on about having a duty in this world tend to also be the people who die.'

'I am the Princess.'

'So? They locked you up, didn't they?'

'But…'

'…Sir, I'm feelin' a bit funny, sir,' Niclas added.

'Keep drinking, boy. We shall go to the docks. Take a ship north. Hide out for a year, until I am able to perform my ritual, then, perhaps, perhaps then, I will help you.'

'A year! A whole year!'

'I know. Painful isn't it.'

'I've never bin outside the city…' said Niclas.

'I can't leave. I have to go home. My mother needs me.'

'She can't protect you from them, you know?'

'But…'

'If you want my help, Princess, you have to do as I say. Else, the boy and I shall leave you here. And you can go home to your palace, until they come for you with the black, crimson cloth waggons and drag you away to… where was it… the Hall of Atonement? Not a pretty holiday for a pretty girl like yourself. Imagine the worst of all possible worlds. It's worse than that.'

Niclas was staring into the bottom of his glass. There was a frothy bit of ale left but it was moving around and he couldn't lock it down. He couldn't help but think that maybe he'd drank it a bit too quickly.

'I fink I'm drunk…' he said.

'Nonsense. You've only had a half,' said the cat.

'Why would they send me there?' said the Princess.

'Isn't that obvious? Someone wants to get rid of you.'

'Who?'

'Well don't ask me, I don't know.'

Cassandra pondered on her list of enemies. She couldn't think of anyone who would want to do her harm. She was always such a nice person to everyone, who would possibly want to… Unless, she thought, unless it had something to do with Rufus. Maybe there was a connection there, something she couldn't quite make sense of yet.

'So? Are you coming with us or staying here?' asked the cat.

'You promise to help me if I come with you?'

'Yes, Princess, I promise to help you if you come with us.'

'What's with the change of heart?'

'Heart?' said Balthazar. 'Heart's got nothing to do with it.'

And so it was decided that they would set off for the docks in hope of finding a ship to take them north. But as they stumbled to the door, the barman called out after them.

'Hey, who's fittin' the bill?'

Niclas patted down his empty pockets, then looked at Balthazar. Cassandra shrugged and looked as well.

And the barman too.

'Well don't look at me,' said Balthazar, 'I'm just a cat.'

And with that, they walked out the door, leaving behind a tavern of mystified, open-mouthed faces.

They took the Queen's Road. An artery of Laburnum, it was the widest of roads and ventured deep into the ventricles of the city. At that time of the morning it was crowded with coaches and carts, paperboys and plebeians, people who looked like they were on official business and a handful of people who had gotten lost and were trying to make their way home after a considerably heavy night on the barrel.

The Queen's Road was always busy, but it was busier than usual. The Watchmen were out in force. They were patrolling up and down in troops of eight, marching in unison, boots thudding as one, rifles held upright against their shoulders. Niclas saw that each of their patrols had a red cloaked inquisitor walking at the helm. But these were not like the inquisitors Niclas had seen before. These were men who wore amongst their crimson robes golden plated armour and carried golden scrolls that were held out in front of them, as if to ward back anyone who stood in their way. Cassandra knew of them, but she had never seen them, not until now. They were the justiciars. The militant men. The soldiers of Logic.

'They lookin' for us?' asked Niclas.

'Probably,' said Balthazar. 'Keep your heads low.'

Niclas had filched a pair of cloaks from a market on the way there, and he and the Princess had their hoods up. It wasn't the best way to hide, it just made them look suspicious. And by the looks of it, the guards were stopping suspicious people on every corner, asking questions and searching bags.

'We're going to be caught,' said Cassandra.

'Shhh! If you think it, you make it so,' said Balthazar.

A little further up the road lay the entrance to the Guard's Square. It was rammed with people from all classes, beggars to clerks, all vying to get a good spot.

'What do you suspect is going on?'

'I don't know. Some sort of get together by the looks of it. Whatever it is, it is of no concern to us. Now, if my bearings are right the quickest way to the docks is through the square, it's going to be a tight squeeze so let's try not to lose each other.'

'Shouldn't we... maybe... go another way... like a back way?' said Niclas, 'I mean, they're all out lookin' for us ain't they?'

'This way is fine,' said Balthazar. 'It's best to be right under their noses. They don't have whiskers to tell them what's right in front of them, and with all this commotion, it'll make spotting us that much harder.'

They squeezed between shoulders, waists and shins, manoeuvring like worms through wet soil.

People were standing on each other's toes trying to see over heads. There was whispering and gossiping coming from every mouth, but it was impossible to hear, it all mushed and mashed into a noisy pulp.

Niclas wasn't concerned with this, he was trying his best to keep an eye on Balthazar as the cat weaved ahead. But Cassandra, the curious one, was trying to listen out for, or see something that would explain it. She'd never seen the Guard's Square so crowded. Something was going on. Maybe a speech? Could it be something to do with her?

Then she saw it.

It rose from the crowd like a black obelisk as she drew closer; the top of the wooden frame a silhouette against the grey, clouded sky.

A little hoop of frayed rope hung in the air from the oak beam.

The Princess raised her head up and bobbed it left and right. Then, fleetingly, through a gap between two tall gentlemen, she saw something she definitely didn't want to see. Something she knew she would see. Something that scared her more than anything she had seen in the Narrows.

The prisoner was standing with a black bag over his head, his hands tied behind his back, his feet shackled together in rusty chains.

Then the two men came together to whisper and the viewpoint sealed.

Niclas turned around just in time to see only a glimpse of the Princess' cloak plunging into the throng.

He looked back.

'Sir! Sir!'

The cat was gone. Empty faces stared back at him.

'Sir!'

'What?' said Balthazar, appearing by his ankles.

'She's…'

'Blast! What is she doing?'

'I dunno, sir, she just went off innit.'

'Well, that's the end of it. Nothing we can do now.'

'Wot?'

'What?'

'But?'

'But?'

'We can't leave her, sir?'

'On the contrary, she left us.'

'But…'

'Moons!' cursed Balthazar. 'See that black lamppost? Wait under it. Wait under it! No running off, no distractions. Just do as you're told.'

And with that said, Balthazar leapt into the forest of trousers and dresses after the Princess.

Niclas looked across at the lamppost. There was more than one. They lined the square like black coffin nails.

'Err… lampost?' he mumbled.

Cassandra pushed her way through the crowd.

Balthazar wasn't far behind, and was able to weave through the legs and dresses far more easily than the Princess could through shoulders and waists; though, it was certainly more dangerous. One wrongly placed foot could crush him. It was a malodorous place to be too. He hated the fact that feet, especially those of the common folk who were ill acquainted with baths, smelt like cheese. In particular, vintage cheddar. It reminded him of the rats and their obsession with the stuff. Perhaps that's why they were notorious for biting toes, he thought, a simple mistake any purblind individual might make.

But this wasn't the place for that sort of thinking. He had to focus. He was nearly at the front and he could see, what could only be Cassandra, apologising to people as she squeezed past them.

A rosy cheeked orator had taken to the gallows like a stage. He was gesticulating and shouting out something about treason, traitors, corruption and justice. The sort of stuff orators are exceptionally good with. And the sort of stuff that woos an audience, making them forget all about decorum, and turning them into a wake of vultures, crying for blood.

The words and cries washed over the Princess. Her eyes were fixed on the prisoner with the black bag over his head.

She was near the front now. City Watchmen were standing in a line with muskets raised to the sky, pushing the crowd back.

'Pssst, Princess,' said Balthazar.

Cassandra looked down.

'It's Rufus,' she said.

'This is a terrible idea, you must come away at once.'

The Princess wasn't listening. She moved forward.

'No, not that way.' Balthazar pounced in front of her.

'Out of my way. I have to do something. I can stop it.'

'No!'

'Out of my way!'

The crowd nearest looked round at the girl in the hood. They'd got there early and had the best standing seats in the square. There was no way a haughty toned girl was going to get them to move.

Balthazar could smell her will. It was strong. Beyond reasoning with. He sprung his claws on his right paw and dug them deep into her ankle. She yelped and pulled her foot away, crossing her eyes with the cat's.

They washed black.

Come away... you must come away... there is nothing you can do here... come with me... with me... come... follow...

The Princess dithered, shook her head and closed her eyes. She tried to fight it, but she couldn't escape his voice, and when she looked again, his black orbs poured into her. They grabbed hold of her thread, winding it and twisting it around like cotton in a spindle, pulling her towards them, winding her in, drawing her away.

Turn around... come back... this is not the way... this is the way.

She walked in a dream-like state, forgetting where she was, who she was, why she needed to do something, or what that was.

The orator had said something grand, a punchline that made the crowd roar.

There was a wooden clunk.

The groaning stretch of rope.

Gasps.

Cheers.

A faint choking sound.

Cassandra nearly regained herself and turned back to look, but Balthazar kept her gaze and lured her away.

Behind, over her shoulder, Rufus' legs were kicking and convulsing at the knees. His body wriggled like a headless snake.

Then, over to one side, a group of peasants battered like a ram through the line of guards and made it to his flapping legs.

'The Queen's justice!' they were yelling.

They took hold of each leg and pulled with violent downward jerks. Pulled hard to make his suffering short. By the time the guards had recovered the line and fought the crowd back, it was too late.

Rufus' spluttering and struggling had been silenced.

He hung there, spinning under the creak of the wooden beam.

He was dead.

Cassandra blindly followed Balthazar through the clamour as it closed after her.

Just a bit further, a little more.

But then something happened the cat hadn't planned for.

A hand shot from the crowd, grabbed the Princess' shoulder, moved to her head and pulled down her hood.

The trance shattered.

'Cassandra! It is you,' said Mr Eccleston, darting cautious looks left and right. He put her hood back up. 'It isn't safe here. You must come with me.'

The Princess looked around confused. She had moments ago been about to do something important. She couldn't remember what. There was the crowd, the shouting. What was her tutor doing there? And… Rufus.

She turned to look back and shrieked, hand over mouth lest all the city hear her scream.

It was over.

The crowd's reaction confirmed it. People were starting on the difficult task of leaving the Guard's Square, complaining about "leg pullers" and "too short a death".

Mr Eccleston grasped her arm fiercely.

'You must come with me, Cassandra, you're in great danger here.'

'But… you… you're one of them!'

'Cassandra. You must trust me. Your mother would want you to trust me. Rufus would want you to trust me.'

'But you had me taken away! You told on me!'

'That is a lie Cassandra, a hideous untruth. My only ever desire is to protect you.'

'How can I trust you?'

'You must. I am your only hope.'

The Princess thought about it for a second. That was about all the time she had. She didn't want to go with him, she didn't trust him, but amidst the horror of it all, it felt right.

'Wait,' she said.

Balthazar, who had no intention of sticking around, was trying to creep away unnoticed. He didn't have the strength to charm both the girl and the man, and an onslaught of trampling legs was coming his way.

He got about a foot's distance before the Princess grabbed him under his belly and lifted him to her chest.

He hissed and moaned.

'My cat,' said the Princess.

Your what? thought Balthazar.

'Very well. Come,' said Mr Eccleston.

And with that, the tutor, the Princess and a reluctant Balthazar made off out of the crowd.

That wasn't so good for Niclas.

He was waiting under a lamppost watching the horde of people move like a body of water to every exit in the square. He couldn't see his master anywhere. Trying to spot a black cat in a mass of hundreds of people was like… well… trying to spot a black cat in a mass of hundreds of people. Really, really hard. It didn't matter how much he squinted, there was no sign of either the cat or the Princess.

Several thoughts occurred to Niclas. Firstly, that he'd picked the wrong lamppost and Balthazar had left him there because of it. Secondly, that the Princess and Balthazar had been caught by the guards and were by now already en route to the Academy. Then he had the idea that Balthazar had never liked him much in the first place and had ditched him at the first opportunity. That was a tough one to stomach. The other thought was that Balthazar had taken a little longer than planned to get the Princess back, but was making his way over right at that moment…

He picked the latter of these, not because it was the most logical, but because it was the nicest.

But after another minute, the other three options became hard to ignore. And after ten minutes, even harder still.

But Niclas wasn't really in the business of making decisions for himself, so he continued to do as he had been told, and waited.

That was until the guards spotted him. At least, it looked like they might have spotted him. One pointed his way and whispered something to the other. Then they exchanged words with the pompous looking, pointy-nosed Inspector Forsyth, who was up on a big grey horse.

It could have just been coincidence. Surely they hadn't made him out from so far away. But then, he was the only person not trying to leave the square; and a suspicious cloaked figure standing at the perimeter of a public event looks… well… like a suspicious cloaked figure standing at the perimeter of a public event.

Niclas tried not to stare, but he couldn't be certain they weren't on to him, so his eyes lingered on them until their passing gaze lingered on him. When that happened, he made a pathetic attempt to pretend he was looking up over their heads. They didn't fall for that old trick and soon enough, the Inspector gave the nod and the two guards started on his position.

He looked back into the crowd. Now would be perfect dramatic timing for Balthazar and the Princess to appear, then they'd make haste together, to the docks and beyond.

But now the guards were nearing closer, shouldering their way through the mob, hands on the twisted handles of their silver rapiers.

He had to run. As soon as he did it would give him away for sure, but it was probably too late anyway.

He backed away from the lamppost and moved sideways, like a hesitant crab, in the opposite direction.

Their pace increased. His increased.

There was no use trying to blend in, he had to make a break for it. If he could just get out of the crowd, then he could follow the Queen's Road to the Brewery Quarter and cross back into the slums. They'd never find him there.

He stopped.

His heart began to pound.

Ahead of him, he'd seen another Watchman moving towards him. They were closing in around him like a net. He changed direction, started to move back towards the gallows. But the solitary Watchman came to meet him, cutting across the crowd.

'You there, boy! Stop!' he said, reaching out. Now he was only two or three people away, and reaching for the steel curved handle of his rapier. But his hand would never touch it. For between him and the boy came a man from seemingly nowhere. He gave the Watchman an open armed embrace, as if the two knew one another. But through the flash of moving people, Niclas saw the embrace for what it really was, and watched as a short sword was driven deep into the guard's armpit, between the plates of his bronze, leather armour, and angled upwards into his heart. Once. Twice. The attacker's other hand stifled the watchman's mouth. No one had even noticed. And just like that the guard stumbled backwards and was dead.

Niclas didn't have words. The Witchhunter turned to face him, grabbed him, and dragged him back into the direction of the swarm.

He looked for the other guards. They'd lost him. They were stood still, searching the square.

Niclas and the Witchhunter made it ten feet, maybe twelve, before a woman screamed. The guards hurried to her and found their dead comrade.

There was no panic in the crowd around the body. The corpse looked so peaceful, that for all anyone knew, the dead guard could have fainted. It was not uncommon for members of the Watch to faint at public events. The crowds and the leather cladding of their armour made it stuffy and hard to breathe.

But then, when Niclas and the Witchhunter had made it another ten feet, the guards noticed the blood seeping from the man's side. At once they stood. One drew his sword. The other, his pistol. Then came the sound of a hollow whistle ringing out. Two long blows, followed by two more.

Guards all over the square knew what two long blows, followed by two more meant. They unsheathed their swords and advanced into the crowd on all sides.

Now the public were waking up to it. Everyone was starting to look back, all except the Witchhunter and Niclas, who were too busy getting away to look back.

Up ahead, guards were pouring into the wide streets leading out of the Guard's Square. They were slowing the crowd down, inspecting people as they left. It was only a few minutes before every road leading out of the square had a checkpoint assembled around it.

'Crikey! Wot we gonna do, gov,' said Niclas.

'Act normal,' said the Witchhunter.

'Normal?' said Niclas. What was normal? He couldn't help but stare at the guards and their guns and their swords and their searching eyes. Some were sat up high on horseback and watched over the crowd like falcons.

'You got a plan, gov?'

The silence suggested that either the Witchhunter had a very sound idea to escape, or, that he had nothing.

As they neared the checkpoint, Niclas saw guards passing round wanted posters between each other. Then he saw ones stopping and searching people, asking questions, telling people to remove hoods and hats.

'Steady' said one of the searchers, lifting his hand to the Witchhunter's chest. The great coat was so big and long that it was destined to be searched.

'Stay close,' muttered the Witchhunter. And Niclas became his shadow, turning his face down away from the guard.

'Open your coat,' the Watchman ordered.

The Witchhunter reached inside his coat and squeezed the handle of his short sword.

There were at least eight or nine of them close by, all armed with enough ammunition to fight a small war.

Niclas thought he might wet himself, and probably would have, had he not taken the liberty of relieving himself in the canal earlier.

There was a shout from behind, back where the guard had been stabbed. It was hard to hear what was said, or if it came from the public or the Watch, but it sent a trembling wave of unease through the square. The people furthest back began to push forward. Amongst the nearest people, there were whispers of murder, of a killer in the crowd. Everyone could feel it, the shuffling, jittery smell of uncertainty.

'Keep calm!' called out one of the guards on horseback. 'Please continue to exit the square in an orderly fashion. You may be stopped and searched as you do so. The Watch demands your utmost cooperation.'

'Excuse me, sir,' said the haughty guard before the Witchhunter, 'I asked you to open your coat.'

'You should let me pass.'

'I'm sorry, sir. Your coat, if you'd please.' The guard stepped back, clutched the pistol at his waist and brought the whistle hovering up to his mouth.

'You don't want this,' said the Witchhunter in a low voice, 'don't you have a family? Something to live for?'

'I beg your pardon, sir?' said the guard, trying to remain authoritative, but paralysed, unable to blow the whistle or pull the pistol; and there was a tremble in his voice that was only to be expected. Some men have eyes that when you look into them, you know to do exactly as they say. Some men have dangerous eyes, killer's eyes. The Witchhunter's eyes were this very flavour. Murderous.

'What's the holdup there?' shouted the guard on horseback.

And then all of a sudden, Niclas could see where things were going. The Witchhunter was going to kill them. As many as he could. He'd certainly kill the man in front of him. Perhaps slit his throat, steal his gun and shoot the guard on horseback with it. But he wouldn't be able to kill them all, and there were musketeers at the back, with rifles to pick them off. A bloodbath was about to erupt in the Guard's Square. It was going to end badly, messily, bloodily. But worst of all, they were going to die.

There had to be another way, a way that didn't lead down that road.

What would a reasonably minded person do, thought Niclas? What would Cassandra do? She'd probably try and bribe the guard, offer him money, assert her status, say something smart, something clever.

That wouldn't work.

Then, Niclas thought, what would Balthazar do?

Yes. That seemed about right.

Without warning, he stepped away from the Witchhunter, put his hands around his mouth and shouted as loud as he possibly could, so loud he shredded his vocal chords. "ELP, HE'S GOT A GUN. MURDERER! MURDERER IN THE SQUARE!"

At first the Witchhunter turned and struck him with a look of betrayal.

Then he looked up.

The crowd around them swelled like an ocean current. Panicked expressions leapt from one face to another. Then the swell broke. One or two people started it. They pushed and shoved and sent those around them pushing and shoving. Soon, thirty, forty people were shouting, cursing, forcing their way to the exits. Then a hundred. Then two hundred.

The guard nearest drew his pistol but was washed aside by the surge of human bodies. He tried to resist the wave, went under and was crushed to death.

The guard on horseback was flung backwards as his horse reeled up in fright, its front hooves clobbered the nearest woman and knocked her to the ground dead.

More screaming ensued.

More panic.

And now people lost their wits and all sense of their wits. They pushed against the small wooden blockades, and when they wouldn't break, the people behind that pushed against them and so on and so on, until it was the people themselves who broke. Arms dislocated. Legs crushed. Ribs popped out.

The line of Watchmen were following orders and their orders were to detain people within the square. And so, when one highly ranked guardsmen readied his sword, the others thought nothing of it, they readied theirs and the rapiers cut down on the crowd as if cutting back a hedgerow.

Blood splattered and flicked into mouths and into eyes. It fed the panic, like oil to a flame. Some turned, tried to run the other way. Some fell underfoot and were trampled to death.

'Get back! Back you fools!' cried an officer of the Watch. But the crowd was unable to listen. They were frightened and completely out of control. So he ordered his musketeers to have one off over the top. But they mistook his order. They fired level. Bullets split heads and cut through necks. Women, children, men; rich folk, poor folk, servant folk, all were caught equally in the barrage.

And now, like a squeezed pimple that wasn't quite ready to come out, the crowd ruptured and the cobbled floor shook.

They smashed into the guards – through the chopping swords and thrusting bayonets. They crashed through the wooden barriers, and spilled into the streets. It was every person for themselves. They ran and leapt and bounded down the streets as far as they could get from the bedlam. And when they got far enough, they looked back, some with blood on their faces and shook their heads because that was all they could do.

In the centre of the square, there were still shouts for calm, for order, for people to remain reasonable.

No one had ears to listen.

It was chaos.

Utter chaos.

And in that chaos, the Witchhunter, and Niclas, the boy with absolutely no talents, disappeared.

Widdershins

will continue...

Acknowledgements

Thanks to Tom, Georgia, Greg, and Vivien, without whom this book would still be possible, but not nearly as good.

About the Author

Alex Alexander is a London based writer of weird, hapless unwonderful tales.

A quasi master of the Dark Arts, he spends his evenings summoning demons, talking with the dead and translating long lost occult texts.

He's also slave to a cat called Albie, who is by no means any relation to the cat featured in this book.

Made in the USA
Lexington, KY
13 November 2018